Backstretch Baby

Bev Pettersen

Editor: Pat Thomas
Cover Art Design: Hot Damn Designs

DEDICATION

To Marie Snarby
In celebration of all the lives she touched.

ALSO AVAILABLE FROM

BEV PETTERSEN AND WESTERHALL BOOKS

Jockeys and Jewels

Color My Horse

Fillies and Females

Thoroughbreds and Trailer Trash

Riding For Redemption

Studs and Stilettos

A Scandalous Husband

A Pony For Christmas (Novella)

Repent (Thriller Novella)

CHAPTER ONE

Eve Lewis knew the thud of pounding feet meant trouble. No groom would sprint down the barn aisle and startle a bunch of hot-blooded Thoroughbreds unless there was good reason.

Ashley skidded to a stop in front of Eve, her face flushed from her mad dash. "The bridles are gone!" she said. "Every single one."

Eve stiffened, then bolted to the tack room. It wasn't much, just an old stall crammed with tack and grooming supplies. But the little room was definitely emptier than it had been last night. The nail hooks were bare. Not a single bridle remained.

She gaped in disbelief, struggling to absorb the empty wall, stripped of everything except a lonely martingale and her dented white helmet.

She twisted, checking the saddle racks, and her breath oozed with relief. At least the rest of the tack hadn't been taken. Her exercise saddle was still perched in its regular spot, along with all their girths, pads and grooming kits. It was strange the saddles hadn't been stolen as well but clearly the thieves had been on foot and limited in what they could carry.

A liniment jug had been kicked aside, thickening the air with its pungent smell. She picked it up from the wooden floor, trying to tighten the cap before replacing it on the shelf with the rest of the medical supplies. But she fumbled, almost dropping the top, and realized her hand was shaking.

"Did you lock the tack room last night?" she asked, trying to keep her voice steady.

"I think so." However, Ashley averted her eyes. "Can't really remember."

Eve sucked in a shallow breath. Ashley was six months pregnant and already reeling from the loss of her jockey job. It was tough working as a groom when one's dreams revolved around riding. She understood that all too well.

Still, this loss was devastating. The horses couldn't be exercised without bridles, and losing a day's training could be critical. Even more so for a novice trainer at a strange track. At first, she'd been ecstatic when her boss had entrusted her with accompanying a string of Thoroughbreds to this small racetrack north of LA. But so far, the three weeks here had been filled with nothing but bad luck.

"Boss will blame me for this," Ashley said, her voice plaintive. "He's been a prick ever since he got married. They're looking for a reason to trim staff. Think I'll be fired?" She cupped a protective hand over her stomach and stared at Eve, desperate for reassurance.

"Don't worry," Eve said. "Jackson won't fire you." But she grabbed a rag and blotted up the puddle of liniment, trying to hide her concern. Ashley wasn't a very good groom. However, she was an extremely talented rider and when her pregnancy was over, Ashley would be back in the saddle where she didn't make many mistakes.

Unfortunately, Eve had begun to suspect their boss had relegated them to this track at the insistence of his new wife. And that perhaps the temporary assignment wasn't really an opportunity but a warning.

Ashley wrung her hands. "But Jackson isn't making the decisions anymore. And Victoria doesn't want other women around, especially single ones."

Eve tossed the sodden rag into a bucket. There was considerable truth to that statement, but she didn't want to fan gossip, especially now that she was an assistant trainer. She had six horses under her care, and it was critical to prove she could handle the job.

She'd ridden for Jackson Zeggelaar's barn for four years, and she loved being a jockey. But high speed falls left too many broken bones, and jockeys weren't paid when they didn't ride. Her son would be starting school soon, and she needed a safer career, one better suited for a single mom.

The scar from her latest surgery was still pink and itchy, and she rubbed her wrist while making a mental list—call Jackson, notify security, replace tack.

She snapped several pictures, angling her phone to include a shot of the metal padlock dangling from the tack room door.

Her eyes narrowed on the lock. It wasn't broken or jimmied, and the door still sat solidly on its hinges. It had been Ashley's turn to feed this morning. They shared a dorm room and Eve had heard the buzzing alarm clock, the thud of boots when Ashley had left for the barn.

"I don't understand how the thief got in," she said. "You were the first one here. Was the door open when you arrived?"

Ashley looked down, suddenly preoccupied with brushing hay off the front of her jeans. "I was a little late today," she muttered.

"But was the door open when you came?" Eve asked, struggling to remain patient.

"Not sure," Ashley said. "Don't really remember."

She must have sensed Eve's frustration because she shook her head, her voice strengthening with indignation. "I sure didn't expect other track people to steal from us. Who would have thought that?"

Eve palmed her phone, forcing herself to wait out the stream of excuses. She'd always found it easier dealing with horses than people. But she was improving. Certainly a four-year-old son had left her softer, more aware of other people's vulnerabilities. Sometimes though, it was tempting to climb on a horse and gallop away. Escape employees and all their personal issues.

"So you're saying the door wasn't locked?" she asked.

Ashley replied with an infuriating shoulder shrug.

"If you forgot to lock up last night," Eve said, her voice tightening, "I need to know."

"But I was tired last night, and my legs are swollen, and Stinger was banging the wall, and it's so hard to remember."

"Try."

Ashley flinched at the sudden whip in Eve's voice. "Sorry," she said, her bravado disappearing. "Maybe I forgot to lock up. I'm sorry." She hung her head in genuine misery.

Eve clamped her mouth shut and looked away, hating to see her friend upset. Ashley was barely twenty and even though Eve was only five years older, she often felt like the girl's mother. However, this wasn't the first time Ashley had been careless. She was simply disinterested in anything but riding.

Fortunately, Jackson and Victoria weren't around to witness Ashley's mistakes. Rumors swirled that both Jackson's race stable and his marriage were struggling. And that they wanted to reduce staff.

"We have to establish the facts," Eve said, calming her voice. "Before I call security, the police. Our boss."

Ashley gave a glum nod. "Well, I left the dorm about four-thirty. But maybe I didn't get here until five." Her voice rose, turning defensive again. "It's easier getting out of bed to gallop horses than to shovel shit. And pregnancy makes me tired. So lately I've been stopping at the guardhouse for a visit. Just for a minute. But Liam always gives me free coffee."

"Liam? The guy with the thick neck?" Eve shuddered. "You didn't do your job because of coffee with some bulked-up rent-a-cop?"

"I know he gave us a hard time our first week." Ashley crossed her arms. "But he's really nice once you get to know him. And it saves me a dollar at the kitchen. You don't understand what it's like to be broke and alone and pregnant."

Eve rubbed the back of her neck. She didn't discuss personal details with many people, but she certainly knew what it was like to be broke. On the other hand, she'd never been truly alone. She'd always had the support of her mother as well as Megan and Scott Taylor. Ashley had nobody. And the reality was that being a single mother was tough, especially when one relied on horses to earn a living.

"Okay," she said, trying to stay calm. And clearly this wasn't the best time to remind Ashley about the dangers of too much caffeine. "So you had coffee with some guard—"

"Not just any guard," Ashley said. "The *head* guard."

"Right." Eve pulled in a deep breath. "You came a little late, around five. But you still arrived before Miguel? You were the first one here?"

Ashley gave a reluctant nod.

"So," Eve said, feeling like she was pulling teeth, "last night you were here for the eight o'clock check. That means the theft happened between eight and five this morning. And you don't remember if you locked the door?"

"Think I did." Ashley scuffed at the floor with the toe of her boot. "I really think I locked it," she added, as if trying to convince herself.

Eve rubbed her throbbing wrist. Only three people knew the combination to the lock. Ashley, Miguel, and herself. Miguel was old and arthritic, but he was a long-time employee of Jackson's and rarely made mistakes. And then only if he'd been drinking. But he hadn't touched liquor since last summer. This past Friday, she and Ashley had helped him celebrate his eight-month anniversary.

She glanced down the aisle. Miguel limped into Tizzy's stall, oblivious to the drama. As always, his attention was focused on the horses. He began unwrapping bandages, diligently checking the gelding's legs and readying him for his morning gallop. Only there wouldn't be any exercise today.

If they'd been back at Santa Anita, Jackson would simply borrow a few bridles from a neighboring trainer, at least until he had time to visit the tack store. But at Riverview Racetrack, she was a newbie. She didn't know anyone. They'd been assigned stalls in the overflow barn at the southeast end of the track. It wasn't even a shedrow, just a small building leased from an absentee farmer.

At first, she'd been delighted with their location, pleased that Jackson had made such thoughtful arrangements. The barn was a horseman's dream. It had a patch of grass with plenty of shade, as well as a small walking ring and even a fenced sandpit where the horses could roll. A colorful hammock and two picnic tables were clumped beneath a sheltering oak tree.

Taking a horse to the track required a fifteen-minute walk along a solitary path, but it was a ride she enjoyed. Not only was it an excellent warm-up, it gave her a feel for each horse before they started their daily exercise. The isolated location had seemed perfect.

She hadn't realized track workers used the picnic tables in the afternoon, lugging their babies and lunches, and letting the toddlers play in the deep sand. Unfortunately, Ashley had turned Banjo out in the sandpit and the horse had rolled, slicing his back on a rusty metal truck. That had left them with five sound horses...until last week when the gray mare had developed a nasty stone bruise which had reduced Eve's string to four. At this rate, she wouldn't have a horse fit to race by the end of the month. And Jackson demanded results.

"I can't believe *they'd* steal our tack," Ashley said, yanking back Eve's attention. "You shouldn't let them hang out here anymore. They're robbing us blind."

"We have no idea who did this," Eve said. "It's not fair to assume."

She turned and walked toward the wide end door, tired of Ashley's constant sniping about the local workers. But Ashley followed.

"Those women know we sleep at the dorm," Ashley went on. "And that our barn is empty all night. They're here every afternoon. Now more of them are coming, especially since you arranged for that second sand pit."

Eve's gaze drifted to the fresh pile of sand, covered by a protective tarp. She hadn't the heart to banish the kids from their favorite play area. Safe spots were scarce at a racetrack. But she couldn't risk having her horses hurt by their toys. Besides, it wasn't sanitary for children to play in a pen frequented by Thoroughbreds.

So last week, she'd dug into the last of her money and ordered a truckload of premium white sand to create a pit solely for the children.

"And what is the reason for that big tarp?" Ashley went on, scowling at the sand.

"The orange cat is hanging around again," Eve admitted. "And I want to keep the sand clean. A few of the women are pregnant and shouldn't be around cat feces. Besides, the tarp doesn't just keep out stray cats. It helps despook the horses."

"Yeah, right." Ashley snorted. "You're just looking out for those kids." But she smiled for the first time that morning. "I didn't even think about the cat using our sand as a litter box. Or how that might not be good for pregnant women. Shows how little I know about babies."

She dragged a hand over her flaring belly. "I can't wait to get back to riding. If you weren't proof that a baby doesn't kill a jock career, I wouldn't even consider keeping it."

Eve bent and scooped up a stray piece of baler twine. Sadly, she hadn't proven anything. Motherhood had affected her in a variety of ways. She just hadn't admitted it—not yet, not to anyone. But Ashley was determined to return to her jockey job, even with a baby. And Eve had to tell her the truth.

"Being a mom does change things though." She wrapped the twine around her fingers. "I ride differently now. It's no longer just me and the horse. I…worry a lot more."

She peeked at Ashley's face. She didn't confide easily, and it was difficult to talk about something that had taken her so long to accept. But Ashley just nodded— waiting and listening. She was always a good listener when it had anything to do with riding.

Eve wet her lips, hating to show vulnerability. She'd worked too hard, sacrificed so much. She certainly didn't want to start rumors that she'd quit a successful jockey career because of nerves. But Ashley was responsible for two people now. And she deserved to know.

"Sometimes in a race I'd see an opening," Eve went on. She fiddled with the twine, yanking it tighter around her hand. "But then I'd hesitate, wondering if it was safe. Worrying about clipping heels and maybe going down and causing a wreck. And that fear was because of Joey. Knowing he needs me. And that the most important thing isn't the win, but to come home at the end of each day."

She blew out an achy breath, thinking of Joey's sweet face. He'd lost his father. No way was he losing his mom too. "And then that hole was gone," she added, her voice strained. "And the horse and I had lost our chance."

The twine was pinching her fingers now, and she pulled it off and jammed it alongside the hoofpick in her back pocket.

Ashley just stared, her baby-blue eyes wide with incredulity. "But you were riding great. It was the accidents that forced you to retire."

"I wasn't as brave though," Eve said. "I knew it. The horses knew it too. And their confidence was affected. That's why I need this training job to work out."

Ashley's mouth opened and closed. "That's awful," she sputtered, her eyes filled with horror. "No one wants a scared jockey on their horse."

"No," Eve said quietly. "Nobody does."

"But that won't happen. Not to me. It can't!"

"You need to know though," Eve said. "Maybe you'll be different. But there's a reason that an ambulance follows the riders. It's not if we're going to get hurt, but when, and how badly. My son is the most precious person in my life. I have to think of him."

Ashley just gaped, as if struggling to reconcile her image of a fearless Eve with this new admission. "But I was modeling myself after you," she finally wailed. "And I don't want to work as anything but a jockey. The only time I feel really alive is when I'm on a horse."

Eve gave an understanding nod. She loved the adrenaline rush too, the feel of a powerful Thoroughbred, the thrill of straining together to reach the wire first. Nothing matched it. But at least she could still exercise the horses in the morning.

"Maybe it won't be that way for you," she said. "And there are other jobs at the track. An exercise job is fun. At least then you'd still be riding."

"But that's another three months away. And it sucks being a groom." Ashley's lip curled with distaste. "Crappy pay, long hours, no benefits. I get kicked and bit and stepped on. No one cheers me on, or even appreciates me."

"I appreciate you," Eve said. "But you're right about the challenges of working here. And that's why I'm going to keep welcoming the local women. They need a place where they can gather and feel comfortable."

She crossed her arms. "And I don't want to hear any more talk about how they're robbing us blind. Not without proof. Everyone needs a little help sometime."

Ashley kicked at a rock, sending it bouncing over the gravel. "Maybe they're not the thieves," she said. "And it is a nice thing you're doing." She paused, then her words escaped in a rush. "It's just that they all speak Spanish. I don't know what anyone is saying. I know it's stupid, but you're my only friend. And you can talk with them…and I can't."

Eve sighed and lowered her arms. Ashley never used to be so self-centered. But pregnancy seemed to have left the girl's emotions churning. And no doubt she was feeling isolated.

They'd both moved from the racetrack at Santa Anita, and the dorms here were dominated by Hispanic workers. Eve hadn't even thought about it. Half of her family spoke Spanish at home, and she'd been more preoccupied with how the horses were settling in than her two staff members. Little wonder Ashley had sought companionship with the English-speaking guards.

"I'm just helping the women understand American social programs," Eve said. "There's a lot of assistance they don't know about. And they like to practice their English. You should join us in the afternoons. Maybe even learn some Spanish."

Ashley's nose wrinkled. "I've tried but my mind always blocks the words." Then she brightened. "But it might be worth the trouble if it'd help me become a better jockey. Half the time I don't know what the groom is saying. What they're telling me about the horse might be important."

Eve gave a wry nod. Understanding Spanish would definitely be helpful. Most of the grooms and hotwalkers were from Mexico, Guatemala, Ecuador or Peru. Some were illegal. The jobs were low-paying and grueling, which made it even more compelling to help the Hispanic mothers, many of whom felt totally isolated.

She reached out and squeezed Ashley's shoulder. She was responsible for the girl being here. Up until last month Ashley had been hiding her pregnancy from Jackson and his wife, afraid they wouldn't let her ride anymore. Or even work in their barn. So it had been prudent to whisk her away, before Jackson made any more staff cuts.

'It doesn't look good for our stable to have pregnant people handling racehorses,' Victoria had said to Jackson, loud enough for Eve to hear. 'Owners don't like it either. Just think of the potential lawsuits.'

Jackson had just mumbled some appeasement. He'd bent over backwards to accommodate Eve's pregnancy. But that had been over four years ago, before he'd married Victoria. Things had changed.

She squared her shoulders and pulled out her phone. Time to call their boss.

"Are you calling Jackson now?" Ashley backed away, her voice rising in alarm. "Victoria is going to freak. Want me to talk, apologize about the bridles?"

"No," Eve said. "That's my job. Go help Miguel with the wraps. Then start hand walking Stinger. I'll be along soon to help."

Ashley gave a relieved nod and hurried away, clearly confident Eve could handle their boss.

But as Eve trudged toward the privacy of the picnic tables, she pulled in a fortifying breath, aware it wouldn't be quite so simple.

CHAPTER TWO

Jackson answered Eve's call without any sort of greeting. "How's it going up there?" he asked. "How did Tizzy work today?"

Her grip tightened around the phone. "I couldn't gallop any of the horses," she said. "Our bridles were stolen."

"Dammit. They can't miss any days, not with two races this weekend."

She circled the picnic table. She'd hoped her boss might have some suggestions, something a little more positive. In the old days, he'd been a problem solver, one of the reasons she enjoyed working for him. But it was becoming more and more apparent that this splinter barn was isolated by more than geography.

"We'll hand walk them under tack," she said, keeping her voice calm. "They're already in good shape."

"I suppose," Jackson said grudgingly. He was silent for a moment. Then he gave a wry snort. "Tizzy is probably broke enough that you can ride him without a bridle."

Her fingers loosened a notch. Clearly Victoria wasn't around. Jackson almost sounded like his old self. "Tizzy's certainly well trained," she said. "But the outriders wouldn't tolerate a bridleless horse."

"No," Jackson said. "They'd write you up for sure. But what happened with the tack. Was the door kicked in?"

"No. I must have forgotten to lock it."

"That doesn't sound like you. Or Miguel." He made a sound of disgust. "It was Ashley, wasn't it? I have to let her go."

"But she's pregnant." Eve's voice rose. "And she's a good rider. It's only three more months. You gave me time."

"That was different. You were competent and the barn was making money. Besides, Victoria told me about a trainer who was sued when a pregnant groom was kicked."

"I'll look out for Ashley," Eve said quickly. "We're careful here. And all the horses are quiet except for Stinger."

"I don't know…"

"And the two most important owners really like her," Eve said. "They might even move their horses if she were fired."

She crossed her fingers, uncomfortable with the little lie. Scott Taylor and Dex Tattrie barely knew Ashley. But both men were fair and they wouldn't want a pregnant groom kicked to the curb. More importantly, Scott's wife, Megan, was Eve's sister-in-law, or would have been if Megan's brother hadn't died.

"Bullshit," Jackson said. "If those men saw how Ashley handles their horses, they'd probably dump me as their trainer. She might be good in the saddle but she's useless on the ground. And they don't suffer fools gladly."

"True," Eve said. "But Megan likes her, and like most men, Scott listens to his wife." She couldn't keep the accusation from her voice.

"You don't understand," Jackson said. "Victoria wants things: a new truck, bigger house, regular vacations. At least she wants to help out more. She applied for her trainer's license and even convinced Eddie Blake to ride for us. He had a win yesterday on the Barkeeper colt."

Eve's hand tightened around the phone, almost smothering the small mouthpiece. She'd ridden that colt three times last fall, never finishing better than fourth. No doubt Eddie Blake was one of California's top jockeys. But if he was riding for Jackson's barn now—and Victoria wanted to assist with the training—where did that leave Eve? And while it was a relief the topic had switched from pregnant grooms to horses, this certainly wasn't reassuring news.

"Wow," she managed. "A new wife really does change things."

"Don't worry." Jackson's voice lowered. "You've earned your spot. Ashley and Miguel might have to go, but you'll always have a job. *She* can't change that."

A lump clogged Eve's throat, and she slumped against the picnic table. Jackson was a decent man but Victoria was like water on a rock. And in time, rocks crumbled. Victoria had already changed his name from Jack to Jackson, insisting he needed a more distinguished handle. And the way Jackson was whispering now was totally unsettling, as if he'd already relinquished control.

"Just make it easy for me," Jackson went on. "Win some races. Then Victoria will be happy. With her, it's all about the bottom line."

"It's not that," Eve said. "She's insecure, jealous—" She clamped her mouth shut, wishing she wasn't always so outspoken. Jackson had enough problems dealing with his demanding wife. And Eve wanted them to work it out so his race stable could function smoothly again.

"We need to find you some bridles," Jackson said, thankfully ignoring her outburst. "Victoria was a hotwalker there but I don't know if she still has any contacts. Probably best if you buy what you need. We're screwed if we lose another day of training."

Not him, Eve thought glumly. But she certainly would be.

"Give me an hour to arrange some credit," Jackson said, speaking a little faster now, clearly in a hurry to end the call. "There's a tack store a couple miles south on the highway. Carries everything. Buy what you need to win."

"Thank you," she said gratefully.

"How's the motel?"

"We only stayed there the first week," Eve said. "Ashley qualifies for a dorm room and it's easier for us to sleep on the grounds." Especially since some lowlife had lifted Eve's car battery, leaving her Civic grounded.

"Our room is close to Miguel and the horses," she added, hoping to distract him. But what kind of trainer didn't have a car? She could no longer pick up supplies or help out her staff. However, she didn't want to tell Jackson about every single problem. It would be total failure to be ordered back to Santa Anita without running a single race.

"Good," Jackson said. A woman's authoritative voice sounded in the background and it was clear his attention had shifted. "Good luck," he added hurriedly. "Keep Ashley away from the owners."

He cut the connection without asking how Banjo's back was healing, or if Eve had found a female jockey for Tizzy, or even to help pick out a suitable race. It was probably wise not to bring up race conditions though. Victoria had already insisted Stinger be entered for a mile and an eighth, even though the horse was a dedicated sprinter. Eve didn't want Victoria picking a poor-fitting race for Tizzy as well.

She jammed the phone against the palm of her hand and checked over her shoulder. Ashley was trying to lead Stinger around the small ring, in lieu of his morning gallop. But it was debatable who was in control.

The horse was dragging Ashley around, and she was doing little to correct him. The chain wasn't wrapped the traditional way around his nose, and the lead shank was too low to be effective. Stinger was a bulldozer, a horse who would take advantage if he could. As usual, Ashley was going to need help. And soon.

Eve pressed Megan Taylor's number, trying to squeeze in one more call before she rescued Ashley.

"I won't be working Stinger until Wednesday," Eve said, after dispensing with their usual round of greetings. "But I'll let you know how he gallops."

"Thought you planned to blow him out today," Megan said. "Is he okay? Is everything all right?"

"He's fine," Eve said. She hadn't planned to talk about the latest setback, but Megan's interest was always hard to deflect. And within minutes she'd confided the details of the most recent theft.

"That track is a den of thieves." Megan's voice bristled with indignation. "First they steal your car battery, then the hay and buckets, now the bridles. How can you possibly train? Is that amount of theft normal?"

"It's a small track," Eve said. "Everyone here struggles." But a wave of misery swept her because it did seem their luck had been unusually bad. It was exhausting trying to put on a brave face for her staff, her boss and the owners, along with the constant worry about when she could send money home to Joey. And she wouldn't earn anything until the horses did. She gulped, clearing the sudden thickness from her throat.

"Maybe you should make friends with the security guys," Megan said. "It would make their day to flirt with a pretty woman trainer. Although you probably prefer thefts to the guards."

Eve gave a weak smile. They both understood and accepted her aversion to men in uniform.

"Seriously though," Megan added, "just chat them up a bit. Throw them a smile or two. It won't take much. Just enough so they don't forget your barn during patrols."

Eve wrinkled her nose. Megan was far more pragmatic than she could ever be, even remaining tactful with the cops who'd botched her brother's murder investigation. But Eve couldn't pretend to respect someone if she didn't. People always knew how she felt.

"Our barn is quite isolated," she said, trying to be fair. "And the guards are busy with their regular patrols. But we'll keep the tack room locked. And the feed room. And anything else that can be picked up and carried off."

"It doesn't sound like a very safe place," Megan said. "Can't Jackson hire a watchman?"

"Victoria has him on a tight budget. She's making changes."

"Wives tend to do that," Megan said. But her laugh sounded troubled. And that wasn't good. She tended to be over protective, worrying about Eve and Joey, and always rushing in to help.

It made Eve feel incompetent.

"We'll be fine." She spoke a little more crisply than she intended. It was best to change the subject before Megan suggested that Eve quit the horse industry and start a safer occupation, something like basket weaving or making jewelry.

"Mom is looking after Joey while I'm up here," Eve added. "But I'm driving home after the races on Sunday to see him. We can talk more then."

Megan hesitated. "I planned to visit my mother this weekend," she said. "And I was hoping Scott and I could take Joey. I know the timing isn't good, especially with you working away, but it would mean a lot."

Eve jerked away from the picnic table. Megan was Joey's aunt, and it was important that he spend some time with his other grandmother. She lived on a farm, and Joey always enjoyed the visits. But it meant Eve wouldn't see her son for two whole weeks, fourteen days that they couldn't hug and laugh and hold hands.

"Sure," she said, trying to sound upbeat. "He'll like that. It's probably good not to drive home this Sunday anyway. I can stay and guard our stuff. Maybe sleep in the barn and catch the thief."

"But you need your rest, especially if you're galloping all those horses. I'll have Scott send an investigator."

"No need," Eve said. "I have two grooms and only four horses to ride."

"Thought you had six?"

"I do, but a couple got hurt. The two that were entered to run last week."

"So you haven't even raced yet?"

"No." Eve squeezed her eyes shut, hating the reminder. She must be the worst trainer ever.

"The two horses that were supposed to run last week? They're the ones that were hurt? That's weird."

"Just bad luck," Eve said.

"Maybe," Megan said, her voice troubled. "But we both know things aren't always what they seem. I think it's best if Scott comes up. Checks it out. I'll talk to him and call you back."

"No," Eve said quickly. "He'd be bored here. And he has an investigative business to run." She rounded the table in time to see Stinger rear. One of his big hooves waved perilously close to Ashley's stomach.

"Maybe someone else then—"

"Sorry, but I have to go," Eve said. "I'll call you back."

She didn't fully exhale until she'd cut the connection and rushed over to grab Stinger's lead line. Didn't want to admit that her staff was extremely limited in its capabilities. And that right now Megan and Scott's unruly horse posed the biggest threat of all.

CHAPTER THREE

The police dog whined with excitement, his quivering nose pointed at the ground. His handler raised an arm. "We've got something," he called.

Rick Talbot felt little satisfaction. They'd already recovered a bloody ball cap, and he'd been confident the corpse had been buried beyond the stand of trees. But once again, discovery came too late for the victim. And despair hollowed his chest.

He pulled his gaze off the sniffer dog and his triumphant handler, gave a brief nod to the lead detective and trudged away from the circle of officials. He was certain there was only one male in that shallow hole, one adult male. But just in case...

Bile climbed his throat. He swallowed and walked faster, trying to control his reaction.

A uniformed officer stepped in front of him. "Going to hurl? Think the head is off?"

Rick gave a non-committal grunt.

"You'll get used to it," the officer said. "This is my fifth. Besides, it's nothing but bottom feeders in those holes. No sense feeling sorry for them."

Rick ignored the man's blathering. His gaze shot back to the grim knot of people. Already the corpse dog and his handler had been relegated to the fringe of the crime scene, beyond the yellow tape. The black lab sat quietly now, tongue lolling while a man in plastic-covered boots used a spade to scoop away the clinging earth.

Moments later a foot appeared, a big boot encased in dirt. Had to be at least a size twelve. Definitely an adult. Rick's breath escaped in a whoosh of relief.

"Haven't seen you before," the garrulous cop went on. "Undercover?"

"PI," Rick said.

The man stiffened. His gaze slid from Rick's black jacket down to his faded jeans and worn leather boots. When the officer spoke again, his voice rang with fresh authority. "This is a crime scene," he said. "Secured by LAPD. You need to move back to the road. Immediately."

"Trying to," Rick said mildly. "You're blocking my way."

The cop's eyes narrowed. His hand shot to the top of his bulky holster. "What are you doing here? How did you get past security?"

"Came with the investigators." Rick flipped open his agency ID. "We supplied the information about the dumping ground."

The officer studied the ID with a suspicious expression. Seconds later, his head shot up. "You're the guy who was involved with the Cache Creek gang? That one with Taylor Agency?" His voice turned hopeful. "Any chance they're hiring? I heard about their cases. High-octane stuff. Are the rumors about their pay true? I'm single so I don't mind going deep. A few years of that and I could move to an island..."

The man's mouth was still moving but Rick had quit listening. He couldn't stop looking at the corpse. Fortunately, it was intact. But like all bodies, it shared a peculiar flatness, a distinct smell. And dirt always made them look pitiful, smaller somehow. Even if they were already small.

A familiar band tightened around his chest. He struggled to breathe through his mouth, but couldn't suck in enough oxygen. The air was too clotted with dirt and death and decay. Even the grass was ugly, a greenish brown with tips bleached to bone white.

His forehead prickled with sweat, trembles starting in his hands and then moving inward, and the vise around his ribs turned suffocating.

"Gotta report back," he managed. He jammed his hands in his pockets and shouldered past the officer.

He fled up the hill, away from the eager technicians, the smug detectives and that sad broken body. Retreated toward the dented Mazda with mismatched tires and three bullet holes in the trunk.

His chest still ached but at least the air here was cleaner. Eventually his heart stopped its frantic banging and it was no longer necessary to fight for his next breath. He even dared to pull his shaking hands from his pockets.

He sagged against the fender, swept by bone-deep failure. He could start the cases but he didn't want to finish them. And if success was defined by finding a body, what was the point?

His phone vibrated but he ignored it. It wasn't his employer. Scott Taylor would never risk calling on Rick's regular cell. But the man deserved an update. He'd been hounding this particular cartel for years.

Minutes ticked past. Rick wasn't sure how long he leaned against the car, but his shaking had stopped. He drew out his boot knife and pressed the lever to open the hood. Then reached into the air filter, removed his hidden phone and pressed Scott's number.

"It's over," Rick said. "Our snitch was right. They're recovering the body now."

"Excellent." Scott blew out a satisfied sigh. "You can finally leave that hellhole and go home."

Rick squeezed his eyes shut. He had no home. Just a sterile house surrounded by happy families and picket fences and kids kicking a soccer ball. The boys were the worst. He could hear them playing in the street, even when his garage door was shut.

"My plants have all died by now." He forced a chuckle. "So I can stay deep."

Scott was silent for a moment. A phone blared in the background, but the man didn't speak. "I think you should come in," Scott said. "Take some time off."

"No, I want to work."

"You've been out a long time."

"It's okay. I like the street."

"But investigators need time off after deep undercover," Scott said. "Company policy."

"Must be a new policy. You didn't mention that when you hired me."

"Policy is constantly evolving," Scott said.

Clearly the man was too tactful to mention burnout and that left Rick edgy and rather pissed. He appreciated candidness. Besides, did his boss think he was fragile? Well, screw him.

"Fine," Rick said. "If you don't have any cases for me, I quit."

"No," Scott said. "I can probably find something."

Rick flipped his knife, snagging it in midair, relieved the man hadn't forced his hand. He liked working for Taylor Agencies—liked and respected Scott Taylor—but more importantly he didn't want to go through any more job interviews, along with the painful psychological checks. He'd made enough market investments to retire and live on the interest, but free time was exactly what he wanted to avoid.

"I'll take anything." He spoke with a victor's grace.

"Good," Scott said, so quickly Rick wondered if he really was the victor.

"You'll go to Riverview Racetrack," Scott went on. "A small Thoroughbred track a hundred miles north of LA. This job is more low-key than you're used to, but it's important. And personal."

Rick shrugged, then realized Scott couldn't see him. "No problem," he said. "I just want to stay busy."

"My wife's relative has her first training job there. But Megan thinks Eve is experiencing an unusual amount of bad luck."

"Someone stopping her horses?" Rick asked. "Doping maybe?"

"Nothing like that. None of her horses have even made it to the starting gate, including ours. But her boss is having marital problems, and Eve is single. There might be blowback. I'd go up myself, but she refuses that." His voice softened. "She's proud and extremely independent. I don't want to tangle with her."

"So you want me take a day or two? Look around?"

"No. Stay up there for the month. There's been some theft so help her with whatever she needs. I'll have Megan tell her you're coming."

Rick dropped into the driver's seat. He refrained from slamming the door. But it seemed Scott had maneuvered him into taking a vacation after all.

"Sounds boring as hell," he muttered.

"Maybe. But stay alert." Scott's voice was oddly pensive. "I've always found racetracks to be full of surprises."

CHAPTER FOUR

Eve studied her forlorn car, parked by the side of the barn. The little Honda Civic hadn't moved for six days, not since someone had stolen her battery. But the tack store was five miles away, the sun directly overhead, and it would be a hot and blistering walk.

"We can get the car going," she said, giving Ashley and Miguel an encouraging smile. "It doesn't weigh much. I'm sure it will start with just a little push."

"Too bad it's not parked on a hill," Ashley said, gloomily tugging at her baggy shirt.

"You get behind the wheel," Eve said. "Miguel and I will push." Which meant she'd be the main muscle. Miguel was lean and wiry but his fastest gait was a shuffle. On the other hand, Ashley was pregnant. No way was she letting her push.

"Let's go," she said, feeling like a cheerleader. "We can do this."

Ashley maneuvered behind the steering wheel while Eve and Miguel took their place behind the dented back bumper. With a little straining, and after Ashley remembered to depress the clutch, the little car started rolling, slowly at first, then picking up speed.

Eve's wrist ached, but she bent lower, pushing harder and running faster as the car gained momentum. At some point, Miguel was left behind but the car was really moving now and crunching over the gravel.

"Okay," she called, giving a last shove before stumbling to a halt and staring hopefully.

Ashley popped the clutch and the car jerked, then sputtered forward. A black cloud spewed from the exhaust. But today it was a welcome sight.

Eve turned and flashed Miguel a triumphant thumbs up. "I'll pick up your chewing tobacco," she called. "After we buy the bridles."

She jogged to the car, ignoring the ache in her wrist.

A grinning Ashley moved from behind the wheel to the passenger's seat. "This is awesome. We're not stranded anymore."

Eve nodded, sharing her excitement. The luxury of leaving the track, even just to run errands, was always appreciated. More importantly, she could postpone buying a car battery until the horses earned some money. And despite losing a precious day of training—most of the morning had been spent filing a report about the stolen tack—the mood in her little car was upbeat.

They cranked the radio, joining Kenny Chesney in a raucous country song. Eve even waved at the thick-necked guard as they passed the security booth at the entrance to the track.

"Liam's probably an okay guy," she said, studying the burly guard in her rearview mirror. "But he made the horses wait for hours our first night. And that's hard to forgive."

"Even harder since you don't like anyone wearing a uniform," Ashley said.

"That's not true."

Ashley arched a pale eyebrow. "Sure it is."

Eve tightened her grip on the steering wheel. It was totally true but she liked to think she concealed her bias. "It's just that if someone's a jerk," she said, "a uniform only makes it worse."

"Do you really think that?" Ashley twisted in the seat, her eyes curious. "Have you had much experience with the police?"

Eve shrugged. A cousin murdered in prison, a brother on probation, friends arrested on trumped-up charges, and of course her son's father, killed and dumped in Mexico. None of the guards or police work in those cases had been stellar.

However, as Megan suggested on the phone, it was probably smart to cultivate better relations with the guards. And Ashley had been lonely ever since they arrived, craving male companionship as well as free coffee.

"From now on," Eve said, "I'll help with morning feedings. You can do lunch."

"Really?" Ashley's blue eyes widened. "But you're already swamped."

"It's okay. Most of the time I'm just worrying about Joey and the horses anyway. And it will give you time to have a coffee with the guards."

"Awesome! That is so nice."

"It's not about being nice," Eve said, uncomfortable with misplaced gratitude. "Megan thinks it'll protect the barn. With all the theft, it makes sense to be on good terms with the guards. I sure wouldn't be any good at chatting them up."

She gave a wry smile but enjoyed seeing Ashley's happiness. And it wasn't just the prospect of free coffee. Ashley was the type who needed attention.

"Better not drink too much caffeine though," Eve added. "It's not good for the baby."

Ashley gave an agreeable nod. "Liam says that too. And that I should get regular checkups and buy a better vitamin. He sure knows a lot."

Eve refrained from rolling her eyes. Give any fool a little authority and they always seemed smarter. "We'll go to the tack store first," she said, changing the subject. "Then the grocery store. I have twenty dollars to spend on tobacco and maybe some chips and chocolate."

She whipped past a slow-moving transport truck and merged into the middle lane. "If there's no hill to park on," she added, "we can leave the car running. Although around a tack store, there's usually no shortage of guys to push."

"Sounds like you've driven a lot of clunkers," Ashley said. "I know a jockey's pay is like a rollercoaster and that you haven't had a check in months. But at least you have rich relatives. Wouldn't Megan and Scott help?"

"They already have," Eve said, her voice clipped. The last thing she wanted was to beg for help. "Besides, Joey and I have everything we need. And with this training job, we might eventually be able to rent a house." She jammed a tendril of hair behind her ear. "I can look after my son just fine."

"Didn't say you couldn't. But if I knew people like the Taylors, I'd take better advantage. Especially since they like Joey so much. Heck, whenever I see them, they act like his parents."

Heat warmed Eve's face, and she stared fixedly over the steering wheel.

"Oh, I see," Ashley said. "You're afraid they'll want to take him more? Maybe demand shared custody?"

"Of course not," Eve said quickly. Sometimes Ashley was surprisingly astute. But Megan and Scott wouldn't do that. They were the most ethical, generous people she'd ever met.

On the other hand, Joey's father had been Megan's only brother, and it was clear Megan wanted to be a bigger part of Joey's life. And Scott would do anything to make his wife happy. That man was formidable.

"Of course they don't want custody," she repeated, her voice a little too sharp.

"But what's wrong with that? It might be good. Especially since you only have twenty dollars in your pocket. And they seem like nice people—"

"There's the store." Eve gestured at a horse-shaped sign.

"Wow, it's big." Ashley leaned forward, distracted by the massive tack store.

Eve swerved into the parking lot, relieved that line of conversation had been avoided. She felt guilty even thinking that Megan and Scott had designs on her son. And she certainly didn't want to discuss Joey. Talking about him when he wasn't around only filled her with an aching loneliness.

Ashley shaded her eyes, peering at the sprawling building and the sign that boasted the best prices in California. "It looks awesome. No wonder Jackson told us to come here."

Eve nodded but privately thought it would have been better to support the small store at the track. And perhaps create some badly needed goodwill with the locals.

"If there's a secondhand section," she said, "we might spot our stolen tack. Maybe the thieves are looking for a quick flip."

"This doesn't look like a store with a used section," Ashley said, studying the newly paved parking lot. "There are some expensive vehicles here. And no hill."

"I'll leave the engine running," Eve said. "At least there are nicer cars to steal."

She parked close to the entrance, wedging between a burly black Hummer and an Audi convertible with a bumper sticker that proclaimed polo players have bigger shafts.

They climbed the steps. A stocky man pulled open the door. He wore white breeches that clung to his muscular thighs, and his buzz cut seemed out of place. "Good afternoon, ladies. Do you want a cart today?"

"No," Eve said. "We just need a few race bridles."

"Racing section is at the back," the man said. "Down the steps, past the hunter and polo sections." His eyes skimmed over their worn jeans and then outside to the little Honda spewing exhaust. His nose lifted and he dismissed them, stepping back to resume his wide-legged stance by the entrance.

"Thanks," Eve said, striding past him.

Ashley giggled and hurried along beside her. "I've never been in a tack store with a doorman before. And such an arrogant one. He didn't even look like a rider. Think they make him wear those tight breeches?"

"He's just a pimped-out security guard," Eve said.

"How can you tell?"

Eve glanced over her shoulder, her mouth tightening. "I just know the security type."

She softened her expression and turned her attention to more important things. They should be able to get by with four bridles, especially since she was the only rider. But the bits needed more thought. Stinger was tough to control and required a ring bit, even for morning gallops. The lazy bay mare was happiest in a loose ring snaffle and the gray gelding preferred a racing D-ring with a copper mouthpiece. Dex and Dani's horse, Tizzy, would be happy with anything, but he was the exception. Tizzy was a rider's dream.

"Look, they have maternity clothes." Ashley jerked to a stop, pausing to admire some shirts with a flared waistband. She checked the tags, then grimaced. "I need some bigger clothes, but these prices are crazy."

She moved to the discount rack, fingering a pretty coral shirt, then pulled her hand back as though burnt. "Sixteen dollars. Even the sales stuff is expensive. And I have those old men's shirts. They should fit for another month."

"I'll buy that for you," Eve said, remembering how grateful she'd been when Megan had brought her something new to wear. "It's payment for staying late last week when the vet came."

"It's still sixteen dollars," Ashley said. "And you're short of cash too."

"But Jackson arranged credit for the bridles." Eve scooped up the shirt. "And you need one nice thing to wear. Is this the one you want?"

Ashley nodded, her eyes glowing. "Yes," she said. "I love it."

Eve smiled, her optimism returning. It had been a few rough weeks but things were improving. Sure, they'd lost a training day but she'd make it up. And with a little luck Tizzy and Stinger would both be ready to run this weekend, even if she was uneasy about the distance of Stinger's race.

Their mood remained upbeat as they selected the bridles, a larger one to fit Stinger's big head, a loose ring snaffle for the mare, and supple race reins with rubber backing.

"These are the easiest to knot," Ashley said, expertly shortening the reins. "What do you think?"

"Yes, those are the best." Eve nodded, enjoying shopping with another knowledgeable rider. Ashley seemed back to her usual buoyant self and they'd done a thorough job of selecting good but inexpensive tack. Jackson would be satisfied.

They walked to the sales register by the entrance and laid their items on the counter.

"I believe Jackson Zeggelaar called," Eve said to the clerk. "You should have his credit card on file."

The gray-haired lady frowned. "No, I don't remember that name."

"Maybe it was his wife, Victoria," Ashley said helpfully.

"Sorry. No one with those names called." The clerk looked past them, smiling at the next customer, a short man in a suit who carried a gleaming saddle with jumping knee rolls.

Eve leaned over the counter, reclaiming the clerk's attention. "Jackson said he'd call. Perhaps you could check with your other staff?"

"Let me ring in this gentleman first." The clerk nodded and reached for the man's saddle. "This is a lovely Stubben. Handmade in Germany. Your daughter will love it. Thirty-five hundred is an excellent price."

Eve's mouth tightened but Ashley clearly didn't share her irritation. She dragged a finger over the brushed cotton of her new shirt, adjusting the collar and even opening and closing the buttons. Eve controlled her impatience, even giving a polite smile as she stepped aside for the father buying the expensive saddle.

Five minutes later, the clerk turned back to them. But her smile was gone now, her mouth a flat line. "You can't buy on credit," she said. "Store policy."

"We're not asking for credit," Eve said. "But our boss planned to arrange payment. He probably left his credit card number."

The woman's face pinched in horror. "We wouldn't do that. He has to be personally present. Otherwise it could be a fraudulent transaction."

Eve blinked. She was accustomed to the tack store at Santa Anita where everyone knew Jackson. "Of course," she said. "Sorry. I'll call him and we can figure out the best way."

"Yes, but move to the end of the counter, please. I have other customers waiting."

The security guard stepped closer, his arms flexing. "Is there a problem?"

"Not yet," Eve said, pulling out her phone. She pressed Jackson's number.

Victoria answered on the first ring, as if expecting the call. "Hello, Eve. What do you want now?"

"I need to talk to Jackson for a sec," Eve said, shocked that Victoria was now controlling Jackson's cell phone. "He was going to arrange for some replacement bridles. But we're at the store now—"

"He's busy with important things," Victoria said. "And your budget doesn't include new tack. You'll have to wait for the insurance check."

"But that could take months. And the amount isn't much. Just five bridles."

"If it's not much," Victoria said, her voice silky but no less threatening, "you should be able to cover the cost. And if you're not capable of handling such a routine matter, maybe I should ship those horses home."

Eve twisted away from the clerk's curious eyes, dismay leaving her movements jerky. Victoria had joined Jackson's stable last year as a lowly hotwalker. Three months later, they were married. Eve had always thought that landing Jackson was the woman's main goal, but perhaps taking over his business was her real intent. He seemed to regret the marriage, and the last few months he'd turned increasingly morose. Now that Eve was away from Santa Anita, Victoria was clearly making a power move.

"I can handle things here," Eve said, her voice tight. "In fact, both Tizzy and Stinger will be entered for the weekend."

"Good," Victoria said. "Be sure to run Stinger a mile and an eighth. And don't call back until Sunday, when you finally have some race results. Understand?"

"I do understand," Eve said. She cut the connection then smacked the phone against her hand.

"What's going on?" Ashley's eyes widened. "Won't she let Jackson pay?"

"She won't even let him talk," Eve said.

"Can you ladies pay for these items, or not?" the clerk asked, a little too loudly.

Eve raised her head, conscious of five other customers straining to catch the drama. Unfortunately she couldn't afford a single bit and bridle. "Not today," she said, reaching for her twenty-dollar bill. "We'll take the shirt though. I'll pay for that with cash."

Ashley reached out and stopped Eve's hand. "No," she said. "I don't need the shirt as much as you need the bridles." She folded the shirt, laying it on top of the counter and walked toward the exit.

Eve followed, hating to see her disappointment. But Ashley was right. Her finances were stretched to the limit, and tack was critical. Somehow, she had to find enough money for at least one bridle.

They walked toward the exit, both of them holding their backs carefully erect. But this time the guard didn't open the door. In fact, he blocked their way.

"I need to check your purses," he said.

"We don't have purses," Eve said.

"Your friend has a backpack. She needs to open it, please."

"It was for bridles," Eve said, "which we didn't buy—"

"Never mind." Ashley pulled off her pack and thrust it at the guard. "Here, take a look. It's obviously empty, except for my water bottle."

The guard glanced inside the backpack, then jabbed his thumb at the door. "Fine," he said. "You're free to go."

"How very kind," Eve said. She pushed open the door and held it for Ashley. Clearly the man's services as a doorman didn't extend to non-paying customers.

She scowled back at the guard but once outside immediately began texting.

"What are you doing?" Ashley asked. "Texting Jackson?"

"No sense," Eve said. "Victoria has his phone. I'm checking with a few friends, trying to figure out what's going on."

"It won't matter," Ashley said glumly. "Haven't you noticed the rest of Jackson's staff are all men now? Every groom, exercise rider and hotwalker. Victoria is cleaning house. And we're next."

"Don't be so pessimistic," Eve said. But her dismay grew as text messages pinged in reply. It wasn't quite as bad as she feared, but everyone confirmed Victoria was leading Jackson around by his dick, even proclaiming she owned half his business since she hadn't signed a prenup.

"I didn't see this coming," Eve said, her spirits plummeting as she scanned her screen. "Poor Jackson."

"You were out with a broken wrist, busy with your son. And Victoria assumed you were married. Now that you're back, as Jackson's assistant trainer no less, she sees you as a threat."

Eve yanked open the car door, her mind whirling. She could probably find riding work at another stable, but once again, she'd have to claw her way up from the bottom. The only horses she'd be given to exercise would be cheap claimers, usually the most dangerous to ride. And danger was exactly what she was trying to avoid.

Unfortunately her recent injury had been costly. Not only had she lost months of earnings but other riders had taken her place. Unless one was a top tier jockey, trainers had notoriously short memories. Of course, they had to please their owners, and it was only natural to favor the hot jockey.

"Luckily you're friends with two of Jackson's owners," Ashley said. "If Victoria manages to chase you off, they'll probably move their horses."

Eve slammed the driver's door, struggling to think. Dex and Dani owned Tizzy, and Scott and Megan had Stinger. But that was only two horses, not a big consideration for Victoria when Jackson managed a stable of forty. And Eve would never ask her friends to switch trainers just because Jackson no longer had a job for her.

"Men are such wimps," she said, clicking her seatbelt tight, trying to downplay her concern. Both Ashley and Miguel had put their trust in Eve, following her from Santa Anita to Riverview. And as the trainer in charge, she felt responsible for her employees, every bit as much as she did for the horses.

"What are you going to do?" Ashley's face was so pale, tiny freckles showed up on her nose. "The horses can't race if you can't exercise them. And even you can't ride without a bridle."

"Don't worry," Eve said. "I'll think of something." She pushed in the clutch and forced a reassuring smile. "At least the car didn't stall while we were inside," she added. "And there's still lots of gas in the tank."

CHAPTER FIVE

Eve propped her elbows on the picnic table, watching three determined boys struggling to build a castle. They filled a bucket with sand and tipped it on top of a growing mound. The sand collapsed to a chorus of groans, and they promptly started the process all over again. One boy looked about four, his dark eyes filled with such lively intelligence, he reminded her of Joey. It almost hurt to see him, and her chest gave a little twist.

She'd never been away from Joey for more than three days. But she had to make this job work. Had to create a better life and stop scraping just to meet monthly expenses. The last round of medical bills for her wrist had consumed her savings. If not for her mother babysitting, the new training career would be impossible.

And her mother was slowing down, better with babies than an energetic boy. Megan and Scott would be happy to help, but Eve hated to turn to them. Again. Her chest gave another kick. They would never try to take Joey. Would they?

"We didn't see you riding this morning."

Eve glanced at the stocky woman seated beside her. Juanita was one of the few ladies that came in the afternoon who could speak English. While the other women conversed in rapid-fire Spanish, Juanita had switched to English, clearly making an effort to include Ashley.

"She couldn't ride today," Ashley said, leaning over the table, eager to join in. "Our bridles were stolen."

Juanita's eyes widened. "But that is terrible. Horses need exercise. How will you train?"

The entire group of women silenced. Clearly they understood some English, or perhaps it was the alarm in Juanita's voice that sparked their attention.

"I'll find a bridle somewhere," Eve said.

She gave Ashley a warning head shake. Up until last year, Victoria had worked at Riverview. She probably still had contacts here, and Eve didn't want rumors spreading. Owners liked their horses with successful trainers, not struggling ones. And there was something about Juanita's expression, as if she knew much more than she pretended.

"Maybe we should fill some buckets with water," Eve added. "So the children can wet the sand and make it stick."

"I'll get the hose," Ashley said, rising from the table.

Juanita waited a moment, then her voice lowered. "You don't have the money to buy a new bridle?"

Eve studied the woman. Despite her sense that Juanita knew more than she let on, she seemed trustworthy. Eve had never heard her gossip, not once.

"I'm broke right now," she admitted. "And my boss has too much going on to help. But it'll be all right once we run a couple races."

She wasn't going to complain, not to Juanita and the other women. Their lives were hard enough, and she wanted this play area to be a spot they could enjoy. Besides, on the poverty scale, she was better off. They worked back-breaking jobs for minimal wages. Juanita helped in the track kitchen so at least she had access to plenty of food, and conversation. But some of the women looked lost and despondent. In fact, Camila, one of the younger women, barely spoke.

"If anyone here has children," Eve said, switching back to Spanish, "there's a new program that might be helpful." She leaned over the table and waved a form. "It's based on need and helps single mothers."

Camila looked up, her usual coolness replaced with interest. "It would help with baby care?"

"Yes," Eve said. "And it's partly subsidized by the racetracks so the eligibility requirements aren't as steep. The wait period isn't very long either."

Eve passed her a form, rather surprised at the girl's interest. Camila was barely twenty and whippet slim. However, while there were only twelve ladies who came to the sand pit regularly—and Camila wasn't one of them—Juanita had confided that they all shared Eve's information with other backstretch workers. Some women were currently pregnant but too shy or afraid to come forward. Or maybe there was just no room to sit.

"Should I try to find another picnic table?" Eve asked. "In case other women want to come? Maybe just to hang out and watch the children play?"

"*Si, gracis.*" All the women gave a vigorous nod. "*Bella princesa,*" someone called.

Their enthusiasm surprised her, warming the otherwise bleak afternoon. Her job might be in peril, but the women's social club was thriving. Unfortunately that didn't pay the bills. And if Tizzy and Stinger didn't step on the track soon, it wouldn't be fair to race them on the weekend.

A fact of which Victoria was no doubt aware.

Eve rubbed her wrist, barely noticing its ache as she skimmed her options. Depressingly few. However, Jackson had mentioned that Tizzy could be galloped without a bridle. He'd been joking, of course, and it was against the rules to take a horse on the track without approved equipment. Outriders were always vigilant. But they were only present during training hours.

And desperate times required desperate measures.

She folded her hands, accepting she was most certainly desperate. And tonight seemed a good time to discover if Tizzy was as well trained as everyone believed.

CHAPTER SIX

"Sure you want to risk this?" Ashley's voice squeaked as she tightened Tizzy's girth another notch. "You don't want to end up back in the hospital. Or worse, suspended."

"It's the perfect time," Eve said. "Almost midnight. No one will be around."

Training hours were from six to ten in the morning. The track was strictly monitored then, and it was impossible to exercise a horse without a bridle. She'd be banished. However at night, the track was deserted. Besides, she didn't have much choice. Tizzy needed to stretch his legs.

But even Miguel, who always seemed to understand a horse's psych, appeared worried. Leathery grooves fanned the skin around his eyes and his gnarly fists gripped Tizzy's lead shank much tighter than usual.

Eve shoved aside her own misgivings. She adjusted her helmet and safety vest then reached up and snapped two rope lead lines to the sides of Tizzy's halter. Of all the horses she'd ever galloped, he was the only Thoroughbred she'd dare ride on a track without a bit in his mouth.

Tizzy's owner, Dani Tattrie, had spent a lot of time training this horse before he'd been sent to the track. The gelding was as well trained as any ranch horse. More importantly, he was the special type who always wanted to please his rider.

"We'll be fine," Eve said. "He can't stand in his stall any longer. It's not fair to him if he's going to be entered for Saturday."

"Don't fall off," Ashley said as she legged Eve into the saddle. "They'll catch you for sure."

"Want me to lead another horse over?" Miguel asked, his eyes still grave. "For company?"

She shook her head. Having another horse waiting by the gap might draw attention, especially if they started calling. Besides, Tizzy was one of the most confident horses she'd ever met. He didn't mind being ridden off alone.

Of course, she'd never taken him out in the middle of the night before.

"Let's go." She shoved aside her own misgivings, knotted the two ropes into makeshift reins and settled into the saddle.

They headed down the aisle and into the crisp night. Ashley led Tizzy from his left side with Miguel on the horse's right. And it worked fine until they left the open area and entered the dark path leading to the track.

First Miguel stumbled, then Ashley, both humans walking so tentatively that Tizzy started to prance, picking up on Eve's frustration with the tortoise-slow pace.

"I'll take him alone from here," she said, keeping her voice low. "And meet you two at the gap. You can cut across the parking lot and open the rail. Keep the flashlight off, unless you need to warn that someone's coming."

She couldn't see their expressions, just the outline of their bobbing heads. Then they faded into the darkness, and she and Tizzy were alone.

The horse stepped out, his walk long and relaxed now that he wasn't encumbered by two grooms hanging onto his halter. He had excellent night vision, and her eyes slowly adjusted as well.

It was a cloudy but serene night. Through the trees, barn lights glowed in neat rows, set against the taller lights of the parking lot. The horse path was a dark ribbon, but Tizzy knew where he was heading. He felt strong and solid, and she drew in an appreciative breath, enjoying the feel of a good horse, as well as the solitude. This wasn't so different from a pre-dawn gallop, except that the track wasn't lit.

She stroked his velvety neck, grateful for his obliging nature. He flicked an ear but continued his long-reaching walk, obviously focused on reaching the track. And no wonder. Other than being led around the tiny ring by the barn, Tizzy hadn't been out of his stall for thirty-six hours. They hadn't dared let him loose in the sandpit, afraid his pent-up energy might result in energetic bucking and cause an injury.

She sat easily in the saddle, looking straight ahead but absorbing the night sounds, alert for any movement. Tizzy's behavior without a bridle wasn't even her biggest concern. Riding on a closed track was a serious offense, and she couldn't afford to be fined or suspended. But as Jackson stressed, it was past time to run some races. And no horse could safely compete if he were stuck in a stall all week.

She tightened her hold on the two ropes, putting tension on the halter, experimenting with her control. Tizzy arched his neck, giving to the pressure on his nose. She loosened the ropes and gave him another approving pat. If he listened like that on the track, there'd be no problem.

Traffic hummed in the distance, joined by the sound of frogs chorusing from the nearby river. Overhead, a blinking plane carved a path in the dark sky. Other than that, their world was insulated from any intrusion. It was Tizzy's raised head, the shortening of his steps, which alerted her to someone's presence.

He stared straight ahead, ears riveted. Alert but certainly unafraid.

Ashley stepped from the shadows. "You made good time," she whispered. "We just got here. The rail is open."

Eve peered past her, straining to see the track. It was darker than she'd anticipated, the white inner rail barely visible.

"I'm going to stick to a trot," she said. "If all goes well, I'll turn and gallop a mile. Flash the light if you have company, and I'll know to stay away."

"Okay," Ashley said. She and Miguel stepped aside, and Eve walked Tizzy through the gap.

He tossed his head, fresh and eager to run. She turned him clockwise, the opposite direction of a race, letting him know this wasn't a speed work.

She guided him to the middle of the track, away from both the inner and outer rail, and he settled into a beautiful floating trot, his ears pinned forward, as if searching for another horse. The makeshift reins felt odd, the ropes thick and lifeless in her hands, but she quickly adjusted.

They rounded the clubhouse turn. Tizzy's steps were muffled in the deep dirt and fortunately his dark coat blended into the night. He only broke stride twice—once when a rabbit darted across the track and the second, when a loud motor roared aggressively from the parking lot entrance.

"You're a good boy," she murmured, slowing him to a walk.

She stopped and stood for a moment, listening to his breathing, feeling the slow beat of his heart. It was obvious he needed more exercise.

She turned, still staying in the middle of the track but now headed in a counter-clockwise direction. This was the moment of truth—when she'd discover if she really had any control. She hummed a soothing children's lullaby, Joey's favorite, and the one she always relied on to keep a horse calm.

But Tizzy's head rose. His nose jutted out and he rocketed into a gallop, veering toward the inner rail so quickly he almost whipped the rope from her weakened wrist. She rose in the stirrups, letting her weight fall on his nose, frantically trying to steer him back to the middle of the track. He resisted, but only for a moment.

Then he gave to the pressure on his nose, his stride steadying, as if they were partners once again and he was used to being galloped in a halter. And he might have been. Dex and Dani Tattrie were mighty fine trainers.

She grinned, relishing the cool air whipping her cheeks. The wind always eased away her worries, but it didn't get any better than this. She'd never had a big racetrack all to herself. There were no distractions—no pounding hooves or riders' hollers or other animals to avoid. It was just her and this obliging horse. Pure magic.

The inner rail was a blur of white now. His rhythmic breathing blended with hers, his powerful stride long and even, and if he missed balancing against the bit, he didn't show it.

Just past the finish line, she rose in the stirrups and leaned back on the rope. Tizzy slowed to a canter and then down to a trot. He barely pulled at the ropes, as if aware her injured wrist hadn't regained its strength.

She leaned forward and gave his damp neck a delighted pat. "You're a prince of a fellow," she said, her breath mingling with his.

A few more nights like this and he'd definitely be ready to run on Saturday. The ride had gone more smoothly than even she'd dared to hope. It hadn't taken long either. Tizzy would be cooled off by the time they walked back to the barn. Now, she just had to make her escape and get him off the track.

But a light flashed, and her satisfaction flipped to a chilling fear. She was only fifty feet from the gap and couldn't see Ashley or Miguel. However, the light flickered again, clearly a warning.

She straightened in the saddle, alarm turning her ramrod stiff. She pulled Tizzy in a circle, straining to see through the dark. It was probably just some backstretch workers returning to the dorms after a night out. They'd be gone soon.

The light flashed again, more frantically now.

Moments later, Ashley's loud voice cut through the night. "Oh, hello. I'm so glad to see *security* around. I dropped my wallet somewhere. Trying to find it."

Eve's throat turned bone dry. She wheeled Tizzy in the opposite direction and trotted away, grateful for the starless night. But now everything seemed cannon loud. Tizzy's hooves, his heavy breathing, her own thrashing heart.

And Tizzy was not happy. He'd expected to leave through the gap, return to the barn and finish his hay. Now he was confused, and irritated. He balked, and she nudged him forward with her legs.

"It's okay," she whispered. "We'll find another way out."

He swished his tail but stepped forward. At least he wasn't nickering. They'd have to circle to the tractor entrance, the one at the far end of the chute beyond the starting gate. It was a long walk but no problem.

But she wiped her sweaty palms against his mane, trying to soothe her apprehension. Because if they'd stationed a second security guard by the tractors, it would be a problem. A very big one.

CHAPTER SEVEN

Rick killed the bike's engine in front of the security booth and tugged off his helmet. It had been a relief to ditch the drug car and climb back on his Harley. To drive as he wanted, simply enjoying the solitude. In fact, the ride to the track had been so liberating he'd explored several side roads, stretching the one-hour drive into six.

The pudgy guard slid the window open a scant inch, studying Rick with obvious alarm. "Lost?" he asked, keeping well back from the opening. "Need directions?"

"Nope." Rick hooked a leg over the seat of his bike. "Not if this is Riverview Racetrack."

"It is," the guard said. "But slot machines are closed."

"What about the horses?"

"Next races are Saturday afternoon."

Rick stepped off the bike and gave a lazy stretch. The guard edged back, his hand slipping below the counter.

"I'm looking for a woman," Rick said, remaining by his bike and giving the guard plenty of space. "She lives in the dorms."

The guard's twitchy fingers returned to the counter. "I see. But we can't let people in without credentials. You understand?" He cleared his throat. "So late like this…"

Rick remained silent. If they let him in at midnight, they'd let anyone in. Which would explain the thefts plaguing Scott's trainer.

"Maybe you could call her?" the guard suggested. "Have her come to the gate?"

"And then you let me in," Rick said. It wasn't a question.

"Well, no." The guard shook his head. "Sorry but you'll still need credentials. There's a bar a couple miles down the road. Open late. And it has a motel that rents rooms by the hour."

A radio buzzed from within the guardhouse.

"Just a moment, please." The man turned and picked up a handset.

Rick yawned and replaced his helmet. He'd learned what he needed to know. Security was in place, at least at the front gate. He'd head over to that motel, enjoy a few beers, and pick up his creds in the morning. Nothing was happening here, not tonight.

"Yes, sir." The guard spoke into the radio mouthpiece, his head nodding with fresh urgency. "Heading there now," he said. He replaced the handset and stuck a yellow note in the window: BACK IN TEN MINUTES. Then he scooped some keys from a wall hook.

"Think you'll be able to find that motel?" he asked, glancing at Rick.

"Think so," Rick said.

The guard hurried from the building, his keys jingling. He glanced at Rick and made a show of double locking the door, then jogged to a compact Jeep parked just inside the closed gate. The engine started and the vehicle sped down the paved drive toward the track, its roof lights streaking the sky with amber.

Rick studied the sky, tracking the warning beacons. It appeared two security vehicles were on the move, one at the east end of the track, the other by the barns in the north end. And then a third set of lights stained the night. Those ones came from the south end of the track.

Interesting. Three vehicles on full alert. Track security was definitely out in force, even calling their man in from the front gate. Maybe they were close to corralling the thieves and Scott Taylor's investigative agency wouldn't be required. Perfect.

He revved his engine. The security bar was lowered over the entrance but it was designed to stop cars. Not bikes. He eased his motorcycle over the side of the concrete onto the grass, skirted the closed gate then rolled back onto the pavement.

The bike's powerful headlight outlined a square reflective sign, its arrows indicating that the clubhouse and grandstand were to the right. The guard had headed left, toward the backstretch.

Rick veered in the opposite direction of the guard. He cruised through a deserted parking lot and into the owners' section, only a stone's throw from the saddling paddock.

He cut the engine, sat back and checked the sky. The towering clubhouse blocked his view of the track but judging from the yellow streaks, the guards had the oval surrounded. Clearly they were going to considerable effort to catch this culprit.

He stared through the gloom at the saddling enclosure. An equine walkway tunneled beneath the clubhouse, leading from the paddock to the track.

He removed his helmet and gloves, stepped off his bike, and walked into the tunnel. Except for some random horse droppings and a program that fluttered in the breeze, the place was eerily empty. A line of white outlined the track with a smaller rail marking the winner's circle. Otherwise, the grandstand was completely dark.

All the action appeared to be on the opposite side of the track, close to the barns. A security vehicle was parked in the chute, its yellow lights bouncing off the starting gate. Obviously the guards were more interested in the gaps by the backstretch, as opposed to the public grandstand where he stood.

It was a mystery why they blocked the gap and not the roads. But having a sprawling grandstand all to oneself was certainly a moment to be savored. Besides, watching the guards chase down their man was much more interesting than lying on a seedy motel bed, waiting for the sun to rise.

He ambled to the front row and selected a prime seat adjacent to the winner's circle. Then he stretched out his legs and leaned back, enjoying the rare luxury of being a spectator.

CHAPTER EIGHT

Unbelievable. Eve sucked in a ragged breath, shaken that the guards were already blocking the second gate. She wheeled Tizzy away from the tractor chute, away from the security vehicle with the flashing lights and back into the friendly darkness. But now she was truly stuck.

Only two gaps opened to the backstretch and there were vehicles watching both gates. In addition, yellow lights flashed at the entrance of the horse track leading to the barn. Ashley and Miguel definitely had company.

She fought to control her panic. But her options were limited. Walk Tizzy around the track until morning? Then pretend she'd just arrived when it opened? However, that wouldn't be healthy for Tizzy, and it certainly wouldn't be fair to ask him to race on Saturday.

And soon the guards might wise up. If she were trying to catch someone, she'd simply turn on the overhead lights and spotlight the horse and rider. It would be impossible to hide. The guards might be a little dull but they weren't complete morons.

She gulped and glanced over her shoulder. Security was certainly on high alert. It would be nice if they devoted half as much energy to preventing the thefts at her barn. No doubt they already suspected her identity, after seeing Ashley and Miguel waiting by the gap.

Obviously the guards hadn't believed Ashley's excuse about looking for a wallet, or maybe they'd heard Tizzy's hooves. Didn't matter what had alerted them. It was apparent she'd be caught. Only a matter of time. She wasn't sure if the racing commission would hit her with a fine or opt for suspension. Either way, it could be a career killer, something that would thrill Victoria.

She eyed the three and a half foot rail. "Too bad you can't jump," she whispered, almost tempted to try. Tizzy had probably hopped over logs at the ranch. But there was concrete on the other side and she would never risk injuring him. Broken legs were reparable with humans, not so much with horses.

Tizzy just flicked an ear and walked faster. He'd already been disappointed once, thinking the ride was over, so this new eagerness was rather baffling. Especially since they now headed away from the backstretch, away from the barn with his food and buddies. Strange, since horses were creatures of habit, and on training days they always left the track through the gap.

And then she understood. Tizzy was heading for the finish line. He thought she'd get off and remove the saddle there, close to the weigh scales where the jockeys dismounted after every race. And of course there was a removable rail by the tunnel, so the horses could parade from the paddock onto the track.

"Smart horse," she said, hope lifting her higher in the saddle. There didn't appear to be any guards by the clubhouse. Not yet. In fact, the entire grandstand was dark. The guards were watching the track adjacent to the barns. They hadn't even considered the paddock entrance.

All she had to do was walk Tizzy through the tunnel and off the track. The saddling enclosure had no time restrictions. It might be odd to have a horse by the paddock at midnight, but it wasn't illegal.

Tizzy sensed her new eagerness and broke into a trot. She feared security might hear the telltale thud of his hooves so she slipped her feet from the stirrups, letting him know it was time to relax. Besides, it wasn't much further. A green and white pole gleamed, the markings indicating there was only an eighth of a mile remaining between her and escape.

She squeezed her palms tighter around the rope reins, just praying she'd reach the clubhouse before the guards realized there was another way out.

Rick heard the horse before he saw it. He leaned forward, eyeing the dark shape that materialized from the shadows. One horse, one rider.

They stopped a scant ten feet in front of him, then expertly sidepassed until they were alongside the rail. The rider leaned down, groping to open the gate. The horse twisted, shoving at the rail with his nose, clearly trying to help. But his fidgeting only moved the rider's hand further away.

"Easy," the rider whispered. Her voice was calm, determined and distinctly female.

The horse stilled. But he pawed at the ground as if trying to hurry her up. He didn't wear a bridle, just a halter with two attached ropes. And the rider didn't carry a backpack or even saddle pads. Clearly this wasn't the tack thief.

"Need some help?" he asked, careful not to move from his seat. He knew he'd startle the rider, but he certainly didn't want to spook the horse.

They surprised him with their composure. She barely twitched, just swiveled in the saddle, scanning the darkened seats, trying to pinpoint his voice. Then she wisely checked her horse, tracking his pricked ears, letting him reveal Rick's location.

He could see her eyes when she spotted him, noted their resignation. No fear at all, which rather surprised him. Even the security guard had assumed he was a badass. Living the life of an outlaw, he'd grown accustomed to being treated with a certain degree of caution, from both men and women.

But she gifted him with a beautiful smile, as if relieved by his appearance. And that shocked him even more.

"Hi," she said. "I thought you were security."

"Not security," he said.

"Yes. I can see that." Her laugh was soft and musical, and full of such delight it left him grinning back.

"I'm surprised they let you in this late," she added.

"They didn't. I rode my bike around the gate after the guard left."

She gave an approving nod. "Good for you. Some of the guards can be control freaks. They always give strangers a hard time."

"They're chasing someone else tonight."

She glanced across the track. "Yes," she said wryly. "They're after me."

"Really? What did you do?" Maybe he'd been wrong and she'd stashed the bridles elsewhere. But he sincerely hoped she wasn't his tack thief. It had been years since a woman had been so relaxed around him. Undercover required a certain appearance. He could clean up, of course, but his heart wasn't in it. And this type of acceptance was utterly refreshing.

"The track is only open in the morning," she said. The horse pawed again, and she placed a steadying hand on his neck. "I needed to get this guy out and stretch his legs."

Rick blinked and leaned back in his seat. And then he laughed. A big booming belly laugh. "*That's* the reason for all those vehicles," he finally managed, still chuckling. "They're looking for someone who's riding a horse at the wrong time?"

"It seems like overkill to me too." She leaned forward, her voice lowering to a conspiratorial whisper. "But could you please tone down the laugh. Because they will suspend me if I'm caught."

He squeezed his mouth shut, still grinning at the absurdity. There was no major crime here—no felons or bodies or blood. It was the type of place where they sent three security vehicles roaring after a tiny woman on a docile horse. Maybe Scott Taylor had been right about a vacation. *This* was what normal people worried about—riding after hours.

He couldn't keep his lips straight, and another laugh leaked out.

"I'm glad you find this amusing," she said. "But if you can't be quiet, could you at least cover your mouth? Sound does carry."

There was a new edge to her voice and clearly she didn't suffer fools gladly. And suddenly it was important she not consider him a fool.

He unfolded from his seat and stepped up to the rail. "I'm not laughing at your predicament," he said. "Just astonished they'd pull all the guards for this...horrendous rule breaking."

"Well, they do need to keep the horses safe. That's everyone's goal. And the track was freshly harrowed so it'll be smooth for tomorrow morning." Her slim shoulders lifted in a shrug. "But yes, their reaction is surprising."

She was trying to be fair, and he liked that. He didn't really want to open the gate and let her vanish into the night. Talking to her was much more fun than nursing a beer in another dirty bar.

But she probably wanted to scoot. Now that he was standing next to the rail, she'd be able to see every inch of him, from his worn leather jacket to his scruffy hair and jaw. And no amount of scrubbing could wash away the stench of his work. It hung over him like a cloud. No doubt she was terrified.

"Are you going to just stand there?" she asked. "Or are you going to open that gate?"

He grinned. Not terrified at all, just impatient. He studied her face, the regal tilt of her head, the determined press of her lips. She was spunky, fearless and so tiny he could probably wrap one hand around her waist. But best of all, she treated him like he was normal.

"Certainly I'll open it." He spread his hand over the rail, stalling for time. "But what will you do with that horse in the parking lot? Is there a pathway back to the barns?"

He'd already memorized the layout and knew the answer to that question. There was no way around the guards.

She shook her head. "No, but I can wait in the saddling enclosure until morning. It's good ground there and it will be fine on Tizzy's feet."

"You're going to stand there all night?" he asked, deciding he definitely wanted to stay and keep her company. "Doesn't sound like much fun...alone."

"It'll be fine. It's worse for Tizzy than me. Especially since I hoped to race him on Saturday."

She hadn't picked up on his invitation, or else had chosen to ignore it. He suspected the latter. There was a focus about her, a clarity of purpose. She was clearly concerned about her horse, as if she were used to responsibility and didn't intend to shirk it.

She placed her hand on the horse's neck again, reassuring him that he'd be okay. That she was going to take care of him. And that little gesture moved Rick, even more than the desire to talk her up.

"The race on Saturday," he said. "Is that important to you?"

"Very." She shot a wistful look across the track. "Hopefully the guards will give up and leave, so I can get him back to his stall."

"Maybe I can help with that." He raised his helmet, setting it on top of the rail. "And have some fun in the process."

Her eyes flashed with hope. Then she shook her head. "A bike diversion might work but if they catch you, they'll give you a hard time. And if it's on the public lot, they'll call in the real police. And they're usually bigger assholes than the security guards."

"They won't catch me," he said.

She looked at him more carefully, her gaze traveling from his head to his boots, absorbing him with feminine awareness. "Probably not," she said, and her voice sounded a little husky, a little more promising.

"I'll draw them off. You get your horse home." He leaned closer, sensing the new vibration in the air. "And then I'll come back and see you on Saturday. Maybe we could have dinner? Or find something else we'd both like to do..."

She'd been leaning forward, closer to his face, but abruptly straightened. Even the horse raised his head and turned all indignant. "Or you won't draw them off?" she asked. "You expect some sort of payment?"

"Not at all," he said. "I'll get you off the track, no strings. But I will be around on Saturday. And I would like to see you again."

She scanned his face, still wary, but after a moment her shoulders softened. "All right," she said. "I'd like that too. So you better not get caught."

CHAPTER NINE

"Tell me more." Ashley swung the bucket with such excitement that water splashed Eve's leg. "Was he on a bike or a car? The guards are so pissed."

She adjusted Tizzy's bucket then turned back toward Eve. "When I stopped at the security booth this morning, everyone was complaining about being up all night. They said two guys were stunting in the parking lot, but they couldn't catch anyone."

Eve rocked back on her heels, swept with relief. She'd worried all night about her unlikely savior. The security Jeeps had fled their posts at the first taunting roar of his engine. Then it had been simple to ride Tizzy through the unmanned gap and return to the barn. She hadn't told Ashley and Miguel many details—just that someone had kindly offered to create a diversion.

"Liam isn't even certain about the vehicle," Ashley went on. "The driver seemed to know where all the security cams were. But Liam asked where you were last night. And if you trained a black horse."

Eve studied Tizzy who was tugging at his hay, seeming none the worse for last night's escapade. Fortunately, bay horses often appeared black. She wasn't too worried about Liam and the security guards. It had been a dark night and she'd been wearing a helmet and vest. Identity would be hard to prove.

"He asked a lot of other questions," Ashley went on, "like if we were able to replace our bridles. And why Miguel and I were looking for my wallet so late last night. He's definitely suspicious."

Eve shrugged. She didn't want her staff fretting. It was a trainer's job to absorb the worry. She gave Ashley a grateful smile. "Thanks for your warning. If I didn't see the flashlight and hear you talking, I would have ridden right into them."

Ashley's forehead wrinkled. "It was like they were expecting us."

"We filed a report," Eve said. "Obviously they know our bridles were stolen."

She tugged the water hose in a tight coil and gave a regretful sigh. She'd escaped this time, but it would be too risky to ride again at night. Especially if the guards were watching. And she didn't have enough money to buy replacement tack.

"We're going to have to leave, aren't we?" Ashley asked. "Liam thinks I might be able to find a job here. Catching urine. Just until I have the baby. After that I can go back to Santa Anita and find jockey work." She jammed a tendril of hair behind her ear and peeked at Eve, as if gauging her reaction.

"That's great." Eve gripped the water hose with both hands. Her training career was imploding before it even began. But a pee catcher's job would be perfect for Ashley. It mainly consisted of holding a container on the end of a long stick and gathering a horse's urine for drug testing. Best of all, the Thoroughbreds were tired and relaxed after a race so it was relatively safe.

At least Ashley would have a job. It was clear Victoria wanted all three of them gone: Ashley because she was pregnant, Miguel because he was old, and Eve because she was friends with Jackson.

She swallowed, trying to gather a more encouraging response. "You should probably grab that job. But I'll sure miss you."

"Me too," Ashley said glumly. "There's so much more you can teach me about riding. If only they hadn't stolen our bridles. That was the lowest. Guess the women want the sand area to themselves."

"I can't believe it was the women," Eve said, fighting her sense of betrayal.

"But I saw someone creeping around in the woods earlier, and everyone knows the locals don't like newcomers. Liam says we should stay away from them. Luckily I locked the feed and tack rooms last night."

"Very lucky," Eve said dryly, "considering that's your job."

"Yes, but I was up late helping you escape the guards." Ashley covered her mouth and gave a theatrical yawn. "So of course I'm extra tired this morning."

"Go on back to the dorm," Eve said. "It's still dark, and I can't ride. You can catch up on your sleep."

"Awesome!" Ashley didn't need a second invitation. She dropped her bucket, turned and hurried down the aisle. "You're the best boss ever," she called over her shoulder before disappearing into the dark.

Eve finished coiling the hose, appreciating the break from Ashley's chatter. She was grateful the guards hadn't caught her bike rider, and was a little surprised with her impulsive agreement to meet on Saturday. But there was something appealing about him and she couldn't deny the flare of attraction. She'd felt the same way when she first met Joey's dad, five years earlier at jockey school.

She walked down the aisle, checking each animal, making sure they were all watered and happily chewing hay. They required grooming and stalls needed to be cleaned. However, the hectic morning schedule was vastly altered now that no horses could be exercised. It felt all wrong to have downtime in the early morning, like her life was out of sync.

She trudged back to the entrance, dropped onto a chair by the door and checked her phone. Jackson hadn't answered any of her texts. No surprise there. But Victoria had replied for him: *If you don't race by Sunday, horses will be shipped home.*

She dropped her head in her hands, trying to push away the beginning of a headache. Maybe she should give up and return to Santa Anita. At least she'd be with Joey. A part of her felt bereft without him. She missed his hugs, his gap-toothed smile, the trusting way he clutched her hand. But he'd be with Scott and Megan this weekend—his doting aunt and uncle who never had time or money problems. And who were eager to be a bigger part of his life.

Maybe too eager.

Fear banded her chest, matching the pain pulsing in her forehead. If they realized she hadn't had a paycheck in four months, they'd offer her money. And she hated accepting charity. Hated that she couldn't give Joey as much as they could.

A trainer's job had seemed perfect. Earning a percentage of a horse's winnings, while keeping both feet safely on the ground, was better for a mom. She'd thought the earnings would be more dependable, especially after a rash of injuries stopped her from race riding. But training was challenging too, especially when she had no cash cushion for unforeseen events—like stolen car batteries and bits and bridles.

She wasn't inclined toward self-pity, but her usual confidence was shaken. The only bright light was that she hadn't been caught last night, thanks to the big biker with the sexy voice and irreverent laugh. She'd always felt more comfortable with men who weren't afraid to bend the rules, unlike Ashley who gravitated to the lily-white security guards, guys in crisp khaki uniforms who freaked out over a little riding curfew.

Movement flickered by the trees. She quit analyzing her taste in men, and jerked forward in the chair. Someone was definitely out there, indecipherable in the predawn. But a second shadow darkened the sand pit. And another. Then three more.

For a second, she simply stared, too stunned to move. So Ashley was correct. It was the locals who were stealing. She couldn't tell if they were men or women but they were definitely working as a group. Trying to drive her away. And their theft had tanked her career.

Adrenaline shot through her, fueled by white-hot fury. She jerked from the chair, too angry to be afraid. Grabbed a pitchfork and charged toward the picnic tables.

"*Buenas dias, princesa*," someone called. A woman's voice. And shockingly familiar.

"Juanita?" Her steps faltered. She never would have suspected the older woman was linked to the thieves. Of all the ladies who gathered in the afternoon, she had become closest to Juanita. Even though they were both reserved, they'd already shared a few confidences. Eve had even talked about her son—something she rarely did around the track— and confided how she hoped to bring Joey here to visit.

Helplessness replaced her anger and her fingers loosened around the wooden handle. No way could she report Juanita and her band of women. Some of them didn't even have green cards. A conviction could wreck their lives. And it wouldn't recover the missing bridles. No doubt, the tack had already been flipped.

"We didn't want you to see us," Juanita said.

"I bet not." Eve jammed the pitchfork into the ground, her shoulders sagging.

"Even my cousin helped," Juanita went on. "In Guadalajara, he worked with metal. If this doesn't work for your devil horse, he'll make you another."

"Devil horse?" Eve tilted her head. "You mean Stinger?"

"*Si*," Juanita said, excited now and reverting to Spanish. "We hope it's enough." She stepped sideways and gestured at the picnic tables.

Eve blinked.

Bridle parts covered both tables. Countless pieces of leather and nylon and metal buckles, enough to make twenty bridles. The leather was cracked and worn, the buckles discolored, but every piece was precious.

Her knees caved and she leaned against the pitchfork, unable to move or speak, stunned by their thoughtfulness. The women must have tramped around for hours, collecting discards from every single shedrow.

"Is it okay?" Juanita asked.

And then Eve was able to move. She shot forward, clasping Juanita with arms that shook.

"*Perfecto,*" she said, her throat impossibly thick. *"Muchas gracias."* She hugged each woman in turn, the delight on their faces almost matching her own gratitude.

Even Camila cracked a rare smile. "I collected the blue reins," she said.

"Now maybe you'll be able to ride your horses today," Juanita said, her eyes hopeful. "Then you can stay and race at our track."

Eve gave an excited nod, already fingering the mixture of leather and nylon. She'd piece together a bridle now, then groom and saddle the first horse. Miguel could rouse Ashley, and they could tack up the others while she rode. Her barn was back in business.

The women smiled and drifted away, heading back to work as silently as they'd appeared. But they seemed to carry themselves a little taller, their shoulders a little more square.

And even though she was eager to assemble a bridle, her fingers shook far too much to manage any buckles. She sat at the table long after the last woman disappeared, simply savoring their unexpected gift and blinking back her grateful tears.

CHAPTER TEN

Rick parked his motorcycle by a tired Honda Civic, its red roof bleached from too many years in the sun. He pulled off his gloves and helmet, placing them on his seat, all the while absorbing every detail of the little horse barn.

According to Scott Taylor's file, the barn was leased to the racetrack by a disinterested farmer. It was well built but different from typical shedrows, the building more square than long, with only one aisle and a single entrance.

A chain link fence ran behind the barn, disappearing into a tall stand of trees. The fence looked solid, with three strands of imposing barbed wire stretched along the top. The barn was a considerable hike from the other shedrows though, as well as the dorms. Certainly at night it would be vulnerable, and its isolation probably made it unpopular for the guards to patrol.

No doubt though, the horses loved this spot. There was plenty of grass for grazing along with an enclosed sandpit where they could be turned out for a roll. Further back, a stately oak tree shaded a second unfenced pile of sand. An empty hammock drifted in the morning breeze, and two picnic tables were strewn with pieces of tack. But it was strangely quiet. Birds chirped and a curious bay horse stuck his head out the barn window. Other than that, there was no movement.

Rick's mouth flattened with disapproval. This woman didn't seem very committed. Race barns were always hectic in the morning. It was odd that a man like Scott Taylor would tolerate incompetence, although having a relative as a trainer explained a lot. Perhaps the bridles hadn't really been stolen, and it was simply an excuse not to gallop.

He dragged a hand over his jaw, trying to calculate a low-level trainer's salary. Usually it was a base price per horse with approximately ten percent of the winnings. Definitely purse money was a keystone of earnings, so it was critical to have your horses racing—and finishing in the money. But horses didn't run well if they weren't exercised.

He shook his head with fresh irritation. This wasn't just laziness. Running horses that weren't in shape was abusive. And he had to stay here for a month. *Damn you, Scott.*

Not only was this a dead boring assignment but it would be hard to hide his aversion. And he needed to stay busy. Needed to keep his body and mind tired. If it weren't for his intent to track down the little rider from last night, he'd quit Scott Taylor's agency right now.

He strode into the barn, hot and irritated. At least the building was shaded. Each stall had a window, and there was a pleasant breeze. He pulled in a breath, his steps slowing as he absorbed the coolness, the primal smells, the refreshing company of animals.

He gave an appreciative sniff. It had been a decade since he'd moved to LA, and the smell of hay and horse surprised him with its welcome, like an old friend he hadn't realized he missed. Two horses poked their heads over their stall doors—a friendly gray and a big-headed chestnut who flattened his ears in warning.

He avoided the aggressive chestnut and checked the gray's stall. The water bucket was full but manure soiled the straw. He grimaced and walked down the aisle, calling out a greeting.

However, the barn was devoid of humans. There was no tack or feed in sight, although two doors at the far end were padlocked. Next to the locked doors was an empty stall that contained a rickety card table and a green army cot. No obvious drugs or alcohol. A container of vitamins sat on the table alongside a wrinkled condition book that listed upcoming races.

He picked up the container of vitamins and checked the label. They were clearly vitamins—prenatal, if the label could be believed. He returned it to the table and stepped back into the aisle.

The gray tossed his head and pawed, eager to escape his stall.

Rick paused to pat the horse. "Wish I could help you, buddy... His words trailed off in a rush of sympathy when he spotted the ragged cut on the horse's back. It was pink and puckered. The wound was healing now but it must have been painful. Stabled horses didn't generally receive that type of injury. Maybe it had been an ill-fitting saddle. Something any competent trainer would notice long before such damage.

He scratched the gray's jaw a little harder. If he ever had the privilege to own a racehorse again, he'd never entrust it to someone like Scott's trainer. Little wonder the woman was being robbed. There was no staff around, at a time when every other barn bustled.

He walked outside, kicked the chair out from the wall and sat.

Five days—he'd give Scott until Saturday. He'd tighten up this barn, track down the bridle thieves, and then insist on returning to the streets for some real work. He didn't want to be stuck babysitting, and he certainly didn't need a vacation. He had no desire to rejoin polite society. Didn't mean there was anything wrong with his head.

The highlight here would be going to the races on Saturday and meeting up with his intriguing night rider. She was the only appeal. It had been awhile since he'd been so interested in a woman. Maybe he'd stay until Monday before splitting. Because the air last night had definitely been crackling.

An orange cat rubbed against his boot, then jumped up and settled on his lap. He stiffened, then realized it wasn't necessary to shoo it away. Mad Dog wasn't around, looking for cats to toss to his pit bulls.

The cat started purring even before he dragged a finger over its ragged ear. Behind him, horses contentedly chewed hay. It was rather peaceful. Maybe it wouldn't be such a chore to take some time off. A few days though, not much. Just to have a little break when there was no need to worry about a knife sliding between his ribs. But he'd call Scott tonight, make sure the man understood there was no way he was staying past Monday.

He stretched out his legs and leaned back, taking care not to jostle the cat. The poor thing was just looking for a safe place to sleep. And he could certainly provide that.

CHAPTER ELEVEN

The thud of hooves jerked Rick awake. He straightened in the chair, surprised he'd napped. He hadn't even noticed when the cat left.

He was even more shocked by the gaudy bridle on the approaching horse. Part nylon, part leather, in colors ranging from faded blue to bright green. With a neon pink brow band.

He leaned forward and adjusted his sunglasses.

"A little blinding, right?" The rider laughed, a tinkling familiar laugh. "Everyone on the track was snickering, but the outriders had no real reason to kick me off." She glanced at his motorcycle. "I'm glad to see you—thanks for the diversion last night. But this is only Tuesday…?"

Rick rose, blinking. He was accustomed to thinking fast on his feet. His life often depended on it. But his usual smoothness seemed to have vanished. He hadn't expected to see *her* until Saturday. In the daylight, her attractiveness was even more apparent. Not a traditional beauty but rather exotic, with flashing dark eyes, a sexy mouth and interesting curves that couldn't be concealed by the protective vest.

But it was her aura that was most compelling. Fire and light. She sat her horse with regal authority, and if he'd met her in a gang clubhouse he'd be moving very carefully right now.

He cleared the huskiness from his throat. "You ride for Scott Taylor's trainer?"

"No," she said, still smiling. "I'm the trainer. At least at this track."

Her genuine smile, totally absent of reservation, turned his mind to mush. He had the weird compulsion to look for a mirror and check his appearance. In his experience, women were either looking for drugs, thrills or no-strings sex. Their smiles were tight and scared, or else blatant come-ons. But she was definitely unafraid. And regrettably, she didn't look ready to hop off her horse and unbuckle his belt. She just acted like he was normal.

"You're Eve Lewis?" he asked. "Not a rider, but Scott's trainer?"

"That's what I said." She frowned, as if disappointed in his mental acuity. She glanced once again at his motorcycle, her lively eyes flashing with intelligence. "Oh, I see. You're not even a real biker. You're Rick, Scott's man. Megan said he was sending someone, even though I told them not to. Well, as you can see…" She gestured at her colorful bridle. "You're not needed."

She unfastened her helmet with an authoritative click. "I'm really sorry you came all this way. But it's best if you go back to LA."

A half hour ago, returning to the streets was exactly what he'd wanted. But her quick dismissal irked him. And left him oddly disappointed.

"I can't leave yet," he said. "The agency pulled a lot of strings to arrange a groom's license. They want me to stay and stop the thefts."

"We're careful to lock the doors now. So there's no longer a problem. And I don't want to waste Scott's time, or yours."

"But there must be other things that need…doing." He gave a suggestive smile that generally worked on women. "I can even be a real biker if that's what you want."

She looked down at him, her expression cool. In fact, it felt like he'd been totally dismissed. Clearly he'd misread their rapport from last night.

"I'm sure Scott has more important cases," she said.

He shook his head, realizing he needed to change his approach. "No." He made a glum face. "This is the only job he offered. And I'd hate to be fired before I'm even a year with the company."

"Is Scott worried about his horse?"

Rick gave a swift nod, although Scott hadn't been at all concerned about his horse—only about Eve. "I'm supposed to watch him gallop," Rick said. "Then report back." He kept his face carefully solemn. Hell, he didn't even know the horse's name.

"All right." She gave a resigned shrug. "I'll take Stinger out next so you can see him. I was hoping Ashley and Miguel would be back by now." She twisted in the saddle, checking the pathway.

"Are they your barn help?" he asked. So it was the staff who were slacking, not her. The realization made him feel better, although he didn't know why. Only that he wanted to jump over himself to help. And maybe earn another one of her beautiful smiles.

"I didn't expect to have a bridle today," she said, "so I gave Ashley a few hours off. Miguel walked over to the dorms to find her."

"I can cool that horse out," Rick said, "while you tack up Stinger."

"You can handle a Thoroughbred?"

"Yes." He stepped forward and reached for the reins, waiting for her to dismount.

She shot another reluctant look down the path, her posture not quite so rigid. But there was a wariness in her voice, something that hadn't been there last night.

Didn't matter though. His quip about losing his job had moved her. Obviously, she was too kind-hearted to chase him off the property. And from the look of the patchwork bridle, she was definitely struggling.

So he intended to stay and provide a little help, whether she wanted it or not. And if, in the process, he could bring her around to a more receptive way of thinking, that would be a definite bonus.

CHAPTER TWELVE

Eve tightened the girth, keeping a wary eye on Stinger's teeth. Some horses play nipped when they were saddled, but he did nothing in play. It was ironic he was the fastest horse Scott and Megan had ever owned. He certainly wasn't much fun.

And she was a little distracted this morning, a little too aware of the man outside.

Scott's man.

She blew out a regretful sigh. He was a big, good-looking guy and she appreciated his easygoing manner, but she couldn't have him hanging around and reporting her struggles back to Scott and Megan. Lately they'd been taking Joey way too much, then sending him home with shoes and toys and Disney passes, as if she weren't capable of providing for her own son. As if she were too broke to afford a babysitter. Too busy with work.

Something twisted in her chest. She had to get these horses racing, make a little money and hang on to her job. Then she'd be able to make a better life for Joey. Now that she had a bridle, nothing was holding her back. But she certainly couldn't tolerate a spy in the barn. No way. Even if he was a dangerously attractive one.

"Be good," she said to Stinger, tying him to a ring in the stall. "I'll be back with your bridle."

She dodged his sneaky kick, left the stall and stepped outside.

Rick was walking Bristol around the dirt ring. It was evident he'd handled a horse before. He'd shed his leather jacket and no longer resembled an intimidating gang member. With his jeans and T-shirt, he looked like a horseman, albeit with a rebel's shaggy hair. No wonder Scott had hired him. An investigator who could change his appearance to fit his surroundings must be very useful.

But there was something in his walk that drew attention. Not a swagger exactly, simply the impression that he possessed more than his fair share of confidence. His shirt hinted of hardcore muscles and he moved like an athlete although she doubted he'd acquired that fitness level in any gym. The gray ink extending below his sleeves certainly wasn't the product of any sophisticated tattoo parlor. She knew the look of prison ink.

"Spent some time locked up?" she asked, shading her eyes and studying the crude tattoos.

"Some." He reached down and checked Bristol's chest with the back of his hand.

"I didn't think licensed PIs could have prison records."

"I'm not licensed."

She edged a step closer. Scott sometimes relied on outsiders for street work, but all his permanent employees were licensed investigators. "So you don't know Scott very well?" she asked. "Do you have an office in his building?"

Rick shook his head, his expression hidden behind his dark sunglasses. "No. Our communication is generally over the phone."

"So you were sent because you know horses?" she asked. "And prisons?"

"And because he thought I could figure out the thefts," Rick said mildly. "Or at least stop any more from happening."

Some of her resentment eased. He seemed like an up-front guy, probably more biker than investigator. He didn't seem the type to run back to Scott with schoolyard tales. But she had to know for sure.

"The reason Tizzy was on the track last night," she said, "was because I had no bridle. It's against the rules. But I wouldn't want Scott to know." She paused, but it wasn't her nature to prevaricate. "And that's the reason I'm not comfortable having you around."

She wished she could see his eyes. His mouth certainly wasn't giving much away. It was hard and flat, slightly larger on the bottom. A gunslinger's mouth. But the corners abruptly lifted, completely changing his face. He looked amused now, with laugh lines bracketing his mouth. He chuckled, that same deep sound that had sparked her awareness of him last night.

"Now I understand why you're trying to run me off," he said, smiling as if relieved. But there was more than relief circling that mouth. His grin was sensual and rather wicked, and it made her skin hot.

"Tell me this," he said, still grinning. "Did you ride Scott's horse when the track was closed?"

She shook her head, flustered by her physical reaction.

"Then it wasn't his horse that was breaking the law," Rick said. "So there's no reason why Scott needs to know about your little brush with security."

"But I would have ridden Stinger," she said, "if he were manageable. Tizzy was the only horse I trusted."

Rick chuckled again. It seemed all he did was laugh and while she liked looking at him, having a man like that around could be very distracting.

She crossed her arms. "I just don't see why you have to be here," she muttered.

"I'm only here to help. Can you let me do that? It's all Scott wants." He pulled off his sunglasses, revealing grayish-blue eyes that were so calm and level he appeared to be telling the truth. "It's what I want," he added, his gaze skimming over her body.

"I suppose," she said, unable to pull her eyes away from his smiling mouth with words that seemed to have a double meaning. And she was way too aware of his teasing. Now her breath was uneven and it seemed as if every part of her was humming.

"Guess we should switch this bridle now," Rick said. "So you can get Stinger out before they close the track?"

Eve checked the path again. Still no sign of Ashley and Miguel, and she did need help. Rick seemed willing, and extremely able. "Stinger needs a larger cheek strap," she said slowly. "And a stronger bit."

She gestured at the picnic tables. "Friends gathered some old tack. And they made a special replacement bit. That's the reason I'm able to ride today."

"Okay." He gave an agreeable nod, as if using discarded tack was the norm in every race stable. "I'll put this horse away and make you a larger bridle."

She hesitated. He seemed useful, at least for now. But was he trustworthy? She didn't want him carrying tales back to Scott.

"What sort of bit do you want?" he asked, as if sensing her indecision.

She nibbled at her lip then blew out a resigned breath. "The ring bit," she said. "There's one on the picnic table."

"Okay, boss. I'm on it. Just give me a couple minutes." He winked and led Bristol past her toward the barn.

She couldn't help but smile back. It seemed she had acquired a new groom. One that was tough, capable and pleasantly cheerful. And while she wasn't delighted that Scott Taylor was his employer, admittedly she was very happy with the employee Scott had sent.

CHAPTER THIRTEEN

Rick liked most animals but Stinger was a brute, quick to take advantage and not caring who he hurt. Little wonder the locals called him the devil horse.

"This is Scott's horse?" He straightened Stinger's head before the horse could turn and grab a chunk of flesh from Eve's leg. "Why would you want to train an animal like this?"

"He's a bully," Eve said. "And it's true, you can't trust him. But under a mile he's hard to catch."

Rick frowned. "Probably other horses are afraid to get too close."

"Maybe," she said. "But that works too. Because when he gets in front, no horse ever wants to pass."

He tightened his grip on the lead line and led Stinger down the aisle. Eve looked so small sitting in the saddle. Small and vulnerable. "Seems like a relative should find a nicer horse for you to train," he said.

She laughed as if he'd made a joke, and he had to admit she sat easily in the saddle, appearing to be an extension of the horse. But she had a fresh scar on her wrist so clearly injuries did happen, no matter a rider's skill. And he didn't like to think that she might be hurt.

He felt Stinger tense a split second before the horse leaped into the air.

"Sorry," a woman's contrite voice called from just outside the door.

Rick muscled Stinger back under control, biting back his curse. The horse's reaction was excessive but nobody should ever rush into a barn like that.

"This is Ashley and Miguel," Eve said, pointing toward the newcomers and introducing Rick.

Ashley looked like a Barbie doll, her tiny frame concealed by an oversized shirt, while Miguel was stooped and wizened with a twisted leg that made Rick ache. Miguel was probably knowledgeable with horses, but he certainly couldn't move very fast.

Miguel greeted him with a cautious nod, but Ashley gave a big smile, her hand flicking to her hair. Her gaze darted from his motorcycle to the bridle parts on the table and then back to his face, her curiosity obvious.

"Rick is here to make sure nothing else is stolen," Eve said. "He works for Scott's agency so give him whatever help he needs. I'll be back in thirty minutes for the next horse." Her gaze turned toward the path and it was clear she was in a hurry to ride to the track.

"Want me to lead you over?" Ashley asked, her voice less than enthusiastic. "Stinger's going to be worse than usual after being cooped up."

Rick turned Stinger in a tight circle, keeping his face impassive. But Ashley looked much too small to handle a rambunctious horse. He couldn't see how she'd be much help. He glanced up at Eve. "I'll walk over with you."

"I don't need anyone's help," she said. "Just let him loose—"

Her voice cut off as Stinger kicked out with a series of bucks, a rather athletic feat since Rick was still holding his head. But her relaxed seat didn't change. She clearly was an accomplished rider.

Still, he kept his hand clamped on the lead line. No way was he letting her ride this nasty horse alone to the track. But he didn't want to rouse her stubborn streak. Or challenge her pride. Even Scott felt the need to tread lightly.

"I have to watch Scott's horse gallop," Rick said mildly. "This seems like a good time."

"All right," Eve said, clearly as impatient as the horse. "Let's go then. We only have another hour before the track closes. And I have two more horses to squeeze in."

Neither Ashley nor Miguel spoke, but they looked relieved that she'd have help. Or maybe they were just happy to avoid Stinger.

Rick led the horse along the path. Stinger continued with his unmannerly ways, trying to ram him with his shoulder and then kicking out with ill temper when Rick corrected him.

"Ever tried him with a lead pony?" Rick asked.

Eve laughed. "We never found one that wants to get that close. At Santa Anita all the escort horses are scared of him. He's actually behaving better here. Probably likes the isolation."

Rick scanned the path. The horse trail was definitely quiet. The other barns were all situated in the north end and no one else used this walkway. It didn't even feel like they were at a track. It was actually rather nice. And though Stinger was still prancing, he'd stopped trying to run Rick over.

"This is how Stinger behaves once he's on the track," she said cheerfully. "He's not difficult at all."

Rick chuckled. Stinger wasn't his idea of an easy horse. It was apparent Eve had been sent to Riverview with a bunch of misfits, both human and equine. The Thoroughbred she'd ridden last night had behaved more like a cowhorse than a racehorse, while Stinger appeared rodeo ready. And Miguel was too arthritic to be much help while Ashley resembled a jockey, not a groom. Clearly Eve was being set up for failure, just as Scott had mentioned in her case file.

"Who chose the horses you brought here?" he asked, keeping his tone casual.

"My boss. He picked six Cal-breds who'd fit the races here. And whose owners wouldn't mind if I was in charge."

"And who chose your staff?" He turned slightly, studying her face. One thing he'd learned was that she spoke her mind. And after years of working undercover, that honesty was refreshing.

"I did," she said.

He stared along the pathway, hiding his confusion. It was obvious she was doing the bulk of the work, acting as trainer, exercise rider and groom. Naturally an assistant trainer wouldn't be given the best horses in a barn but why had she saddled herself with such inept staff? If her workers were broke and desperate, they might even be responsible for the thefts.

"Were Ashley and Miguel at the track when you were riding last night?" he asked. "I didn't see them."

"They were waiting by the gap." Her voice warmed. "They flashed a light. That's how they warned me about the guards."

So they were a tight group. The pair had been standing in the dark, long past their bedtime. Loyalty compensated for many flaws. It still didn't explain why she'd burdened herself with needy employees. But if he were too critical, he knew she'd jump to their defense.

"Miguel looks like he has lots of experience," Rick said, picking his words carefully.

"Yes. He came from Panama. Worked with horses for over sixty years. Probably forgotten more than I'll ever know."

"Your boss must miss him."

She was silent for a moment, the only sound the steady thud of Stinger's feet. "Yes, but Miguel has mobility issues, and Jackson is trimming staff."

Her concern was obvious, and it wasn't necessary to probe any longer. She was simply trying to help Jackson and Ashley, a desire to protect that he understood all too well.

"Guess it's important for everyone that these horses run well," he said, keeping his eyes on the curving path.

Stinger was prancing again but at least, after four corrections, the horse had quit trying to run him over. In fact, Stinger hadn't thrown any more dirty bucks and just seemed eager to reach the track. Obviously he loved to race, and while that was understandable for a Thoroughbred, it was a tough way for humans to make a living.

Salaries at the track were rock bottom. Owners received sixty percent of a purse with ten percent of that going to the trainer and jockey. Eve's boss would probably give a portion to Eve, as assistant trainer. And Ashley and Miguel might receive a small bonus. But if the horses weren't winning, it didn't leave much, only a base salary. And some assistant trainers liked to gamble and work for a percentage alone.

Eve seemed the gambling type.

"I'm guessing you work solely on a percentage?" he said, glancing over his shoulder.

"Yes. Boss promised six percent." She gave a rueful smile. "So far, that's six percent of nothing."

He blew out a sympathetic breath. No wonder the thefts had been catastrophic. The barn was on a shoestring budget. Owners paid a monthly fee to the trainer, but that didn't funnel down to Eve. His eyes shot toward the multi-colored bridle, held together with rusty buckles. If not for her resilience, the horses would still be standing in the barn—unable to train, unable to race, unable to earn. And it must be especially tough for a rookie, who everyone would watch and criticize a little more closely.

"You need a real bridle," he said. It would be the first race of her career, and no trainer wanted to be the joke of the paddock. "I'll buy you one for Saturday."

"Not necessary." Her words were so clipped he instantly knew he'd made a mistake.

"You can pay me back after you win," he said. "I'm sure Scott prefers his horse in conventional tack."

"I don't know if he's coming this weekend."

"But he might see a win picture. And don't trainers have to please their owners?"

She turned silent and Rick peered over his shoulder. Her expressive face was filled with so much conflict he regretted criticizing the bridle. He'd been warned she was proud, a fact he needed to remember.

"I'll put it on my expense account," he added. "Your boss will never know."

"Absolutely not," she said, startling him with her fervor. "Scott is *not* paying for another bridle. He's already paying Jackson enough."

Rick clamped his mouth shut. Somehow he'd muddled this even worse. But she'd accepted gifts from the local women—all the bridle pieces and the special bit for Stinger. So it seemed help was acceptable if it was essential for the horse. Just not for her.

They walked another twenty feet before he tried again.

"Too bad Stinger's face is getting chafed," he said, reaching up and fiddling with the horse's head. "This bridle is way too tight."

She leaned forward, trying to see from her position on his back. "Is it rubbing his cheek?"

He gave a glum nod. "And I apologize. I'm the one who put the bridle together."

"Don't worry," she said. "His head is huge. It's hard to fit."

"But I owe Stinger an apology...as well as a suitable bridle."

She looked at him with narrowed eyes. Then her mouth lifted in a reluctant smile. "You're messing with me. It's not really chafing, is it?"

He just smiled, relieved she wasn't the type to sulk. He could handle stubborn, but didn't deal well with moodiness.

"You're right," she added, blowing out a sigh. "The horses deserve to race in a proper bridle. I'll call my boss again."

"I'm sure he'd be mortified if his stable raced without proper equipment."

"One would think," she said, "because Jackson's worked hard to establish his race business. But he has a new wife and his biggest concern is keeping her happy. I'll look around and see if someone has a secondhand bridle for sale. I don't want to embarrass any owners...or kind volunteers."

She bestowed him with such a grateful smile it made his chest swell, and it was obvious if she looked at other men like that, she'd have no shortage of guys clamoring to help. In fact, if her barn hadn't been so isolated, she probably could have borrowed a truckload of tack. He yanked his gaze from her mouth.

"How did you end up in a barn so far from the other shedrows?" he asked, his voice gruff. They'd finally reached the track, but even with Stinger's eagerness, it had been a fifteen-minute walk.

"They were the only stalls available," she said.

She pointed at the gap in the rail. "You can let me go there. No need to wait once you've seen enough. I'll walk back alone. Stinger's always better behaved after his exercise."

Rick had no idea how long she'd be on the track but he certainly intended to walk back with her. And he was curious to see her ride. Scott said she'd been a well-regarded jockey before too many accidents forced her to the sidelines.

He unfastened the lead shank and stepped back. Stinger bucked twice, seemingly out of sheer excitement, then settled into a high-stepping trot, hugging the rail and heading clockwise.

Several trainers lingered around the gap, lead shanks draped over their shoulders. On Rick's right, two men with coffee and binoculars stood on a wooden viewing stand. Everyone seemed engrossed with the horses. Certainly no one waved a sign advertising stolen bridles for sale.

He walked up to a gray-haired man who was mouthing a thick wad of tobacco. "Is there a tack store on the grounds?" he asked.

"Yeah, white trailer by barn two." The man gestured with a stained thumb. "But he doesn't have much. You might have to go down the road."

Rick nodded and checked on Eve. Stinger's colorful bridle made her easy to spot. The horse was moving nicely, still trotting, seemingly not inclined to give any more trouble. It looked like the beginning of her warm-up considering that the faster moving horses were on the inner rail and galloping in the opposite direction.

He turned toward the tack trailer, accepting that his groom's work was on hold for a bit. And now was a good time to do some sleuthing.

CHAPTER FOURTEEN

Rick stepped into a compact trailer stuffed with horse liniments, shampoos and a wall filled with a selection of farrier supplies. The rectangular sign above the door said: WOODY'S TACK.

"Need any help?" a wiry man called. He was missing two front teeth, his nose was misshapen and it looked like he'd been on the losing side of more than one argument with a horse.

"Looking for some bridles," Rick said.

"Got a few over here." The man led him around a rack of horse dewormers and an assortment of fly sprays. "Cheapest is sixty dollars. I don't carry many now that the big box store opened up. Have lots of grooming supplies and shoes though."

Rick fingered the bridles, all standard size. Nothing that would fit Stinger's coarse head.

"Do you have a used section?" he asked. "Can people sell on consignment?"

The owner shook his head. "Nothing like that. Too tight on space. But you can check the board." He jabbed over his shoulder at a bulletin board crammed with notices, colored thumbtacks and one black riding glove.

Rick scanned the board. It was unlikely the thieves were rash enough to post stolen bridles at the track, but sometimes people were complete boneheads. However, most of these notices were legitimate: retired Thoroughbreds needing a good home, a hotwalker looking for work, and a signup sheet for a caps tournament.

"What's a caps tournament?" he asked.

"A drinking game that involves a lot of skill. It's way more challenging than beer pong. You get a point for knocking the cap off a beer bottle." The owner pointed at two huge trophies proudly displayed behind the counter. "We won that tournament the last couple years."

"Sounds like fun," Rick said, noting how the man's eyes had lit up. "You probably know everyone around. With this store and tournaments like that..."

"For sure," the man said. "I know all the regulars anyway. Not the big shots that come from Santa Anita, trying to steal a win. But our horses are tough. And most of the outsiders leave pretty damn quick. They don't stay long enough to meet anyone, or support the track."

Rick gave an agreeable nod, still studying the bulletin board. Eve's boss, Jackson Zeggelaar, was from Santa Anita. And he'd definitely sent his second-string horses here, hoping to find some softer competition. No doubt there was some animosity toward outside trainers. But was it enough that the locals would resort to stealing?

"Thinking of signing up for the tournament?" the owner asked, studying Rick with an assessing eye. "Looks like you could be a top player. It's good to have some size to help handle the beer. How's your aim?"

"I generally hit where I'm aiming," Rick said, realizing he could learn more by chatting up this man than wandering around the barns. And he could still watch Eve and Stinger through the window.

"Here." The man reached into a jar on the counter and pulled out a shiny beer cap. "Try hitting the top of the blue brush on the second shelf. Use an overhand action, like this."

He took considerable time to demonstrate the proper technique, holding the cap between his thumb and index finger, and arcing his hand in the air. It took several minutes of enthusiastic demo before he finally handed over the cap, deeming Rick ready to shoot.

"Sounds like a big-league tournament," Rick said, solemnly fingering the cap.

The man's head pumped. "Yes, there are plenty of rules. Folks around here take the game seriously. We're going for the Guinness Book of Records for largest game. Have to beat out the Corkum Road players for that though."

Rick took aim and shot. The cap landed squarely on the back of the blue brush then ricocheted to the floor.

The man jabbed his fist in the air. "Just like I figured," he said. "A natural. No one else ever made that shot their first try. And I need a partner for Thursday night. So, what do you say?"

"I'm not really in shape for a big caps tournament," Rick said, trying to keep a straight face.

"You have a few days to practice. And everyone on the backside will be there. It's big bragging rights. Along with gift certificates from here, and the tack store down the road."

Rick stiffened. "What's the value of the certificates?"

"Two hundred dollars each." The man's eyes twinkled. "That's why it's important for me to win. So I can keep my gift certificate in the drawer. My name's Woody. So, are you in?"

Rick reached out and shook the man's hand. "My name's Rick," he said. "But you can call me partner."

CHAPTER FIFTEEN

Rick left Woody's store with a wealth of information on all the barns and trainers, along with strict instructions about how to prepare for the caps tournament. He felt unusually relaxed, had stopped checking over his shoulder, and realized he was looking forward to the day instead of dreading it. Life here was simple. No one worried about last names or your education or what kind of vehicle you drove.

Best of all, there were no children. Just adults and horses. He strode to the rail and checked the track for Eve and Stinger. They were on the far side now, in front of the clubhouse and moving counter-clockwise.

Stinger appeared eager, his head tucked almost to his chest, and for a moment Rick feared she wouldn't be able to hold him. But then he remembered the special bit her friends had left and its extra stopping power. Stinger wasn't the type who could be ridden in a halter—unlike Tizzy. But the horse was moving powerfully, and even though Eve made it look easier than it was, Stinger didn't seem to be fighting her control.

She was a beautiful rider and a pleasure to watch. But galloping in the morning, far from the glamour of the starting gate, was different from race riding. There was no fame, no adoring crowds, no glory of the winner's circle.

Some people might consider it a step down, much like the changes in his career—from decorated street cop to fighting organized crime to private investigator. Now here he was, at a minor racetrack, reduced to probing a theft that didn't even reach a paltry grand. On paper, it seemed trivial.

But it wasn't trivial to Eve. Or to her staff. In fact, it had been a body blow. If not for the generosity of some backstretch ladies, her horses would be stuck in their stalls, instead of powering around the oval in a patchwork bridle.

He shook his head. If the locals resented outside horses and were responsible for the thefts, why had the women taken considerable trouble to scavenge pieces of tack? And it appeared congenial out on the oval. No one was trying to cut Eve off or crowd her horse. In fact, there was a definite sense of camaraderie, from the cheerful greetings of riders to the laid-back trainers waiting at the gap, sharing conversation and coffee.

He strode back to the tack trailer and pushed open the door.

"Hey, Woody," he called. "Do you have much theft here? In your store?"

Woody glanced up from the counter. "Nah," he said, shaking his head. "I don't even lock up when I step out. People around here are broke but honest. Why?"

"My boss had a bunch of bridles stolen. Just wondered where to look."

"So that's why you need the gift certificate." Woody nodded in total understanding. "Sure hope you don't find those bridles until after the tournament. You won't back out on me, will you?"

"No," Rick said. "I'll be there."

He turned and headed back to the rail, wishing he could be as single-minded as his new caps partner.

Eve was walking Stinger about fifty feet from the gap. He pulled the lead shank from his back pocket and stepped out to meet her, feeling like a genuine groom.

"You didn't have to stay," she said, slightly breathless. Her cheeks were flushed, her eyes bright with pleasure, and it was apparent she loved the speed work every bit as much as Stinger. "But I imagine you have to make a full report on Scott's horse?"

"That's right." Rick gave a solemn nod. "I do. But it's also good to hang around the backstretch and meet the people. And it gives us a chance to talk."

He led Stinger through the gap and along the walkway, waiting until they were thirty feet down the path and safe from prying ears. "Any chance your bridles were taken by someone you know?" he asked. "Maybe someone who wants you gone?"

She shook her head and it was clear she'd already considered that angle. "I don't know many people here. Neither do Ashley or Miguel. And Victoria is too far away."

"Who's Victoria?"

Eve winkled her nose. "My boss's wife. Lately she's been making life miserable for Jackson. And Tizzy and Stinger are good horses, but they're not likely to scare the competition. The horses here are tough."

"So I hear," Rick said. "But why did your boss send you to Riverview, if it wasn't for some easy races?"

"He was short of stalls and they have some nice purses here for California breds. And," she pulled in a regretful breath, "Victoria is pushing to trim staff, and Jackson wasn't quite ready."

"Do Ashley and Miguel know they're on the chopping block?"

She nodded, her eyes flashing with passion. "But Ashley's pregnant and Miguel's old. It's not right to treat people like that."

"No," he said. "It's not. But maybe they can find jobs with other stables."

"Maybe, but they'll need some bonus money to tide them over."

He understood now why it was so important to get the horses racing. She wasn't just trying to establish her credentials as a trainer. She was desperate to look after her friends.

It might be possible to have Scott lean on her boss, encourage Jackson to treat his staff a little more ethically. But that could create even more animosity and merely hasten the pink slips. Besides, for some reason she shied away from accepting Scott's help. She didn't even want him paying for Stinger's bridle, a purchase Scott would no doubt be happy to cover. He was already absorbing the cost of an investigator. And Rick's services didn't come cheap.

However, Rick wanted to keep her happy. And there was more than one way to bridle a horse. He glanced up at her, his smile slightly wicked.

"I might have a solution for our race bridle," he said. "But first you need to drive me to the store so we can pick up some beer."

CHAPTER SIXTEEN

Eve pulled her hood lever and leaned out the window, trying to watch Rick. He hadn't looked surprised when she admitted her battery had been stolen and her car wouldn't go without a push. Had acted as if this type of jumping was the normal way to start cars. And she appreciated that.

He was bending over her engine, tinkering with something. But moments later he strode around to her window. "Looks like only the battery was taken," he said. "Do you lock your car doors?"

"I do now."

He nodded, not even chiding her for leaving the car unlocked. "Okay," he said. "Push the clutch in and let's go."

"Should we get Ashley and Miguel to help?"

"Think I can handle it," he said.

Her gaze shot to the ridged muscles beneath the tattoos. No doubt, he could tuck her car beneath one arm and carry it away. In fact, there didn't seem much he couldn't do. He'd helped tack up and cool down five horses that morning. Even mucked out stalls. Best of all, he'd joked with Miguel and Ashley, making them smile and lifting everyone's spirits.

He was imminently capable, but it was his easy-going nature that attracted her the most. Not his looks or killer body.

Right.

The car was already moving and she yanked her mind back to her job. Waited another moment as it built up speed, then popped the clutch. The little engine sprang to life. She immediately slowed, but Rick slipped into the passenger's seat before the car stopped rolling, as if he had considerable practice leaping in and out of moving vehicles.

Which, of course, was quite likely. One didn't end up in prison without a good reason. Of course, people could reform.

"Do you know Dex Tattrie?" she asked.

"I know some of the Tattries." Rick adjusted his dark sunglasses. "Believe they have a club north of here."

"That's right," she said. "Dex and his wife own Tizzy."

Rick made a non-committal sound.

"Dex is a farrier who teaches at the state prison," she said, watching Rick's mouth. Absolutely no change. He didn't give anything away unless he chose.

"He's a good guy," she added. "You remind me a bit of him."

Rick glanced at her then, as if trying to figure out what she meant.

Heck, she didn't know what she meant either, except to let him know that a prison record was okay with her. And why was she assuming he even cared? She gripped the steering wheel and stared straight ahead, oddly flustered.

But he reached over and touched her bare arm. "Good," he said, and it was clear he did understand. "I like how no one here worries about the past...especially you."

Her skin tingled from the brush of his hand, and her face felt hot. She fiddled with the air conditioning, even though it hadn't worked for years.

He held the back of his hand over the air vent. "Nothing's coming out," he said. "I'll take a look at it after we find a battery."

"But I can't spend money on my car," she said. "Not yet."

"There's a junkyard just twenty miles south," he said. "They'll have cheap parts. Worth checking."

She swallowed, fighting a well of panic. She had little more than twenty dollars left, and it was more important to invest in the horses than a battery. And Rick's plan to win bridle money in some caps tournament was sweet, but a definite gamble. Maybe he was broke too, and this was just his way of conning her into buying beer.

Of course, he deserved something to drink. He'd been doing way more with the horses than she'd ever expected from one of Scott's shadowy investigators. On the other hand, beer was a luxury she couldn't afford.

She slid him a suspicious look. "How much practice beer do you need? For the tournament?"

"Not much," he said. "I have plenty of practice drinking beer. It's shooting a cap off an opponent's bottle that needs work. So I'll need your help tonight."

"You want me to sit and hold a bottle?"

"No holding. The bottle has to be between your legs, an equal distance from both your knees." He chuckled. "Woody made me promise to duplicate a game situation."

She laughed and zipped her car into the outer lane. It was amusing that after one morning, Rick had been roped into a caps tournament and was already good buddies with Woody, a gruff man she'd only spoken to once. "I guess Woody thinks he's found a real ringer."

"Yes. He'll be truly disappointed if I don't hold up my end. He was just waiting for a prospect to walk into his store."

"You're the right size for drinking beer," she said, a little wistfully. "No one's ever asked me to be their caps partner."

"And no one's ever asked me to gallop their horse." He gave a teasing smile as if picking up on her competitive nature. Then his voice turned serious. "Do you miss it? The race riding?"

"Sometimes. But I had a few accidents and they affected my psyche. It's hard to win when you're worrying about getting hurt. Ashley is a better jockey than me now." She blinked, surprised by her admission. But Rick had a way of listening that drew her out, as if what she was saying was the most important thing in the world. And he didn't want to miss a word.

"I guess your first win as a trainer will be doubly sweet," he said.

She nodded. "Yesterday I had doubts I'd ever get a horse to the starting gate. But now it looks like it will happen."

"And you're going to have a nice bridle for the weekend."

He proceeded to tell her about the rules of the caps tournament and how Woody was intent on defending his title, and then they went on to discuss their favorite types of beer and how nothing could tear up your eyes like the Budweiser ads. And the lost puppy on the Super Bowl commercial made her think of Joey, and her eyes really did tear up, but he seemed a little moved too and the silence was oddly comforting.

"We're here," he said, scanning the GPS on his phone. "Turn right just past that rusty Ford."

She veered onto a gravel road, surprised they'd already reached the junkyard. The driveway was tree lined and rutted, the ridge in the center so high it almost tore the muffler off her car. She slowed to a crawl. Judging from the shape of the road, the owner didn't encourage retail traffic. They passed a handwritten NO TRESPASSING sign, its letters black and aggressive. Then another sign: THAT MEANS YOU!

She glanced sideways at Rick.

He seemed unconcerned so she drove on. The barbed wire gate was open. A white trailer sat inside, appearing to double as a home and an office. Beyond sat a graveyard of cars, every color, make and model. Some looked in pristine condition. Others had clearly been in a wreck. It was sad and rather creepy.

"That one looks recent." Rick pointed at a lime green Honda Civic with a parking sticker still hanging behind its cracked window. "Stop here. I'll see if it has a working battery."

He stepped out and raised the hood. Bent over the engine, fiddled with something, and flashed her a thumbs up. Then he pulled open her car door and gestured at the trailer. "Let's see what he wants for it."

They walked across a patch of dirt spotted with scraggly dandelions and ripped tennis balls. The trailer looked deserted, the blinds pulled. But something thumped. The screen door opened and a huge black dog burst out, his growls menacing.

Her knees buckled.

Rick grabbed her hand and tugged her behind him. "Keep walking," he said.

Her breath stalled, but she gripped his hand like a lifeline, forcing her legs to move. He didn't look at the dog, so neither did she.

A man in a camo shirt filled the doorway. "Rebel, quit!"

The dog stopped growling but continued trotting toward them. She studied him from the corner of her eye. He was massive, his neck framed by raised hackles. Red drool hung from the side of his jaw, as if he'd been chewing on something bloody.

She tried not to stare, knew she should hide her fear, but when Rick reached out and tucked her protectively against his hip, she sagged with relief.

"Nice yard you got here," Rick said. "We need a battery for a Honda Civic. Thought the one from that 2006 Civic might work."

The man stepped further onto the sagging steps. "Yeah, that's a good one. Just came in last week. Teenagers around here put a lot of cars in the ditches." His eyes narrowed on Rick's jacket. "Got a hog? What'cha ride?"

They went on to talk about Harleys, the best kind of bike polish and a mutual acquaintance called Boomie. Rick kept his arm around her the entire time, except now he scratched the dog's head with his other hand. She remained motionless, trying not flinch at the reddened teeth so close to his hand.

"All right," Rick said, finally ending the conversation. "I'll stop in on the way out and pay."

When he turned Eve back toward her car, the dog followed.

"Rebel likes you," she whispered, gripping Rick's arm. "But he looks at me like he's eyeing his next meal."

"I think he has a bone stuck in his mouth after chewing up the last visitor." Rick smiled down at the dog. "Clearly he's trained to spot troublemakers. You better stick close."

She swallowed. "Maybe I should just sit in the car."

"No." His arm banded around her. "You're not afraid of a little Rottie, are you?"

"He's not so little. And I was bitten a few times when I was a kid. It hurts." She squeezed between Rick and the grill of her car, peering at Rebel the entire time. "Let's do this fast," she said. "There's some tools in my trunk."

"No, I'm good." Rick pulled a compact wrench from his back pocket. He adjusted her in front of him, keeping his legs between her and the watchful dog. Then he leaned over the engine, so close his minty breath tickled her neck.

"I want to clean the cables first," he said. "Your old battery was quite corroded." He pointed at the white residue around the terminals. "If I were going to steal a battery," he added, "I'd choose a new one. Isn't it strange someone took yours?"

She nodded, but it was difficult to think about thieves and what they might take or not take. And it wasn't just concern about the hovering dog. Rick's closeness jumbled her senses. His belt rubbed her hip, and his muscled thighs blasted off so much heat, her nerves tingled.

She'd never been so enveloped by a man. So aware of his touch, his feel, even his smell. If that dog wasn't so close, she'd scoot away. Just so she could breathe again.

"See the corrosion on the posts," Rick went on. "Maybe someone didn't want you driving from the motel to the track?"

"But the car didn't affect anything," she said, staring down at his lean fingers. Square tipped, capable, ringless. She fought the impulse to wet her lips. "Ashley and I just moved into the dorms."

"But trainers aren't usually allowed to sleep there. And most of them wouldn't bunk with hotwalkers and grooms. It's not the lap of luxury."

"I'd sleep in the barn before giving up."

"Of course you would," Rick said. "But not all trainers would do that. Maybe someone underestimated your resilience."

He reached down and suddenly there was a lethal-looking blade in his hand. It didn't even have a real handle. Her eyes widened, but he only scraped residue off the battery posts, his movements relaxed, even though his buckle, or something equally hard, was brushing her thigh.

She stared down, feigning interest in the workings of her car, even though she'd almost quit breathing. She inched to the right, pressing further against the grill. Was it his buckle? Difficult to tell. His entire body was so hard and his breath vibrated against her neck, close and warmly intimate.

He didn't appear conscious of how she was sandwiched between him and the bumper. He just talked about her car— about the importance of locking doors and how driving without a battery wasn't good for the computer components.

"Looks like your alternator is okay," he went on. "We just need to grab the other battery."

He curved his arm around her hip and guided her over to the wrecked car, thoughtfully staying between her and the dog.

She didn't notice when he put away his knife, but it had been replaced with the shiny wrench that he handled with similar ease. He had beautiful hands, his nails short and surprisingly clean. Most bikers she knew had permanent oil stains. And he didn't smell of exhaust, more of spice and leather and the outdoors.

She pulled her head away, flustered by her growing awareness. He was here to help, yet she was eyeing him like he was a breeding stallion being led around the auction ring. And he was only trying to do his job. Worse, he worked for Scott.

"I appreciate all the extra things you've done," she said, crossing her arms. But that only pressed her elbow into his ripped abs, and she quickly dropped them. "For leading Stinger and helping with the horses. It'll be great to have a car that starts. But I'm going to tell Scott it's not necessary that you stay—"

"I'm going to lift the battery out now," Rick said. "And switch it to your car. Stand back so you don't get acid on your clothes."

She froze, her eyes shooting to the Rottweiler. Seconds ago, she'd wanted to step back. Put more space between her and the press of his virile body. But now that he'd suggested it, she was loath to step away. Didn't want to admit she found the big dog terrifying.

Rick studied her face, then pointed at the trailer. "Go home, Rebel."

The dog lowered his head, his expression crestfallen. Then he turned and trotted back to the trailer.

She jerked away from the bumper, shaking her head in disbelief. "Why didn't you do that ten minutes ago? Then I wouldn't have been hanging on your arm like an idiot."

"Not a chance," he said, his eyes locked on her face.

She flushed and took another step back.

He gave a dismissive shrug. "I'm here to look after you. Can't have you telling Scott I'm not needed."

She nodded then eased around the fender, putting more distance between them. Obviously he wanted to keep his job, not let her be chewed up by a junkyard dog. That explained why he'd kept her pressed against his hip. Totally understandable.

However, she didn't want to analyze her tug of disappointment or question why part of her wished the dog hadn't been quite so obedient.

CHAPTER SEVENTEEN

Eve pointed at the tack store on the side of the highway. "That's our final stop," she said, still laughing at Rick's last story.

She couldn't remember when she'd indulged in such a carefree afternoon. Rick was totally engaging: funny, smart but amazingly kind. He even helped the junkyard owner remove a jagged splinter from the inside of the dog's mouth. And Rebel was really a gentle soul, licking both Rick's and Eve's hands in gratitude.

She wasn't sure when Rick ended up driving. It had been after he bought the battery and beer, but before they stopped for a hamburger. She hadn't planned to stay away from the barn so long, but now it felt like she'd just enjoyed a two-week vacation. And she wanted to take something back to Ashley and Miguel, and share the pleasure.

Rick turned into the parking lot. "This is the tack store that's donating the gift certificate," he said. "But we can't get the bridle until after the caps tournament. Maybe we should come back Friday."

"I'm not buying tack today," she said. "But they have a maternity T-shirt that Ashley wanted. I just hope it's still there."

"This is the place your boss sent you?" Rick stared over the steering wheel, frowning at the store. "Where his wife cut off your funds?"

"Yes." She patted her pocket. "But Ashley needs one nice shirt that fits. And since you found that cheap battery and bought the beer, I can afford to buy it now."

"Okay," he said, reaching over her lap and opening the door. "Let's go."

She'd stopped being surprised at his gentlemanly behavior. Had stopped jumping whenever his hand brushed her skin. Not that her body had quit reacting. Even now, her leg tingled from the brush of his arm. But it was a nice tingle.

They walked across the pavement, and it seemed normal that his hand cupped her hip. Totally normal that they'd be shopping together.

He reached for the door, but the security guard rushed forward and yanked it open. It was the same short-haired man as before, but today he was dressed in cream breeches and a black polo shirt. His welcoming smile faded when he saw Eve. His gaze skittered over Rick then dropped to the floor.

She bit back a smile, wishing Ashley could see the guard's discomfort. Rick wasn't the type of man any sane person would mess with. It wasn't just his size or obvious fitness, but a cool confidence that hinted he could handle himself in a fight.

She gave the doorman a regal nod and strode through the open door to the sale rack.

There were a lot fewer clothes and for a moment she feared Ashley's shirt was gone. But she clicked through the hangers and found the coral shirt stuck behind some discounted maternity jeans. Even better, the price had been slashed another twenty percent.

"It's still here." She smiled over her shoulder at Rick. "And it's even cheaper. Because of you I still have my twenty dollars. That means I can buy her some real maternity jeans and pay it forward. She'll be so happy."

Rick didn't say anything, just stared at her with an odd expression.

She held up the shirt. "It's pretty, isn't it? Bet she'll wear this to the caps tournament. When we come to cheer you on."

"It's very special," he said, but he wasn't looking at the shirt. In fact, his eyes never left her face. When he spoke, his voice was gruff.

"We should get you a bike helmet," he said. "So you can ride with me. Okay?" He held out his big hand and waited.

It was obvious he was talking about more than a motorcycle ride. And she knew nothing about him except that he had a prison record, made her laugh and was good with animals.

She reached out and took his hand.

Ashley pirouetted in the barn aisle, raising her arms and showing off the fit of her new shirt and jeans. "Thank you, Eve! I can't believe you went back and bought it."

She clasped her stomach, almost hidden now by the flare of the maternity top. "Now I have something to wear tonight. One of the security guards has a birthday, and there's going to be cake."

"That's great," Eve said, relieved to see her happy and bubbly like she'd been before the pregnancy.

Ashley tilted her head, her eyes mischievous. "You've never been gone all afternoon before. Juanita and the other ladies asked where you were."

"Rick and I ran some errands," Eve said. "We found a battery for my car, bought some beer...did some other stuff."

Ashley snickered.

"Not that," Eve said. "We haven't even kissed."

"Doubt he's the type to stop at a kiss." Ashley peered out the door to where Miguel and Rick were hosing Stinger's legs.

Eve crossed her arms. "You can't judge people by appearances. Bikers can be more mannerly than security guards."

"I didn't mean it like that," Ashley said. "But if he moves on a woman, it probably means something. I was checking him out this morning—you know, just letting him know I was interested." Her voice turned defensive. "After all, he's hot in a scary sort of way. But he totally shut me down."

A warm glow spread through Eve's chest, rising up her neck and leaking from her mouth. Because he hadn't shut her down, not at all. He'd even bought her a bike helmet, one that fit perfectly and had a special fog resistant insert. He hadn't let her see the price but she'd tried on at least six, and judging from the smile on the salesman's face, the helmet must have been one of the more expensive brands.

"Maybe it's because I'm pregnant." Ashley's voice turned plaintive. "Men don't look at me the same way, even though my boobs are much bigger. I can't wait until I get rid of this baby."

"Rid of the baby?" Eve jerked back, her smile disappearing. "What do you mean? I thought you were keeping it."

Ashley shrugged. "I don't know. Lately I've been considering putting it up for adoption. But then I hung out with the women at the sandpit today, and the children were playing, and it was kind of fun. And I could even imagine being a mother. I'm just not sure if I want it fulltime, you know, because I really want to be a famous jockey."

Eve rubbed her forehead. The only thing Ashley didn't waffle on was her commitment to becoming a top jockey. But at least she was getting to know the other workers now, instead of throwing out slurs and accusations. And it helped for the young mothers to get together, to have some support and learn all their options.

"I learned a few more Spanish words," Ashley went on. "And Juanita showed me how to change a diaper. It stinks and it's way worse than mucking stalls." She gave a mock shudder. "But at least I can do it. And that second sand pit was a good idea. If all big trainers were like you, life would be a lot easier."

"I'm not exactly a big trainer," Eve said.

"But Tizzy is running on Saturday and Miguel is going to give him a special massage. The purse is twenty-five thousand with a bonus for California breds. And we know he'll win after a massage. Miguel thinks so too."

Eve smiled but worry wormed through her chest. Ashley and Miguel were already counting on the bonus Jackson had promised. This was a small track but the race had some very tough competition. And Tizzy was in a slump. Vets had never found any physical ailments. But he hadn't won a race in six months. Not even close. In fact, his best finish was an uninspiring fourth. And it was never wise to rely on one horse.

"We'll have to let Miguel rest up," Eve said. "It takes a lot of energy working on that big horse. And his hands are already stiff."

"Sure." Ashley nodded, so vigorously strands of hair spilled from her jaunty ponytail. "I'll do the stalls the rest of the week. That will save Miguel for the important jobs. The stuff that makes horses win. Besides, Rick helps with the barn work."

Eve picked up a halter, then re-hung it in the exact same position, her gaze shooting down the aisle to the men outside. Ashley and Miguel were polar opposites, so it was great they were getting along and working toward the same goal. And since Rick's arrival, their entire situation seemed much improved. He was so helpful, so optimistic, so utterly grounded. He lifted everyone's spirits. And she couldn't keep her eyes off him.

"Bet he wins that caps tournament," Ashley said, following Eve's gaze. "Seems like he's good at everything."

Good at everything. Eve jammed her hands in her pockets, trying to straighten her increasingly wayward thoughts. She'd always been disciplined, not letting anyone but Joey sneak into her head. And this was not a good time to start drooling over a man. "He plans to practice tonight," she said, keeping her voice businesslike. "And win some bridles for the barn."

Ashley didn't answer, not even to make a suggestive comment. She stared toward the entrance, watching as Rick led Stinger down the aisle. The horse had clearly accepted Rick's leadership. His neck was low and relaxed, and he didn't push or try to bite.

"The scenery is sure a lot better now." Ashley blew out an appreciative sigh. "They say you should watch how a man treats his horse. Because that's the way he'll treat his woman." Her voice lowered. "You should totally go for him."

Rick glanced sideways, sending heat flooding to Eve's cheeks, even though there was no way he'd heard. Ashley hadn't spoken very loudly.

But his gaze locked with Eve's, his eyes twinkling. He kept one hand on the lead line. Then he reached out and, very deliberately and very gently, stroked Stinger's neck.

CHAPTER EIGHTEEN

"The bottle has to be between your knees," Rick said, placing a cap upside down on his beer bottle. "And we have to sit so our feet touch. Tell me if my arm extends too far. I need to release the cap on my side. No leaning allowed."

Eve sighed and moved her bottle the requisite inch, adjusting it to halfway between her knees.

They sat crosswise in the aisle, with every horse in the barn watching. She'd played caps before, but never so seriously. And she certainly hadn't realized there were so many rules.

"We used glasses when I played," she said. "Knocking the cap off the bottle looks harder."

"Yes." Rick gave a mischievous wink. "But we're in the big leagues now." He pulled back his wrist, took careful aim and shot. The cap arced through the air, hitting the top of her bottle and sending her cap spinning.

"Great shot." She leaned over and retrieved the cap. "Now what?"

"Now you drink," he said. "And I get a point."

She contentedly took a sip of cold beer. There were obvious benefits to giving up her jockey career. Even though her weight hadn't changed much, she didn't have to step on the scales and analyze every ounce. It made life simpler. "How much do you drink in the tournament?" she asked. "One sip?"

"One bottle."

"What?" Her jaw dropped. "That could end up being a lot of beer."

"Yes," he said, way too happily.

She frowned and scooped up another cap. It would be great if he won the gift certificate, but this tournament didn't sound like a walkover. At least he'd have a good time. He certainly deserved some fun. There wasn't a thing he couldn't do. Even Miguel was impressed.

'He's a good hand,' the old man had whispered, nodding his head in approval.

"So Woody won this tournament before?" she asked, aiming her cap. "What happened to his last partner?"

"Moved back to Mexico. He and Woody won the last two years."

She shot at Rick's bottle, missing the target by at least six inches. "So you're helping him defend a title," she said. "Heavy responsibility. Think you can do it?"

"I like to win. Do what I'm supposed to do." He paused and even though he was smiling, the shadows in the barn made his face look oddly grim. "Whatever it takes," he added.

And then she understood. This tournament wasn't really about winning a bridle. It was just a quick way to infiltrate a tightly knit society. Talking, drinking and camaraderie. He already knew more backstretch workers than she and Ashley combined. And after Thursday night, he'd probably be able to track down the bridles and provide the thieves' names to Scott. Job complete.

She pinched her beer cap against her palm. She'd had such a good time this afternoon. Couldn't remember enjoying a man's company so much. Other than Joey, she'd never let anyone lure her away from the horses. But it was important to remember that Rick's thoughtful attention wasn't personal. He was on the job. And naturally he was good. Scott only hired the best.

"Does Scott make all his investigators do this?" she asked. "Go shopping, drink beer?" She smiled, hoping Rick would reassure her that this wasn't just work. But he didn't speak. "Do you ever do anything just for fun?" she added.

"Scott assigns our jobs. We choose how we want to do them. But results are the only thing that matters."

Her smile froze and she struggled to hide her hurt. Yes, he was here on a job, but he'd been so charming and she'd been falling so fast, and she'd thought he liked her a little bit too. Heck, he'd even bought a second helmet. Acted like it was so important. No doubt, he'd be laughing about this later with Scott.

She didn't mean to shoot her cap at his head, but her aim was off, probably because she was blinking so much. It didn't matter though. His quick hand reached up and snapped the cap in midair.

"I'm tired," she said, rising and brushing some hay off her jeans. "But you should keep practicing... Scott expects results. Just be sure to hide any leftover beer. Miguel's an alcoholic."

She didn't realize Rick had even moved until his hand wrapped around her hip. "What's wrong?" he asked, turning her around.

Her pride called for a shrug and a smile, but she'd never been anything but forthright. And his eyes were so concerned and he still was a nice guy, even if he was entertaining her on someone else's dollar.

"I was having too much fun," she admitted. "I keep forgetting Scott's paying you to do a job."

"If I was really doing my job," he said, "I'd be over in the cafeteria right now. Having a beer and talking with the guys. Instead of doing this."

He traced her lower lip with his thumb, his eyes locked on her face. "Which, for the record, is what I wanted to do ever since I saw you riding in the dark. Before I could even see how beautiful you are. In every way. "

His hand splayed around her hip while his thumb stroked her lip, and sensations shot through her body. His touch was so gentle, so knowing. Little wonder the animals loved him. She tilted her head, anticipating his kiss.

But he didn't move. Didn't touch her anywhere else. He just caressed her lip, staring down at her mouth as if it were the focal point of his existence. As if nothing else mattered, not the horses, or his job…and certainly not the caps lying at their feet.

His thumb was soft but rough, with a callus on the pad, and somehow his slow touch made her lips feel bigger, pouty and it turned utterly, crazily erotic. She trembled, her mouth parting. And finally when every quivering nerve seemed hot wired to her mouth, his head lowered.

His mouth was hard and hungry, and fit hers perfectly. She clutched at his shoulders, losing herself in the kiss. He groaned, or maybe it was her. But she didn't care. Already their tongues were entwined, as if they knew each other and had just been waiting for their time to dance.

A languid pool of heat spread, dipping to her very core, and she pressed against that hard body. His hand had moved up her back, along her ribs, and now that clever thumb stroked the tip of her nipple, taking as much time there as he had with her lips.

She arched with impatience, and he obligingly cupped her breast, his thumb strokes matching the movement of his tongue. She quivered with wanting, and if he hadn't been holding her up, her legs might have buckled. Nothing mattered anymore, only that big masculine body that was making her senses sing.

But outside tires crunched over gravel, the sound jerking her back to awareness. A man's voice rumbled. Then a woman called good-bye.

Ashley. Precisely on time for night feed. Of all the evenings to be punctual. And Eve, the professional trainer, was making out in the barn aisle, on legs too buttery to move. She'd never live this down.

However, Rick swung her around, easing her into the shadows of the tack room. She clung to his arms, disoriented after his kiss. Kisses. She didn't know how long they'd been standing in the aisle, only that it was clear he didn't rush and she'd been the one in a hurry. And that left her stunned and more than a bit embarrassed.

Probably this was the time to make a joke, to let him know she didn't usually lose control like that. Or maybe she should just say "wow," let him know it was special. One of them should say something.

But he just pressed her head against his chest, his hand stroking her hair. She could feel the thudding of his heart, pounding a duet with hers. Could hear their mingled breathing. And no words were necessary.

Ashley strode into the barn, calling out a cheery greeting to the horses. Hay rustled and one of the horses, probably Stinger, slammed the wall with impatience. Soon she'd have to walk to the end of the aisle and grab another bale of hay.

Best to step out now. Eve squared her shoulders, checking her legs. They didn't feel quite so boneless. Rick had given her a chance to regain her composure, but now it was time to get back to work.

A phone chirped.

"Hi, Victoria." Ashley's voice sounded in the aisle, a scant fifteen feet away.

Rick's arms tightened around Eve in silent warning.

"No. We haven't raced yet," Ashley went on. "Entries are tomorrow... Of course the horses have been training... I'm not sure about the jockey." Her voice turned clipped. "Shouldn't Jackson speak to Eve about this? Well, if you're looking after it, you'll have to talk to Eve directly. Try her cell."

Eve didn't realize she'd been holding her breath until it escaped in a relieved whoosh. She glanced up at Rick who gave a nod of encouragement.

She stepped out into the aisle.

"Oh, hi," Ashley said, turning and shoving her phone back into her pocket. "I didn't know you were here. Victoria just called. Pumping for info. She wants to know the name of Tizzy's jockey but I didn't tell her anything—" She stopped, tilting her head in confusion. "Why are you grinning like that?"

Eve just shook her head. She'd always trusted Ashley, ever since the horse-crazy girl had shown up three years ago, determined to become a jockey. But lately she'd been questioning her instincts, and to overhear that phone call was utterly reassuring. Clearly Ashley was staunchly on Eve's side. Although it was sad that a race barn even had sides.

Rick stepped forward, a bale of hay tucked under his arm, and Ashley's puzzled expression turned to a knowing smile. "Oh, I see. You're both here. Were you practicing caps?"

"Yes." But both Eve and Rick spoke at once, a little too emphatically.

Ashley tilted her head, studying them. The silence stretched.

"Rick has great aim," Eve added hurriedly. "I'm sure he'll represent Woody well. How was the guard's cake?"

"Good. Liam gave me the leftovers so I brought it back to share." Ashley jabbed her thumb at a foil-wrapped plate by the door. "But that pee catcher job is no longer available. And he said there's nothing posted at the race office. So I need to do some serious thinking about what I'm going to do about... You know."

Eve nodded. She couldn't imagine giving up a baby. Joey was the center of her life. But it hadn't been easy, and what was good for her might not be the best choice for Ashley. Or her unborn child.

But tonight wasn't a good time to be discussing anything so important. Her body still sizzled from Rick's attention, and her brain felt sluggish, alert only to his magnetic presence at the far end of the aisle.

She glanced over her shoulder. He'd already begun topping up water buckets, moving with a lazy grace, rather unusual in such a big man. His arms rippled as he uncoiled the hose. Only minutes ago, those arms had been around her. And it had been wonderful. She couldn't hide a little shiver.

"Did I come at a bad time?" Ashley whispered.

"Of course not." She flushed and jerked her head away. "I was just heading back to the dorms. Besides, there's never a bad time for someone bringing cake."

But clearly she wasn't fooling anyone. Because Ashley snickered.

CHAPTER NINETEEN

Rick's eyes jerked open. He remained motionless, absorbing the night sounds: a horse slurping water, another shuffling in the straw. Nothing abnormal. But something had jarred him awake.

He pushed the blanket back and swung his feet onto the cool floor. The cot had originally been at the far end of the barn, but he'd moved it to an empty stall closer to the horses. It was the ideal place for watching the aisle, as well as the feed and tack rooms. He'd see any intruders long before they spotted him.

It was clear someone wanted Eve to fail. And at this point his money was on Jackson's ambitious wife. It hadn't taken him more than half a day to dig up Victoria's background. The woman had started at Riverview Racetrack walking cheap claimers for small-time trainers, but absorbing knowledge like a sponge. She'd climbed the ranks here, then moved to Santa Anita as a hotwalker where her physical attributes had caught Jackson Zeggalaar's eye.

Woody said she was smart and capable but unfortunately for Eve, she didn't like to share the limelight. Whether she had enough power to disrupt a stable from a hundred miles away was still the question.

Rick had added surveillance cameras to the barn entrance, as well as over the tack room, but they wouldn't help much if someone wore a hoodie. And they certainly wouldn't stop an intruder determined to hurt the horses. If Victoria was the source of mischief, the horses were probably safe since it was doubtful she'd deliberately harm her husband's business. On the other hand, emotional people were unpredictable and could be dangerous.

He tugged on his boots and edged to the front of the stall. From across the aisle, Stinger stared, his ears pricked. Rick remained still, studying the horse.

Stinger nosed his empty hay net, then swung his head away and peered down the aisle. Looking for more food or had he heard something too?

Rick wasn't sure yet what made the big horse tick, or if his reaction was significant. When he'd been working with Stinger, the horse hadn't seemed at all sensitive to his environment. The ill-tempered gelding appeared to have only one thought in his head, and that was to pound around the track.

However, Bristol, the bay mare with the star on her forehead, had a much different personality. She acted liked the matriarch, and when he led the other horses down the aisle, they all tried to keep a respectful distance.

She was definitely on watch now. Her head was stuck over the stall door, her nostrils flaring. She didn't look at him. Her attention was locked on the dark shadows beyond the end door.

But there wasn't anything outside worth stealing. Eve's car was locked, and he'd pushed his bike into an empty stall. Whoever was out there would have to come inside. When he did, Rick would nab him, and they'd finally learn the identity of her tormenter.

His breath quickened, pumped by a hunter's adrenaline and the prospect of an aggressive chase. But along with that came a spike of regret.

He liked it here. Enjoyed the simple way of life, of working with the horses and with the caring people who obsessed over those horses. He was curious how Stinger's raw power would convert to a race and if Tizzy would run better after Miguel's massage. It was refreshing not living with brutal criminals and not being hit on by desperate women craving their next fix. He really liked not finding dead bodies.

And he liked Eve.

Tomorrow he'd take her on his bike. Injuries had stopped her from race riding, but the motorcycle might fill her need for speed. She was the type who appreciated an adrenaline rush. Maybe some day, she'd even want her own bike. But soon that sweet body would be pressed against him. She'd be holding tight and he'd be in the driver's seat. And they'd be away from the barn and its untimely interruptions.

He blinked, realizing he was staring into the liquid eyes of the bay mare. She no longer watched the door. She was staring at him. And her expression was complacent, as if they were alone again.

Dammit. He charged from the stall and ran outside.

A fat white moon hung in the sky, illuminating the gravel road and darker horse path. Both were empty. He crept across the grass, careful to avoid the noisy gravel, then paused to listen.

Nothing moved along the chain link fence. But beyond the picnic tables, the fence was hidden by trees. Earlier he'd found a gap beneath the mesh, but the hole was at least two hundred yards away, and the woods were thick and overgrown. It was too silent for someone to have approached the barn from that route.

Unless, like him, they were standing still. Also waiting.

He shot forward, this time making no effort to hide his noise. Few people could remain still when faced with an aggressive charge. And once the intruder bolted, Rick was confident he could run him down.

He was halfway through the wooded path when he realized he was alone.

He stopped, snorting in disgust, then turned and jogged back to the barn. The visitor must have come from the other direction and either walked along the horse path or the paved road. Which meant he wasn't an outsider, but lived on the backstretch.

But what was the point of this night visit? Nobody had entered the barn, and there was nothing to tamper with outside.

He stiffened then hurried into the fenced sandpit, using the light from his phone to spotlight the sand. Eve said the gray gelding had cut his back rolling on a razor-sharp toy. Maybe it hadn't been an accident. He kicked at the sand, searching for any sharp objects. Found nothing.

Perhaps he'd been imagining the visitor. But he shook his head, dismissing that possibility. He trusted his instincts, and he definitely respected those of the boss mare.

However, he was alone now, and the tension slipped from his shoulders. Probably best to grab some more sleep. This wasn't a life or death situation. The horses were safe, turnout was safe, the feed and equipment were safe.

Nobody would be planting a bomb or lining Eve up with a sniper rifle. Victoria might have aspirations to be top dog, but she certainly wasn't a killer.

Still… His gaze drifted to Eve's car, parked beyond the barn. It was easy to sabotage a car and cause an accident, minor or major. He'd done it several times. But only to scumballs, never to someone like Eve.

His fists tightened and he strode toward her car. Before she drove it again, he'd run a thorough check. He wanted to fix her air conditioning anyway. And he'd have her park in front of the barn, or possibly by the guardhouse.

He stopped making his list, stopped worrying about where she should park at night. Because when he rounded the Civic's dented fender, he saw the reason for the sneaky night visit.

A sheet of paper fluttered on the windshield, pinned in place by the left wiper.

He lifted the wiper blade and pulled out the paper. The printing was so big and dark and angry that the letters were visible in the moonlight.

We don't want city snobs here. Leave now. Or die, bitch.

Not a bomb or sabotage. Just a note. And he couldn't stop grinning. It was so juvenile, so personal, and a refreshing change from the outlaw gangs that would kill a small boy without a second thought.

He stuck the note in his pocket and ambled back to his bed in the barn. Clearly, Eve had stepped on someone's toes. And though this type of work was far beneath his pay grade, at least here he could make a difference. He might even help out someone who deserved a boost. Someone he liked.

Best of all, there wouldn't be any guns or blood or bodies. His steps lightened and for the first time in years, he felt truly optimistic.

CHAPTER TWENTY

Eve bounced from the race office, filled with euphoria. She'd done it. She'd entered her first horse. She'd managed Tizzy's training and picked the day, the race, the jockey. All without any help from Jackson.

She'd always thought her career would start and end as a jockey. She loved the rush of racing, of partnering with her mount in order to reach the wire first. But this sense of satisfaction was every bit as heady.

Now her job centered on getting Tizzy to the starting gate on Saturday, healthy, happy and ready to run. And it was just as challenging, except that she'd leg another jockey into the saddle and watch the race from the rail.

Rick pushed himself away from the wall and raised his sunglasses, further tousling his hair. He'd insisted on accompanying her to the office after morning gallops despite her assurance that it wasn't necessary. But he seemed to be taking the car note seriously. Which was okay with her.

Generally she was irritated by men hanging around too close. But she doubted few women would be bored with Rick. He was smart and fun and made her see things beyond the track. And it had nothing to do with last night, the way his kiss had rocked her world. Not a thing. *Right.*

Her cheeks felt hot, and she jerked her gaze away from his mouth, aware that he was studying her lips too. Clearly they were both remembering.

"All done." She waved her hands in the air, hoping to distract him. "First time ever. My palms are sweating."

"Congratulations," he said, obviously understanding the enormity of the occasion. "So Tizzy's in?"

"Yes. Sixth race on Saturday, an allowance. And the rider is a woman. I think he'll like her."

Rick folded his hand around hers. "We should celebrate," he said. "Let's take my bike, do a little sightseeing, then have a nice dinner."

She opened her mouth to protest. She hadn't seen Juanita and the children in two days. Banjo's back needed be checked, Tizzy's whiskers should be trimmed, and Stinger needed to stand in ice water. Plus she was exhausted from riding this morning.

Rick's thumb traced the inside of her palm. Odd, how his body was granite hard, yet his touch so gentle. It made his embrace the night before doubly hard to forget, even though her mind should be filled with Tizzy. And if she didn't have so much to do, it might be fun to go for a little bike ride.

"Miguel already hosed Stinger," Rick said, "and I looked after Banjo's back. Ashley will stay until the five o'clock feed, and Miguel will take over until we return. Most trainers watch their horses from the gap, but you've galloped all morning. You need a break."

"I was going to take a break," she said. "A little nap."

"That's not really a break," he said.

And now his thumb circled the sensitive underside of her wrist. It was hard to think when he touched her like that. Just his finger grazing her skin, but it made her remember what it was like to have all his fingers, both hands, his mouth…

"This way we can be alone," he added, his voice persuasive. "We need to talk about who might want you gone. Until we figure that out, I'm not leaving your side. But if you're tired, sure, we can stop somewhere and nap."

The inflection he put on the word 'nap' made the sun feel even hotter. When she'd stepped down from her last horse that morning, she'd been exhausted. Didn't want to do anything but grab an apple and hole up in the dorm for an hour. Now though, she felt a lot of things. And not one of them was tired.

"I think you know the note writer," he went on, his thumb stroking a trail over the pounding pulse in her wrist. "So we need to decide how to proceed. Getting away from the track will help you analyze things more clearly."

It was hard to analyze much when he was touching her like that, making it hard to breath. And it was certainly hard to think.

She freed her hand under the guise of tucking a strand of hair behind her ear. When he'd first shown her the note, she'd been baffled and hurt. Then angry. What distressed her most was how it sucked away the barn's positive energy. All Rick's conversations this morning had been less about the horses and more about people. And he hadn't just peppered her with questions. He'd quizzed Miguel and Ashley too.

It was disruptive and draining. They'd already spent too much time worrying about bridles and batteries and Victoria. Rick was probably frustrated as well, but too conscientious not to follow her around. No wonder he wanted to figure this out.

And she wasn't helping. Instead of thinking about the possible note writer, she was melting at his touch and breathlessly wondering what else those capable hands could do.

"Okay," she muttered, stepping back and gathering her composure. "Let's go somewhere and talk. I realize you're in a hurry to finish this bodyguard job too."

His mouth lifted in an amused smile. "That's not what I said."

The powerful engine throbbed as they cornered another hairpin curve. Eve tightened her arms around Rick's waist. She'd started out holding his hips, but he'd adjusted her position with a warning rev. She rested her head against the soft leather of his jacket, keeping her weight centered, determined to be a good passenger.

It was weird to have no control, to rely on someone else to look after her safety. But a bike didn't buck or bolt or spook, and he was an excellent driver. With the horses far away, and nothing to do but sit, her mind began to relax.

The note he found on her car changed everything. The bridles, buckets and car battery could no longer be dismissed as simple thefts. Maybe even Banjo cutting his back hadn't been an accident. And anyone who would deliberately hurt an animal had to lack the smallest shred of decency.

But she didn't know anyone like that. Victoria might want to discredit her as a trainer, but she'd never hurt a horse. And did Victoria even know anyone at Riverview who'd do her dirty work. An old boyfriend maybe?

She closed her eyes and rested the side of her helmet against Rick's broad back. Her mind, soothed by the rhythmic rumble of the bike, skipped over a myriad of possibilities. However, it kept circling back to Victoria. No doubt, the woman was power hungry and quite likely still had influence at Riverview. It shouldn't take long to track down her old acquaintances. Eve didn't know how to go about questioning Victoria's friends, but she was quite certain Rick did.

At some point, the hum of pavement changed to the crunching of gravel. She peered at the towering redwoods, relishing the invigorating air. They followed a narrowing trail, much too small for cars. Passed a sagging fence and bumped into a meadow filled with weeds and wildflowers.

Rick cut the engine. He pulled off his helmet, then twisted on the seat, and helped remove hers. "Able to do any thinking?" he asked.

"Yes." She sighed. "But the only person that makes sense is Victoria. And she's my boss's wife so I'm not sure how it can be resolved. Any way it shakes out, I'll lose my job."

He helped her off the bike, not saying a word. And the fact that he didn't dispute her statement was rather depressing.

She circled the bike, weighing her options. No matter what Victoria did, or how much proof Rick found, Jackson would always side with his wife. And animosity toward Eve would spill over to Ashley and Miguel. So all three would lose their jobs.

Possibly she could quit and train on her own. Then she could hire them back. But that would be impossible to do now. She hadn't competed in a single race. It would be difficult to convince owners to send her their horses, especially since Santa Anita had an abundance of good trainers and most people still viewed her as a jockey.

Rick pulled a coffee thermos from his saddlebags, still silent. Usually she barged forward, with little thought of consequences, but he was encouraging her to stop and think. And clearly in this case, what was right might not be what was best.

He sat down on the grass and poured two cups of coffee.

After another moment, she sank down beside him. "Hopefully it's not Victoria," she said, appreciating his patience. "But even if it is, I guess I don't want you to prove it."

Rick nodded. "That's what I thought too."

"But you realized it way before me."

He passed her a coffee mug and draped a comforting arm over her shoulders. "Seems like it's Victoria who's causing you all this trouble. But there's less than a month left in the meet, and no real harm done. If accusations are avoided, you and your friends can return to Santa Anita and hang onto your jobs. At least it gives you time to work out some options."

"Being on a tight budget doesn't give much wiggle room," she said.

"Just get some races in," he said. "Make a little money, build up your creds. I'll watch the barn and horses. Seems the best option is to let this blow over."

She sighed. It didn't seem right to ignore Victoria's vindictiveness, but he was correct. There was no advantage to be gained by nailing her to the cross and forcing Jackson's hand. Rumor was that their marriage was headed for the rocks. It was probably easier to just wait her out.

"Maybe it's good we're at Riverview," she said, closing her eyes, soothed by the warming sun. "Not closer to Victoria's line of fire. You're sure it's her too?"

"Ninety percent."

"Does this mean you're leaving?"

"Not a chance." He pressed a kiss on the top of her head. "I still have to watch the horses. And you. But now it involves preventative measures…day and night."

He shifted, positioning her between his hard thighs, leaving little doubt as to what he wanted those night measures to involve. And she couldn't hide her own shiver of awareness.

She swallowed, glad he couldn't see her face. He was so confident, so certain with everything he did. And while she didn't want to fake coyness, she wasn't in the habit of hooking up with someone who would be in and out of her life so quickly. On the other hand, she had no doubt where this would end. If Ashley hadn't walked into the barn last night...

She glanced around, pretending to be absorbed with the meadow and the colorful golden flowers. It was private here, much quieter than the barn. She wondered if he'd brought a blanket. Probably not. The saddle pads behind the bike weren't that big.

She took a swift sip of coffee, wishing she wasn't so jumpy, wishing it were possible to relax.

He certainly could.

One tanned forearm, sprinkled with darker hair, was casually looped around her waist. She could feel the steady beat of his heart, absorb the masculine scent of his skin. But he didn't seem inclined to make a move. Wasn't trying to spread her out in the grass, checking how far his skillful kisses would take him.

He was just drinking from his mug. And holding her.

She took another sip, actually tasting the coffee this time. It was excellent, with a hint of hickory. Her favorite. Obviously he hadn't bought it at the track kitchen. Or maybe it tasted so good because this coffee break was unexpected. She wasn't chugging it down in a mad rush, injecting caffeine before her first gallop of the morning.

There was no reason to rush here. Rick was good company, able to appreciate silence. The meadow was interesting and full of life. Even if there were no horses to watch, there was still plenty to see. Like the agile squirrel scampering from tree to tree, and the rabbit that nibbled on the clover, ears constantly twitching.

She relaxed against his chest, liking that he didn't rush to fill the quiet. The sun was warm, the buzzing of the bees comforting. And slowly the stress seeped from her body. Her eyelids lowered, only flickering open when a shadow blotted the sun.

She peered up at a circling hawk. Rick lifted his boot and thumped it onto the ground, sending the rabbit scooting to the safety of the trees.

She jerked upright. She'd thought he was as relaxed as her, but his reaction said otherwise. He was a natural protector, even of little bunnies. But if he wasn't tired, why didn't he try to kiss her?

"That was nice of you." She touched his knee. His jeans were pleasantly warm from the sun and she left her hand on his leg, telling herself it was a more comfortable position. "I wasn't even thinking of the rabbit," she said. "And what could happen."

"Good." His breath fanned her hair. "Means you're not worrying."

"This is actually quite nice. Getting away like this."

"Then I should probably stay around," he said. "Make sure you keep relaxing. Scott wants me to help out any way I can, so this is progress."

There was a little innuendo in his voice, as if the progress wasn't solely related to his job. Although maybe she was misreading him again. Maybe his desire to stay at the track was more about earning points with Scott than scoring with her.

"Admit it," she said, keeping her voice light, pretending his answer wasn't all that important. "You just want to stay and play in the caps tournament, wow everyone with your great aim and guzzle free beer."

He chuckled. "There is that."

But then he placed his hand over hers before she could even formulate another question. "Let's get back on the bike," he said. "There's a waterfall close by. Supposed to be quite a sight."

She nodded and scrambled to her feet. She didn't like feeling out of control and it was easier on his bike. Not so confusing. She could still wrap her arms around those hard abs, but she didn't have to peek at his face, wondering if and when he might kiss her.

She waited for him to rise, and caught him watching her with eyes full of such sexual intensity, she flushed. But he merely rose and led her to the bike. And it was clear that even though the air was crackling, he sensed her uncertainty and was prepared to give her a little more time.

A little more time…but probably not much.

CHAPTER TWENTY-ONE

Rick lifted his mouth. His hand still cupped the back of Eve's head. He stared for a moment, his eyes glittering. Then his mouth swooped back down for another hungry kiss.

If there had been a course in the art of seduction, she thought, he must have aced it. She'd never been wooed so thoroughly. From the bike ride to the scenic stops and romantic restaurant, the entire day had been perfect.

He didn't rush. Ever. He'd merely been waiting, with every touch of his hand turning a little more familiar. Obviously an effective technique since she was now plastered against him, so tightly she could feel every ridge of his chest. His other hand was splayed over her bottom, holding her close, and it was clear—at least to her—that she was his for the asking. His body filled her senses, even as he angled her head further back, so he could more deeply explore her mouth.

Which was all wonderful, except for that little voice in the back of her head reminding that he worked for her. Or rather for Scott. And that this was a very short-term affair. A more cautious woman would probably step back and think things through.

Rick lifted his head an inch. "Let's go home," he said.

"Where's home?"

"Wherever you are." And he spoke so sweetly, his voice so thick with emotion, that the last of her reservations melted away.

She wanted this. Enjoyed being with him, whether it was working at the track or cruising on his bike or simply sitting on his lap and enjoying the scenery. Usually she didn't like being away from the horses for long, but they'd already been gone eight hours. And she wasn't at all anxious.

She wasn't obsessing about Banjo's back or Tizzy's race or Victoria's next scheme. She was no longer brooding about missing her weekend with Joey. Even the fear that Scott and Megan might be eyeing joint custody no longer seemed insurmountable. Instead, she felt weirdly content. Happy.

A door slammed, and voices drifted from the front of the restaurant. A man guffawed.

Rick immediately twisted, his wide shoulders sheltering her from curious stares. His hand grazed the underside of her breast, making her nipple tighten, and she ached with longing. There was no denying their chemistry.

But she shared a cramped room with Ashley, and the thought of grabbing a sexual tryst in a darkened stall didn't feel right. And there wasn't enough time to check into a motel, even if they could afford to splurge. Miguel was only on duty until eight. It was seven o'clock now, already dark, and the horses couldn't be safely left alone. Maybe they could figure out something for later in the week. Perhaps another bike ride.

Maybe next time he'd bring a blanket.

She lowered her hands from his neck, taking a moment to steady her breathing. "Thank you," she said. "For this day. It's been awhile since I wasn't worrying about something. About everyone," she added, thinking of Joey.

"Me too," he said.

She doubted that was true. He was too easygoing to obsess about much. In fact, it was his very levelness that kept her grounded. He'd never complained once about sleeping with the horses. And he was doing work way outside his job description. Heck, he'd rarely let her out of his sight. He probably needed some down time.

"If we hurry," she said, "we can get back before eight. I can watch the barn until midnight and you can grab a shower at Miguel's dorm. It's your turn for a break."

He picked up her helmet and buckled it beneath her chin, his intent gaze never leaving her face. "A break isn't really what I'm wanting now," he said.

"But I don't think tonight will work. We don't have a place, a proper place—"

He pressed a finger over her mouth. "Stop worrying so much," he said.

And so she did.

She climbed onto the bike, wrapped her arms around his lean hips and simply savored their closeness. His body was familiar now. And totally safe. She knew every inch of his broad back, the slope of his shoulders, and the deft way he avoided potholes, taking care of his motorcycle as thoroughly as he took care of her.

Riding at night was just as enjoyable as the day, maybe more so since there was an added risk. She couldn't see the curves of the road until the bike abruptly cornered. And the rushing roadside was full of mystery. She found herself pretending they were racing from danger, just like she sometimes imagined when she was galloping a horse. And that gave her more reason to press closer, to clutch him even tighter.

But the intriguing roads turned to wider highways, crammed with creeping traffic, stinky exhaust and blaring car horns. And all too soon the ride came to an end.

The entrance to the track was empty of traffic, except for a lone Jeep parked by the security building. They slowed at the barrier. She peered into the illuminated room, searching for Ashley's blond hair, hoping she might be having coffee with the guards so that their dorm room would be empty.

But only Liam was inside, his thick shoulders unmistakable.

He slid open the glass window, his gaze skipping from Rick to Eve. Then he nodded and raised the bar without even requesting a show of credentials.

She blinked in amazement, then waved her thanks. Obviously it helped that Ashley was friends with the guards.

The motorcycle rumbled along the line of shedrows. Horses stared over their stall doors, watching their passage with complacent eyes. Workers often relied on bicycles for transportation, but clearly the animals were accustomed to a variety of traffic noises.

They wheeled past the worker dorms where boots dried on windowsills and rusty bikes rested against clapboard walls. The smell of cilantro and chili peppers wafted in the breeze, mingling with the sound of mariachi music.

The light was on in Ashley's room. She must be home, sprawled on the narrow bunk bed, and Eve fought a rush of disappointment. She'd known this night would end. But she'd harbored a faint hope it might be prolonged.

However, Rick didn't glance sideways at the dorms. Didn't ask which door was hers or whether she shared a room or if there was any way to find some privacy. Which was just as well.

The helmet had left her hair plastered to her head, and she was probably covered with grit. She definitely had sand between her teeth. In fact, it felt like she'd been race riding. Rick had made her feel so desirable she'd forgotten how she must look. And she probably smelled earthy too.

She loosened her hold and sat a little straighter. He immediately swerved to the right, bouncing the bike over a shallow rut. She gave his helmet a warning rap but looped her arms back around his waist. She felt him chuckle.

They circled the hammock and picnic tables with her still gripping his waist. She was certain he took the darkest and bumpiest route possible, or maybe he was checking the grounds for trespassers. With Rick, she was never sure of his motives.

Miguel shuffled from the barn, nodding a greeting. The light from the doorway outlined his stooped shoulders, but he seemed relaxed. Of course, his workload was much lighter now and it helped that Rick spoke fluent Spanish. Miguel wasn't even reserved with Rick, not like he was with most newcomers.

Rick cut the engine.

"Everything's quiet, boss," Miguel said to Eve. "Legs all good. Horses ate up."

"Great," she said. "Thanks for watching the barn." She pulled out the tobacco she'd bought and slipped it into his gnarly hand.

Miguel gave a rare smile. *"Gracias."* He turned to Rick, still smiling.

"Any problem with the trailer?" Rick asked.

Miguel shook his head. "Security came but I gave them the phone number. And it's all hooked up. There was no trouble."

The two men kept talking while Eve fumbled with her helmet. She turned and pulled it off, then stiffened, startled by the huge white shape barely distinguishable in the gloom.

A horse trailer? But all trailers had to be parked in the common area. And this didn't look like horse transport. The windows were darkened glass, and human-sized steps led to a screen door.

"I need to watch the entire area," Rick said from behind her, his voice cautious. "An RV will help keep things safe, so you don't have to make accusations to your boss. Like we discussed."

She gripped her helmet. She didn't remember discussing any RV, only that it was important to keep Victoria at bay, without alienating Jackson. But a trailer would definitely help control trespassers. The tinted windows made it hard to see if a watchman was inside. Still, it must be against the rules. People couldn't just park trailers wherever they wished.

She stepped closer, admiring the gleaming structure. It was the biggest RV she'd ever seen and she definitely wanted to look inside, before security roared up and insisted it be moved.

"We have special permission," Rick went on. "The RV can stay until the end of the meet."

She made a sound deep in her throat, a ragged sigh of approval and distress. Scott had powerful allies throughout California and his investigative firm was well respected. He'd probably only needed to make a single phone call to the track owner, the same way he'd expedited the process for Rick's groom's license.

Clearly Scott had spent a lot of money. An RV like this wasn't cheap. And part of her knew she shouldn't accept it. He was already covering the cost of an investigator.

But an onsite trailer was the perfect solution. As Rick pointed out, it would keep Victoria's accomplices at bay without forcing Eve to make any accusations. And they could concentrate on the horses.

Footsteps shuffled on the road to the horse path. Miguel was already limping back to the dorms. He'd stayed late to watch the barn, a loyal employee who certainly deserved to keep his position. If they could lie low and wait for Jackson to sort out his marital problems, maybe they could all keep their jobs. This RV would help achieve that.

Still, Scott's presence hung like an oppressive cloud, his long reach now extending to her job. And closer to Joey.

She glanced at Rick. "If you'd asked me about this," she said, "I would have refused."

"I know," he said. He'd placed his helmet on the seat but remained by his bike. And it was clear he wasn't going to influence her. As he could, so easily. With a mere three-second kiss, or the brush of his finger, or that sexy chuckle. She swallowed, accepting she was already committed. She'd made the decision to sleep with him when they were sitting in the first meadow. He'd been the one who'd chosen not to rush.

"I suppose an RV would make things easier," she said. But that sounded all wrong and she winced, glad it was too dark for him to see her embarrassment. "Not for us," she added quickly. "But you probably don't like sleeping in a stall."

She didn't hear him move, but within seconds he was standing beside her. He tilted her head, studying her expression, and for the first time since they'd met, he seemed uncertain.

"I don't mind where I sleep," he said. "If it's too much, I can make a call. It will be towed away within the hour. But I wanted something better. For you... for us."

His quiet words swept away her uncertainty. Sometimes he said such sweet things, and they always left her speechless. She hadn't dared hope this might last longer than the meet. And maybe it wouldn't.

But when he held her like this, his big hands cradling her face as if she was the focus of his world, she truly believed love was possible again.

"Just go inside and check it out," he said. "There's chocolate, wine and food in the fridge. The shower even has special jets. Supposed to ease muscle pain."

He went on about how the pulsing spray might help her wrist and that the king-sized bed even had a magnetic mattress, and how important good health was for her job. If he were any more persuasive—and if she had an extra thirty grand stuck in her back pocket—she would have bought the RV on the spot. And now he was speaking about a reclining massage chair with zero gravity and heat therapy, but her mind simply couldn't absorb any more.

Nobody had ever looked after her like this. She'd pushed most men away, too focused on Joey and her career, and the strain of carving out a living in a very competitive industry. But she didn't want to push Rick away. Not one bit.

At some point he'd stopped talking, and she could feel the tension in his hands. "Too much?" he asked. "Or too soon?"

"Actually," she said, happiness bubbling in her chest until it leaked from the corners of her mouth. "You had me at chocolate."

CHAPTER TWENTY-TWO

Eve followed Rick into the RV. She let go of his hand to pull off her boots, then gawked at the kitchen. Everything was sleek and sophisticated, from the stainless steel appliances to the built-in wine cooler, already fully stocked.

It was even more luxurious than anticipated, and she'd expected a lot, based on Rick's pitch and the gleaming exterior. The fridge reminded her of Scott and Megan's, smaller but equipped with the same type of shaved ice dispenser that Joey always spoke about.

"Beer? Wine? Water?" Rick asked, flinging open cabinet doors and searching for glasses.

"Beer, please," she said. "But where's that chocolate?"

He smiled and dropped two foil packages on the table, along with a bag of peanuts. "There's dark and milk. I wasn't sure of your favorite."

She studied the buffet of chocolate: the dark truffles wrapped in gold and the miniature Swiss chocolate bars. She'd always been a sucker for sweets. But when she was a jockey, she'd rarely indulged. The weigh scales were too unforgiving.

Now it felt like a fairy godmother was waving her wand. And the beer Rick expertly poured into a tall glass was her favorite, the same kind she'd ordered at the restaurant today.

He'd remembered everything—even how she'd wistfully eyed a milk chocolate bar when they stopped for Miguel's tobacco. And his thoughtfulness moved her even more than the luxurious RV. But it was incomprehensible how he'd arranged everything. He'd been with her all day. And the few times he'd used his phone had been noticeably brief.

She took a sip from her chilled glass, noting the compact massage chair in the corner. Her doctor had recommended one of those but the price had been much too steep.

"This is amazing." She gave an appreciative smile, still absorbing all the features. "But how did you arrange it?"

"Scott's assistant, Belinda," Rick said. "She's super efficient. Keeps a file on everything."

Eve's fingers tightened around the glass. Of course. Rick would have been given extensive information. About the track, about the staff, about her. So it wasn't surprising he knew how to push her buttons. The warmth in her chest disappeared, replaced by a chill that matched the beer.

He wasn't looking at her. He moved around the kitchen with easy authority, expertly checking his phone and a computer screen, looking less like a prison parolee but perhaps someone more lethal. She knew from media coverage that Scott's company was known for tackling dangerous criminals. And those reports were always blunted as Scott tried to keep details of his cases private.

Megan had once said investigators who didn't have an office were the ones Scott relied on to handle the most dangerous assignments. Those types of men were wasted on mundane track theft. She'd already noticed Rick's sheer athleticism, his surprising quickness. Only that morning he'd snapped a horsefly in midair, before it could even think of biting Stinger. No doubt, those hands had done much more than snag flies.

A shiver ran down her back. He wouldn't stay around long, that was certain. Perhaps he wasn't bored yet, but he would be. Unfortunately, she was totally smitten. After a day of being pressed against him on the bike, she'd memorized every one of those hard ridges, knew exactly how fast his hands could make her quiver, and how the feel of his hungry mouth left her gasping.

They both knew they were going to end up on that king-sized bed with the goose down pillows and magnetic mattress. They'd gone too far to stop now. It was evident in the possessive brush of his hand when he passed her the beer, the timbre of his voice, even the sexual undertones crackling in the kitchen.

He pressed a key on the laptop and closed the lid. His hot gaze returned to her face, seeming to lock on her lips. "Want to check the horses first?" he asked quietly.

She shrugged, pretending a casualness she didn't feel. "First? As in before the shower, or before bed?"

"I'm not caring much about the shower," he said.

"Okay," she said. "I better check the barn now. In case I don't get back out until morning."

He nodded, his eyes so dark now they appeared black. He set down his beer and tugged her toward the door, and if the air had crackled before, it now seemed even more alive. Almost painful.

This was always a scary time. Trusting a man. And he was not the average railbird variety. His knuckles were ridged with scars, the palms of his hands callused. Yet she'd seen them soothe a horse, had felt their gentleness.

He hadn't asked any of her history, and it was clear he didn't wish to discuss his. And good men sometimes ended up in prison, just like Dex. So the past didn't really matter. Not to her.

But when she walked beside him into the barn, her heart was thudding so loudly she feared it would frighten the horses. However, they didn't seem to notice her racing heart, or her quickened breath or Rick's barely concealed urgency.

"All good?" he asked gruffly, after she'd checked every animal.

She nodded, her throat dry.

"Thank God." He scooped her into his arms and carried her past the sleepy-eyed horses. Strode to the RV, climbed the steps with a single bound, and used his boot to push open the door.

He carried her into the bedroom and she could feel his steely focus, the pulsing tautness of his body. He didn't seem to mind that her hair was flattened, her face streaked with dust, her clothes tired and rumpled. No doubt, a man like him had enjoyed a smorgasbord of women, from biker babes to perfumed thrill seekers with red lips and perfect hair. And she didn't want to stress over anything as trivial as dust and helmet hair and how she might not match up...but somehow she did.

"I'd really like a shower first," she whispered. "Just so I feel better."

She guessed he'd try to overrule her on that, maybe reassure her that it didn't matter. And while it would be nice to wash off the road dust, if she were honest, she was just as eager to try out that magnetic bed. It was time to stop worrying, stop thinking, and just feel.

But his patience surprised her. He didn't sigh or grunt or argue. "Okay, sweetheart," was all he said.

He turned and carried her into the bathroom. Deposited her on the shower floor and stepped back. Clearly he wasn't as eager as her, or as attracted—

Seconds later, a shocking spray of water drenched her face. It wasn't cold but it wasn't warm either. She squealed and scooted sideways, hurrying to escape the pulsing jets.

But he blocked her way. He'd already whipped off his shirt and now stepped from his jeans, grinning with mischief and something else. A raw longing that left his eyes dark and smoldering, his mouth utterly sensual.

And she no longer noticed the streaming water or how the temperature was warming, or that the pulsing shower really did invigorate the skin. Because he was utterly and mouthwateringly magnificent, like a statue that had captured a warrior's physique. His chest appeared carved from granite, although several white scars proved he was indeed human.

She could only gape, her breath choppy. As an athlete she appreciated fitness but his utter steeliness was remarkable. She couldn't help but reach out and slide her hand over that rippled chest, with skin surprisingly smooth and unmarked. Except for a few scars the size of bullet holes. And a barbed wire tat around his lower back.

She stepped back, silently inviting him to join her beneath the spraying water. His entire body was rigid and it was apparent it would have been much more sensible to move directly to the bed. There wasn't much room in the tiny shower and she'd always needed considerable foreplay. But judging by the urgency radiating from that virile body, he'd be unlikely to linger.

He stepped in, swallowing up the space, his erection so huge its bulbous tip jabbed her hip.

She drew in an uneasy breath, guessing she'd be sore for riding tomorrow. But his head dipped, lingering over a particularly sensitive spot of her collarbone. His mouth was warm and slow and tender, and the feel of his tongue sent familiar quivers shooting to her core.

He raised her wet shirt, inches at a time, stroking her skin with his mouth, his tongue, his hands, first with a butterfly touch and then more demanding. He moved as if her body was meant to be appreciated and he had the experience to do it. And by the time his thumb finally reached her taut nipple, she quivered with longing.

And it was apparent the cramped shower wouldn't be a problem at all.

CHAPTER TWENTY-THREE

The sound of restless horses seeped into Eve's consciousness. But she didn't want to move, too entangled in Rick's arms and legs, her head too comfortable, pillowed against his warm chest.

She peered up. His eyes were half-lidded, but his smile was gorgeous. Thick stubble covered his jaw, extending along his neck. She hadn't noticed it last night, but she'd certainly felt it. All over.

"Awesome night," he said, his mouth still lifted in a smile. "You don't even snore."

She doubted either of them had slept enough to snore. It seemed she'd had her year's quota of sex in one night. He might be accustomed to a little more though. Already he was stiffening against her thigh, and surprisingly, her own body tingled in response.

But someone was rattling buckets in the barn, and horses stomped, impatient for their breakfast. It was time to stop marveling at how he'd made her body sing, and turn her concentration back to riding.

She wasn't sure how he wanted to handle this though. Was he even allowed to have a relationship when he was on a job? If they hurried, perhaps she could sneak out of the RV. Pretend they hadn't spent an amazing night together.

"I have to go," she said. "Sounds like Ashley is here. Or maybe Miguel."

"Let's stay in bed," Rick said, running his warm palm over her hip. "Wait until they saddle your horse."

"Then you're okay with this?"

His eyes whipped open. "On them knowing we're together?" He spoke like it was an ongoing thing, certainly not a one-night fling, and her heart gave a little skip.

"I just wondered if this was allowed," she said, "you know, with Taylor Agency. And Scott being your boss."

"I can do what I want." He scowled, his voice almost testy. "The only boss I need to please is you."

"And you did please me," she said. "Repeatedly."

He still looked offended at the idea of Scott telling him what to do, and she totally understood the feeling. She pressed a soothing kiss against his cheek. "I have to get up now," she said. "And you're not going to get out of cleaning stalls today, no matter how magnificent you were."

"I was magnificent?" His smile returned, a rather smug one, but she figured he deserved a little praise.

"Not sure if I like the whisker burn," she said, prying her leg out and edging to the side of the bed. "And a couple areas need improvement. But overall you were very satisfactory."

His hand hooked around her waist. "But I feel obliged to work on those areas now," he said. "Just until I get it right."

"Can't. I have horses to ride. And it's always a rush fitting them in before the track closes."

She lifted his arm and eased from the bed, putting a more prudent distance between her and temptation. Surprisingly, she wasn't a bit sore, just utterly sated and ready to climb into the saddle.

It would be nice to gulp a coffee first but it would take too long to make, and she wanted to be the first rider on the track. It was safer for her young horses when the ground was freshly harrowed. Less chance of them pulling a tendon, straining a ligament, or worse. Usually she stopped at the track kitchen on her walk to the barn, but last night was an unusual event. And well worth missing her usual wake-up coffee.

And then she smelled it. The distinctive smell of hickory.

She twisted, surprise mingling with delight. "You made coffee? When did you do that?"

"Turned the timer on last night." His gaze drifted over her naked body, his eyes glittering with appreciation.

She blinked, rather chagrined he'd had the presence of mind to prepare coffee, while she hadn't been able to think of anything much. Except him. Even the drenching shower hadn't cooled her passion—

"Oh, no." She jerked back in dismay. "My clothes are wet. I have to run back to the dorms. I'm going to be so late."

He rose from the bed, all gorgeous naked male, and padded from the room. His tight butt disappeared around the corner. Something clicked in the hallway, and he ambled back with her clothes draped over his arm. "They're dry now," he said.

She took them, clutching them to her chest. Great sex, fresh coffee, clean clothes. This guy was a dream. But it was rather embarrassing how he'd turned her into a quivering mass of desire, with no thought of anything after he'd pushed her against the shower wall and hooked her legs around his hips.

"Thank you," she said. "You were certainly thinking much clearer than me last night."

"Not a chance." He slid his hand around the back of her neck and gave her such a tender kiss, she stopped worrying about his surprisingly organized mind—and his utter, and totally distracting, nakedness.

"Are you riding Stinger first?" he asked, tugging on his jeans.

She shook her head. She was in too good a mood and far too relaxed to waste it on Stinger. "He'll go last today." She peered sideways, watching as Rick pulled up his zipper. It was a little disappointing to see that magnificent body concealed.

"Good," he said. "I'll lead him over when you go. It'll give me a chance to talk to Woody. See what he can tell me about Victoria's friends."

"So we still have to worry?" She fumbled with her bra, trying to hurry, realizing she'd soon be the only one naked. "You don't think the RV will keep her people away?"

He buckled his belt, his eyes on her face. "It will help," he said. "But nothing's a certainty. Don't worry. Just concentrate on your horses."

She gave a little nod. If the barn was safe, there was no reason to fret. The horses never went anywhere, except to the track where she was always on their backs. And no matter how reckless Victoria's henchmen were, they couldn't do anything there. So it seemed the only thing left to worry about were Tizzy's and Stinger's races this weekend. And how long she'd have to wait to see Joey.

Rick slid his hands over her back and deftly fastened her bra, as if he'd been helping her dress for years. His warm breath feathered her skin. And even though they'd shared an intensely satisfying night, his touch left her hungering for more.

She swallowed, aware she had a tight schedule. The sun was almost up, horses needed conditioning, and successful trainers didn't lie around in bed during training hours.

Besides, Rick was fully dressed now. He seemed to have no trouble moving on, once he made a decision. She wasn't even going to beat him to the bathroom, and that would slow her even more.

But he pressed a kiss against the back of her neck, and she could tell his mouth was smiling, as if reading her mind. "Bathroom's all yours," he said. "I'll pour your coffee. Then I'll get at those stalls."

He turned her around and even though he was still smiling his eyes looked darker, more serious. "Ride safe," he said.

"He's gorgeous," Ashley said, adjusting her hold on Tizzy's lead shank. "But way too scary a ride for me."

"Don't be ridiculous." Eve dipped a sponge into the sudsy bucket. "Tizzy's easy. Like a dependable cow pony."

"I'm not talking about Tizzy."

Eve sloshed the sponge over Tizzy's sweaty back. Ashley had been making snide comments all morning, ever since she recovered from the shock of seeing a luxurious RV parked beside the barn.

"I heard biker clubs share their women," Ashley went on, her eyes bright with curiosity, and perhaps a touch of maliciousness. "And that they earn a colored wing for group sex, a skull-and-bones patch for murder. But I'm sure you already know that. And that you've checked his jacket..."

Eve scooped up the hose. She sort of pointed it in the direction of Tizzy's neck, but most of the water drenched Ashley. "Oops," Eve said.

Ashley squealed and scrambled back, almost stumbling in her haste.

"Sorry," she said, shoving the sodden hair back from her face. "I deserved that. But Rick is intimidating. I know he works for your brother-in-law and he's a big help around the barn, but we don't know anything about him. Liam is concerned too. He thinks Rick might be hiding from a gang. And that he's probably packing a gun or two."

"No guns are allowed at the track," Eve said.

"Yes. But he's not the type to worry about rules. Bet he's used to lots of different stuff too. You know, like kinky things." Ashley's voice lowered, turning almost wistful. "Did he tie you up?"

Eve dragged a sweat scraper over Tizzy's neck, her strokes jerky. She and Ashley had been jockeys together and they'd shared a few bawdy jokes. But Rick was off limits. Besides, there were all kinds of bike clubs. Gang members might follow a different code, but they weren't all promiscuous.

Still, Ashley's comments left her feeling vulnerable. Uncertain. And she certainly didn't want to hear any more. "We can talk about the horses," she said. "Or you can be quiet."

"Sorry. I'm just worried. This is so unlike you. I figured you two were together when you didn't show up last night." Ashley hesitated then made a wry face. "You and Rick haven't stopped grinning all morning. And that RV is like a hotel. Guess I'm just jealous."

Her burst of honesty soothed Eve's temper. Jockeys were a competitive bunch, but Ashley was incapable of guile. Probably why they were friends.

"You can go inside and take a shower," Eve said. "And there's lots of coffee. Including decaf. Help yourself."

"Really?" Ashley brightened. "You don't mind? What about Rick?"

"He won't mind either. Just be careful of his chains and guns."

Ashley gave a sheepish smile. They both looked at Rick who was cooling out Stinger, stopping every second circle to offer the horse a sip of water.

The two had definitely hit it off. Stinger didn't give him a speck of trouble. And both Miguel and Ashley were relieved to avoid handling the challenging horse.

"Is he ready for the caps tournament tonight?" Ashley asked, clearly trying to make amends. "I heard Camila's boyfriend won last year. He used the gift certificate to buy her a pair of paddock boots."

Eve pulled her gaze off Rick. "But Rick said Woody won last year."

"Yes, but Camila's boyfriend was Woody's partner. They won two years in a row."

"Where's he now?"

"Back in Mexico." Ashley edged away from the sudsy water pooling by Tizzy's hooves. "They found drugs in his room. He didn't have a green card so he left before he was charged."

Eve grimaced. No wonder Camila rarely smiled. But at least Ashley was opening up to the Hispanic women. She'd stopped blaming them for all the barn's problems and had even learned some Spanish. It would be nice to see the women this afternoon, hear the laughter of the children. Since Rick arrived, she'd been away in the afternoons. She didn't know what his plans were for later that day, but she hoped it included relaxing by the barn.

Her gaze drifted back to the small walking ring. Rick seemed to sense her scrutiny and glanced over Stinger's head. His smoldering smile left no doubt about what he wanted to do later.

She fumbled with the sweat scraper, surprisingly flustered, but happy. The day was much brighter with him in it. All her senses seemed on full alert. Even the soap smelled sweeter. Most certainly her breasts felt more sensitive.

Ashley caught Rick's heated look. "I've never seen two people more obvious," she grumbled. "Maybe Scott will pay Rick to go to Santa Anita. Then you'll be able to see him longer."

Eve's pleasure drained. She scanned Ashley's face, wondering if this was just another barb. Granted, the words were totally true. And maybe Rick routinely hooked up with women on his jobs. He clearly didn't worry much about Scott's rules.

She tossed the sweat scraper into the bucket. "Walk Tizzy around now," she said, her voice crisp. "And you're in charge of the five o'clock feeding instead of Miguel. He'll have to stay late to massage Tizzy, so he needs some time off."

Ashley gave such an agreeable nod, Eve decided she was being too thin-skinned. Of course she realized Scott was paying Rick. And whoever Rick slept with before was history. Besides, she wasn't in the habit of asking nosy questions. It certainly didn't bother her if he routinely picked up women. Or if the whispers about club orgies were true.

She jammed the water hose in a tight coil and tossed it beside the barn. No, she told herself, Rick's past didn't bother her at all.

It shouldn't bother her… But somehow it did.

CHAPTER TWENTY-FOUR

Rick twisted the kitchen faucet, staring through the RV window as yet another kid materialized. There must be at least fifteen of them now, from toddlers to five-year-olds, all playing tag and squealing and poking sticks in the sand. The mothers looked relaxed, crowded around Eve at the picnic table, their conversation flowing in rapid-fire Spanish.

He hadn't realized the second sandpit had been created for children. It must have swallowed a big chunk of Eve's limited funds, yet another example of her generosity. And while it was nice she'd created a welcoming place for the women, he sure wished it was somewhere else.

He concentrated on regulating his breathing, hating how his hand shook when he filled the pitcher. But deep breathing didn't help the constriction in his chest. He swiped at his clammy forehead, accepting he couldn't take this much longer. He'd been serving coffee and ice water, nodding at the women, all the while despising the artificial smile pasted on his face.

It had been impossible to look too long at the kids. Their innocent eyes and fragile little bodies made his gut churn. The shrinks claimed that when he let go of the guilt, the panic attacks would fade.

Clearly they'd been wrong.

Eve passed Juanita a black marker, smiling at the English version of the poster: *HAIRCUTS (FOR HUMANS) YOUR BARN, YOUR TIME, ONLY $9.00!*

Opinions on the best price for a cut ranged from eight to twelve dollars, but after much discussion it was decided that most customers would leave the extra dollar in a tip, letting them offer a more competitive price.

Juanita gave Eve such a grateful smile it lit up the woman's round face. "This is a good idea. Life is better since you came. We have more joy, more hope. This business will help our income, our families, everyone."

"You could also offer massages," Ashley said. "The horses get rubbed all the time. But grooms get sore too. I'd love for someone to rub my back."

That started another round of conversation with Ashley in the middle, and everyone valiantly trying to stick to English. Even Camila nodded and grabbed the marker, keen to make another poster that included massages.

Eve rose from the table. She'd provided several ideas to earn extra money. But now her help was no longer needed. They were already making posters, in both English and Spanish, demonstrating a new confidence as well as a shrewd understanding of price points.

She removed a pointed stick from a toddler's pudgy fingers and replaced it with a plastic scoop borrowed from the feed room. They desperately needed more toys. Barn utensils were only a temporary solution, and every day more children appeared, shyly clinging to their caregivers' hands and then embracing the sand pit.

Perhaps if Tizzy finished in the money, she and Rick could drive down the road and find a cheap store. Most backstretch workers were limited, not only with funds and time, but also with transportation. If she could visit a mall, she could pick up some shovels and buckets, real children's toys, instead of the bulky barn equipment.

And now that she was at a small track, away from Victoria and her stifling rules, she could bring Joey for a visit. Maybe he could even come after his weekend stay with Megan and Scott. Then it would only be nine days she wouldn't see him instead of fourteen. It would be wonderful to have him close by while she worked, to be able to see him from the moment he woke.

She could introduce him to all the animals, help him build a sand castle, and even put him to bed every night. Best of all, she could let him sit on Tizzy's back and share the joy of just how wonderful it was to ride a horse.

Certainly some details needed to be ironed out, like finding a good babysitter. But if Megan and Scott came to watch Stinger race on Sunday, they could drop off Joey then.

She pulled in an excited breath, flushed with gratitude. This could all work out beautifully. She also needed to thank Scott in person, for renting the RV and especially for sending Rick. There hadn't been any more theft since he'd arrived. Victoria had pulled back her horns.

Rick was exactly what the barn needed. What she needed.

Her heart beat a little faster and she glanced toward the tinted windows of the RV. He was so thoughtful, making coffee for the women and having Miguel help bring over ice water for the children. But then he'd disappeared, joking that the men had to rest up: Miguel for his massage of Tizzy, and him for the caps tournament.

But it was almost three o'clock and while she'd seen Miguel head back to the dorms, she hadn't seen Rick again, not since he'd carried over the last pitcher of ice water.

She walked toward the RV, automatically smoothing back her hair. The door opened as if he'd been waiting for her. He carried work gloves and wire, and a tool belt hung around his lean hips. The heavy belt tightened his shirt, flattening it against his ridged chest, and the impulse to touch him was overwhelming.

She stuck her hands in her pockets. "Moonlighting somewhere?" she teased.

"Going to plug those holes in the fence," he said, not cracking a smile. "Just a stopgap until security brings in their regular contractor."

"I see," she said, a little disconcerted by his flat tone. But maybe he'd learned something this morning. He'd been lingering by the little tack trailer the entire time she was riding. "Did Woody say anything today?" she asked. "About Victoria?"

"He doesn't think she has many friends here," Rick said. "Apparently she wasn't well liked. Mostly he talked about carbing it up for tonight."

The little boy that was teething let out a cry and Rick's gaze shot over her head. He seemed aloof. Like a man who'd picked up a woman the night before and now regretted it. But he'd been fine this morning, even grabbing a kiss when they'd been alone on the horse path.

She stepped back, confusion mingling with her hurt.

"Come with me," he said, his voice almost rough. "To the hill."

"Sure," she said, relieved he wanted her company. "I've never walked beyond the trees. Do you think someone's sneaking in from outside?"

"Not sure." He took her hand and tugged her toward the east side of the woods, skirting the picnic tables. "But if the gaps are fixed, there'll only be two ways to reach the barn, the horse path and the road. So I don't want to wait for the contractor to fix it."

She gave a good-natured shrug. Theft wasn't a big concern anymore. No one would be foolish enough to sneak into a barn with an RV parked by the door, manned by someone as imposing as Rick. And while they were at the tournament tonight, Miguel would be giving Tizzy a massage. The horses would never be alone.

She waved at the women. But they didn't even notice her departure. They were clustered around Ashley's blond hair, their conversation a mixture of Spanish and English, punctuated with giggles and bawdy massage jokes. The posters would be funny, if nothing else. Hopefully the flyers wouldn't be too suggestive, or security might order that they be removed. Although Ashley, who was so tight with the guards, could probably hang anything she wanted.

"They're adding massage to the hair business," Eve said, trying to keep up to Rick's long strides. "Should be a good side business. Maybe in a few months it will develop into something more. Juanita's cousin is amazing. Did you notice the haircut on the boy in the striped shirt—"

"The first hole is just over there," Rick said, holding back a branch so it wouldn't poke her in the face. "I'm not sure what's on the other side, but there's definitely a path. Looks like it was well used at some point."

He was clearly focused on more important things than haircuts, and she glanced past him, searching for the hole. The break at the bottom of the fence didn't look new. In fact, the steel mesh was curled with age, leaving a two-foot gap. Beyond, a narrow footpath cut through the field and disappeared over the hill.

"You think someone comes this way?" she asked. "Looking to steal tack?"

"Maybe." Rick bent and tested the wire. "It's loose. Anyone could fit through here."

"I wonder where it goes," she said, intrigued by the path leading over the ridge.

"Let's find out." He unbuckled his tool belt, dropped it on the ground and held up the mesh. "After you."

"Okay," she said gaily. "Maybe we'll find my bridles. Or a cache of saddles."

She slipped beneath the fence, then stopped and held up the bottom of the mesh, waiting for him to edge beneath the wire. Her gaze kept shooting toward the mystery hill, her imagination racing.

Maybe they'd find more than tack. Possibly even a stolen horse. Or maybe it would lead to a ring of thieves who collected Thoroughbreds capable of winning stakes races, or Kentucky Derbies, or even the Triple Crown. She'd read every Dick Francis mystery, and things like that always happened in England. It *could* happen here.

"Maybe we should have weapons," she said. "Maybe take a wrench or something. Or I can use that pointed rock over there—"

"Maybe," he said, rising and pulling her into his arms, "you should just stick close."

He tucked her head against his chest, and she could feel the thud of his heart, and it was clear that whatever had been distracting him earlier was no longer a factor. He certainly didn't feel like a man who wished he hadn't made love to a woman. No doubt she'd let Ashley's comments stir up her uncertainty, something she wouldn't let happen again. Mind games didn't interest her. And she sensed Rick wasn't into them much either.

"I don't mind sticking close," she whispered. "For as long as you're around."

His arms tightened. He seemed to have forgotten all about climbing the hill and checking for thieves. "Maybe when this meet is over," he said, inching back and studying her face, "I could ask Scott for work closer to Santa Anita."

She gave a little nod, too stunned to speak. She'd feared he regretted sleeping with her. But now he was talking about moving so they'd be closer. This relationship might last a lot longer than she'd dared to hope.

She nodded again, much more emphatically. "That would be great." Then she tilted her head, her initial happiness dampened with worry. "But do you need to stay somewhere small? Should we avoid the city? Is there a gang looking for you?"

"No." His chuckle was slightly rueful. "But I appreciate your courage. And that it wouldn't scare you away."

"So you were just in a riding club?" she asked. "Nothing illegal...lately?" She didn't want to ask details about his prison sentence. Would save that question for another time.

He skimmed her cheek with his thumb, his eyes tender. "I worked different types of undercover. But it's been almost two years since I rode with a motorcycle club. I came here directly from a job with Scott, tying up some loose ends. Some of that work was south of the border, a cartel case. It's over now."

"But when did you do the biker job? You only worked with Scott for a year. And you don't have a full PI license."

He hesitated and his tanned throat rippled. "I was with LAPD for nine years." He spoke so low she could barely hear. "Gang and Narcotics for three."

She blinked. He wasn't a biker at all, but a cop. It was amazing she hadn't picked that up. Generally she had a radar for police, and it usually sent her bolting in the opposite direction. But Rick didn't walk or talk or think like a cop.

"But you have prison tattoos," she said slowly. And then she groaned. "Now I understand. You don't have a record at all. The tattoos are just for show."

She must have sounded disappointed, because his voice strengthened with amusement. "Sorry," he said. "No record."

A squirrel scolded from a nearby tree, but their eyes remained locked, neither of them speaking while she struggled with the implications. He was a cop. She was sleeping with a cop. She rolled that thought around for a moment, trying to absorb it, wondering if her lip was curling with distaste.

"I never thought I'd hook up with a cop," she finally said.

"Ex." His eyes twinkled.

"I suppose that's okay then. At least it was undercover, no uniform." Her eyes narrowed. "You didn't wear a uniform, did you?"

"Well, yes, I did." He chuckled. "But only for the first two years. Sorry, sweetheart."

"At least you don't wear a uniform now," she said, trying not to smile, but it was hard not to feel happy when he called her sweetheart. It didn't sound like a casual term of endearment either, but something he sincerely meant.

Besides, he'd probably been a good policeman. That was definitely a safer job than working undercover and dealing with the constant fear of having your throat slit. Her heart kicked with empathy.

"It must have been terrifying living with criminals," she said. "Wondering if this is the day you might get caught. Worrying that someone you know could say hello. And accidentally give you away."

"I was pretty deep," he said. "Didn't run into many acquaintances."

"So you lived with outlaws. Laughed and talked and made friends." A lump clogged the back of her throat. "And then you had to turn them in. That must have been hard."

"It wasn't too bad. Most of them were murderers." He shrugged, but she could feel the muscles cording in his arms.

"But not all of them," she said. "And I know that must have hurt a kind person like you."

He stared down at her, and for a moment he let her see everything in those dark eyes. The regret, the anguish. The way a muscle spasmed on the corner of his jaw. "It did," he admitted.

He looked away, abruptly engrossed with the scolding squirrel. Then he pressed her head against his shirt, his fingers splaying beneath her hair, and it was clear the talking was over.

Her heart ached for his obvious ambivalence, but it was significant he'd even confided about his work. And for now, that was enough.

CHAPTER TWENTY-FIVE

Rick turned at the crest of the hill and studied the scene below—the barn, the RV, Eve's car. If he had his binoculars, he'd probably be able to spot the orange cat sunning itself beside the barn.

"What a great view," Eve said. "You can see everything from here... Her voice trailed off and it was clear her quick mind understood the implications. "So that's how they always knew when we were gone," she added glumly.

He gave her slim hip a comforting squeeze and checked the other side of the hill. It was a beautiful property and clearly had once been a well-loved farm. A driveway led to a sturdy farmhouse with a sweeping verandah, then curved down the hill to a dirt road. Obviously the track had leased the barn but didn't want the house, and had separated them with a chain link fence.

But someone had visited recently. The long browning grass was flattened by tire tracks. The vehicle had parked below the crest of the hill, above the farmhouse but out of sight for anyone in Eve's barn.

He studied the squashed grass. Not wide enough for a tractor or farm vehicle. And there were several larger areas where the vehicle had parked, and then turned. Something glinted in the sun. He bent and pulled a bottle cap from the tangle of grass.

"Someone was cocky enough to enjoy a beer while they were watching you," he said, studying the cap. "A Corona.

Probably not teenagers. They're more inclined to toss the bottles. Let's see if we can find anything else."

He tucked her arm beneath his and they walked along the grass, checking the ridge. Insects droned and butterflies fluttered, but there was no other sign of people. Whoever had parked here had been very careful, which was puzzling in itself.

If Victoria had begged or bribed an acquaintance to cause trouble, he would have expected a more rushed job, something they did when they weren't working at the track. Yet the person, or people here, had been very patient. And judging from the grass, they'd been here many times.

"I hope they wasted three weeks of their life sitting here," Eve said. She wrinkled her nose like she did when she was disgusted, but it was clear she was a little spooked.

"No one's been in the barn since I arrived," he said, cupping her arm a little tighter. "So it's more of a nuisance than anything else."

But even as he rushed to reassure her, something didn't sit right. It felt like he was missing a link. Maybe he wouldn't fix the hole in the fence. That way he could sneak up the hill and catch the creep.

He didn't want her worrying. She had enough problems dealing with the horses and her wimpy boss. Scott had already warned it was critical that Eve's horses run well this weekend.

"Is Tizzy ready to race?" he asked, steering her away from the bruised grass. "It looked like he galloped well today."

She gave a grateful nod, as if aware he was changing the subject but happy to do so. She'd sent Tizzy for gate training, and everyone had been all smiles afterwards. It was interesting that she thought the horse would try harder with a female jockey, but it made sense. If he were a horse, he'd prefer a woman rider too.

"Miguel's our secret weapon," Eve said. "He's going to rub Tizzy tonight. We've tried different masseuses and chiropractors, but it's Miguel who always gets results. His massage might add an inch to Tizzy's stride. And if that happens…" She shrugged but her face glowed with anticipation.

"I'm surprised your boss doesn't hold Miguel in higher esteem."

"Jackson won't admit it," she said. "He prefers to think it's his training that makes a difference. But I ride in the morning, and it's always apparent when Miguel has been rubbing a horse. He's too arthritic to give many massages and he's busy with all his other duties. But Dex and Dani—Tizzy's owners, they think Miguel makes a difference too." Her eyes sparkled. "It's going to be a great race. Especially if you win the tournament tonight and Tizzy gets to wear a normal bridle."

"Then let's hope Tizzy and I both win." He gave her hand a reassuring squeeze, amused his worries now revolved around massages and tossing a beer cap. And he was happy about that. Life at the track was utterly absorbing, leaving no time to brood about past mistakes. His head was too crammed with horses.

Or maybe it was filled with the woman by his side. Now that he'd told her about his work, he felt lighter, as if he finally had the chance to start fresh. He hadn't been truly open with anybody since leaving the Police Academy.

He glanced down the hill at the empty picnic tables. A red bucket sat in the middle of the sand pit, but thankfully the women and children were gone. It was safe to return.

"Getting hungry?" he asked, swinging Eve around and nuzzling her neck. "Let's go back and order supper. Woody recommended pizza, but warned me not to eat or drink anything after five."

She laughed, fitting into his chest as if she'd been built for him. "Woody's sure serious about winning. There'll be a lot of teams though. You'll have to keep your eye out for someone who drinks Corona and knows Victoria."

"I'll be keeping my eye out for a lot of things," he said, "but I do plan on winning you that gift certificate."

"Good. And I'll cheer you on. But shouldn't we check the farmhouse first? Just in case my tack's there?"

He could already see the house was deserted. The grass around the building was undisturbed, the doors and windows boarded and dust covered the steps. But if she wanted to explore around the house, then he was all for it. In fact, he was all for anything that made her happy.

"Sure." He obligingly veered to the left. "Seems like the house is still solid. Even the roof looks good. That verandah could hold a lot of people."

"It's a beautiful property but my favorite part is the field." She blew out a wistful sigh. "Joey would love it here. We don't have a yard where we live."

His chest tightened. What the hell? A boyfriend? But he kept his voice level, his eyes studiously fixed on the house. "Who's Joey?"

He felt her look at him, felt her pretty smile, but he just stared at the house, feeling like somewhere an axe was flying through the air, heading toward his back.

"Joey's my son."

"Oh," he said, staring at the house like a roofer counting nails. But his mouth turned bone dry and the front of his head began to throb, and he couldn't manage another word.

"That's how I know Scott and Megan," she went on. "Joey's father was Megan's brother. We all met at jockey school. I assumed you knew. That it was in my file."

"Nope," he said, still staring blankly at the shingles.

"That's nice Scott took out my personal info," she said happily. "At first I was resentful he sent you. Afraid they wanted to apply for joint custody. Especially since I've been struggling lately. That's the real reason I didn't want you around."

She went on to talk about heroin and bad cops and how Joey was named after his dad and that it wasn't surprising he'd wanted a pony since both she and his father loved horses. But the pain in his forehead drowned out her voice, and his jaw clamped so tightly his teeth hurt. And the middle of his chest felt gutted, as if someone had carved a hole then yanked out his beating heart with both hands.

Because this was worse than a boyfriend. This was…impossible.

CHAPTER TWENTY-SIX

"Joey's fine," Eve's mother said. "I don't think you should talk to him though because he'll just start missing you again. But he's excited about spending the weekend with Megan and Scott."

"Great." Eve gripped her phone a little tighter and edged away from the picnic table. "How's everything else? How's your knee?"

Her mother complained for another ten minutes about her aching leg, the doctor's outrageous prices, and how the tenants in the adjacent apartment made too much noise. By the time Eve cut the connection, her stomach was churning. Her mother did her best. But Joey needed a younger, more positive caregiver.

If only she had some of Tizzy's purse money right now. Lately though, Tizzy had been unreliable. And everyone knew banking on winning only brought bad luck. It wasn't fair to raise doubts with her staff but she needed to talk to someone. Needed to reassure herself that Tizzy really would run better with all the changes she'd made.

Jackson was the head trainer. He'd understand her nerves, the constant second guessing. She checked the time then pressed his number. Victoria answered his phone in the morning but hopefully Eve could reach Jackson when he was doing night rounds. It'd been three days since she had talked to him, and either Victoria didn't pass on her messages or else he'd chosen not to respond.

Jackson answered on the fourth ring. "Yup," he said.

Eve sighed with relief. "I'm so glad to have reached you."

"Yeah, well, hurry and talk. Got a vet waiting."

"Sure," she said quickly. "Just want to let you know Tizzy's entered in the seventh on Saturday, an allowance race. Julie West is riding."

"Sounds good," he said grudgingly. "Surprised she agreed to ride him. His record this year sucks."

"She worked him from the gate today and loved him. He likes her too. I really think he goes better for a female rider. Dex and Dani think that's possible too."

"Don't talk to the owners," Jackson said. "That's Victoria's job now."

"But they're my friends. And Tizzy's their only racehorse. They want to stay involved, have fun—"

"Don't talk to the owners," he snapped. "Can't you follow orders?"

"Of course I can." She swallowed back her hurt. This conversation wasn't going the way she hoped. Jackson was the experienced horseman and she had so many questions. Should she wrap Tizzy's hind legs? Run him in blinkers? Switch his shoes to ones with a rounder toe? Mainly she wanted reassurance, to talk to someone who understood a trainer's constant angst.

"I won't call them," she said, clearing her throat. "But they'll want to watch Tizzy's race. Are you sure Victoria will let them know he's entered?"

"Of course she will. And not making owner calls will save you time. You're struggling enough." His voice turned accusatory. "Just get those horses running. Don't worry so much about little cuts and bruises. They're not pets."

"I just want to make sure they're healthy. We had a few problems but everything's good now. Ashley and Miguel are working hard." She hesitated. "Victoria picked a race for Stinger. I don't agree with the distance though. It's over a mile and he's never run that far. I've been trying to get more air into him but…"

"Good." Jackson grunted. "Run him long. Just get him in a race on Sunday. Make me some money." His voice lowered. "It's getting tight here. I had a couple owners move—"

A woman's authoritative voice sounded in the background, and he muttered an unintelligible oath. Seconds later, his words turned crisp, and it was clear Victoria was within earshot.

"Remember not to let Ashley in the paddock," Jackson went on. "It doesn't look good to have a pregnant groom handling a horse."

"But you said Miguel's too old to be around the public."

"Then maybe it's time they both look for another job. We're not running a charity."

He cut the connection without asking anything more about Tizzy or Stinger or even about Banjo's sore back.

She shoved the phone back in her pocket, stiff with despair. First Rick was acting weird. Then she wasn't allowed to talk to her son. And now Jackson was sounding more and more like Victoria.

She pasted on a smile, determined to hide her misery, and walked back to the picnic table. Miguel and Ashley were happily munching pizza, unaware of Victoria's toxic influence. There was no need to wreck their night.

"This is delicious," Ashley said. She picked up another piece of pizza, stretching a line of cheese from the box to her hand. "Nice of Rick to pay. And it will give plenty of energy for Tizzy's massage, don't you think, Miguel?"

Miguel nodded and wiped his mouth with the back of his hand, saved from answering by the food in his mouth.

Eve picked up a slice. But it tasted like cardboard, and she had to force it down with sips of water.

"Look at all these toppings." Ashley waved her pizza in the air. "That's why Liam and the guards always order from Gus's. It gets here quick too because they know the driver and don't hassle him at the gate."

Eve nodded, pretending to care about the guards' preference in takeout and how the cheese was extra generous. Her gaze drifted back to the barn. Rick had paid for the pizza, then offered to feed the horses, delighting both Ashley and Miguel with his offer.

But now he'd holed up in the barn. Clearly he'd lost his appetite too.

"Rick better eat something," Ashley said, following Eve's gaze. "It's important to have food so it soaks up the beer. They have him and Woody at five to one."

"People are betting on this?" Eve asked, yanking her gaze away from the barn door.

Ashley gave a happy nod. "Last year, Woody and Camila's boyfriend were bet down to even money. Rick is the dark horse. But even though he's new, people are backing him because he looks like such a badass."

Eve nibbled at a piece of pepperoni. Rick did look tough, but his appearance was usually softened by his affable smile. That smile had disappeared though, ever since they'd returned from checking the hill. Or maybe it was before that.

She picked up her pizza with both hands and gamely tried another bite, determined not to let Rick spoil her supper. She had to tiptoe around Jackson. But he was her boss. Rick wasn't. And she didn't have the time or inclination to deal with moody people. Temperamental horses were tolerable. Moody men, not so much.

So it really didn't matter what had wiped the smile off Rick's face. Or when. She wasn't going to let it bother her.

But the pizza stuck in the back of her throat and no amount of swallowing could force it down. Drinking water didn't help either. Because no matter how many times she replayed the afternoon, there was no denying that his silence had started when she spoke about Joey.

"Juanita and the gang are coming over to do our hair," Ashley announced, grabbing a paper napkin and swiping at her chin. "They need customer quotes for their posters, along with a volunteer for a buzz cut. How about you, Miguel?"

Miguel's eyes flashed with alarm, and Eve smiled despite her despondency.

"He doesn't have time for a haircut," she said, earning a grateful look from Miguel. "He's massaging Tizzy tonight. Why don't you get one of your guard friends to volunteer? They already like their hair short."

"I asked Liam," Ashley said. "He planned to volunteer but when I told him Camila needed the practice, he changed his mind. Which is crazy because these women have always cut hair. They just never charged money before."

"But most of their experience is with horses," Eve said wryly.

She fingered a strand of hair. She couldn't remember the last time she'd had it cut. It would be convenient to have a trim without leaving the track. She didn't want a buzz cut, but she didn't mind the ladies practicing. It was good they were pursuing the business with such enthusiasm, and it was important to help as much as possible. Even Ashley had stopped complaining about her pregnancy and was thinking more of others.

"Before and after pictures might work better," Eve said thoughtfully. "Then they wouldn't have to rely on customer quotes."

Ashley's head bobbed. "You're right. Pictures would be best. Then they can advertise to all languages on the same poster." She pushed away the pizza box, her voice lifting with excitement. "We can wear makeup for our after photos and really look hot. Maybe they could even do makeup as a sideline. And some men might pay for a shave."

Miguel touched his chin and eased from the table, obviously keen to escape before the hair brigade arrived. And that was convenient as they tried not to talk much about events with liquor while in his presence. However, the local women were excited about the caps tournament, constantly chatting about their favorite team and the generosity of the beer sponsors. Eve didn't want Miguel tempted. It was a good thing he shunned most social occasions.

"I want to check the horses," she said to Ashley. "Call me when the women arrive."

She rose and caught up to Miguel as he limped into the barn.

"The owners will be grateful," she said, "when they learn you stayed late to give Tizzy a massage." She was sure they'd tip him, but she didn't know their plans and now Jackson had forbidden her to call. Which was crazy since Dani had been her friend long before they sent their horse for training. But she wanted to remind Miguel he was appreciated, even if Jackson seemed to have already cut the loyal groom loose.

"They value your touch," she went on, "and I know Tizzy will run better. Even though it's a mystery."

"*Si.* The horse is healthy. But," Miguel tapped his head, "he needs to be happy here too."

She gave a dubious nod. Vets couldn't explain it, but whatever the reason, there was no doubt Tizzy galloped better after Miguel's magical hands. Tomorrow would be the horse's first massage in a while, and she hoped it would bring results. Tizzy's ability wasn't in doubt, but lately his race efforts had lacked much enthusiasm.

"I'll be back tonight about ten," she said. "Can you stay at the barn until then? Maybe have your nap until seven, then do the massage?"

"*Si.*" Miguel's head pumped, clearly relieved he now had another reason to avoid a buzz cut. "Will you bet two dollars for me?" he added, almost shyly. "At the tournament?"

"Sure," she said, glad he could stay involved even if it was from a distance. "Which team do you like?"

"The big man's." Miguel gestured at Rick who was at the far end of the aisle, tossing hay bales into an empty stall.

Probably a good choice, she thought, watching as bales flew through the air like toothpicks. But it was strange he was restacking hay. She and Miguel had piled it near the end, and they were only staying at Riverview for three more weeks. The stay would be much shorter if Tizzy and Stinger didn't run well. Jackson had made that clear.

She turned her concentration to the horses, determined not to fuel any negative thoughts. The horses were going to give a good effort and they'd be able to stay, and everyone would keep their jobs.

She visited each horse, checking leg wraps and feed bins, making sure every one was healthy and content. Banjo's back was healing well and Stinger needed a farrier, but everything was in order and eventually it was impossible to avoid Rick any longer.

She walked down the spotless aisle, impressed at the amount of work he'd completed. Every bucket had been scrubbed, there wasn't a cobweb in sight and he'd double bedded each stall. The hay was the focus of his attention now.

She paused at the front of the stall. He didn't stop working. His muscles rippled as he tossed a bale to the top of the pile, then angled it with an engineer's precision. He was completely engrossed in his work. In fact, he didn't look up.

She swallowed back her hurt. "Why are you moving the hay?"

"Better ventilation," he said.

She eyed the window. It was the exact same size as every other stall window.

"I see," she said, her voice dubious. "Thanks for ordering the pizza. Don't you want any?"

"Nope." He stepped down and adjusted his work gloves. "No time to eat. Woody wants to review game strategy. I didn't realize caps was such a thinking game." His smile didn't reach his eyes. In fact, he looked at her with something akin to resentment.

Her hurt and confusion bubbled together, and she couldn't hide her feelings any longer.

"Is something wrong?" she asked. "Because for the last couple hours, you've been really quiet."

"Nothing to say."

She swallowed, but the tightness in her throat wouldn't go away. And she hated that she was reacting like this. Hated her horrible suspicions. She blew out an achy breath. "Are you really so put out that I have a son?"

"Of course not." He yanked off his gloves and tossed them onto a bale of hay. "Your life beyond this track isn't my concern."

Something moved, pushing the lump further down her throat until it jammed in her chest. Because only two hours ago he'd been talking about working closer to Santa Anita. He'd kissed her like he couldn't get enough. They'd held hands and smiled and teased like teenagers. She'd thought they were in this together.

But he worked undercover. He was trained to pretend. Besides, it was no big loss. Cops were never her favorite anyway. At least he was working hard, lightening the barn work and delighting Ashley and Miguel. There wasn't anything he hadn't been prepared to do.

Even her.

She took a stumbling step backward, relieved he'd turned to the hay and couldn't see her reaction. Because she was blinking much too fast and dust stuck to the back of her eyes, and her entire body felt chilled.

"Hey, are you ready?" Ashley called from the doorway. "The women are here."

Eve turned back to Rick. "Good luck in the tournament tonight," she said, surprised her words sounded composed, or that they came out at all, considering how her throat felt so dry and tight and bruised.

Then she squared her shoulders and walked away.

CHAPTER TWENTY-SEVEN

"Wow, look at me. I'm gorgeous!" Ashley stared into the mirror, her darkened eyelashes fluttering. "The lipstick matches my new shirt. Did you take plenty of pictures? Both sides?"

Juanita gave a tolerant nod, freed the mirror from Ashley's grip and replaced it in the pink bucket.

Eve gave Ashley a thumbs up. It was remarkable what the women had accomplished with just some water, scissors and makeup. They hadn't been able to round up any male volunteers. But the women were content to concentrate on Eve and Ashley since they didn't want to risk being late for the caps tournament.

"This business is going to be a huge moneymaker," Ashley said, her gaze swiveling to Eve. "I love what they did to you too. How they feathered your hair and showed off those gorgeous cheekbones. You look like a movie star."

Eve's smile was forced. She didn't feel like a movie star. More like someone who'd been kicked to the curb. And her love life was the least of her worries. Jackson had made it clear that if Tizzy and Stinger flopped this weekend, there'd be no second chance.

Maybe she could return to race riding. But her fingers balled in panic, and she knew that wasn't really an option. She was too obsessed with rider falls now, too worried about Joey and his future.

Of course, if something happened to her, Scott and Megan would adopt him. Maybe they'd feel compelled to step in sooner. No doubt, Rick had updated them on her lack of money, her precarious employment.

She clasped and unclasped her hands, absorbing the irony. Here, she was being thanked for making life better for the backstretch mothers. Yet she couldn't even look after her own son. Or her staff.

"Stop worrying about Tizzy," Ashley said, rising from the table. "Miguel's massage will fix him. And we should walk over to the rec room now. We don't want to miss anything."

Eve gave a little nod. Tizzy would win on Saturday and keep Jackson happy. Her training career was going to work out, and she and Joey would never have to be apart again. And the ache in her chest would go away, and she wasn't going to hurt anymore about Rick.

"Wait," Juanita said. "I need more pictures of Eve." She grabbed her phone and bent down, her voice lowering. "You are beautiful but I think you are sad too. You miss your son, *sí?*"

Eve looked into Juanita's compassionate eyes. Everything seemed to be crashing down, but she'd tried to hide her fears. Certainly Ashley hadn't noticed. Juanita, however, was much more perceptive.

"This is the longest I've been away from him," Eve admitted. "It'll be two weeks before I see him again. And my mother isn't the most energetic babysitter. But the only one I can afford."

"You can't go home and see him after the races on Sunday?" Juanita asked.

Eve shook her head. "He's spending time with relatives this weekend. But he'll have fun. It'll be good for him."

"Not good for you though." Juanita's eyes flashed with concern. "And you are worrying about so many horses and people. You don't even have an exercise rider. It is too much for one person." She turned quiet for a moment, then her face brightened.

"I work nights next week," she said. "So you can bring Joey here. I'll look after him in the morning while you're training."

Eve blinked, stunned by such a generous offer. Everyone at the track worked long hours, whether in a support service or directly with the horses. Most people grabbed naps whenever they could, and vacations were non-existent. For Juanita to give up her precious downtime was astonishing.

"It will be good," Juanita went on. "Because of you, we have this meeting place. So he will have lots of children to play with."

Eve leaned over the table, her heart pounding with hope. It might work. Certainly her mother would be relieved to have a well-deserved break. And Joey would have fun being outside, playing with the other children and seeing the horses. To have him here for a whole week, twenty-four seven, seemed too good to be true.

"Really?" she asked.

Juanita's eyes twinkled. "Really," she said.

Eve gripped the edge of the table. "I don't have any cash now," she said. "But I can pay you from my bonus, if either Tizzy or Stinger finish in the money. As soon as Jackson sends it, if not this month then—"

"But I would not take money from a friend." Juanita scowled, her voice rising so sharply that the other women stared. She turned, raising her arms for attention.

"Eve's son, Joey, will be visiting next week," she announced. "We will help with his care, *sí?*"

All around the table, heads nodded with enthusiasm. "Of course," they called.

Two women who worked with Juanita in the kitchen immediately pulled out papers to compare their work schedules. And it was clear that even if Eve had to spend extra time on the track, Joey wouldn't lack babysitters.

She placed a hand over her chest, her heart thudding. To have Joey close by, to be able to hug him every night would be an unexpected gift. She could see him in the mornings too. She'd be able to ride a horse from the track, look over at the sandpit and watch him play. In the fresh air, with other children.

The entire four years at Santa Anita, she'd only had six days off. She'd left for the track every morning before sunrise, long before he woke. Then she'd sat in traffic, trying to make it home before his afternoon nap. Most days, she had to return to the track for evening races. Weekends had been even busier.

She'd always hoped that working as a trainer, instead of a jockey, would give her more time with Joey. And now it was happening. But only because of this secluded barn and these generous women. Her gratitude welled, and she gave them a tremulous smile, overcome with emotion.

Juanita saw her watery eyes and raised her arms again. "Tomorrow we'll finish the posters with our new pictures," she said. "And start advertising our business. But tonight we will go to the rec center and cheer on our favorite teams."

She switched to Spanish. "And we will toast our old countries and families who can't be here. But be grateful for our new friends in the United States."

"What's she saying?" Ashley whispered.

"Just that they're missing people and places tonight," Eve said, her throat still thick. "But like us, they're grateful for new friends."

"Awesome," Ashley said.

CHAPTER TWENTY-EIGHT

Eve followed Juanita into a room throbbing with music and the smell of beer and peanuts. The ping pong and pool tables had been pushed back, and rows of competitors were seated in front of the karaoke stage. Most teams wore matching T-shirts with their sponsors' names written on the front, although some appeared unsponsored. A few women wore skimpy tops, the shirts almost hidden by their official back numbers.

"How many teams are there?" Eve asked.

"Almost fifty," Juanita said. "Half these teams have been playing together for years. The ones that made it to last year's semi-final have a bye. So they're in the food room. That's a real advantage because they're eating, instead of drinking. They can also watch the new teams and figure out their moves."

"Caps teams have moves?"

"Of course," Juanita said. "See the Pink Vipers, the women in the tank tops. Teams find them distracting, especially when they lean forward for a shot. They also have a trick of tapping the inside of their thigh, just when the men are about to shoot. The judges are supposed to stop that, but of course they can't see everything. Especially after a few drinks."

"Of course." Eve laughed with delight. This was a bustling spot. She could see the judges sitting on the sidelines. It looked like there was one judge for every two teams. Each judge had a beer in his hand and wore a complacent grin.

A man wearing a faded ball cap updated the scores and odds on a whiteboard which also showed which teams had already been eliminated. A woman beside him appeared in charge of the bets. Eve couldn't see Rick anywhere, but since Woody's Tack had won it last year, maybe they hadn't played yet.

The room erupted in cheers and the Pink Vipers scrambled to their feet and slapped a triumphant high five. The two men they'd beaten shook their heads and looked sheepish.

Both of the Vipers were toned and fit, and she recognized one of the girls from riding in the morning. It was doubtful they'd be able to keep up with the big men, but they'd certainly won this round.

"The Vipers are more successful against men," Juanita said, "but now they're playing another women's team. The draw was probably rigged to get them out early. Men hate to lose, especially to women."

Eve checked Juanita's expression, but she didn't seem to be joking. Clearly everyone took this tournament seriously, and like other sports there was always a question of bias.

Ashley sashayed over, flicking her hair and clearly feeling good about her appearance. She pressed a cold beer into Eve's hands. "It's free," she said. "The beer companies sponsor everything. Wish I could drink too. This is the best night ever."

Eve glanced around the crowded room. Everyone was having fun but she rather hoped Tizzy's jockey wasn't competing. She didn't want Julie West drinking a lot of beer and having to sweat it out before Tizzy's race. But judging by the size of the teams, most participants were grooms or hotwalkers. Except for the Pink Vipers, who were small enough to be exercise riders.

"Liam says the guards always drop by to watch," Ashley went on. "They're not allowed to enter a team though. The backstretch workers don't like them much."

Eve wasn't surprised. Their first night at Riverview, Liam had held them up at the gate, examining their papers in excruciating detail and forcing their hot horses to remain on the trailer. She remembered him cruising past their barn, scowling and being singularly unhelpful. But now, thanks to his friendship with Ashley, he was much nicer. Clearly he was the type of over-zealous guard who'd worked at this property a long time and didn't welcome newcomers.

"Ashley," Eve said, tilting her head in sudden thought. "Did Liam know Victoria? Would he remember her friends?"

"Maybe," Ashley said. "I already told him about our troubles. He's not surprised. Said Victoria was power hungry."

"I should have thought to ask him about her connections," Eve said. "Maybe he could even track them down and ask some questions."

"But you never wanted anything to do with the guards," Ashley said. "And now Rick's here. He's already met most of the workers."

"But this way he could leave." Eve crossed her arms. "We wouldn't need him anymore."

"But he can't go." Ashley's eyes filled with dismay. "He did all the stalls for me today and even fixed a plank in Stinger's stall. And he's going to win us a bridle. Besides," she said, shaking her head, "I thought you two were an item."

"No," Eve said. "So it would really be helpful if I could ask Liam some questions. Can you help me with that? Introduce me again?"

"Sure." Ashley glanced over her shoulder. "He said he was coming about eight. I'll let you know when he arrives."

Eve nodded and edged away from the blaring speaker. It was hard to see the game floor, with all the spectators milling.

But at least she could grab this opportunity to talk to Liam. Figure out if Victoria really could be responsible.

She just needed to figure out her questions so they wouldn't spike Liam's interest and start rumors that might hurt Jackson's business.

Cheers rang out and two more teams rose, one dejected, the other jubilant. Then the next contestants paraded in. And her mind blanked as the oxygen seemed to drain from the room.

In the line of smiling men, Rick towered over everyone. But it wasn't just his height or the imposing width of his shoulders but more the way he walked, the jauntiness of his stride. It gave the impression that anyone around him was going to have a very good time.

Or maybe it had nothing to do with how he moved. Maybe it was his sheer physicality, the way the Woody's Tack shirt outlined each ridge. Clearly the shirt had been made for a smaller man, no doubt Camila's boyfriend. But it was almost indecent the way it showcased the six-pack on Rick's chest.

Of course, Woody had supplied the shirt so that wasn't really Rick's fault. Still, it was very distracting for the women, and there definitely should be rules against that.

She huffed in annoyance and yanked her gaze away, determined to focus on more important people. Ashley was watching the door, talking to three spellbound men while she waited for Liam. Juanita was trying to convince the oddsmaker to hang one of their makeover posters on a corner of his board. And Camila was speaking to a wiry man drinking by the bar. His head was shaved, he had a scar on his cheek, and for a moment his eyes locked with Eve's. But he quickly looked away, his gaze settling back on Camila who stood in front of him, her hands waving as she spoke.

And then Eve couldn't help it. Her gaze shot back to Rick.

He was staring. She didn't know how he found her, standing at the back of a crowded corner, but his level gaze cut through the cheers and chatter, and for a moment it felt as if they were the only two in the room. Then he politely inclined his head and took his position on the floor beside Woody. She couldn't see the opposing team but it was clearly an important match, judging by the press of people.

A sharp elbow jammed her in the ribs, and she glanced around, surprised to see Ashley. Liam stood beside her. Obviously he'd said something, but she had no idea what it was.

"That would be great, Liam," Ashley said, shooting Eve a confused look. "And if you can remember the names of any of Victoria's friends, that would help too."

"I only saw Victoria when she drove in and out of the gate," Liam said. "She mainly hung out with the trainers."

Eve gave a quick nod, hoping to encourage him. Ashley said Liam had been in charge of security for the last five years, and that he knew everything that happened on the backstretch.

"What about when you did your patrols?" she asked.

Liam shook his head. "Victoria didn't talk to the guards. It was like she was above us. But there was one man I remember because he wasn't her usual type. There was talk he always had something for sale. We never caught him with anything illegal though."

His voice was lost in the music, and she stepped closer, straining to hear through the hubbub of the room.

"... jeans were always wet at the bottom," Liam said. "He was probably a groom or hotwalker. She seemed to like him. So the rumors probably weren't true."

"What rumors?" Eve edged even closer.

"That he tended to get rough with the women." Liam sighed and rubbed the back of his thick neck. "But no one ever complained. A lot of workers are here illegally. We protect everyone as much as we can, of course, but we can't help if they don't report it."

"But do you remember the man's name?" Eve asked. "Or where he worked?"

"First name was Marcus," Liam said. "I don't remember his last name, but he works at one of the barns on the west end. We probably have it recorded somewhere. He had a little scar here." Liam touched the side of his left jaw. "Where a horse reared and caught him in the face. I remember the ambulance took fifteen minutes to get there that day. But one of my guys got there in two, way before the paramedics."

"Was it that guy over there?" she asked, snagging Liam's arm, trying to keep him on track. "Standing by the bar. Is that Victoria's friend?"

Liam stared across the room. "Yes," he said, his mouth flattening with distaste. "I do believe that's the man."

CHAPTER TWENTY-NINE

Rick leaned forward, took quick aim then shot. His cap arced through the air, hitting the top of his opponent's bottle and sending the beer cap spinning across the floor. The man groaned and reached for another full beer.

"Great shot, partner." Woody grinned and slapped Rick on the back. "Keep it up. Let's not give them a chance to get back in the game."

Rick wistfully eyed his beer. It was hot and crowded in the room, and it had been awhile since he'd had a drink. But as long as he was knocking off caps, the rules specified he was allowed to keep shooting. He only needed three more points to end this game.

No reason not to. He'd already talked to most of the players here, and it was clear the backstretch workers had nothing in common with Victoria. Apparently she'd been very aloof, only hanging out with other trainers, and not spending any time around the rec hall or kitchen.

But in this position he could see Eve. For the next match, he and Woody would be seated on the opposite side. Teams always rotated since the glare of the lights could impact the outcome, and organizers didn't want anyone to have an unfair advantage. But he wouldn't be able to see Eve when he was seated on the other side.

Not that she seemed to care. Supposedly she'd come to cheer him on, but she'd hardly looked at him. Didn't seem to notice he'd barely missed a shot. And he was playing this game to win her some tack. She could at least show some gratitude.

He fingered the bottle cap, twisting it beneath his thumb, knowing he was being unfair. Her new reserve simply matched his. Totally understandable. He'd tried to act like everything was normal when they returned from the hill, but he'd seen the confusion on her face. And the hurt.

But it would hurt him even more to talk about it. The simple fact was she had a child. And he didn't do kids. Not anymore.

"Plan to shoot anytime soon?" the man seated across from Rick asked. "Or are you trying to delay the game?" He waved his arm, signaling the ref.

"Hurry up and shoot," Woody whispered. "We don't want them counting the seconds between throws. Once they start that, they'll be watching us like hawks."

Rick sighed. There were a lot of rules to this tournament. And he just wanted it over. The room reeked of sweat and yeast and beer farts, and he'd give anything to roll back time and be back on the hill with Eve. With the fresh smell of her skin, the taste of her sweet lips…with a woman who had a kid.

He tightened his mouth and snapped off a shot. Once again his opponent's cap ricocheted off the bottle.

The man groaned and threw up his hands. Then he and his teammate proceeded to guzzle another beer.

Rick's gaze turned back to Eve. She was still talking to Liam Turner, head of security, a man the backstretch community preferred to avoid. Understandable, as most of the workers distrusted people in uniforms. It was rather surprising she was even giving Liam the time of day, as her opinion of law enforcement was extremely low.

The man wasn't wearing his uniform though, and he looked younger and more relaxed than when he was controlling the security booth. He gave Eve a smug smile, leaning even closer when she placed her hand on his arm.

What the hell? Rick jerked his head away, wishing now he was seated on the opposite side of the room.

"Your shot again," Woody said, nudging him in the ribs. "Nice of you to give them time to drink. But don't let up. Make this throw and we're onto the finals."

Rick blasted a shot so hard it knocked over the beer bottle.

"Hey," the opposing team protested. "What's the ruling on that? It hit the bottle, not the cap."

The ref's forehead wrinkled and the man took a fortifying sip of beer. "Not sure," he said, wiping his mouth.

"It's a good shot." Woody's face flushed with indignation. "The cap came off."

The ref pulled out his phone. "I'm going to make a call," he said. "You guys can relax a bit."

Rick's finger remained locked around his next bottle cap, but he concentrated on chatting with the men, determined not to look at Eve. Or scowl at Liam.

However, it wasn't surprising the guard was plastered to her side. She always looked achingly pretty, but usually she was sitting on her horse, out of reach of other men. Tonight though, she looked different.

He stole another look. Maybe it was her hair, not stuffed under her helmet but fluffier. Dark tendrils feathered her face, outlining her cheekbones, making her look sleek and dramatic. Even from this distance, he could see the curve of her mouth, that full lower lip, the color a little pinker than usual.

He leaned forward, wishing he were closer so he could read her expression. Make sure that persistent guard wasn't bothering her. He couldn't blame Liam for making a move— any man would—but there was a limit. Soon she'd stiffen and edge away.

Wait, was she smiling?

"Drop by next week," the player opposite Rick said in Spanish.

"Yeah," his teammate added. "We play cards on Monday, pool on Tuesday."

Rick pulled back his attention and made an agreeable sound while Woody beamed like a proud parent. The tournament had definitely boosted his acceptance, and he did enjoy the occasional game of poker. But he wasn't any closer to finding Victoria's henchman, and it was frustrating to be stuck on the game floor while Eve was forced to deal with an over friendly guard.

His gaze shot back to her. He couldn't figure this out. Her body language said she was quite content talking to Liam. Maybe she'd forgotten her aversion to uniforms. Forgotten Liam was the man who'd ordered a barricade of the track the night she'd been trying to train Tizzy. An ineffectual search too because Liam was an idiot. It had been child's play to draw off the guards.

He snorted and looked away.

"Won't be long now," Woody said, misinterpreting Rick's disgust. "The ref is calling Liverpool. They deal with all international rulings."

"Good," Rick said. He hadn't intended to look back at Eve. But she was smiling and chatting, and it was obvious she was having a very good time. He grabbed his bottle of beer and took a hefty swig.

Woody's face blanched in alarm. "What are you doing, partner? Wait until you have to drink."

"I'm thirsty now," Rick said.

The crowd silenced, every man enthralled as the Pink Viper leaned forward, flashing a spectacular display of cleavage. She shot but missed, and her cap bounced off Rick's thigh. He snagged it, gave the woman a teasing smile, then made his return shot.

A square hit.

The Viper shrugged and reached for her bottle.

"Your groom doesn't miss many," Liam murmured, his mouth close to Eve's ear. "Even with all the feminine distraction."

"He's clearly had lots of practice," Eve said.

"Where did he come from? I checked his background but didn't find much. Ashley wasn't sure either. She said some investigator type?"

"My boss sent him," she said, cutting off Liam's questioning. The man had been a big help, but he'd been hanging over her all night and now she just wanted him to leave.

She edged back a step. Obviously the locals were wary of him. Even Juanita had stayed away, remaining on the opposite side of the room. It was amusing how a little makeup and a good haircut could change a man's attitude. Liam had dropped his dogmatic attitude and was actually being helpful, even offering to dig up more of Marcus's background. Of course, men were always drawn by feminine flash.

Except for Rick who seemed to prefer her fresh-faced with helmet hair and a horse in hand. And generally that was a positive. But a sour taste rose in her throat. Because although he wouldn't admit it, it was also clear he preferred she were childless.

A spontaneous round of clapping pulled back her attention. "What happened," she asked. "Is the tournament finally over?"

Liam shook his head. "No. The Vipers were supposed to drink another beer, but your groom waived it. He's drinking for them."

"How very kind," she said, reluctantly glancing across the room.

Woody looked annoyed but the rest of the men were enthused, clearly enjoying the continuing flash of breasts. Someone patted Rick on the back, and a couple others gave him fist bumps.

"It's taken me years to get to know those people," Liam said, his voice thickening. "Yet he waltzes in and they accept him like a brother."

"Because he doesn't think of them as *those* people," she said.

Liam gave her a narrowed look but she ignored him. Beneath Rick's tough appearance, he was one of the kindest men she knew. He had the ability to relate to everyone. And he listened when people spoke, really listened.

But she didn't want to discuss that with Liam. She was tired of the cheering crowd, tired of this tournament that seemed to drag on, and she was especially tired of watching the pretty Pink Viper flirt with Rick.

"I have to go and check the horses," she said, easing toward the door. Miguel would be finished Tizzy's massage by now, and it was quite clear Rick and Woody were going to win. They'd controlled every game from the initial toss. Woody obviously had an excellent eye for choosing caps partners.

"Want a drive home?" Liam asked.

"No, thanks," she said, glancing around the room. Ashley was still by the bar, flirting with an outrider in a cowboy hat, but Juanita and Camila were nowhere in sight. Camila was probably missing her boyfriend, especially since he'd won the tournament last year. Drugs could really screw up lives, even innocent ones.

"Did you notice if Juanita and Camila left?" she asked.

"Juanita is hanging a poster in the men's washroom." Liam gave a disapproving shake of his head. "But Camila and that guy left ten minutes ago."

"What guy? You mean Marcus? The one who's friends with Victoria?"

"That's right," Liam said.

CHAPTER THIRTY

Eve strode along the horse path, relieved to escape the tournament and finally breathe in some fresh air. This route was quicker than the road, and once her eyes adjusted to the dark, it wasn't necessary to use her phone light.

She was eager to hear Miguel's report on Tizzy. Maybe he'd found some muscle kinks, a soreness the vets had missed. She had complete faith in the old groom. Even though he'd never had any formal training it was noticeable that whenever he worked on a horse, the animal always seemed to do better.

She could never pinpoint the change, but she'd ridden the horses he'd rubbed, and they stepped out a little further. Had a little strut to their walk. And she needed Tizzy healthy. Needed him to run like he had last year. Time was running out.

Her steps quickened just thinking of Victoria and her far-reaching tentacles. The woman would obviously do anything to discredit perceived rivals, and the fact that Marcus had been her closest friend here was troubling. The man looked a little sketchy. His eyes had been flickering between Camila and the Vipers the entire night, as if trying to decide who to take home. He'd even been studying Ashley like she was low-hanging fruit. And according to the security guard, he was more than just a creep.

Something rustled in the underbrush. Something small. At least, she told herself it was small. But thoughts of Marcus left her jumpy, and goose bumps chilled the back of her neck.

She pulled out her phone, squeezing it in her palm, all the while chiding herself for the paranoia. No matter how creepy Marcus was, Victoria wouldn't send someone to rough her up. That would be too extreme. Victoria's style was sneaky sabotage, not physical brutality.

Still, she kept her finger over the phone, ready to call security. Rick had programmed both his cell number and the guardhouse into her speed dial, and a guard's Jeep could squeeze onto the horse path. Of course, Liam and his crew would take several minutes to arrive.

She checked over her shoulder, relieved she'd turned off the phone light. Her boots were silent on the dirt and if she hugged the edge of the dark path, she'd be difficult to spot. And even though the urge to bolt to the safety of her barn was overwhelming, she forced herself to move slowly. Quietly. She even paused several times to check the night sounds.

Whatever had been rustling in the bushes was now silent. Probably a rat. There were plenty of those around the track. But the darkness abruptly shifted, revealing a man-sized silhouette. Her knees buckled.

The shadow was huge. And she could hear his breathing, as if he'd been running. And now that he'd caught her, he was content to stand on the path. Waiting.

She swallowed, tasting the dryness of her throat. She could wheel and bolt to the main road. She was a fast runner and in shape. But it wouldn't solve anything. Besides, she was tired of this harassment. Tired of Victoria causing problems for her horses, her staff, and ultimately her son.

She was tired of being afraid.

Anger blasted through her body, strengthening her legs and blowing away her fear. She launched forward, yelling and balancing for a forceful kick where it would hurt a man the most.

"Hey," Rick's voice said.

She skidded to a stop, landing awkwardly in front of him, her right leg extended.

"Oh." She sagged with relief. "It's you. I was going to—"

"Hurt me badly." He sounded amused. "And then I hope you were ready to run like hell."

"Yes," she said, her voice shaky. "If my legs worked. I was a little scared."

"Sorry," he said. "Thought you could see me." And then his arms wrapped around her, and for a moment she let herself slump against his chest. He was strong, familiar and comforting, and he smelled of leather and beer and male assurance.

And perfume.

She pulled away. "Is the tournament over?"

"Yup." He dropped his arms. "We wrapped that last game up quickly. I didn't want you walking home alone."

He'd left the adulation of his fans, his partner, even the Pink Vipers, to make sure she reached the barn safely. Her voice softened. "It must have been hard to leave."

"Ashley offered to fill in for the trophy presentation."

Eve smiled. "She'll love that. She misses the winner's circle." But then she sobered. This was his moment and he deserved to enjoy the night, the entire night.

"You should go back," she said. "This is a big event. They'll want you there."

"But I wanted to leave," he said. "I don't like crowds much. They teach us how to get along, but it's only pretend."

He spoke slowly, enunciating his words too carefully, and it was clear he was a little buzzed. Or maybe a lot. But the fact he was sharing information about himself was very revealing as to his sobriety.

"And you don't like kids either, do you?" she asked.

She heard his quick intake of breath. Knew she'd hit a nerve. But it was important to know, and now was the ideal time to ask some questions.

"Sorry," he muttered. "I wouldn't have slept with you if I had known...wouldn't have let myself feel like this."

His words were definitely slurring. Of course, he had downed a lot of beer. But drunk men told the truth. And even though it was a relief he didn't deny their attraction, she was filled with an aching sadness. Because he spoke with such finality.

She swallowed back her despair, forcing herself to speak crisply. "Joey is the most important thing to me. The reason for everything I do."

"As he should be," Rick said.

They walked in silence. His steps were generally even, although he did stumble once. She automatically reached out to steady him, then pulled back her hand. It was tragic that she enjoyed his company so much. That their relationship was doomed. Because she was still intensely attracted. She'd have to find ways to avoid him. And just hope he left the track soon.

"I'll sleep in the barn the rest of the meet," he said. "I want you to use the RV."

She shook her head. "I have a bed in the dorm."

"No. Ashley told me your son is coming Sunday. The RV will make it easier. And a lot more fun for him."

She opened, then closed her mouth. Rick was always so thoughtful. It would be much easier if she could dislike him. She didn't try to speak again. Could only walk in the achy silence.

The barn loomed in front of them. Whinnies sounded a greeting and she lengthened her steps, eager to be with something that wanted her, even if it was only horses.

"Wait." Rick caught her wrist. "Don't you usually have night lights?"

She stilled. There was always a light by the door. Yet the building was totally dark. Not quiet though. Straw rustled and an impatient animal slammed the wall, the sound shattering the night. The horses should be more content. Miguel would have filled their hay nets.

"Stay behind me." Rick shifted forward so swiftly he was almost ten feet away before she could hurry after him.

He paused in the doorway, his head bent.

"What is it?" she asked, bumping into him.

She peered around, straining to see. Recognized Miguel's wiry shape sprawled in the aisle the same time as she absorbed the harsh reek of booze.

"Oh, no." She pushed past Rick and sank to the floor.

Miguel's eyes were closed but he clutched an empty bottle of tequila and wore a beatific smile.

Rick switched on the aisle lights then kneeled down and checked Miguel's vitals.

"Just drunk," he said, easing the groom onto his side. "I'll get a blanket from the RV. He'll be all right once he sleeps it off."

But when Rick looked at her, his expression reflected her concern. Miguel was an alcoholic and while it was good to be optimistic, this was definitely a setback.

"He was doing so well," she said, prying the bottle from Miguel's hands. "It's been eight months since his last drink. And he avoids any place with liquor. Someone must have brought him this."

"I'm quite sure someone did." Rick pointed at the surveillance camera, now ripped from the ceiling. "Someone who didn't want Tizzy to have the massage."

"But that's despicable." She jerked to her feet, the bottle clenched in her fist. "Victoria can't play with Miguel's life, just to hurt me. I'm calling Jackson right now. I don't care if I'm fired."

"Hang on," Rick said. "Did Victoria even know about the massage? And maybe Miguel rubbed the horse before he started drinking."

Eve looked at Tizzy and the blue cooler still folded in front of his stall. "No," she said. "Miguel would have blanketed him afterwards. Would have wanted to keep his muscles warm."

She glanced down the aisle at the row of empty hay nets. "And he would have fed the horses. Banjo is a slow eater and even his hay is gone. That tequila must have been dropped off right after Ashley and I left with Juanita."

Rick nodded, his eyes on her face. He didn't look at all drunk now, just extremely focused. "And did Victoria or Jackson know about the massage?" he asked.

Eve rubbed her forehead. Jackson always hired professional therapists and then charged the owners on their monthly bills. She and Ashley only knew about Miguel's magic because they rode the horses and had felt the difference.

"Who else knew?" Rick asked, his voice steely.

She lowered her arm, unable to speak.

"Who knew?" His tone softened. And it was the gentleness in his voice that helped her say the unimaginable.

"Only Ashley," she said.

CHAPTER THIRTY-ONE

Eve rolled onto her back, punched a pillow beneath her head, and stared through the dark skylight. Despite the comfort of the RV, it was impossible to sleep. Had Ashley been responsible for all the stable's misfortunes? And if so, why? It didn't make sense.

She reached for her phone and checked the time.

Just after midnight. Ashley might still be up, celebrating with the others at the rec hall. It was tempting to walk over now and confront her. But Ashley and Victoria conspiring together? The thought made her stomach lurch.

She dropped the phone back on the bedside table, feeling like her entire world had tilted. She didn't trust many people. But she'd trusted Ashley. And how did Marcus fit into this? Ashley hadn't seemed to know the man. She'd chatted with Eve and Liam and then an outrider, before moving closer to the wagering board and enthusiastically cheering on the players. Marcus had been talking with Camila, on the other side of the room.

Gravel crunched. She jackknifed up, straining to listen. Not a car but someone was definitely walking along the road. And moving clumsily.

She crawled over the bed to the window and peered through the blind. There was so much noise now, it could be two people. And they were definitely heading toward the RV.

Coming for her.

She rolled off the bed and rushed down the hall, cold with fear. The door wasn't even locked. She'd thought Rick might decide to sleep in the spare bedroom, instead of the barn, or that he might want to make an early morning coffee after his night of drinking. Or that...he might just want to come in.

Her fingers fumbled to turn the lock. It would be close. Already boots bumped on the step. She could hear breathing, a feminine giggle.

Ashley?

She stiffened, then yanked open the door, ready to confront her.

A woman in a tiny pink top swayed on the step. "Where's Rick?" she asked, with a breathy giggle.

Eve closed her eyes, overcome with relief. Not Ashley or any of Victoria's goons. Just a Pink Viper—a good rider in the morning, a harmless drunk at night. And then another emotion filled her. One not so pleasant.

"Rick's not here," she said.

"Oh." The woman leaned sideways, peering past Eve as if expecting him to materialize. "Where does he sleep?"

"Not here," Eve said.

"In the barn?" The woman swayed, flattening one hand on the wall for support. Blue ink covered her wrist, the sloppy numbers indecipherable. "Okay. I'll go there." She paused, then tilted her head, staring at Eve with eyes that matched the color of her hot pink top. "You don't mind, do you?"

Eve squeezed the door knob. Rick's blatant masculinity would appeal to many women and no doubt he'd enjoyed more than his fair share of booty calls. But she did mind. She minded very much. On the other hand, their fledgling relationship was over. And she had no right to interfere in his personal affairs.

"Just don't disturb the horses," she said. Then she pulled the door shut.

She slipped back into bed, numb and cold and alone. At least it hadn't been Ashley, sabotaging something in the barn. That was a positive. But she tugged the pillow over her head, making sure to cover both ears. She didn't want to hear the woman's satisfied groans. Because she knew just how wonderfully Rick could satisfy a woman.

She had the pillow in good position, strategically clamped over her head, but only five minutes later the door clicked again. The woman was back.

Eve sat up, groaning. "Are you lost?" she muttered. "Check the third stall from the end."

There was silence, then a heavy sigh.

"It's me," Rick said. "Is it okay if I sleep here tonight?"

She froze, her mind disconnected to her body. Rick and that woman. No way. That would hurt too much. She opened her mouth to speak, but no sound came out, only a horrified squeak.

"And I can't believe you'd tell her where I was," he added.

He stomped down the hall, past her bedroom and into the adjoining room. Definitely disgruntled. Definitely alone.

She sank back on the bed, limp with relief. From the room next door, boots thudded. Clothes rustled and a buckle clinked. Then she could hear nothing but his breathing. It sounded ragged, upset.

She waited a moment, not sure. "Sorry," she whispered. "I wasn't sure what you'd want—"

"If someone came looking for you like that," he said thickly, "I'd want to hurt them. Not give directions."

She stared through the skylight. The night wasn't quite so dark. She could even see a few stars, faint but twinkling. "I felt like that when I saw her," she admitted, matching his honesty.

"I suppose you weren't thinking clearly. A bit groggy." Rick sounded much less truculent now.

"Yes, that's right." She smiled against her pillow, even though he couldn't see her. "And obviously I wasn't too keen to mess with a Pink Viper."

And now his laugh rumbled through the thin wall. She smiled and inched to the side of the bed. Closer to his voice. "What did you do with her?" she asked.

"Tucked her in beside Miguel. They'll both have a headache in the morning. She'd been celebrating."

"Guess it's not every day a girl comes second in a big caps tournament," Eve said, full of good will now. Rick's voice sounded as if it were only inches away. He must be lying close to the wall too. In the dark she could pretend he was right beside her.

She closed her eyes, soothed by his presence, deciding she might fall asleep after all. "Good night, Rick," she whispered.

"Good night, sweetheart," he said.

CHAPTER THIRTY-TWO

Eve stretched, then shoved aside the sheets. She never used an alarm, the habit of waking early was too ingrained. But it was obvious that today she'd overslept.

The sky was already a colorless gray, the sun inching toward the horizon. And she had five horses to ride and two grooms who would be of limited help. And then there was Rick. He'd been drinking heavily. Who knew how he would feel this morning?

She dressed quickly, listening for his breathing, but the RV felt deserted. And when she smelled the hickory coffee, it was obvious he'd risen long ago. He'd even left a box of granola bars on the counter.

She poured a cup of coffee, stuck a bar in her back pocket, and hurried from the RV.

A woman in a scanty pink shirt wandered from the barn, rubbing at her puffy eyes and further smearing her mascara. "What a night," she muttered. "What time is it?"

"Almost six," Eve said.

"Damn." The woman rubbed at her spiky hair. "I have five to exercise this morning. And my head feels like shit."

"Here. Take this." Eve thrust out her coffee.

The Pink Viper grabbed it with a grateful groan. "Thanks, girl," she said. "See you on the track."

She headed toward the horse path, the mug pressed to her mouth.

Eve hurried into the barn, understanding the Viper's dismay. Losing time in the morning meant every ride was rushed. And quite likely she'd have to do the feeding and grooming today, as well as the riding. Worse, horses like Stinger were always in a nasty mood when their breakfast was late. It wasn't a good way to start the day.

However, the horses barely looked at her. They tugged at their hay nets, their expressions content. She walked down the spotless aisle, checking each horse. Their stalls were clean and freshly bedded. Better still, they were groomed, with stable bandages removed and neatly rolled. Her sense of urgency faded, replaced with gratitude. She wasn't off schedule at all. But Rick must have been up for hours, despite last night's revelry.

The aisle was empty. However, the rumble of men's voices drifted from the end of the barn. She walked down the aisle toward the third stall from the end.

Rick and Miguel sat on the cot. Miguel's hands were shaking almost as much as his voice.

"Sorry, sorry," he kept muttering to Rick. His thin shoulders were hunched in misery, his trembling hands clasped.

"We all have our setbacks," Rick said, his voice so gentle it tugged at her heart. "Later we'll go see the chaplain. See what programs they have. The important thing is to not give up. Take one day at a time."

He stared over Miguel's head, seeming to sense her presence. "We have to keep trying." His gaze held hers. "And not give up."

She saw the plea in his face. His eyes were slightly bloodshot, his hair shaggy, and his heavily stubbled jaw resembled that of an outlaw on the run. But one tattooed forearm supported Miguel while he tilted a bottle of water to the man's mouth. And there was no doubt he was a kind man, a good man. Someone who cared.

Besides, people could change if they wanted. And Rick could learn to like children. To like Joey.

Her throat was impossibly tight but she gave a little nod and backed away. Miguel was in the best possible hands. And she still had a lot of horses to ride in a very short time.

She hurried back to the whiteboard and reviewed her training notes. A jog and paddock visit for Tizzy who was racing the next day, a three furlong blowout for Stinger who was entered on Sunday, and a mile and half gallop for Bristol and the rest. They could probably start walking Banjo under tack since his back was healing so well, but staff were spread too thin to start that today.

Ashley burst into the barn, wearing a wide smile and lugging a huge trophy. "Woody wants to display this in his store," she said. "But I convinced him that Rick should have it for a week. Where do you want to keep it? Maybe in the tack room?"

Eve just stared. She'd always thought she was a good judge of character, both horses and people, but she'd been terribly wrong about Ashley. Never dreamed she'd be the backstabbing snitch who was relaying their information to Victoria.

She didn't intend to confront Ashley yet. The horses deserved to have a level-headed rider in the saddle. But she couldn't hold back.

"I know it's you," she said, through clenched lips. "You're the only other person who knew everything. When we were gone, details about our horses, and what would hurt the most. What did Victoria promise you? First-call jockey maybe?"

"What are you talking about?" The smile slid from Ashley's face, and she gave a blink of dismay. However, Eve wasn't fooled, not any longer.

"It was despicable to give him the liquor." Eve's voice shook now. "Miguel didn't deserve that."

Ashley just gaped, the shiny trophy almost slipping to the floor. And now Eve shared her confusion. Ashley was always easy to read and rather childlike with her emotions. But now the girl looked—not guilty or defensive—but genuinely bewildered.

"Someone gave Miguel a bottle of tequila last night." Eve stepped closer, studying Ashley's expression. "He's in rough shape. Rick's with him now."

The color leached from Ashley's face. She set the trophy on the floor. "But he hasn't had a drink in eight months. And he was fine when we left for the tournament." She wrung her hands, her voice rising. "Are you sure about this? Where is he?"

Eve rubbed her forehead. Maybe it wasn't Ashley. Her concern for Miguel was too genuine. And she'd been in the rec hall the same time as Eve. They'd walked over together after their haircuts. Probably she should have thought this through before tossing out accusations. Should have talked it over with Rick first.

"We can't let Jackson find out," Ashley went on, still clenching her hands. "Horses are Miguel's life. He needs this job." She turned back to Eve, her eyes hopeful. "Did he massage Tizzy first? Before he started drinking?"

"Rick thinks that was the reason for the liquor," Eve said, still studying Ashley's reaction. "To stop him from giving Tizzy the massage."

"Guess Tizzy won't win now," Ashley said glumly. "Victoria is a bitch but she sure is smart. Surprising she'd even think to go after Miguel."

Something tightened in Eve's chest, an uneasy feeling triggered by Ashley's comment. Victoria was smart, but like Jackson, she never gave Miguel any credit. She'd scoffed at riders who reported that the old groom's horses seemed happier, preferring to use licensed masseuses who would justify owners' expensive bills. Two hundred dollars a week for a massage would let Victoria pocket a higher percentage for each horse.

And Miguel wasn't even paid to massage. He did it because he used to be Tizzy's groom and still loved the horse. But Victoria would have no reason to stop him, especially since she considered the man insignificant.

"I don't think Victoria would care about Miguel's massage," Eve said, almost to herself. "Even if you did tell her."

"Well, of course, I never told her anything." Ashley's head jerked back and forth, her cheeks flagged with pink. "I can't believe you'd think that."

"But someone is feeding her information. When did you last talk to her?"

"That's a crazy question. After all you've done for me—teaching me to ride, helping me get my first job. You're my best friend. You'd think I'd want to hurt you?"

"But when did you last talk to her?"

"I'm not dignifying that with an answer." Ashley's mouth flattened in a mutinous line.

"She has to ask." Rick's voice came from behind Eve. "And you have to answer," he said.

Eve turned. Rick stood behind her. His powerful arms were crossed, his blue-gray eyes cold and menacing. He said nothing else, just stared.

Ashley wilted.

"I haven't spoken to Victoria since she called about Tizzy's jockey," Ashley said. "And I'm truly sorry about Miguel. I would never give him alcohol." She forced a meek smile. "Heck, I couldn't even afford it."

"Do you know a guy called Marcus?" Eve asked. "Shaved head, scar on his jaw?"

Ashley gave a reluctant nod. "But I never said anything to him about Miguel or our horses. He told me about an alcohol-free beer that pregnant people could drink. And he promised to find me some cheap vitamins. That's all. You have to believe me."

Eve glanced at Rick. "Did Miguel recognize the person who gave him the alcohol?"

"No," Rick said, his expression still grim. "He never saw anyone. The bottle was left in front of Tizzy's stall."

Hair rose on the back of Eve's neck. "So someone not only knows everything about our staff, they also know our horses?"

"Afraid so," Rick said.

CHAPTER THIRTY-THREE

Rick tightened his hold on Tizzy's lead shank, even though the horse was totally relaxed, resting a hind leg as he stood in the saddling enclosure. A maintenance worker emptied a metal garbage can, but Tizzy barely flicked an ear at the ensuing clang.

He forced his hand to loosen. The area was empty, except for the lone worker. And Tizzy wasn't the type to spook. But the horse carried precious cargo.

He glanced up at Eve, intensely aware of her every movement. She seemed warm, fiddling with the snap on her protective vest. Beneath the vest she wore a thin blue T-shirt and probably the pink sports bra, the one she'd washed that had been drying in the bathroom. He wasn't sure of the color of her panties, only that they covered her firm ass. And that he worried about it every time she climbed on a horse.

She was pushing herself too hard, and her wrist still wasn't fully healed. She'd never admit it, never complain, but she always rode Stinger home one-handed, the injured wrist resting on her thigh...the same sculpted thighs that had wrapped around his hips two nights ago in a way that made him want to crawl back into her bed, and never leave.

He felt himself growing hard and forced his attention off the rider and back to Tizzy. But the horse wasn't near as exciting. And it was impossible not to think and hope and wonder about the next time he and Eve might have sex. Or even if they ever would.

"Guess it'll be more hectic here tomorrow," he said, staring fixedly at Tizzy's chest, and not at her leg, with the black boot that covered her tiny toes, along with the dainty arch he knew for a fact was one of her significant erogenous zones.

She leaned forward and gave Tizzy an affectionate pat, her hand almost brushing Rick's shoulder. He shifted back, away from the smell of her skin and the urge to pull her off the horse and do her against the wall of the outrider's stall. But the maintenance worker was only a hundred feet away. Besides, Tizzy would probably trot back to the barn and that would draw all sorts of attention.

"Tizzy won't be much different in front of a crowd," she said. "Not much bothers him. He's a real gentleman. It's just too bad he didn't get that massage."

Massage. Rick forced a nod. Eve gave a great massage too, and he was stiffening just thinking about her hands between his legs, but he was quite sure they were talking about the horse now. Of course they were. He slapped down his thoughts, deciding his intense longing, the total awareness, was because this relationship was so damn fragile.

He flexed his fingers, fiddling with the lead line. Right now, he could almost forget about Eve's son. Pretend it was a minor inconvenience, and he could man up. He didn't want to lose her. Wanted to stick close, day and night.

But when her kid arrived...

A chill swept him, and he stopped wondering if Tizzy would ground tie and if there was a possibility of grabbing some high-noon sex. Because this was going to be tough. And the way she looked at him made him feel like a fraud. She didn't understand he was broken. And that maybe he'd already given everything he could.

"Let's walk him around the paddock one more time," she said, loosening the buckle on her helmet.

"Keep that tight," he said. "You never know when a horse will jump. Even one as quiet as Tizzy."

"Hey, I'm the trainer." She smiled, all teasing and light. "You're supposed to listen to me."

"And I'm supposed to keep you safe." His voice was unexpectedly rough.

"Right." Her smile turned sad. "I keep forgetting. I'm your job."

He swallowed, knew that was exactly what he'd been trying to remind them both. But he didn't want it that way. And he hated to see the sadness in her face, and know that he'd put it there. "You're much more than that," he muttered.

She looked at him for a long moment, as if sensing his turmoil. "And Joey?" she asked, with her typical openness.

"I plan to work on that." He took a ragged breath, knowing she had no idea how the prospect filled him with terror. And because she was looking at him with those beautiful eyes, and he really wanted to please her, he added, "I'm looking forward to meeting him."

He basked in her relieved smile before stepping forward and leading Tizzy around the paddock. And he told himself it would be okay. He could handle one little boy.

But dread pitted his stomach and his sweaty hands stuck to the leather lead shank. And while he was quite certain she didn't pick up on his fear, Tizzy certainly did. The horse jammed his head in the air and skittered around the enclosure, acting far different from the confident Thoroughbred Rick had led into the paddock.

In fact, Tizzy shivered with such nervous energy that sweat darkened his neck, matching the perspiration soaking Rick's forehead. And no matter how Rick tried to control his reaction, it was impossible to stop his hands from shaking.

Eve closed the RV door, sank down at the kitchen table and stared glumly at her phone. Jackson didn't want her dealing with owners, but Dex and Dani were friends. And they'd always promised they'd take Tizzy back to the ranch if their horse wasn't happy at the track.

She'd lose her job if she didn't follow orders. No trainer wanted their staff calling owners and possibly creating problems. That would only give Victoria more ammunition to fire Eve. But every owner deserved honest feedback. And so did Tizzy.

She picked up her phone and resolutely pressed Dani's number.

"Double D Ranch." Dex answered with a hint of impatience. Judging from the clink of tools, it sounded like he was in the process of shoeing a horse.

She pulled in a fortifying breath, wishing it had been Dani who'd taken the call. Dex didn't say much and certainly wasn't one for coddling.

"It's Eve," she said. "You know I have Tizzy at Riverview and he's entered for tomorrow?"

"Know he's at Riverview," Dex said. "Didn't know he was running tomorrow."

She winced. Despite Jackson's assurances, Victoria hadn't even bothered to call the owners and tell them Tizzy was racing. Dex and Dani always enjoyed the thrill of watching their horse run. And Eve liked seeing them. They were good people.

"I should have called," she said. "He's in the seventh, an allowance race, mile and a quarter."

"We can't make it anyway. Dani's brother is coming home. Tomorrow is the family dinner. How are Tizzy's feet?"

"Good," Eve said. "The farrier you recommended came last week. And Tizzy's in great shape, moving well, looks sharp."

"But?"

"But lately he's been acting different," she admitted. "And during paddock training today, he was unsettled. As if he didn't want to be there. You always said if he wasn't happy you'd take him home. Turn him out in the pasture. It might be time…"

Her voice trailed off in misery. She didn't want to lose Tizzy. Hadn't even been sure what she was going to say. But he'd run well in five races and been a flop the last three. And his agitation today was uncharacteristic. Like he was an unhappy horse. He was too talented to run that badly, so like Miguel said, it must be in his mind. Obviously he no longer wanted to be a racehorse.

"The last six months," Dex said, "he lost you as his jockey and Miguel as his groom."

She nodded, even though Dex couldn't see her. Jackson had insisted Victoria be assigned to groom the barn's top horses. At the time, they included Tizzy. But after three poor races, Victoria had dumped the horse, choosing to send him to Riverview. 'He doesn't even try,' she'd complained. 'He's good for nothing but dog food. I'm not wasting my time on a crap animal like that.'

"So you're saying…" Eve paused, not sure what Dex meant, only that anything he said was always valuable. His message seemed to be that Tizzy had run well with Miguel as his groom and her as his jockey.

Miguel was here at Riverview, but he only bandaged Tizzy's legs. Since Ashley was limited to handling the easy horses, she'd taken over as Tizzy's groom. The horse was easy to handle and therefore the first to be shortchanged.

"I thought it was Miguel's massage that made him feel better." She pressed the phone tighter against her ear. "But you're saying it's really Miguel's attention?"

"A horse gives back what he gets," Dex said cryptically. "Just like people."

She rose and peered out the window, studying the grass around the barn. Miguel was in no shape to give Tizzy a massage but he could hang out with the horse all afternoon. Let him munch some grass, make Tizzy feel special.

And while Rick was great with Stinger and the rambunctious three-year-olds, his handling of the horses was more clinical. She'd noticed his agitation when they discussed Joey, and that tension had definitely transferred to Tizzy—a horse who'd spent the first four years of his life on a quiet ranch, eating grass and being cared for by the same well-grounded people. No wonder Tizzy's performance had been erratic.

"Thank you, Dex." She squeezed her eyes with relief. "Guess I should have done a few things differently."

"Nothing that can't be changed," he said laconically. "Appreciate your call."

He hung up before she could ask him not to tell Jackson about their conversation, then realized that was a non-issue. Dex was a man who knew how to keep secrets.

She grabbed a bottle of water from the fridge and hurried from the RV into the barn.

Miguel was raking the aisle. He looked up, his eyes shadowed with embarrassment, and defeat.

She gently took the rake from his hands and replaced it with the bottle of cold water. "You don't need to do anything else today," she said, "except drink water and look after Tizzy. And if you're up for it, I'd like your help with saddling tomorrow."

"You want me?" Miguel's eyes widened. "In the paddock for the race?"

She nodded. Victoria had banned the groom from the public eye, saying he was too frail to control an excited horse before a race. And that it didn't look professional. But that was where Tizzy needed the person he trusted most. And there was no doubt that man was Miguel.

"I'm getting my horse back?" Miguel's eyes turned watery. "Even after last night?"

She nodded, moved by his unusual show of emotion. She hadn't realized how hurt Miguel had been to lose Tizzy, how many people Victoria had flattened with her scorched earth policy.

"Don't worry about last night," she said. "It was just a little slip. We all make them. Rick set up an appointment with the chaplain. Things will work out. Just make Tizzy feel special again, okay?"

"*Si*, boss." Miguel's head pumped "Me and that horse, we like each other."

He turned and limped toward Tizzy's stall. The horse poked his head over the door, his eyes hopeful. Miguel picked up a lead line, then stopped to scratch Tizzy beneath his jaw, over his cheek and even his ears, touching him like he had all the time in the world.

Eve heard his soft crooning, saw how Tizzy pressed his head against the man's chest, utterly trusting in the groom's gentle hands.

Rick stepped out from Stinger's stall. "Looks like a good move," he said, his voice quiet. "Some things are stronger when they're together."

She glanced up. He wasn't looking at Miguel and Tizzy. He was staring at her. In the paddock this morning, he'd claimed he was looking forward to meeting Joey. But his voice had been strained. There'd even been a sheen of perspiration on his forehead. Tizzy definitely had picked up on the tension.

"Yes," she said. "But sometimes it's a leap of faith. We never know what will make us stronger. Or weaker." She squeezed the rake, praying Rick would reassure her that everything would be okay. That he really did like kids.

But his expression remained inscrutable. "That's right," he said. "It's impossible to know."

CHAPTER THIRTY-FOUR

Eve spread the new tack on the kitchen table, stroking the bridle with a reverent finger. "Thanks for winning this, Rick," she said.

While the mismatched equipment was suitable for morning exercise, and she'd be forever grateful to the ladies, it was a relief that Tizzy could appear in public tomorrow with a traditional bridle.

She reached into the second bag and eagerly pulled out the rest of their purchases. Rick's tournament winnings had been enough to buy three bridles as well as a shirt for Miguel. Of course, it was from the sales rack but the T-shirt matched the owner's bright silks. Miguel was excited about handling Tizzy in public, and he'd feel even better if he had the perfect-colored shirt.

Best of all, she'd been able to buy a special toy for Joey—a stuffed pony that neighed when its stomach was pressed. Rick had noticed her wistfulness when she'd spotted it by the counter. He'd scooped it up, ignoring her objections, and added it to their purchases.

He was utterly generous and in no hurry to return to the track, even picking up sandwiches and stopping the bike by a sun-splashed brook for an afternoon picnic. He had a knack for whisking her off to scenic spots. Surprisingly, she'd stopped analyzing the upcoming races, or whether Miguel could really help Tizzy, or what shoddy trick Victoria might attempt next. Life was more fun with Rick around. It was definitely better rounded.

She glanced across the kitchen, still smiling her appreciation. But all she saw was Rick's back.

He stood in front of the sink, gripping the sides of the counter and staring out the window. It was after five, and the women and children were gone. The only movement was Miguel and Tizzy as they wandered companionably around the barn, the horse selecting the sweetest grass while the groom scratched the crest of his shiny shoulder.

It was an idyllic scene. But Rick's legs were braced. Even the muscles in his arms were taut, his posture totally different from earlier today when he'd coaxed her into a leisurely bike ride. To help them both relax, he'd said. To pick up the bridles and escape the hectic pace of the track.

But it wasn't hectic. Not in the afternoon when the horses napped in their stalls and the only sounds were the women and children laughing by the trees.

And then realization dawned. She pressed the toy pony against her chest, trying to ease the stabbing pain. "Is that why we stayed away so long? So the children would be gone when we returned?"

"I'm just watching Tizzy," Rick said, not turning around. "He's following Miguel like a dog. The horse has really locked onto him."

But he didn't answer her question. Didn't even try to deny it. And if he couldn't bear to be within fifty feet of laughing kids, how could he possibly share the RV with Joey? Or a relationship with her?

She sank down at the table, her legs weak.

"I looked for Marcus this morning," Rick added, still staring out the window. "Couldn't find him anywhere on the backside. But a couple of the boys promised to call when he shows up."

She gripped the pony tighter. The caps tournament had cemented Rick's position with the backstretch workers. When she'd been galloping that morning, everyone had been slapping his hand, congratulating him on the win.

And now he had locals willing to call when Marcus surfaced. Rick was the perfect groom, the perfect bodyguard, the perfect boyfriend...except that he avoided kids like the plague.

She squeezed her eyes shut, then slowly opened them, grappling with the enormity of the problem. "Would it help to talk about it?" she asked.

"I don't think Marcus left that tequila," Rick said. "Last night he was at the tournament until just before midnight. And I couldn't find any connection between him and Victoria. He seemed quite smitten with one of your ladies...what's her name? Camila?"

She swallowed. Rick was deliberately misunderstanding her question. And while there was nothing worse than someone digging into private affairs, clearly he didn't trust her enough to confide. Her fingers closed around the pony so tightly that it neighed.

Rick turned at the sound. "Joey's going to like that toy."

She nodded. But she saw his forced smile, and her hopes crashed in a pile of discarded dreams.

"He's always wanted a pony," she said, her voice shaky. "When he was little I was able to take him to the track. But he's not allowed now. Victoria only lets owners' kids visit."

She ran a finger over the pony's soft mane. "That's why I wanted to help the mothers here. Because I know how hard it is. But some things are impossible to change, aren't they?"

She lifted her head, her voice breaking. "Like how you feel about k-kids."

He just stared and for a moment she thought he'd attempt to shrug it off. Then his face changed. He cursed and reached out, pulling her to him with arms so tight they hurt. "Sorry," he muttered. "I want to try. I really do. I just keep seeing Ben."

Her face was pressed against his shirt, and the thudding of his heart was louder than his voice. "Was Ben your son?"

She felt his head shake but he didn't say anything else. Outside a crow cawed, and she heard Miguel singing a Spanish love song to Tizzy. But Rick remained silent.

Slowly though, his arms turned less taut, and she was able to look up and wrap her arms around his neck.

"Maybe it would help," she whispered, "if you talk about it."

"I'm not allowed to." He pressed his face against her hair, and she could feel the raggedness of his breath. "Only to police-approved psychologists. The case is confidential. But please know I would never hurt Joey. Or any of the children here—"

She jerked back, aghast. "I would never think that. You are the most gentle, caring person ever. Anyone can see that. Why would you think you have to say that?" Her voice turned fierce. "Those idiots!"

His mouth lifted in a glimmer of a smile. "Easy, tiger," he said. Then his head dipped, his lips seeking hers, gentle at first then turning more desperate. As if he were looking for something he couldn't quite find.

He finally lifted his head. "You make me feel whole again," he said. "Give me a chance. With you, with Joey. I used to be good with kids."

He picked up the pony and squeezed its stomach, his eyes on her face. "Just give me some time, okay?"

But the pony's happy neigh was swallowed by the roar of a vehicle. It jerked to a stop only feet from the RV. Amber roof lights flashed and dust left a spiraling cloud that blotted the window.

Rick set the toy down, brushed her mouth with a swift kiss, then opened the door. She followed, watching as Liam and Ashley spilled from the Jeep.

Their faces were too grave to be carrying anything but bad news. Even Tizzy stopped grazing, staring at the vehicle with concern.

"It's Camila," Ashley said, her eyes huge in her white face. She ran toward Eve, her voice choking. "She's d-dead."

CHAPTER THIRTY-FIVE

Liam adjusted his gunbelt, his face as distraught as Ashley's. "I should have said something last night, when I saw Camila with that creep. But the workers resent us. They never listen."

Eve's legs felt boneless and she grabbed the door for support. But Rick's arm wrapped around her, his solid presence a comfort. "What happened?" he asked.

Liam shook his head as if bewildered. "This is the first murder we've had at the track. But it's not really the track. She was found in the river, off the property. So I guess it's not our jurisdiction. I mean, how could we be expected to patrol there?"

Rick's arm tightened and Eve sensed his regard for Liam wasn't very high.

"It's a clay flat," Liam went on. "And way too muddy for our vehicles. But I've been gathering information." He fumbled for his notepad, a small coiled book with a picture of a scenic ocean. It didn't look like there was anything on the pages.

"I just have to ask a few questions," he added. "Collecting facts for the police. Piecing together her last week. So," he looked at Eve, his voice turning officious. "When did you last see her?"

"At the tournament," she said.

"And who was she with?"

Eve swallowed, trying to moisten her throat. "Marcus," she said. "But you know that. You saw them too."

"She didn't show up for work at her barn this morning," Liam said. "Weren't you worried when she didn't arrive this afternoon? She's been hanging out here lately. Isn't that correct?"

Eve rubbed her cold arms. She couldn't stop wondering how Camila had died. Had she been drinking too much? Maybe stumbled in the mud and drowned?

"She regularly hangs out here," Liam went on, his tone almost accusing. "With the other women and children. Did she say anything? Did you talk to her about her plans? Her life?"

"She didn't talk much, not really. I—"

"I'll take it from here," Rick said, stepping in front of Eve. "We can talk in your Jeep, Liam."

His voice was so crisp that Liam quit talking. He looked up from his notebook, flushed a beet red, then turned toward his vehicle.

"You and Ashley stay here," Rick said. He gave Eve's arm a squeeze then followed Liam to the Jeep.

Eve looked at Ashley. They hadn't really talked since Eve's impulsive accusations about aiding Victoria, but now that faded into the background. They both hugged, gripping each other for support as they stumbled into the RV.

Eve added water to the coffee machine, her fingers clumsy.

"Someone found her by the river," Ashley said. "Liam said it looked like she'd been beaten. And no one has seen Marcus since last night."

Eve twisted and stared out the window, numb with horror. Rick and Liam were sitting in the Jeep. Liam had put away his notebook and was nodding his head at something Rick said. A moment later, they wheeled away in the Jeep.

"Sit down." Ashley tugged Eve over to the table. "I'll make the coffee. They'll find Marcus soon."

Eve dropped her head into her hands. A murder, not an accident. That was even worse. She didn't want to think about Camila's last moments. What the girl had endured. And she couldn't stop picturing that bleak, brackish river and its creepy inhabitants.

She'd checked the river when she first arrived, wondering if it was safe for a horse to cross. But mud had sucked at her boots, the squelching sound startling a crab. It scrabbled sideways, leaving a trail in the red clay before disappearing down a hole. It wasn't really a river, just a dying creek filled with crabs and catfish and leeches.

She shivered, trying to block the images of hungry bottom feeders. "How long was she there?" she whispered. "Have they removed her body?"

"Don't know." Ashley banged open a cupboard and gathered two mugs. "The police taped it off. Even Liam isn't allowed back. But they'll catch Marcus soon. Everyone's looking."

Eve dropped her head in her hands. Camila had just started to open up. She'd nodded and smiled and seemed excited about the hair business. And last night, she'd been the one to apply Eve's lipstick, carefully selecting a pink shade of lip liner and making a shy joke about Rick and macho men.

She was still reserved but her eyes had been bright, devoid of that haunted look. And Eve couldn't even remember if she'd properly thanked her. What their last words had been.

"She was just starting to look happy," Eve said, her hands slumping to the table.

"I imagine she missed her boyfriend." Ashley set down mugs and filled them with coffee. "Last night I heard her and Marcus talking about him."

"What did they say?"

Ashley took a thoughtful sip. "They were speaking in Spanish, so I only understood a few words. But it sounded like she wanted to find him. And that Marcus didn't think it was a good idea. I gathered he was jealous."

Eve sighed and picked up her coffee, cradling the cup in her hands, needing its warmth more than the caffeine. This was a horrible tragedy but there was nothing she could have done. It wasn't related to her barn, or Victoria.

Her phone pinged, announcing an incoming text. She set down her mug and scanned the screen. Her relief vanished as quickly as it had come.

Rick's warning was brief but chilling: *Stay together until I get back. Don't let anyone walk alone.*

CHAPTER THIRTY-SIX

Eve swept the last piece of straw from the tack room then replaced the broom beside the pitchforks. Leather gleamed, everything in the barn was spotless—even more than normal. But she had to keep busy, had to stop herself from calling Victoria. The police would handle this. Besides, she told herself, there was no way her boss's wife was involved with a murder. No way.

She glanced through the doorway. The sun was lowering, staining the horizon with red. Last night, at this time, Camila had still been alive. Everyone had been smiling and preparing to walk over to the caps tournament. The trophy sat on a chair in the tack room. It all seemed so silly now. And what if they hadn't gone? What if they'd stayed and made more hair posters?

She turned away, her throat impossibly thick.

It was puzzling why Rick wanted them to stay together, but she appreciated the company. Miguel was polishing Tizzy's neck with a soft cloth, not seeming to mind the enforced curfew. Assigning Miguel solely to Tizzy created more work, especially since Rick was off with Liam. But Ashley hadn't once complained. And Eve was relieved to keep busy. The routine barn chores didn't stop her 'what ifs' but they helped.

"Anyone hungry?" she asked. Rick didn't want any of them walking alone, but her staff needed food. Miguel suffered from a hangover, and good nutrition was especially important for Ashley and her unborn baby.

"There's leftover pizza in the fridge," she added. "Or I can make sandwiches or an omelet. Maybe even order something."

This wasn't the time to worry about limited cash. And what wasn't spent on essentials, she'd donate toward Camila's funeral costs.

"Nothing for me, thanks," Ashley said, glancing up from where she was scrubbing buckets. "I'm going to the guardhouse later. They always have extra food."

Eve's chest banded with guilt. Only a week ago, she'd truly believed working with horses was the absolute best job in the world. But running a stable while at odds with the boss's wife was increasingly tricky, creating hardship, not just for her but her staff. It hurt that Ashley relied on the guards to eat. And that Miguel had been plied with liquor. And now Rick warned they shouldn't walk alone.

"What about you, Miguel?" she asked, keeping her voice light. "Want something to eat or drink? Maybe more Tylenol?"

Miguel shook his head, still lovingly rubbing Tizzy's neck. "I need nothing, boss." He looked at her, then his face creased in a smile. "This horse, he will run big tomorrow."

Eve hurried toward the stall, hope flaring. Even Ashley dropped a bucket and rushed to join her. They both studied Tizzy, who'd stretched out his head and rested it on Miguel's shoulder. His eyes were liquid and peaceful, his lower lip sagging. He looked placid enough to pull a milk wagon, not tear around the track competing with nine other toned and powerful Thoroughbreds.

But Miguel was rarely wrong with his predictions. In fact, Eve couldn't remember a time that the groom had promised a horse would run big and it hadn't happened.

Not one of the humans spoke. Tizzy lifted his head, as if questioning the silence. He nuzzled Miguel on the back of his neck, checking on the old man, then gave a sleepy blink.

"He's acting like he did last fall," Eve said slowly. "Before he started losing." Before Victoria insisted on taking over as his groom.

"We made thirty-two dollars betting on the caps tournament," she added. "If we put it all on Tizzy, we might have something worthwhile to donate toward a fund for Camila."

Miguel and Ashley nodded, neither of them hesitating a second about giving up their scarce cash.

"Let's figure out the exotics too," Ashley said. "And really make our bets count. For Camila."

Eve gave Ashley an impulsive hug. Backstretch communities were always supportive, but they were growing especially close to the people here.

"Maybe we can hit the exacta," Eve said. "I'll ask around tomorrow. Find out what other horses might run big. One of the Vipers gallops a horse in Tizzy's race. She said he was ready to fire."

"You're friends with a Viper?" Ashley arched a disbelieving eyebrow. "The one with the boobs that was hanging over Rick?"

Eve shrugged. Stinger had been aggressive this morning and the Viper had jogged her horse alongside, helping to keep him calm. Actually Eve had enjoyed the woman's company. Granted, the Viper had been tired from the tournament and probably didn't want to do much galloping. But her lead pony had been unusually brave, totally unfazed by Stinger's teeth.

Besides, nothing had happened between the Viper and Rick. In fact, the incident had helped demonstrate that he was an honorable man. The fact that he'd walked away from an attractive and willing woman after a night of drinking was no small thing.

Of course, Rick didn't have a problem walking away from things. Jobs, women…children.

And who was the boy he'd called Ben? It would help her understand if she knew more about his background. Unfortunately, his police work was off limits, something he wasn't allowed to discuss. At least with civilians.

But Scott was his employer. Surely he'd know some details. His agency would never hire anyone without an extensive background check. Megan was always joking about how fussy Scott was, and how few investigators ever met her husband's criteria.

"I need to call a few people," Eve said, swinging toward the RV. "I'll make some sandwiches while I'm in there. Just in case either of you get hungry."

She hurried away, already pulling out her phone. Normally she didn't care about anyone's family name, their history, even their prison record. People, like horses, deserved a fresh start.

But this was different. Besides, she needed to talk to Scott. Victoria would have told him Stinger was running on Sunday, but they had other things to discuss. Like finding out when they were getting Joey and where Eve should pick him up on Sunday. So of course she had to call right now. And it certainly wouldn't hurt to slide in a few questions about Rick.

She stepped into the RV and closed the door. Then scrolled down her contact list. Usually she called Megan but for the purposes of this call, Scott would be best.

She pressed his number quickly, before she lost her nerve.

Scott answered on the second ring, and it was apparent by the background music that he was in his Mercedes. And that he was surprised by her call.

"Hi, Eve," he said. The music abruptly lowered. "What's wrong? Is Joey okay?"

"He's fine. I just wanted to check on the weekend."

"Megan's not here," Scott said. "You can reach her at the studio. But we'd like to pick up Joey tomorrow at nine."

"Okay," Eve said. "I'll let Mom know. Her leg is hurting again so afterwards I'm going to take Joey for the week. I'll drive down after the races on Sunday. Unless you plan on coming to see Stinger run?"

"Stinger's running? What race?"

Eve grimaced. Once again, Victoria hadn't bothered to contact the owners, the people who paid the bills. This was no way to run a race stable. She might be trying to discredit Eve, but her actions were also hurting Jackson.

"Stinger's running in the ninth on Sunday," Eve said. "And Julie West is riding. Sorry. There seems to be a little mix-up with communication."

"It's okay," Scott said. "Jackson made a rash decision when he gave so much responsibility to his wife. We'll definitely drive up to watch."

"That's great," she said brightly. "You can just drop off Joey then."

For a moment, there was no sound but the muted strands of music. And Scott's breathing.

"I don't think the track is a good place to leave a four-year-old," Scott finally said. "If your mother isn't feeling well, we'll look after Joey. Megan would love to keep him for a few weeks, more if necessary."

"But I miss him," Eve said. "This is the longest we've been apart."

"This isn't about you. It's about what's best for him."

Eve tugged at her lip, hating Scott's reasoned tone. "But he needs his mother," she said, trying to match Scott's calmness. "He'll want to be with me."

"You can't care for him those long hours when you're working. What would he do?"

"Friends offered to help. And we have a play group here, with a big sandpit. I'm going to find more toys, maybe a soccer ball. He loves kicking that. He won't be too close to the horses." She hated the defensiveness in her voice. And that she had to justify her son's safety.

"Track dorms can be rough. Full of flies and rats." Scott's voice thickened with disapproval.

"But he won't be in the dorms," she said. "He'll be in the RV. It's hooked up right next to the barn."

"What RV?"

She shook her head in confusion. "The one you arranged for Rick. He's letting us use it while Joey's here."

"I didn't arrange for any RV. And Rick's used to roughing it. He's one of my most capable men."

"Oh. I must have misunderstood him." But her legs felt wooden and she plunked down on the massage chair. "Anyway, there's a nice RV here and that's where Joey and I will sleep."

"Sounds okay then," Scott said, as if his approval was necessary.

She clamped her mouth shut, determined not to say anything more. Scott was not a good man to antagonize.

She remained silent as he went on about how she'd have to keep a close watch in case Joey was bored and how the food at the track kitchen might not be appropriate. It was a relief when the topic swung back to horses.

"So you think Stinger likes the track?" Scott asked.

"Yes," she said. "He's training well. Even galloped quietly in company today."

"Good. But I gather from Rick's reports that someone is still keen to cause you problems."

"I guess. But everything's under control. At least Victoria is up at Santa Anita."

"When you go back though," Scott said, "it'll be worse. And a husband-wife team can be difficult, especially if the marriage is already rocky." His voice softened. "You realize that you'll always be our trainer? That Stinger is only with

Jackson because you're there. If they force you to move, the horse goes too."

The back of her throat balled and for a moment she couldn't speak. Scott trusted her to train their horse. He was a smart and savvy man. So his confidence meant a lot.

"We don't care if Stinger ever wins another race," Scott added. "We just want you and Joey to be okay."

Her words of thanks dried. They didn't expect her to succeed as a trainer. It was just a way to give her money. More charity.

"Maybe you should reconsider working with Megan," Scott said. "Her jewelry line is expanding. Then you could stay home, and Joey would have a…better environment."

"Thanks," Eve managed. "But I have to go."

"All right. We'll see you Sunday. And if the track doesn't look suitable, we'll take Joey home with us. Just until you move back to Santa Anita."

"No." And she could no longer keep the crispness from her voice. "He's staying at the track. With me. See you Sunday."

She cut the connection before fear turned her words more heated. Scott and Megan had good intentions, and they genuinely loved Joey. But there was a threat in the man's words, and he possessed money as well as clout. In fact, her chest had knotted with such apprehension, she forgot to ask a single question about Rick.

Her gaze swept over the European coffee maker to the fridge with the deluxe ice maker. Scott hadn't known about the RV. Something this luxurious must cost a big chunk of money. Obviously Rick was padding his expense account. And now Scott would see the RV, check the expenses, and no doubt fire Rick.

Groaning, she dropped her head in her hands. It seemed

everyone she cared about was at risk. Her staff, her horses, her son. And ironically Scott now loomed as an even bigger threat than Victoria.

CHAPTER THIRTY-SEVEN

"See you in the morning," Eve called, waving as Ashley slid into the front of Liam's Jeep and Miguel climbed into the back.

Liam lowered the driver's window, his gaze including both Rick and Eve. "I can have someone drive your staff to the barn tomorrow," he said. "If you're still concerned about them walking alone."

She glanced at Rick. Marcus hadn't been found yet, but police had issued an alert, announcing him the primary suspect in Camila's murder. She wasn't sure why Rick was on edge, but he hadn't left her side since he and Liam returned.

"Not necessary," Rick said.

She gave him a little nudge. It was already past everyone's bedtime. If security drove Miguel tomorrow, the groom would have more energy to handle Tizzy. And Ashley would certainly appreciate a drive, especially by a doting guard who would no doubt bring her morning coffee and possibly a breakfast sandwich.

"Drives aren't necessary," Rick added smoothly, "but certainly appreciated. Thank you."

"No problem." Liam gave a courteous nod. "I'll have a vehicle pick them up at the dorms."

The guard was beginning to grow on Eve, no longer reminding her of the Gestapo. And the smile she gave him was genuine and grateful.

Rick looped a hand around her waist, tugging her back a step as the Jeep's headlights sliced the darkness by their feet. "Hope they find Marcus soon," she said, as the Jeep disappeared around the curving bend.

"Me too."

There was an odd note in his voice. He'd been with Liam for over two hours and it probably hadn't been easy dealing with Camila's death. "Did you see the spot?" she pulled in a breath. "Where she was killed?"

"The scene is restricted," he said. "But I spoke with the lead detective."

"Who found her?"

"Someone fishing beside the river bank. The police are interviewing everyone who knew Marcus. Including Victoria."

Eve crossed her arms, fighting a chill. "But this has nothing to do with her."

"Probably not," Rick said, a little too quickly.

"But Camila was beaten. That doesn't sound like something a woman would do." Her voice faded, the back of her neck turning cold as she imagined the brutal fists, Camila's helplessness, her utter terror. "Did she d-die quickly?"

"We'll have to wait for the autopsy," Rick said. He raised his hands and began rubbing her shoulders. "I looked in at Tizzy. If a horse can grin, that horse is doing it. He likes having Miguel to himself."

She nodded. Rick was obviously trying to change the subject. But it was true, Tizzy definitely had a little strut to his walk. Actually, all the horses seemed happy. Contented sounds drifted behind them: hooves shuffling in the straw, a muzzle slurping water, the munching of sweet alfalfa. The normalcy of the barn was reassuring.

And tomorrow Tizzy would finally race. Miguel believed the horse would run well, and best of all, on Sunday Joey would come. She'd be able to keep him close and he could sleep in the RV, and everything would be great.

But no matter how she tried to distract her mind with good things, she couldn't stop picturing Camila's big brown eyes, her rare but beautiful smile. And the brutal fists that had left her lying in the mud like a piece of trash.

She pulled in a choky breath. "I don't know how to help," she said. "Except to try and raise money for her family in Guatemala. Juanita is tracking down her relatives now."

"Good idea," Rick said. His soothing hands continued stroking her shoulders.

He didn't seem in any hurry to go inside, and neither did she. Part of her still felt frozen. She'd lost loved ones to violence before and numbness helped her cope. But she'd never leaned against a man like this, sharing her grief, not talking much, just appreciating his closeness.

The sky stretched above them, a dark mantle laced with pinpricks of silver. Last night it had been beautiful but tonight it made her feel small and helpless and totally insignificant.

"I'm glad you're here," she said.

"Me too."

An owl hooted and a horse kicked the wall, probably Stinger upset that Banjo had hay left while his was gone. And she knew life would go on. It always did. She reached up and squeezed his hand.

He pressed a kiss against the back of her neck. "Scott was right," he said, his mouth warm against her skin. "I needed to slow down. Get off the street. But Camila's death is definitely a twist. We weren't anticipating anything like this. He'll need an update."

She dropped her hand, clasping them in front of her, her fingers fluttering nervously. Scott already thought the track wasn't a safe place for Joey. And now he'd learn of this tragedy.

"I talked to Scott about an hour ago," she said. "He and Megan are coming Sunday to watch Stinger race. They'll bring Joey too."

"Did you tell him about Camila?"

"No," she said. "I wanted to reassure him that it would be good for Joey here. That the place and people are fine."

She twisted. But Rick's face was shadowed, and it was too dark to see his expression.

"And I made a big mistake that you need to know," she said. "When he asked where Joey would sleep, I mentioned the RV. So he knows all about it. And he's a stickler about following rules. So we have to get rid of it before Sunday."

She clasped her hands tighter. "If not, probably the best thing is to scratch Stinger. Then I can drive down Sunday night and pick up Joey, and Scott will have no reason to drive here."

Rick remained silent, his face still shadowed. It was hard to tell if he was speechless at her blunder or simply concerned about his job. But when he spoke he sounded only incredulous, not angry. "You'd scratch your horse?" he asked. "After all the hard work? When your job's on the line?"

"But Scott will check your expense account." She wrung her hands in dismay. "And your job's on the line too."

"Sweetheart." He wrapped his warm palms over her hands, stilling their twitching. "I appreciate your concern. But I bought that RV. Belinda arranged it because she's the office assistant and a whiz with details. Other than that, it has nothing to do with the company."

She blinked, utterly stunned. Almost everyone who worked at the track was broke. She'd assumed he shared the same financial challenges.

"I've been living in some skuzzy places," he went on. "This was a chance to clean up and be normal. And I wanted that RV here. For us."

"But it's so much money."

"I can afford it."

"Then you should be sleeping in it." She shook her head, aghast at how she'd expropriated his property. "I thought Scott was paying, so that made it okay for me to use. And I've been hogging everything. The kitchen, the shower, the magnetic bed."

"Actually," he said, "I was rather hoping you'd consider sharing that again." He skimmed a finger over her collarbone.

In actual fact, he was the one who'd chosen to leave their bed, but it didn't seem ladylike to remind him. And since he was always such a gentleman, she should act with some decorum. But already the skim of his finger was making her insides quiver. She'd never realized that spot was so sensitive. Of course, she'd never known her feet were so sensitive either.

He looked down at her and even though she couldn't see his eyes, she could feel the force of his desire. Darts of excitement charged her body. But he just stood there, so cool. She forced what she hoped passed as a long-suffering sigh.

"I guess we could negotiate something," she said. "After all, it *is* your RV."

"True," he said, and though the word was gruff, his tone was tender.

His finger trailed along the top of her shirt, skimming and looping above the swell of her breasts, dipping, but not quite touching. And she wanted to step forward, wanted him to wrap that hand around her, and make them both forget everything except how well their bodies fit.

He didn't say anything though, just seemed engrossed with mapping the bare section of her skin. One distracted finger, and already her breasts were tightening, but he was totally in the wrong spot, and she wanted to stand on her tiptoes and encourage him to pay better attention.

"So, I guess it's your RV," she prompted, wishing he wouldn't just stand there. In another second, she'd be pulling off her shirt and rubbing against him like the orange cat he seemed to have adopted.

"I own it, yes," he said, spending another frustrating moment examining the angle of her collar bone.

"And you need to shower and make coffee and stuff," she said.

"That's right."

"Then maybe we could share," she said. "Make some sort of arrangement."

"I'll deal on the kitchen and shower," he said. "Even the chocolate and coffee. But not the master bedroom." He looked down at her then, his eyes glittering. "Please, sweetheart, not that."

His voice was so taut she realized she'd mistaken his dawdling for lack of interest. And that he didn't intend to move until he was invited in, even though he must know how easily he could make her melt.

She inched closer, feeling his pulsing heat, the bulge of his arousal. And she gave thanks that their incredible sexual attraction wasn't one-sided.

But she tilted her head, pretending it required some degree of thought. "You want the master bedroom?" She gave an aggrieved huff. "But my sunglasses are already in that room. I can't just *move* them."

"Of course not," he said. "If your sunglasses are there, you'll have to stay." He sobered. "We'll work it out, Eve. Whatever it takes."

He was obviously talking about more than sharing the master bedroom, and it was also clear he thought it would be a considerable challenge.

But when he scooped her up and carried her toward the RV, she could feel the urgency in his body, his unusual clumsiness as he fumbled for the door. And it was clear he was just as hungry as she was.

And for tonight, there was no need to worry about anything else.

CHAPTER THIRTY-EIGHT

Rick curved a hand around Eve's bare hip, wishing dawn hadn't come so quickly. It was still dark, but the horses were impatient for their breakfast, and he suspected it was Stinger who was slamming the wall.

"I heard a car," she whispered, her voice groggy. "Was that a guard driving Ashley?"

"Yes," he said. "Everything's under control. Try to sleep a bit more."

"I hope that isn't Tizzy kicking. They can hurt themselves. And he's racing today…"

Her voice trailed off, her breathing deepening. He pulled her closer and pressed a kiss against her soft cheek. They hadn't had much sleep last night, but he felt amazingly rested. Optimistic. Even happy.

It was an unusual feeling, this contentment that filled his chest but conversely lightened his arms, his legs, his entire body. He hadn't experienced it in a long time. Didn't expect to ever feel it again. His therapists said he should never have been a cop. But he liked people, liked helping. He just couldn't handle the pervasive sense of worthlessness every time he lost someone. Especially the innocent.

He nuzzled her neck, hoping she'd wake up and help him block those darker thoughts. He didn't want to churn up any ugliness. He was at Riverview Racetrack where life was refreshingly simple. Here, horses ruled, and drugs were the biggest crime. Camila's death was tragic but surely an aberration.

However, an insidious fear kept creeping into his psyche, taunting that he couldn't keep Eve safe. That he was missing something. And he couldn't shut off the voice.

He still had no clear picture of Victoria. She definitely had the queen bee syndrome, and she'd been causing trouble for Eve—something he'd never forgive—but sending Marcus after a woman Eve barely knew seemed a quantum leap.

And it was troubling there was surprisingly little chatter about Marcus. Generally there were warning signs, hushed whispers. However, the most Rick had gleaned about the man was that he was a big talker with a weakness for gambling. Sure, he liked the women. But no one had stepped forward with any stories of brutality. The people who'd complained to Liam in the past had refused to file reports and drifted on to other tracks or already left the States. So, like Victoria, Marcus remained a shadowy figure. But a man who didn't seem to pose a danger to Eve. And someone Rick could deal with.

His gaze shot toward the shadowed hallway. Soon there'd be a kid sleeping in the spare bedroom. And he could deal with that too.

But the thought made his forehead prickle and a cold sweat rose on his brow. Moments later, the dampness spread to his neck and back, soaking the pillow and leaving his skin tight and itchy.

I can do this.

But his heart was pounding, his chest turning tight, and he just wanted to flip Eve onto her back and find some sweet oblivion.

He gulped, remaining rigid, trying to control his body, his scrambling thoughts. Possibly he should check out Victoria, see what made her tick. It was never smart to rely on secondhand reports. Scott planned to send an investigator to

Santa Anita but if Rick went up, there'd be no need for an additional man.

Yes, Sunday might be an excellent time to drive to Santa Anita. He could meet the woman, figure out her thought process, and what she was capable of. It would only take a few days, maybe a week... And by then Eve's kid would be gone.

The docs called that avoidance. To him, it was survival.

"What's wrong?" Eve's breath fanned his chest. "You're squeezing my ribs."

"Sorry." He forced his arms to loosen. "I'm just thinking of Tizzy's race," he said quickly. "What's your schedule today?"

"Take Tizzy and Miguel over to the paddock. Let them see it one more time. Gallop the rest. Stinger will have a quarter mile blowout, just to stretch his legs before the race tomorrow."

She spoke casually about the gallops but he knew they were demanding. And he'd kept her up most of the night. Add in all the emotional turmoil and there was no doubt she was exhausted. This was a big weekend too, a last chance for everyone to keep their jobs. And all he was thinking about was how he could keep her in bed for another half hour...and the easiest way to avoid her kid.

"I'll clean the tack after I do the stalls," he said, fighting his utter sense of worthlessness. "And tidy up outside. Any race day superstitions I should know about?"

"Like all night sex before a race?" she asked, her teasing words ended in a yawn.

"Sorry," he said, trying to wish away his erection. She was obviously sleepy but he needed her, so badly. Even he was surprised at the depth of his desire. The sound of her voice, the way her lips moved, the sexy sounds she made when he was moving deep inside her. It made him want to howl at the moon, leap tall buildings and carry her off to a remote cave. All at the same time.

But she was a fit and vibrant woman. Perhaps it was always like this for her, the complete and utter wanting.

"Is it usually good luck?" he asked, keeping his voice light, as if her answer didn't matter so very much. "All night sex, before a race?"

"Let me think." She tilted her head, waiting a beat before smiling and putting him out of his misery. "No, dude. This is the first time I've ever done that."

"Good." And a rush of masculine pleasure loosened the tightness in his chest until his breathing felt almost normal again.

He lowered his head, capturing her mouth, loving the feel of her lips, their shape and taste, how her tongue mated so perfectly with his. And how her very presence blew away his fears.

"So," he said, raising his head a notch, "if Tizzy wins today, we'll have to duplicate this. Every night."

She gave a throaty laugh, wiggling from his arms and clearly ready to turn her attention to the horses. "Even you have to sleep some time," she said.

It wasn't quite the response he wanted. Actually he didn't know what he wanted, except that he didn't want their time here to end. With Eve, he felt whole again. He even slept better, that is, when they weren't making love. No more thrashing or night sweats or staring at the ceiling, waiting for the start of another gray day.

Sure, he'd had a tiny little panic attack at the thought of her kid pattering down the hall. But that hadn't lasted long. Her presence had washed it away. She and the backstretch community were good for him.

This was a different world, a place where obsessions revolved around the horses, with long hours, backbreaking work and unpredictable pay. As consuming as a love affair that delivered grief one day, ecstasy the next. But it was a life he wanted to embrace.

"How much longer are you here?" he asked, rising and groping on the floor for his scattering of clothes. "Twenty-two more days?"

"Twenty-one. But only if Tizzy and Stinger run well."

"Then we'll have to make sure they do." But for a moment, he fumbled with his shirt, because while he could use his unique skills to keep Eve safe, the other elements were beyond his control.

And it was rather unsettling that their happiness depended on two erratic Thoroughbreds. And one small boy.

Eight hours later, Rick was still on edge. Tizzy didn't act like the other horses in the race. He walked around the saddling enclosure, his head so low his nose almost touched Miguel's arm, unaffected by the buzzing crowd thronging the paddock or the colorful pageantry.

Loudspeakers blared, spectators pointed, cameras clicked. All the other horses pranced and one gray horse with white lather on his neck kicked out so forcefully the people by the rail scrambled away. But Tizzy remained oblivious.

Rick glanced at Ashley. "Think he's tired? Or sick? Maybe he hurt his legs kicking the stall?"

Ashley shook her head, not even glancing up from her race form. "Miguel has two bum knees," she said. "Tizzy knows that, so he's walking slow. He's a very obliging horse, especially when there's no rider."

"Great he's so obliging," Rick said. "But does that mean he's going to oblige the other horses by letting them pass?"

"That's always the question." Ashley finally looked up, but she didn't seem surprised by Tizzy's behavior. Her attention locked on the flashing tote board. "We've boxed him with the number two and eight horse," she said. "His times are better than the others. But he might have lost his mojo."

"How do you know that?"

"You don't," Ashley said. "Not until the race."

He grimaced. Tizzy and Miguel acted like they were out for a sightseeing tour, not twenty minutes away from a very critical race. A race that Jackson was insisting Tizzy win.

Granted, they both looked good. Miguel was unusually spiffy in his new shirt, and Tizzy's coat was so shiny it reflected the sun. But they were definitely the odd pair in the paddock. At one point Miguel stumbled and Tizzy came to a full stop, as if waiting for the old groom to regain his feet.

Rick shook his head. "I've never seen anything like that."

"It's the way they trained Tizzy back at the ranch," Ashley said. "And Miguel's doing his best. He's just not used to all the walking. Jackson and Victoria never let him in the paddock. They insist their staff look professional. I don't know how we're going to manage tomorrow with Stinger. I'm pregnant so Eve doesn't have anyone else."

Her eyes narrowed appraisingly on Rick. "And you can't do it. I mean that look totally works for you. But you'd scare the women and children. Victoria would hate that."

He scowled. He didn't scare all women, certainly not Eve. And he was wearing jeans and a T-shirt, simple groom clothes, no motorcycle in sight. Admittedly, there was a big gap between him and the rest of the spectators, as if nobody wanted to risk coming too close.

A little girl with pigtails stood twenty feet away, a hotdog gripped in her hands. Rick gave her an experimental smile. She immediately twisted, hiding behind her father's legs and smearing his knees with ketchup.

Rick ignored Ashley's snicker and looked back at Tizzy. Okay, maybe he was a little intimidating. And usually that was a relief. A tough appearance helped with his job. But he didn't feel relieved. He certainly didn't want to scare Joey. It would be hard enough being around the boy. If they were both frightened, it would be a disaster.

In the saddling enclosure, Eve was giving final instructions to Tizzy's rider. The jockey nodded and flicked her stick against her black boot. He wished he could hear what Eve was saying, instead of being stuck on the outside with the other spectators. Hopefully, she was making suggestions about how to wake up the horse.

Then Miguel and Tizzy shuffled up, and Eve boosted the jockey into the saddle. The line of mounted horses turned from the saddling enclosure and headed through the tunnel to the track. Nine of the runners looked like quality racehorses. But Tizzy just ambled beside Miguel, even with a jockey on his back.

Only fifteen minutes to post. Not much time to remind Tizzy he was headed for a race. Rick rubbed his sweaty palms against his jeans. He'd been less nervous in gunfights.

"Let's join Eve and Miguel," Ashley said, turning away from the rail. "They always watch by the finish line."

Rick wheeled. He didn't want to watch Tizzy—he preferred backing winners—but Eve was certainly going to need his support.

They wove through the surging crowd, past the beer stands and betting windows and found Eve standing by the rail.

Tizzy had joined the post parade and was now being escorted by a pretty rider on a stocky bay horse. The rider looked vaguely familiar, and when she nodded at him, Rick realized it was Dana, the woman with the nice breasts from the caps tournament.

Eve turned toward him. "So, what do you think?" she asked.

He froze, wondering if it were some kind of trick question. But then he absorbed the proud tilt of her shoulders, her confident smile, and his heart swelled. She was smart and brave and didn't give a rat's ass about trivial flirtations, reserving her energy for the horses and people she cared about. No wonder they'd nicknamed her Princess.

"I think," he said, "that you're unique." He could see she wanted to talk about Tizzy so he added, "And that our horse is smart about conserving energy."

She nodded happily. "His last three races he was sweating and agitated. Having Miguel in the paddock and Julie as his jockey is new. And he's not wearing blinkers. Hopefully those changes will help him regain his form. At least I hope they will." Her voice trailed off, and it was obvious she wasn't quite as confident as she appeared.

He nodded, frustrated that she was in such a tough position and there was nothing he could do to help. She was experimenting with a lot of different angles. But it was hard to fine-tune an athlete who couldn't talk. Race results were open to public scrutiny and considerable second guessing. Worst of all, she reported to a head trainer with a very hostile wife.

"Watching is probably harder than riding," he said, noting her clenched fingers.

She pressed a hand over her chest. "My heart's pounding. This is my first race as an assistant trainer. He looks good though, doesn't he?"

Rick glanced back at the parading horses, wishing he could agree. But at this point, it was too late for anything but reassurance. For a moment, he even wished he were a horse. So he could race instead and give Eve a shot at her first win, instead of relying on Tizzy, a too-kind gelding who could be ridden alone in the dark with just a halter and piece of rope.

"No matter how he does," Rick said, "you still have Stinger's race tomorrow."

Someone shuffled up and he glanced around. Miguel stood behind them. His face was impassive but his index finger tapped excitedly at the metal snap of the lead line.

"You did a great job in the paddock," Eve said, instantly squeezing sideways and making a place for the groom between her and Ashley. "Thank you."

Miguel looked down, then back at the horses. A flush climbed his face. Clearly he respected Eve and was delighted with her praise.

"You sure did," Ashley said. "And we have time to get another bet down and make more money for Camila. Do you still like his chances, Miguel?"

Miguel's rheumy eyes gleamed. "He will win today," he said.

Ashley grinned at Eve, then stuck her hand in her pocket and hurried back toward the betting windows.

Rick wrapped his hands around the rail, resolved to keep his mouth shut. It was doubtful Camila's fund would make any money today. But he was enjoying the camaraderie, the teamwork, the sense of accomplishment.

He'd helped get Tizzy to the starting gate. He'd cleaned the horse's stall, filled his hay net, and funded his race bridle. And in the process, he'd developed an attachment to the animals, the people, to the entire community. There was certainly little time to stress about anything except the horses. In fact, he barely flinched when a young boy ran up to the rail, hopping on one foot and gawking at the horses.

Rick looked at Eve. "Is it always like this?"

She nodded, understanding his question. "It's full of highs and lows, but totally absorbing. I can't imagine working anywhere else."

She pointed at the horses nearing the starting gate. "Julie's feet are in the irons. Tizzy knows it's time now," she added, "so you can stop worrying."

Rick followed her gaze. When Tizzy had paraded past the grandstand, the jockey's legs had been hanging by his sides. Now she'd placed her toes in the irons. And the change in Tizzy was remarkable. His body was coiled, his head arched over the bit, his ears pricked toward the gate. He rushed forward, so impatient to enter he almost clipped the assistant starter.

"He's a horse who wants to please," Eve added. "And he knows it's not time to race until the rider's feet are in the stirrups. That night in the dark, when I took my legs out of the stirrup, he quit prancing. That small thing can save a lot of energy."

"Did you tell the jockey that?"

Eve nodded. "Julie is great because she listens. To the horse and the trainer." She glanced at the tote board. "I'm not sure if the bettors were impressed with his quiet behavior though. His odds are the highest they've ever been."

Rick gave a wry nod. He'd also written off Tizzy based on his cowhorse appearance. Yet this was a long race, and it could be won by a whisker. Unlike Tizzy's competitors, their horse had conserved every drop of energy.

Their horse. He stared over the infield, sharing Eve's pride, watching as the rest of the runners loaded. The gray horse balked, refusing to move his feet. But Tizzy waited in the gate, poised and alert, his new bridle flashing whitely in the sun. He looked like a knight's charger, ready for battle.

"Guess there's not many horses like Tizzy," Rick said.

"No," Eve said, "there aren't. He's a pleasure to be around. But he still has to outrun nine other horses. Hopefully hanging out with Miguel will give him back his confidence, his desire to win. Everyone needs to feel special."

Amen, Rick thought. He ached to wrap her slim body in his arms but resisted the compulsion. This was a special moment—watching the first horse she'd every trained, and she vibrated with excitement. When those gates burst open, she'd need to be free, to bounce and cheer and urge Tizzy on.

He didn't know if Tizzy was good enough to win, but there was no doubt Eve made him feel special. Alive. Trusted. And no longer alone.

He lifted his face in gratitude, feeling like he'd escaped from society's seedy underbelly and somehow stepped into the sun. And it was a place he intended to stay. If only he could.

CHAPTER THIRTY-NINE

"They're off!" the announcer called. The horses burst from the gate in a line of flashing colors.

Eve jumped with the crack of the gate, praying for a good break. Tizzy shot from the six hole, running straight and even, his white bridle flashing. She exhaled, relieved all ten were safely out with no mishap. A fair start for all. Now he just had to run his race.

The horses thundered past, galloping by the grandstand for the first time. The speed horse on the outside had taken control, his gray tail streaming as he happily led the runners toward the first turn. Tizzy was racing midpack, fifth, outside a blinkered bay.

She rocked forward, imagining she was on his back. But instead of the reins, she could only squeeze the rail. "Watch the turn," she said. "Don't let him push you out."

She pressed her mouth shut, realizing she was calling instructions to Julie West, one of the top jockeys in the country.

"Don't go too wide," Ashley screeched, jumping almost a foot off the ground. "Grab that hole!"

Clearly jockeys were the worst critics, Eve decided, but then she stopped worrying. Didn't care that she was jumping and hollering and elbowing Ashley as Julie coolly brought Tizzy up on the outside, staying at the gray's hip as they raced down the backstretch. Eve knew she couldn't have positioned him any better.

Tizzy was galloping smoothly. He had a clear view of the track and there was no kickback, no dirt stinging his face. He and his rider looked relaxed and in control. There was only one horse in front of him when they entered the final turn, and the gray was tiring. It was obvious from his straining head, his shortened stride…and the way Tizzy galloped past him.

"Oh, my God." Ashley's voice rose with glee. "He's going to win."

The local favorite, a white-faced chestnut with a big closing kick, was making his move. However, Tizzy spurted loose on the turn, eating up the ground with his powerful stride. And when they straightened down the homestretch, he was five lengths in front, extending his lead without any visible encouragement from his jockey.

"She's not even moving," Eve said.

Indeed, Julie was sitting chilly, just letting Tizzy enjoy his run. And the horse was opening up, galloping away from the other horses, his ears pricked.

He crossed the wire eight lengths in front of the second-place chestnut.

"Tiz A Keeper wins it easy," the announcer said.

Eve leaped in the air. And then Ashley was hugging her, and they were dancing a circle by the rail, and Ashley was talking about the exacta they'd hit. And it was wonderful, and every bit as exciting as her first jockey win.

She grabbed Miguel's arm. His eyes were moist and she'd never seen his face all scrunched up like that but she totally understood, because she felt the same way. And then Rick gave her a big squeeze and whispered something about a wonderful training job, and her face felt like it was glowing.

She took a steadying breath because she'd watched other trainers, and it wasn't cool to celebrate too raucously. But this was her first win and they all loved Tizzy, and she permitted herself another joyous skip. Then she composed herself and hurried behind Miguel, who was already headed out to catch the horse.

Tizzy and Julie trotted up the middle of the track. The horse's chest was caked with dirt but he puffed with pride, enjoying the cheers of the crowd. Julie's teeth flashed in a big smile.

"He's a pro," she said, leaning over the saddle and pumping Eve's hand. "You had him prepared well. Thanks for the ride."

And Eve couldn't stop grinning because Julie West had her pick of quality horses. And trainers. A compliment from her needed to be savored.

Miguel stopped patting Tizzy's neck and tried to pass Eve the lead shank. But she shook her head. "You lead him in. We'll gather around."

Miguel blinked, then led Tizzy into the winner's circle. And even though Miguel moved awkwardly, his limp wasn't obvious because Tizzy immediately quit prancing, shortening his stride to match his beloved groom's.

A woman in a blue suit shook Eve's hand and presented her with a monogrammed cooler. They squeezed around Tizzy and a camera clicked. Everyone was smiling, and Rick chuckled with Julie's husband.

"We're going to Louisville next month," Julie said, pulling her saddle off Tizzy. "But I'd love to ride him again, if we ever cross tracks."

Eve nodded, feeling like she was dancing on air. If a jock like Julie West re-offered her services, it said a lot about Tizzy. She wished Dex and Dani were here. They'd been worrying about their horse, wondering if he should be shipped back to the ranch. No doubt, they'd watched the race online. Still, it wasn't the same.

She pulled out her phone, snapped a picture of Tizzy in the winner's circle, then pressed 'send.'

Dani texted back almost immediately. *Yay. He's back. Thank you! Let us know your plans for next race.*

Of course, the next race would be up to Jackson, but at least Tizzy wouldn't be retired. Eve sent another picture to her boss then slid the phone back in her pocket. She'd have to call Jackson today, but not yet. This moment was too much fun to risk dampening with any barbed comments.

An hour later, Eve and Miguel led a weary Tizzy back from the test barn. She'd wanted to save Miguel some walking, but he insisted on staying with the horse. He'd crooned and whistled and walked, helping the pee catcher gather a sample. And both Tizzy and Eve appreciated him.

"Thank you, Miguel," she said as they approached the barn. "I'm going to suggest to Jackson that you be the sole handler of Tizzy when we return to Santa Anita."

Miguel's face creased in a smile. "I was afraid for my job before," he admitted. "But this big horse, my friend—" He gave Tizzy a look full of gratitude. "He saved me."

"He saved us all," Eve said.

She scanned the barn, rather disappointed not to see Rick and Ashley in the doorway. Horses needed to be fed and legs checked. Once Tizzy was settled, they'd have to discuss how best to celebrate. Maybe go out to eat? They were all hungry, but tired too. And she still needed to call her boss.

Food was important though. She'd been too nervous to eat anything before the race, and she was sure Miguel hadn't been able to stomach anything either. But now her mouth was salivating. It took another few seconds for her brain to process the delicious smell wafting through the air. And then she spotted Ashley and Rick bending over the picnic table. Food sizzled on an enormous silver barbecue, and the table was covered with a bright cloth and plates and bowls.

Miguel's stomach rumbled, and they both laughed.

Ashley bounced over. "Everything's ready," she said, taking Tizzy's lead line. "Why don't I turn Tizzy out in the sandpit for a roll. And you two can finally sit down."

"But where did the grill come from?" Eve asked. "And the food?"

Ashley gestured over her shoulder. "I don't know how Rick did it," she said, her voice filled with glee. "But please keep that man around. There is so much food here. And even the guards don't have their own gas barbecue."

CHAPTER FORTY

Eve gathered the dirty dishes, piling them at the end of the picnic table. Miguel and Ashley were bathing Tizzy, so she'd offered to clean up.

Rick definitely deserved a break. He'd grilled fresh vegetables along with juicy T-bone steaks and wild salmon, although she suspected the fish had been intended for the cat. He'd thought of everything, even arranging for some sparkling apple cider so Miguel could join them in toasting Tizzy's win.

She looked at Rick, her smile simmering with gratitude. "This was the best meal I've had in a long time. Where did you rent the barbecue?"

"Bought it," he said, placing a morsel of steak in front of the cat, who clearly preferred meat to fish. "Thought it would be handy to have a grill, for when Joey's here."

Her hand stalled over a plate. The barbecue was more than just a grill, but a deluxe model with two side panels, a rotisserie and a warming element. Not only would it be hugely useful but it gave the play area a cozy feel, making it seem more like home.

Of course, Rick's other additions enhanced the area too. Somehow he'd found time to gather soccer balls and a net, as well as hang a tire from the big oak tree. And some of his track friends had delivered a third picnic table.

She hadn't asked many questions. Over supper, they'd all been ecstatic about Tizzy's win, reliving every stride. She'd assumed the women had left the balls. Now it was evident Rick had arranged everything, no doubt because of Scott's prodding about having toys for Joey.

She clinked the last plate on top of the stack, then balled the napkins. Rick obviously had more money than she'd imagined, oodles more, but she couldn't let him keep buying everything. And all this would be hard to repay.

She had the horrible feeling Scott and Megan didn't trust her to look after Joey, or even to feed him properly. And sure, maybe she skipped breakfast and ate at weird times, but she was conscious of good nutrition. Heck, she was an athlete. Now that her car was working again, she'd make sure they had plenty of groceries. They could even eat in the track kitchen if necessary. She didn't need a stainless steel barbecue with an attached cooler and triple propane tanks.

Rick stilled her hands, stopping her from shredding the napkins. "It's just a grill," he said.

"And I really appreciate it," she said, looking into his concerned eyes. "I do love the swing. And the soccer balls are great. But tell me...did Scott's office have anything to do with this? With the barbecue?"

"Yes." Rick pried the napkin from her fingers. "I asked for Belinda's help. To make sure it was assembled and delivered on time. And to organize the groceries."

"But whose idea was it?"

He averted his gaze, suddenly occupied with re-stacking the plates.

Her insides twisted. "How many times did you talk to Scott today?"

"Three, four times," Rick muttered. "The police haven't located Marcus yet, and Scott needs updates."

"And that's all you talked about? Did he say anything about Joey?"

Rick paused, clearly searching for words. "A few questions," he said.

"Like what?"

"Like who'd be looking after Joey when you were busy with the horses. Who'd be his playmates. What kind of toys were here. Where he'd sleep. He just wanted information like that. You know, normal stuff."

"It's not normal." She shot to her feet, so quickly her knee banged the table. "I'm Joey's mother. And I expected more of you. I trusted you—"

Her throat clogged and she backed away, not even feeling the numbness in her knee, too hurt by his lack of loyalty to want anything but escape.

She'd forgotten how fast he could move. Somehow he'd glided between her and the barn, not touching but definitely blocking her path.

"Hey," he said, his voice somber. "Scott asked those questions. Doesn't mean I answered them… I didn't."

The lump in her throat shifted. She pulled in another breath, absorbing his words. He hadn't said anything. That was good. And it must have been hard to refuse Scott.

She stared into Rick's shirt, so close her nose almost brushed the soft cotton. Then she leaned forward, letting her forehead rest against his chest. "Sorry," she whispered. "I know I'm too sensitive. But Joey's my son. Not theirs."

His arm lifted but he didn't speak, only clasped her shoulder with a comforting hand. Birds trilled from the trees and a squirrel scolded. He didn't ask any questions, didn't chide her for throwing accusations. He just stood there. And he deserved an explanation.

"Megan and I went through hell together," she said, her voice rusty. "Her brother and I met at jockey school. Joey was my first real love. My son's named after him." She swallowed. "But a cartel was using school horses to move drugs and money, and he disappeared. Nobody would help. The police dismissed him as a heroin dealer who'd run off to Mexico. If not for Scott, we never would have recovered his body. Or known the truth. Joey never even met his dad."

She cleared her throat. "Megan and Scott are family and I'm very grateful, but their interest in Joey is scary. Especially since they can't have children of their own... And obviously they'd make better parents than me."

The squirrel still scolded, a horse thumped the wall from the barn, and something deeper rumbled in Rick's chest. She glanced up, alarmed. Was surprised to see him laughing.

Her eyes narrowed. "You find this funny?"

"Just the part that anyone could be a better parent than you. You're like a lioness, loving, loyal, brave. Maybe a little prickly sometime. But that's good in a parent. I like that. Gotta keep those kids safe."

His grin faded and he lowered his arm. "If you can clean up here," he said, looking over her head at the barn, "I'm going to hang some rubber in Stinger's stall. So he won't hurt himself when he kicks."

It was obvious that children's safety had hit a nerve and she wished he'd talk more, but clearly the subject was off limits. And cushioning Stinger's walls with rubber was an excellent precaution, except that investing in a barn where they'd only be stabled a short time was rather extravagant.

"That's a good idea," she said. "But I know Jackson won't want to pay for the rubber."

"No charge. Barn six had some extra sheets, and one of the grooms who worked with Marcus pushed it my way."

She nodded, no longer surprised by Rick's ability to make friends. He'd visited shedrows when she was galloping horses this morning, and had the rare gift of making everyone feel at ease. But the fact that he could do his investigative work, while so ably filling in as a groom and a handyman, was utterly remarkable. And rather intimidating.

He'd only laughed when she teased him about his supernatural endurance. But right now, when her back ached and she just wanted to tumble into bed—instead of hanging rubber—it was almost irritating.

She squared her shoulders, hiding her exhaustion, trying to muster some enthusiasm. "Great," she said. "I'll grab the drill from the tack room, and we can hang it now."

"Think I can handle it." He slid a gentle hand around the back of her neck. "You've been working with horses all day."

So have you, she thought. But she shifted, sighing as his capable fingers kneaded the back of her neck, hitting spots she hadn't even known were tight. She tilted her head, giving him better access.

"Maybe we can pick up the rubber tomorrow," she said, her eyes already half closed.

"It's already delivered. Liam arranged for a truck."

"Are they close to catching Marcus?"

"Doesn't seem like it. Someone must be hiding him."

"Not even Victoria would help a murderer," she said, her voice sleepy, lulled by the expert rhythm of his hand. "I don't think she's involved in this."

"You think that?" His fingers stopped moving. "In your gut?"

She gave a protesting nudge with her head. "I can think better if you keep rubbing."

He chuckled and resumed massaging. "Camila's murder seems unrelated to everything else going on. But the police think Marcus is good for it. So does Liam. They're not looking at anyone else."

"Police thought Joey was a criminal too," she said.

"Yes. And Scott's a careful man. So he's sending an investigator to Santa Anita. To take a closer look at Victoria."

Eve groaned, but this time not with pleasure. "If Jackson finds out Scott's agency is investigating his wife, he'll be furious." She shook her head, hating to even consider the consequences.

"He won't. Scott has good people."

"Braggart," she said. But she knew the Taylor Investigative Agency had earned immense respect. It was rumored even the LAPD relied on their services.

"Victoria won't give the time of day to a hotwalker or groom," she added. "They'd have to be a trainer or owner to even start a conversation. And the investigator better not be female. Victoria doesn't like women."

"She sounds charming," Rick said dryly. "Scott might send someone posing as a divorce lawyer. But I guarantee your boss will never know." He paused, then slid his finger beneath her chin and tilted her head. "Tell me. Do I scare children? Even away from my bike?"

She laughed. "Just because you resemble a cage fighter with hair and scary ink and ass-kicking boots, heck, no—" Her smile faded at his crestfallen expression. She'd thought he was joking but realized now he was serious. "You might scare kids a little," she said. "But that's only until they get to know you."

He dropped his hand. "I need your ladies to fix me up. So I don't scare Joey."

It was probably exhaustion that made her legs turn buttery. But this macho man with the tender heart was concerned about scaring her son. And that was definitely progress. She'd been worried about his reaction to children, couldn't forget how he'd backed away when he first learned about Joey. But now things were working out beautifully, and happiness left her insides soft and glowing.

She rose on her toes and looped her arms around his neck. "Do what you want. But don't you need that look? For your job?"

He shrugged. "If I go to Santa Anita and help check out Victoria, I need to look like a lawyer."

"But you said Scott already sent someone?"

"That's right." His gaze drifted over her head toward the barn. "But it might need two of us...just for a week, not sure."

"But when would you go? Not until Monday, right? Because I need your help with Stinger."

"Right." His tanned throat rippled. "Okay then. I won't go."

She rocked back, weak with relief. Stinger behaved so much better for Rick. But it wasn't just that. Her stomach flipped in dread at the thought of him leaving, even if it were just for a week. It was an odd feeling, comforting but at the same time disturbing. And along with it came the nagging suspicion that he might be trying to avoid Joey.

"Does Scott want you to go to Santa Anita?" she asked. "Or was that your idea?" She kept her hands on his shoulders, knowing he was skilled at concealing facial expressions, but she might be able to detect something in his body.

"Can't remember," he said. "Besides, it doesn't matter now. If you need me with Stinger, I'm staying." His face gave away nothing, but she caught a telltale tightening across his shoulders.

She swallowed her dismay. "You should know that I want Joey to stay for more than a week. Mom needs a break, and besides, I really want him with me, all the time—"

Shrill voices rose behind her and she twisted.

Juanita stood by the barn, waving her arms at Ashley. Both women looked at Eve and gestured.

"Guess we better talk about this later," she said.

His face remained absolutely expressionless. "Guess we better."

CHAPTER FORTY-ONE

Juanita paced a circle around Eve and Ashley, waving her arms and spicing the air with the smell of onions and kitchen grease. A stained white apron was still wrapped around her waist and her dark hair was tucked beneath a hairnet.

"It's so strange," she repeated, shaking her head in a mixture of confusion and delight. "It's a godsend for Camila's fund, but why did she have so much money in her room?"

Ashley's eyes narrowed. "Liam says there's a big underground economy here. Probably the money is illegal."

Juanita tugged off her hairnet and jammed it into her apron pocket. "Maybe I was mistaken about the amount," she murmured, glancing over her shoulder as if checking for a security Jeep.

"Let's go inside and have a coffee," Eve said, taking Juanita's arm. While Ashley's friendship with Liam was helpful, the Hispanic community still viewed the guards with suspicion. No doubt Juanita feared, quite rightly, that the funds would be seized and tied up in the investigation.

Juanita followed Eve into the RV. She sank down at the kitchen table, her hands folded in front of her. She waited until Eve shut the door, but when she spoke, her voice was low and determined.

"Camila's sister needs this cash," she said. "It was in Camila's dorm. So it's hers. And I'm going to send it to her."

"Of course," Eve said, deliberately casual as she poured some coffee. "Best to send it right away, before everything gets muddled."

"But what if Ashley tells the guards?""

"We'll have to send it quickly." Eve paused. "Camila never mentioned this money, even when you were discussing raising funds for the hair business?""

"Nothing. Not a word." Juanita's face darkened, and it was obvious she felt somewhat betrayed by Camila's surprising wealth. "I was packing up her things and found it hidden in a cracker box. Almost five thousand dollars."

"Do you think it had something to do with Marcus?" Eve set a mug in front of Juanita. "Gambling maybe?"

"I don't think she liked Marcus much," Juanita said. "He's full of big talk. And they always seemed to be arguing." She shook her head and reached for the coffee mug.

Eve joined her, sitting down at the table and taking a little sip. She didn't want caffeine, not this close to bedtime. But she needed to put Juanita at ease. When the woman first arrived at the barn, she'd been happy and excited. Now she just seemed pensive. Even secretive.

"If Camila did anything illegal," Eve said, her voice gentle, "it won't matter now. She can't be arrested or deported. So there's no reason to worry."

"*Sí.*" Juanita gave a weak nod. "And we're still going ahead with our hair business. She'd like that. But we need more customers. Women are interested but not the men."

"Rick might want a hair cut."

"Good." Juanita's smile returned. "Tomorrow I'll send over one of the girls."

"But he wants the most experienced person. So it's best if you cut it." Eve's fingers tightened around the handle of the mug. She didn't want to break Juanita's confidence, but Rick needed to know about this money. And she had no doubt that given twenty minutes with Juanita, he could humor her into providing a detailed list of every item in Camila's room.

Besides, he wasn't hung up on legalities, not like the starched collar guards. He'd be cool about sending it to Camila's family, before it was caught up in a lengthy police investigation.

"We should send the money soon," Eve said. "Before authorities find out."

Juanita's eyes narrowed. "You won't tell anyone, will you?"

"Someone else might already know about it," Eve said. "Or maybe the money has something to do with Marcus. No doubt he'll talk when the police catch him."

Juanita turned her head, staring out the window over the sink. Daylight was waning, the sun staining the horizon with red. It was a pretty sight but even so, Juanita seemed unusually interested in the view.

"I was going to look for a drive to the post office next week," she said, still staring out the window. "Tape up the box and mail the money with her clothes."

"It's safer to send money through a bank," Eve said. "I can drive you after training on Monday. I'll have Joey then. Maybe we can go to McDonalds afterwards."

Juanita tapped her finger against her lip, watching as Rick strode past the window, shouldering a strip of heavy black rubber. The rubber was long and awkward, yet he carried it effortlessly.

Juanita leaned forward, waiting until he disappeared into the barn. "He keeps things safe," she said slowly. "Your man."

My man. Eve nodded, filled with a warm glow. Rick liked to keep everything safe, animals and people. And now she wouldn't have to worry about Stinger kicking the walls and hurting himself. Rick was also astute enough to stay away from the RV, realizing that Juanita wanted privacy.

"He is much liked," Juanita went on. "But feared and respected too. No one would dare steal, not from him. Not even Marcus." When she finally turned away from the window, her smile was back, as if she'd reached a difficult decision. "So I wish to keep the money here," she added, "where it will be safe. And then I will cut his hair for free."

Eve swallowed, moved by the woman's trust. "Sure, we'll keep Camila's money here. But I'm sure he'll want to pay for his cut."

Despite Rick's appearance, it was clear he had a well-padded bank account. And even though money wasn't a challenge, his empathy for the workers was obvious. He understood that every dollar here was well earned.

"No," Juanita said. "His haircut will be free." She gave a knowing smile. "Because then I will have his picture on our posters. And the men will see it and they'll all want haircuts, just like him. It's just good business."

Eve laughed but couldn't argue with that logic. Whether it was Rick's charisma or the tournament or simply because he knew how to make people feel good, he'd definitely made an impact. When she was galloping Stinger this morning, he'd watched from the rail alone.

But he hadn't been alone for long. Within minutes, he'd been surrounded. And it wasn't just the grooms who loved him. At one point his entourage had included a sportswriter and a security guard, as well as the feed man with the pesticide-free oats.

At the time, Eve had been riding beside Dana, the Pink Viper—the woman seemed to appear whenever Stinger turned fractious. Dana was tough and confident, and Eve quite liked her.

Dana had rolled her eyes at Rick and the cluster of people. 'Popular guy,' she said, and then she grimaced. 'I was loaded that night. Looking for love. He said he was honored but couldn't give me the attention I deserved because he was committed to another beautiful woman. Nicest rejection ever.'

'I don't suppose you get many rejections,' Eve had said.

'Not with this rack.' Dana had stuck out her impressive breasts and they both laughed.

And then they'd gone on to talk about horses, and bullet works and Stinger's street-punk attitude. Dana even agreed to pony him on race day, especially helpful since Stinger disliked other horses but was relatively accepting of Dana's gelding, limiting his displeasure to the occasional nip.

Eve realized she'd been daydreaming and yanked her attention back to Juanita, not sure if she should blame her inattention on Rick, or Stinger, or maybe both.

"I'll come right back with Camila's box," Juanita was saying. "And I'll be here at five o'clock Monday morning to look after Joey." She picked up the toy horse, smiling at its neigh. "This trailer is like a mansion. He'll love it here. We'll make sure of that."

Gratitude warmed Eve's chest. The early hours weren't even a problem. Juanita already knew when a trainer was busy. And after morning gallops, Joey would have the chance to ride his first horse. She couldn't wait to see his grin when he looked down from the top of Tizzy's back. To be able to experience that special moment with him would be something she'd treasure forever.

There was little doubt that he'd love the track and want to stay here the rest of the meet. He certainly wouldn't be much trouble. Sometimes he was mischievous but he was generally reasonable, a little reserved like her, but brave and athletic like his dad.

No, the trouble wouldn't come from Joey. And the warmth in her chest was replaced with a chill of apprehension. Because while her son might want to stay, Scott and Megan could pose considerable resistance. And they were much harder to handle.

CHAPTER FORTY-TWO

Rick padded from the washroom, his rumpled hair still damp from the shower. Eve's eyelids had been drooping ever since Juanita left, but now his rampant masculinity prodded her awake. His jeans hung low on his lean hips and drops of water clung to his bare chest. He was battle scarred and magnificent, and she itched to touch him, even though seconds ago she'd been yawning.

He pulled a beer from the fridge and cocked an eyebrow.

"Nothing for me, thanks," she said, still full from the barbecue. What she needed most was sleep. It was almost nine o'clock and she'd been up since five. Tomorrow would be an even longer day, with Stinger running in the eighth and Joey arriving. It was amazing Rick wasn't exhausted too, especially since he'd been in the barn hanging rubber while she'd been sitting with Juanita.

He sat down at the table. His arm stretched behind her, carrying the heady smell of spicy soap and male skin. She noticed he'd left his beer in the fridge.

"No wonder you're tired," he said. "Most trainers are asleep by now. And you pull double duty as an exercise rider."

She snuggled against his warm chest. "Juanita just left," she said. "And I didn't want to fall asleep before talking with you. Was there enough rubber to cover Stinger's wall?"

"Enough to cover the back and both sides."

His finger rubbed an achy spot at the base of her neck and her eyelids drooped again. But she couldn't figure out how he had the energy to be so thoughtful. "Don't you ever get tired? Or are you on some drugs I don't know about?"

He didn't answer and she tilted her head, checking his face.

"I'm used to small amounts of sleep," he said slowly. "Generally I'm just starting work at this hour."

That marked the first time he'd volunteered any information about his past, and curiosity replaced her tiredness. She knew he'd been involved with Scott in breaking up a mafia ring, and before that had infiltrated some sort of biker club. She'd assured herself it was merely a riding club, not the dreaded one percent. But sometimes there was a hardness in his eyes, a cold implacability, that made her suspect he was capable of a variety of things.

"The club you rode with," she asked, "was it an outlaw club?"

"Yes."

She swallowed, absorbing the ramifications. Obviously she couldn't ask any more, but she couldn't stop her mind from scrambling into overdrive, imagining the horrible things he'd been forced to do, simply to maintain his cover.

"I was a prospect," he added. "Never patched in."

She gave an involuntary sigh of distress and gripped his hand. A prospect had to constantly demonstrate his loyalty. Before being patched in, his face was circulated to every chapter. Some clubs also hired private investigators for background checks, and many had informants within the police force.

Scrutiny was intensive, the pressure overwhelming. And when an undercover agent was caught trying to infiltrate a biker gang, death wasn't always quick. But it was usually the result.

She didn't realize she was crying until his finger wiped her cheek.

"Hey," he said gently. "I'm done with it. That was two years ago. And I was pulled before I was made. Don't worry. There won't be any repercussions."

She shook her head, her throat too clogged to speak. It wasn't fear about anyone finding them. It was imagining how he must have felt each time he parked his bike and walked into that clubhouse. The sheer terror of wondering if this would be the day they'd discover his true identity.

"I'm sorry." She swiped at her eyes. "Everyone says a jockey's job is dangerous but I can't imagine what you must have gone through, how you felt."

"It wasn't too bad. I mostly served beer, ran errands. The president liked me so that helped."

His voice was light but she wasn't buying it. Before earning a patch, club members were brought in as prospects and faced a rigorous evaluation period. Dex said it could range from having a brother's back to killing for the club. And like Boy Scouts, patches were awarded for a range of activities. Everything from gang bang to murder.

Her breathing was ragged, the only noise in the kitchen except for the sound of a dripping tap. She hadn't turned it off properly after she rinsed Juanita's mug. She kept her head against his shoulder, not looking at him or the sink, desperate to clear her mind of ugly images.

She tried thinking of something benign, picturing the water pooling at the end of the faucet, even counting the seconds before its weight sent it plopping to the bottom. But soon the dripping water would overflow...like the blood in the sink on *Sons of Anarchy*.

She shivered. It wasn't that she lived in a pristine world. Far from it. One of her cousins had died in prison, and Joey's father had some criminal history before he'd been murdered. However, the real biker gangs, the one percenters, were lethal. To be avoided at all costs. Their patches were an outlaw's road map. Yet Rick had ridden with them, lived with them…been one of them.

And he'd just handed her confidential information. It couldn't be a mistake. A man like him would have learned to measure his words, his actions, and be able to withstand intense scrutiny.

Yet he was so calm, sitting at the table, seemingly ready to field her questions. It had to mean he intended to stick around. Didn't it?

She wasn't sure how long the silence stretched. But his shoulder felt tense, and she was suddenly aware of his edge, like a taut wire. And it was obvious he wasn't calm at all. He was simply waiting for her reaction. Anticipating emotion…maybe revulsion?

And she'd been so silent.

She reached for his hand, raised it to her mouth and kissed it. "If you tell me any more," she said, "you're either going to have to kill me or marry me."

His breath escaped in a half-sigh, half-groan, and he pulled her to his chest, and then all she could hear was his pounding heart.

"I wasn't sure what you'd think." And then after a moment, he spoke again. "Riding with the club wasn't too bad. Prep involved spending time in prison which meant a weekly piss test after release. That gave me a valid reason to refuse the drugs."

She traced a finger along his tattooed arm, tracing the gray lines, then peered up at his hard jaw. "Were you ever asked to…kill someone?"

"Only once, but I had police pick him up in time."

Her breath released in a slow exhale. He was a good man. If he'd ever had to murder someone just to gain the trust of a club, no doubt he'd be irrevocably scarred. But they could deal with this. She didn't care about anything else, and she certainly wasn't going to ask about other women. That was in his past. None of her business. Just like a horse with a troubled history, they could work through it.

But her throat felt tight, and she remembered Ashley's comments about bikers and their interchangeable women. How there was even a badge for having oral sex in front of club members. And Dex had once said that all prospects are given assignments to weed out police plants. She didn't want to think about what Rick had been forced to do, but unfortunately her mind wasn't listening.

A callused thumb brushed the curve of her cheek. And then he raised his other arm, cupping her face with both hands, holding her like she was precious. He stared down, his eyes dark with understanding.

"You should ask about it," he said gruffly. "Anything you want. Let's get this out of the way."

She drew in a ragged breath. "Just one question," she said. "I've heard that women are plentiful. And that they're not treated well. Did you…participate in that?"

"It can be a misogynistic society," he said. "But a prospect is low man on the totem pole. There was always a patch that wanted her first."

"Are the stories about sharing true?"

"Every chapter is different. Depends on the president. Mine was more of a family man." His hands tightened around her face, and for a moment his eyes glittered with something akin to anguish.

"You don't think they'll come after you?"

"The president is dead. Everyone else is in prison."

She gulped. That explained his emotion, the sadness in his voice. Naturally he'd have grown close to club members, even if they were criminals.

"Let's go to sleep," he said, his voice flat. "You need to think about all this."

She automatically rose from the table. It was tempting to head for the bedroom, to enjoy some glorious sex, and then a dreamless night's sleep. But her gaze shot to the closet.

"There's something I have to tell you too," she said. "The reason Juanita came tonight. When she was packing up Camila's things, she found some cash. Quite a bit. Nearly five thousand dollars."

Rick's eyes narrowed. "Small bills?"

"I don't know. But she brought it over while you were in the shower. She thought the money would be safer here."

"Where is it?"

She gestured at the closet. "In a cardboard box with Camila's clothes. The money's in a cracker box."

He pulled open the closet door. With his other hand, he reached beneath the kitchen sink and pulled out a pair of latex gloves. He found the money, fanning it in his hands for an expert count before lifting it to his nose and sniffing the bills.

Eve blinked. She'd been picturing him as a prospect in a biker gang and the switch to a seasoned cop was rather disconcerting.

"I'll have Scott check this out," Rick said. He replaced the money then skimmed through the rest of the box, pulling out a pink ball cap, a small notebook and a T-shirt that said: NUMBER ONE GROOM.

It was tragic seeing someone's possessions reduced to a two-foot cardboard box, and Eve averted her head. "We're going to mail that big box on Monday," she said. "But use a bank to transfer the money."

"Did the police release this?" Rick asked, fingering the notebook.

"I guess so." She studied the tips of her fingers. "Her room wasn't taped off or anything. Juanita just went in and gathered Camila's stuff. Her little sister wants it."

"So will the police," Rick said. "And the money has to be reported."

"We'll report it," she said. "After it's sent."

He replaced the notebook and looked up. He didn't say anything, just gave her a flat-eyed stare that she'd seen him use on Ashley a few times, but never on her. It was rather intimidating.

Her back stiffened and she crossed her arms. "We're sending it on Monday."

"Can't," he said, his voice just as clipped. "We have to turn it over."

"But you know what the police are like. All the legalities. That money could be tied up for years. Maybe forever. And Camila's sister is an orphan. She needs it now."

"That's unfortunate," he said. "But it still needs to be reported."

"But the police were the idiots who didn't find it. And Juanita trusts me to do the right thing."

"Giving it to the police is the right thing." He replaced the box and shut the closet door with a click of finality.

She hadn't seen this coming, and gave a disapproving sniff. "Your cop colors are showing. And I don't like it."

His face softened. He even had the audacity to smile. "I wouldn't have had a chance with you if I wore a uniform. Good thing I'm not still a cop."

"Then maybe you should stop acting like one. Because you know I'm right. Once the police are involved, this will get complicated."

"Maybe," he said.

"So you agree? They'll just mess it up?"

"I have to turn the money in. Otherwise this could blow back on Scott. And I work for him."

"That won't be a problem," she said brightly. "We'll just pretend you didn't see it."

He strode to the sink and yanked the tap tight, stopping the drip. Then he stared out the dark window, his hands gripping the counter.

"But I have seen it," he said.

She recoiled, shocked by the finality of his words. Obviously it had been a mistake to associate his appearance with a sliding morality scale. And probably she should have known better. She'd witnessed how tirelessly he worked for her barn. He'd bring that sense of duty to every job. Of course he'd feel honor bound to Scott.

She didn't quite understand his code. She'd been raised in a world where it was clever to outsmart authorities, and uniforms weren't to be trusted. But she was filled with a grudging respect. And she couldn't ask him to be less of a man, no matter how inconvenient.

She walked over and wrapped her arms around his waist. "Sorry," she said, pressing her cheek against his back. "Don't worry. We'll report the money." She hesitated for a moment but he'd been so open earlier, she wanted to match it. "And I do still love you. Even if you sometimes act like a cop."

His entire body stiffened. He wheeled and scanned her face, his eyes incredulous. "Sweetheart," he said, his voice hoarse.

Then he shifted, wrapping her in his arms, his legs, his entire body, and when his mouth claimed hers, it felt like he was absorbing her into his very being. Filling her senses with his amazing love.

And leaving her with the conviction that she and Joey would never be alone again.

CHAPTER FORTY-THREE

The sun shone especially bright this morning, slanting through the mist and gilding the track. Even the horses seemed burnished with a golden glow. Or maybe Eve was just happy.

Joey was arriving today, and Stinger was racing, and Rick... She couldn't stop smiling.

Stinger gave an exuberant buck, as if sharing her enthusiasm the only way he knew. But she tightened her reins, wanting to save his energy. This was just a morning stretch and one last chance to school in the paddock.

A rider cantering a horse mid-track called out a cheery greeting and a wiry man on a chestnut congratulated her on Tizzy's race. At some point she'd been accepted by this insular community. They were genuinely happy about her win yesterday, no longer treating her as the outsider from Santa Anita. It might have been because of Juanita's influence and the welcoming spot she'd made for the children. But more likely it was because of Rick.

She gave a happy sigh and Stinger gave another buck, his ears pinned on a passing horse. He wasn't being nasty. He was just eager to run. And he didn't like to take orders from anyone but himself. And of course, Rick.

She rounded the turn, her gaze drifting to the railbirds waiting by the gap. As usual, Rick was in the middle, surrounded by an attentive group of people. She understood the feeling. She liked to be close to him too. Even though she was on the track, fifty feet away and separated by a rail fence, his gaze connected with hers. And her heart sang.

It no longer mattered that Jackson still hadn't returned her calls or that Juanita would be upset when she learned the money had to be turned over. With Rick by her side, life was fuller, brighter. Even Victoria's scheming faded into the periphery.

A neon shirt flashed and hooves pounded, sending dust swirling. Dana, the Pink Viper, slowed beside Eve.

"You look happy," Dana said. "Good sex last night?"

Eve's smile widened.

The Viper glanced at the gap then gave a wistful sigh. "Can't remember the last time a man left me grinning like that."

Eve couldn't remember her last time either. She'd loved Joey's dad but it was different with Rick. More trusting. More complete. She was happier now than she'd ever been, in spite of the tumultuous events. In fact, she felt almost weightless.

"I must say," the Viper went on, "you were sure decent the night of the tournament. Even giving me a coffee. I never would have made a run at your man if I'd been sober." She gave a wry shrug. "Didn't matter anyway. We all know how that turned out."

Eve straightened Stinger's head, barely listening. That incident was over and forgotten. It only helped reinforce that she'd found a man worth keeping. And what a man. The way he'd held her last night, the words of love he'd whispered, left her giddy with hope. And she couldn't stop spinning plans.

In a year or so, she might have enough experience to leave Jackson and train on her own. She'd hire Ashley and Miguel and look for some good owners. By then her earnings might be enough to rent a house close to Santa Anita as well as

Scott's investigative office. She'd be able to have lunch every day with Joey, and she'd even learn to cook healthy meals.

Of course, there'd be nights when Rick wouldn't be able to come home. Scott's cases often involved lengthy undercover work. But at least Rick would have a steady job. It was expensive to live around the track but surely between the two of them they'd be able to rent a house. Maybe something with a yard.

She shifted in the saddle, excited at the prospect. Joey wanted a pet so badly. His parents had both been jockeys so naturally a pony ranked at the top of his wish list. Of course, that was impossible. Track stalls were at a premium and reserved for racehorses. But he'd be content with a small dog, or even a cat.

Maybe when she had her own training business, she could justify a stall for a stable pony, one of the dependable animals that escorted the Thoroughbreds. Of course, they weren't actual ponies but often retired racehorses. However, they were good animals with great minds. Safer than a pony and definitely more practical.

She gave a guilty start, realizing she hadn't been listening to a word Dana was saying. Something about the caps tournament and riding with a hangover and how Camila had advised that she drink lots of water.

"Camila?" Eve swiveled in the saddle. "You were talking to her at the tournament?"

"Just for a bit," Dana said. "She was going to cut my hair, layer it a little. I wrote the appointment time on my hand so I wouldn't forget. But then…" She stopped talking and they both were silent, the horses' hooves loud in the tranquil air.

Eve fingered Stinger's short mane, hating to think how Camila's life had ended. She'd barely been in the States a year and was apparently sending every cent back to her younger sister in Guatemala. And yet she had five grand hidden in a cracker box—and a groom only made eight hundred dollars a month.

"Do you know if she had another job?" Eve asked, keeping her voice casual. "Besides her work as a groom?"

"Don't think so. After her boyfriend left, she hung out with Marcus for a bit. She couldn't work as a groom that last month she was pregnant."

"Pregnant?" Eve blinked with surprise. "Camila had a baby?"

Dana nodded. "But even though we worked in the same barn, she never said much. Hid her pregnancy for as long as she could. She was shattered when her boyfriend bolted, and left her with no support. I think Marcus was quick to take advantage."

Eve's mouth tightened. Conditions had been ripe for the exploitation of a young woman in a foreign country. Hopefully Rick or Liam would find Marcus first. They could inflict a little punishment before turning him over to the police, although it was unfortunate their weird cop code might stop from dishing out proper payback.

"Wish we could string Marcus up," the Pink Viper said, echoing Eve's sentiments. "Weird thing is that I hooked up with him once. He never got rough, even when we had heated words about who had the fastest horse."

Eve eyed Dana. The girl was flamboyantly female but like most riders was tough as nails. Marcus probably needed a more vulnerable target. "Everyone seems to think he did it," Eve said.

"Yeah. But jerks are generally consistent. Like your horse." Dana gestured at Stinger. "He's always ornery. We know it, understand it, deal with it. Marcus, he's self-centered but I never thought he'd hurt anyone."

She gave her head a regretful shake. "Camila wasn't the friendliest girl but her last four months were rough. And

Marcus is a smooth talker. Maybe she turned desperate, a little too clingy, and he just blew up. Other than that, I don't see why he'd ever hurt her."

Eve stared over Stinger's ears, hating the darker direction of her thoughts. She didn't even want to voice them. But by all accounts, when Camila had been deserted by her boyfriend she'd been pregnant, alone and broke. With nowhere to turn. And babies were in demand, especially ones from healthy young mothers who worked at a track and were subject to drug testing.

They walked another fifty feet, past the weigh scales and winner's circle, before Eve spoke. "What happened to her baby?" she asked.

Dana shrugged. "Gave it up for adoption, I guess."

Her disinterest was obvious. Clearly Dana had never been pregnant. Didn't understand a mother's all-consuming love. She also didn't seem to know anything about the money in Camila's dorm.

"I'll see you just before the eighth race," Dana went on. "Is your horse worth a bet?"

Eve blinked, struggling to get back on focus. She shouldn't be speculating about black market babies, not when she was trying to prepare Stinger for his race. And she still had to clean up the trailer and play area for Joey, enough to satisfy his very fussy godparents.

"This is Stinger's first start over a mile," Eve said. "He's always been a sprinter, mainly because he's headstrong and refuses to rate. But I've been working with him. And his dam won at a mile and an eighth."

Dana pulled a rumpled condition book from her back pocket. "Not much speed in your race," she said, scanning the page. "He could get an easy lead. Think I'll bet him."

"You might be the only one," Eve said. "Nobody thinks he can run past a mile, even my boss."

"Then why did you pick that distance?"

"Orders from above," Eve said, reluctant to admit Jackson's wife was calling the shots now. "But I've had four weeks to stretch him out."

Dana nodded. "I've seen your gallops. You've made sure he has enough air. If the pace is right, he'll win."

Eve stroked Stinger's neck. If he won, it would have to be considered an excellent weekend. Two wins from two starts. A hundred percent success rate. And since horses ran best when they were healthy and happy, it would be clear that Ashley and Miguel had also done their jobs. There was no way Jackson could justify firing staff with that kind of result, in spite of Victoria's prodding.

Dana knew all the horses at the track. She galloped some, ponied many, and also escorted on race days. Her analysis was more insightful than the track handicapper's. And she wasn't trying to be nice. She had no idea of the importance of Stinger's race.

Eve flipped her reins to the other side of Stinger's neck, wishing she could feel as confident. Hopefully he was ready. But he'd missed a critical day of training, and maybe there were a few mornings she should have worked him faster. Trainers relied on a mixture of experience, instinct and horse sense. But her experience was limited.

When she was a jockey, she'd climbed on and followed the trainer's directions. And morning gallops were also carried out in strict accordance with instructions. Of course, she gave feedback to Jackson. But this was the first time she had sole control over a horse's conditioning.

She'd tried to ask for advice but lately her boss had been unavailable. So it was hard to tell if Stinger was properly prepared. No one would know until the draining stretch run. That's why horse racing remained such a mystery.

However, she loved the challenge, even if it sometimes felt like balancing over a precipice. And Stinger felt ready. His ears were pricked, his walk bouncy and full of attitude. So maybe he could run beyond a mile, and bettors would be wise to pick him.

Time would tell.

She smiled at Dana, pumped now with the familiar anticipation of a competitive race. "I sure hope you cash that bet."

CHAPTER FORTY-FOUR

"Don't move," Juanita said, her scissors clicking perilously close to Rick's ear. "We need to fix you. Women prefer their men less hairy."

Maybe some women, Rick thought, his gaze on Eve who was standing by the barn, talking to the vet. But she'd never asked him to shave, or cut his hair or wear different clothes. Had barely flinched at his history. She saw beneath people, the same way she did with the horses. And despite the setbacks, her training skills were obvious.

Word around the track was that Stinger was a one-dimensional sprinter, and Victoria expected him to run dead last. Wanted to embarrass Eve.

But Rick had watched her gallops. Stinger had some stamina. More importantly, Eve had taught him patience. She was always riding him close to other horses, both behind and alongside, teaching him that it wasn't always necessary to be in front. And that he needed to wait for the rider's signal.

"You are a fine-looking man," Juanita went on, talking over the rapid click of her scissors. "But you've been hiding for a long time. *Si?*"

He made a non-committal sound. Her hands felt good against his scalp, and it was surprisingly pleasant sitting beneath the oak tree, watching his hair fall to the ground.

Maybe he had been hiding. A rough appearance kept people away. It was an effective way to avoid both relationships and questions. Although it hadn't been much of a barrier here. People at the track were different. Like Eve, they didn't put much stock in appearances.

But the little girl with the hot dog had definitely been intimidated. And the last thing he wanted was to scare Joey. It would be tough enough being around the kid. No need for them both to be terrified.

"Stop wiggling." Juanita pressed his head against her soft stomach. "I need you to look good. For the photo."

"Right," he said, trying to slow his suddenly hammering heart. Joey wasn't arriving for a few more hours. There was no need for panic. And Eve had thoughtfully set him up for a private conversation with Juanita. He needed to use this time wisely.

He pulled in a slow breath, then another. *Focus.*

"I saw a hair poster on Woody's bulletin board," he said, after a moment. "What's the name of your business?"

"Camila's Corner," Juanita said. She slapped some shaving cream on his jaw, then pulled a gleaming straight edge from her bucket. "We changed the name last night."

She went on to explain how the women had unanimously voted for the new name, even though it meant they had to change all the posters. He tilted his head further back, patiently waiting for a chance to move this conversation along.

Eve had surprised him with the news about Camila's pregnancy. Apparently the girl had wanted to keep it concealed. She'd done an effective job too, especially since the police and security guards had never mentioned it.

"Camila's Corner is a nice name," he said, once Juanita paused to take a breath. "I'm sure her family will be appreciative..."

"She doesn't have family, just a fifteen-year-old sister." Juanita dragged the straight edge over the side of his jaw, then bent and rinsed it in the second bucket. "Camila was helping her stay in school. Sending money when she could."

"Generous of her," Rick murmured. He crossed than uncrossed his legs, slightly uncomfortable. There'd be no more pay checks coming from Camila. And Eve was correct. It would be a long wait before the money found in her room was released. If the police determined it was from illegal proceeds, Camila's little sister would never see it.

"But that can still happen." Juanita's smile broadened. "Did Eve tell you what I found? All the money?"

He blinked, surprised Juanita was trusting him with the information. Of course, only Eve's barn and the security guards knew he was an investigator. "Yes," he said reluctantly. "She mentioned something."

"Over five thousand dollars," Juanita said. "So the girl will be able to finish her education after all." She waved an excited hand, filling the air with flecks of white soap. "That was Camila's last gift. A big one too. On Monday, Eve and I go to the bank."

Rick closed his eyes. Didn't want to look up at Juanita's relieved face. Eve had looked the same way. Heck, if Scott's business weren't involved, he'd probably whisk the money off to Guatemala too. But there could be other factors at play here.

"I heard Camila was pregnant," he said, filling his voice with nothing but idle curiosity. "Must be hard, giving up a baby."

Juanita's voice turned regretful. "A lot of girls do that. Until Eve arrived, there wasn't much hope. But Eve is so brave, so strong. She believes in us. And that makes us strong as well. Camila was just starting to understand that she had choices."

Rick opened his eyes and checked on Eve. She'd finished dealing with the vet and was now talking to the farrier. If she were paid by the hour, she'd be a millionaire. A trainer's job was never ending, the horses a constant source of worry. Yet she'd still found time to carve out an oasis for the mothers and children, sharing her knowledge and generous spirit. Now the women here were a more cohesive group.

Camila, though, had chosen to remain on the fringe. Some workers labeled her shy, others reserved. But she didn't seem to have any close friends, certainly none willing to talk to the authorities.

"There must be someone who was close to Camila," he said. "Someone who could help them figure out what really happened."

Juanita's hand stilled. "The police and security guards think Marcus killed her."

"Maybe," Rick said. "Maybe not. But they need to talk to him… wherever he is. And to her old boyfriend who returned to Mexico."

Juanita hissed with disgust. "That boyfriend knows nothing. He runs away. Doesn't even say good-bye. Too many men are scared of one little child."

Rick almost flinched. He didn't like this line of talk. Besides, he shouldn't be pursuing it anyway. Scott had ordered that he concentrate on Eve's barn. There was certainly no link between Victoria and Camila.

On the other hand, a young woman had been brutally murdered. And while the police were doing everything possible, the Hispanic community was too closed, too distrustful of authority. He was better positioned to dig out the truth.

He flattened his palms against his jeans and blew out a resigned sigh. The track community had become important to him and so, despite Scott's directions, he knew he couldn't let this go. The last time he'd followed orders that conflicted with his instincts, consequences had been tragic. And there was a randomness about Camila's death that left him uneasy.

Juanita wrapped her hand around his jaw. "Hold still," she said, before continuing with her complaints about Camila's boyfriend and how cowards always run.

He waited for her to take a breath, then forced a teasing smile, as if her words weren't eating at his self-esteem.

"Men run away?" he said. "All men? Or just from this track?"

"That is what they do here." Juanita scowled. "Now don't move." She laid the flat edge against the top of his lip, and it was clear she really meant 'don't talk.'

He waited until the blade was safely returned to the bucket and she was rinsing his jaw. "Do you know other women whose boyfriends left?"

Juanita nodded. "When things get tough, they run and hide. Afraid of the system. Sometimes people hide even when they're innocent... But that's only because they're scared."

Rick studied her face, those dark eyes that seemed so knowing. "A natural thing, to hide." He waited a beat, letting her feel his sincerity. "But the information they have can be important," he added. "Camila didn't own a phone so police can't trace her calls. But if someone found a name or number, perhaps when they were cleaning her room? Or if someone knew where Marcus was hiding, he could help answer these questions. Just in case the investigation is heading in the wrong direction..."

He watched Juanita's face. She'd come directly from her job in the kitchen, the hub of conversation, and the smell of bacon and coffee mingled pleasantly with the shaving cream.

"I could give you my private number," he went on. "Maybe Marcus could call. Let me know what really happened by that river. Just me. No police."

Juanita glanced over her shoulder. A horse nickered from the barn but otherwise the only sound was her ragged breathing. Then she sighed, her big bosom heaving.

"Eve trusts you," she said slowly. "And I trust Eve."

He kept his hands motionless on his lap, careful not to push.

"So I will pass on your message," she said. "But first you need to believe Marcus didn't do this terrible thing. Nobody knows who would beat a woman like that."

She wiped the straight edge, carefully wrapped it in a towel and placed it in her bucket. Then she turned back to him, her eyes blazing with a sudden ferocity. "But we want to know. We are family here. So we hope there is some punishment. Before the police are called. Only then might Marcus be found. Do you understand?"

"Yes," he said, "I do."

CHAPTER FORTY-FIVE

Eve checked Stinger's stall for the fourth time. His hay and water had been removed in preparation for the approaching race. A few hoof prints marked the new rubber on the wall, but otherwise he appeared to have stopped kicking. He flattened his ears now, looking sleek, shiny and ill-tempered.

Rick's familiar chuckle came from behind her. That man could move like a ghost.

"He doesn't have as much fun kicking a padded wall," Rick said. "Think he liked the noise. It made him feel tough."

"Let's hope he's tough enough to go the distance." She picked up a rake, saw the aisle was immaculate and set it back down. "Guess I'm a little nervous."

She glanced back at Rick, paused, then did a double take. He'd been with Juanita for less than an hour but the change was dramatic. His hair was businessman short now, and his face was clean shaven, further emphasizing his killer cheekbones and chiseled jaw. He was numbingly, strikingly handsome, and it was impossible not to gawk.

He gave a wry smile and rubbed a hand over his face. "I know you don't like conventional. And it feels weird. But I can grow it back. For now though, this is better."

She reached up, touching his smooth jaw where the skin was lighter than the rest of his face. Clearly it hadn't been exposed for a while. Just as clearly, he was too damn gorgeous.

"This is just so disappointing," she said slowly.

"Because I look like a cop?" Concern flickered in those grayish-blue eyes.

"No. Because you're much better looking than any of my horses. It will reflect badly on the stable." She struggled to keep a straight face. "It makes everything else look second rate. I expect Victoria will fire us all."

He stood very still as if aware she was teasing, but not quite sure why. She rose on her toes and planted a smiling kiss on his cheek, amazed he didn't realize how gorgeous he was. Better still, that he didn't seem to care.

His shoulders softened. "I'm glad you can laugh about that woman now," he said, wrapping her in his arms.

He smelled of leather and shaving cream, and she didn't want to move, even though it wasn't very professional for a trainer to be cuddling in the barn aisle.

"Did Juanita take a picture?" she asked, unable to resist reaching up and touching his jaw again.

"Several," he said. "She also confided a few things."

"Anything about Camila's baby?"

"She didn't know Camila well enough for that. Not many people did. But they do know where Marcus is."

"They know where he's hiding? And they didn't tell the police?" She jerked back, aghast. "But why? Everyone knows he's the killer."

"The Hispanic community doesn't think so." He paused. "I don't either."

"But you said Victoria wasn't involved. That Scott sent an agent to Santa Anita."

"That's right," Rick said. "And early indications are that Victoria hasn't had any contact with Marcus."

"But is the track safe?" Her voice rose. "Because Ashley walks alone at night. So does Miguel. And Joey's coming—"

Stinger slammed the wall. His hooves were muted by the thick rubber, but he snaked his head over the door, his annoyance clear. He did not like people hanging out in front of his stall, especially if they weren't carrying hay or grain.

She and Rick shuffled further down the aisle.

"Is it safe around here?" she repeated. "Are you going to look into this? What does Scott say?"

"He wants me to concentrate on you, especially since Joey will be here."

"But someone murdered Camila. We can't just forget about her. Or about the rest of the workers. Just because Scott ordered—"

Rick pressed a finger against her mouth. "It's okay," he whispered. "Doesn't matter what Scott thinks. I can't let this go."

She nodded with approval. He may have cut his hair but he still had a rebel's soul. And she had no doubt he'd find Camila's killer. And that he'd keep everyone safe.

Bristol stared toward the doorway, as if she'd heard something. Seconds later, car doors slammed and a boy's voice rang out.

"Joey's here," she said, twisting toward the door. His toy pony was still in the RV. She'd planned to have the present waiting on the chair by the barn, but he'd be just as excited to see real horses. And of course the orange cat would be a hit. The stray had taken up permanent residence since Rick's arrival.

She strode down the aisle and rushed outside.

Joey hadn't seen her yet. He stood by Megan, close to the fender of the silver Mercedes. He wore a white shirt that was surprisingly clean, a tiny pair of crisp jeans and tooled cowboy boots trimmed with black leather. And her heart felt like it would burst out of her chest.

Joey turned. "Mommy!" he called. Then he charged toward her, his arms and legs swinging like a windmill.

She sprinted forward and scooped him up.

"I missed you, honey." She pressed her mouth against his head, pulling in his familiar smell, trying not to squeeze too hard. They were going to have such fun. This was a rare chance for him to experience life on the backstretch, where they could be together from dawn to dark and far removed from Victoria's child ban.

He was already wiggling and she reluctantly set him down.

"I missed you too," he said. He stuck up one foot, almost losing his balance. "Like my new boots? They're just like Uncle Scott's."

"Very cool," Eve said. "You'll be able to ride a horse with boots like that. We have the perfect one here—"

"But I already did. And guess what!" He jumped up and down, his eyes sparkling. "I own a pony now! Her name is Bubbles and she's all mine. And I've been riding, just like you. She has to live at my other grandmother's house but I can see her whenever I want. Aunt Megan promised to drive me and she'll take Rex, so it's like I have a pony and a dog too."

"Wow…a pony. That's great." Eve managed a smile, but her chest gave a funny kick, and her face felt like it was cracking. She'd wanted to be the first person to lift her son on a horse, to experience the joy on his face. But of course, Megan had wanted that too. She saw a lot of her brother in little Joey.

Eve glanced at Megan and Scott. They'd obviously been shopping together. Scott's shirt matched Joey's, and his boots were the same designer brand. He was an attractive man, a good man—even a decent rider—but today she just wanted them to disappear.

"We stopped to eat," Megan said brightly, "so you wouldn't have to worry about Joey's lunch. And we brought some extra wraps, in case you or your grooms are hungry. We know you're busy with Stinger and don't want to get in the way."

"Thanks," Eve said, but her lower lip gave a little quiver. They were probably being thoughtful but it was also apparent they feared she'd be too preoccupied to feed Joey. Even though she'd rushed down the road and stocked up on kid friendly groceries. Cookies and peanut butter and white bread, but maybe she should have chosen whole wheat wraps and alfalfa sprouts.

"How's the horse?" Scott asked, moving around the car to stand beside Megan. They looked like a power couple, beautiful, loving…childless.

"Doing well," Eve said.

But nobody walked toward the barn. They all looked at Joey.

"It's a great place here," she said. "We have lots of grass and a sandpit. And an RV and a barbecue. Even a tire swing."

"Can I go on the swing, Mommy?" Joey grabbed her hand. "Please?"

"Sure," she said. "There are soccer balls too, and a net." But he was already running toward the swing, his legs churning.

"Looks like a nice setup." Scott swiveled, his cool eyes absorbing every detail.

"Rick hung the tire," Eve said. "Made the net. Even rounded up the soccer balls."

"Rick?" Scott turned back, his eyes widening. "Rick Talbot?"

She crossed her arms. Scott rarely acted surprised, always seemed composed, but his shock was apparent. Surely he didn't think Rick was lazy?

"Rick's always working," she said. "When he's not looking for barn thieves," she added, before he thought Rick might be neglecting his real job. "Thanks for sending him," she went on. "He's a big help. And I really needed him. Even when I thought I didn't."

"Probably the first time you ever admitted needing anyone." Scott's mouth lifted in a teasing grin. He looked surprisingly boyish and Eve couldn't help but smile back.

"Rick's helped a lot with Stinger too," she said. "He's the only groom your horse doesn't push around."

"Not surprising," Scott said. "Stinger isn't a complete idiot. Rick's my best man."

Eve's face turned warm. She jammed her hands in her back pockets and checked on Joey. He was already on the swing, one thin leg hooked around the tire, the other scuffing the ground. When Eve looked back, Megan was staring, her head tilted, astute eyes full of mischief.

"I've never met Rick," Megan said, her tone sweet and innocent. "He's your best man? In what way?"

"Lethal," Scott said. "Not someone you want to annoy. But he can go where others can't. And come out alive." He looked at Eve. "You made out okay? He wasn't too surly about being stuck here?"

"Not surly at all," Eve said. She didn't dare look at Megan. Sometimes she wished the woman wasn't so darn intuitive.

"Good." Scott gave a brief nod. "I didn't expect any trouble. But I'll re-assign him now that Joey's here."

"You don't have to do that," Eve said quickly. "Joey doesn't care what people look like. And besides, Rick had a haircut—"

"It's not about Joey," Scott said. "I simply can't ask Rick to be around children."

"Why?" Both she and Megan spoke at once.

Scott folded his arms, ignoring their question. "Snake will replace Rick. He needs some downtime and can watch Joey."

"But I already have a babysitter lined up," Eve said. "A capable woman named Juanita. And I don't need Snake. There's been no more thefts."

"Maybe nothing else has been stolen," Scott said. "But there is an unsolved murder. So I want Snake here to watch over…everyone." His voice hardened. "And if you find you're too busy, he can bring Joey back to LA. We'll look after him until your mother feels better. Or until you return."

Eve looked at Megan. But Megan only gave an apologetic shrug and stepped closer to Scott, clearly in accord with her husband.

"But I don't need you to arrange babysitters." She fought to keep her voice level. "And I'll have lots of time for Joey. My staff is top notch."

"Of course they are," Megan said soothingly. "But you need your time and energy for training. We only want to help. Especially since Victoria is determined to make you fail."

"Look at me, Mommy!" Joey called. He perched on top of the swing, both legs wrapped around the tire, his hands gripping the rope. "Come and push me."

She swallowed and glanced toward the barn. Stinger needed his legs wrapped, and a tongue tie, and the ring bit switched to his race bridle. And she needed to make sure his mouth was rinsed, just in case he'd managed to grab some hay. Rick was looking after the horse, but a trainer needed to supervise.

"Go and take care of Stinger," Megan said. "I'll look after Joey. We'll meet you in the paddock. Then we can watch the race together."

"Okay, thanks," she said, gratitude warring with resentment. Scott undoubtedly had good intentions. And his concern was rather sweet. But he was accustomed to directing aggressive men, and she didn't like anyone tossing out orders, especially in regard to her son.

Even more troubling was his inference that Rick couldn't, or shouldn't, be around Joey. Along with his announcement that Rick would be re-assigned. But maybe Rick had requested a new case. Maybe he didn't want to admit he was bored. After all, Scott should know. The men spoke at least twice a day.

Joey was spinning circles on the tire now, laughing and waving at Megan with every turn.

Eve shot her son a last wistful look then turned and trudged into the barn, frustrated, conflicted and confused.

CHAPTER FORTY-SIX

Eve laid the yellow saddle cloth on Stinger's back, smoothed out the wrinkles, and then followed with the jockey's tiny saddle. So far, Stinger was surprisingly tractable, his ears locked on the spectators jammed around the rail.

She stretched his front legs, making sure no skin was pinched by the girth. He usually acted up at this point, rearing and charging forward, impatient to race. But Rick distracted him by jiggling his bit, and Stinger forgot to throw his hissy fit.

She shot Rick a grateful smile. Maybe Scott was right, and the horse was smart enough not to mess with Rick. Whatever the reason, Stinger was a model of obedience.

Owners were allowed in the paddock and she'd half expected Scott to linger too close, making suggestions and getting in the way. But he remained on the grass beside Megan and Joey, not even approaching until Rick was leading Stinger around the enclosure.

"First time I've seen our horse look so composed," Scott said. "Think it will translate to the race?"

"I have no idea," she said. "He's never acted like this before."

Scott's eyes narrowed. "Any chance someone slipped him some drugs?"

"Not likely," she said. "Rick installed new surveillance cameras. And Stinger was his normal self earlier today. He yanked Ashley all around the grass. Her arm is still bruised from his teeth. I think his behavior is related to Rick's presence, rather than any drugs."

"Okay, good." Scott stared at Rick and Stinger, his gray eyes unreadable. He hesitated then his voice lowered. "You need to be cautious, Eve. He has issues."

She stiffened, realizing he was no longer talking about Stinger.

"If he leaves after all," Scott went on, "call and I'll send Snake."

She stepped back against the wall of the saddling stall. Scott was usually an incisive man. Today, though, he seemed to be talking in riddles.

"So Rick isn't leaving?" she asked. "You're not re-assigning him?"

"I can't assign him anything. Especially since he quit." Scott gave a rueful smile. "And he'll be damn hard to replace." His expression changed and he looked truly troubled. "I just wish you both luck."

Eve leaned against the wooden wall, struggling to sort through Scott's words. Rick had quit? The two men had been talking outside the barn, just before they led Stinger over. They'd nodded and shaken hands. She hadn't had a chance to talk with Rick about Scott's plans to replace him with Snake. Or even to ask Rick what he wanted. Had thought it best to wait until after the race.

But she had no idea what all this meant. In fact, her head was beginning to pound, as if too small for her muddled thoughts. All around, horses were prancing, people were babbling, and Joey tugged at Megan's hand, trying to get closer. And Scott just stared with that grave expression, and now the jockey was striding toward them, expecting coherent race instructions.

Eve pushed herself away from the wall, shaking her head. She needed to concentrate on Stinger now. She'd brought him here, and he deserved her full attention. But she couldn't dismiss Scott's words, his veiled warning. Couldn't ignore how it stoked her own misgivings.

She looked at Scott, knowing he'd either give a straight answer, or say nothing at all. "Why are you wishing us luck? Why do you think Rick will leave?"

"Because of Joey," Scott said.

The jockey apparently decided she'd waited long enough. "Hi," she said, stepping forward and reaching for Scott's hand. "I'm Julie West."

Julie shook his hand then strode over to Megan and Joey, including them in her polite round of greetings.

Eve stared at the tableau of horses and riders, feeling like she was a spectator. She knew Rick had an issue with children, but Scott spoke with such certainty. And not only was he a very intelligent man, but he also knew Rick's background.

And now it wasn't just her head that hurt. Worry wormed through the pit of her stomach, leaving her nauseous. She pressed a hand against her mouth, praying she wouldn't throw up.

"Riders up," the paddock judge called.

She swallowed and stepped forward on stiff legs. Rick and Stinger were circling in front of them. And Julie was looking at her, wondering how to ride the horse. And Eve knew she was a horrible trainer—just like Victoria said—because all she was thinking about right now was her son. And Rick.

"Guess you don't want me to fight with the horse," the jockey said, her voice encouraging. "I see you've taken off his blinkers. Anything else you want to tell me?"

Eve cleared her throat. There was plenty to tell Julie but only seconds left to do it. Stinger was a sprinter trying to run long. He disliked horses and people, but he was brave and full of fight.

"Maybe try to get him settled?" Julie added helpfully. "Save him for a run at the end?"

Eve nodded.

"I know it's hard to concentrate," Julie went on. "My husband says training is the hardest job of all. But I'll do my best for your horse. I've watched his replays and know he doesn't like to be crowded."

Eve struggled to control her nausea. "I've been working him with other horses," she managed. "He'll tolerate them better now. He should have a good finish."

"Your son is really cute. Love his boots." Julie gave Joey a jaunty thumbs up then turned toward Stinger. "We'll try hard to win so you can have a picture together."

"Great," Eve managed. She legged Julie into the saddle, galvanized by the jockey's empathy. She clearly thought Eve suffered from rookie trainer jitters. That she was paralyzed thinking about the race.

This was certainly a poor time to worry if Rick and Joey would ever get along. Besides, if Rick didn't have a job, he'd have to leave anyway. She certainly had no money to pay him.

She realized Rick was staring at her and averted her gaze. But he reached back and tugged her alongside him as he led Stinger into the tunnel.

"What's wrong?" he asked, his voice quiet but concerned.

She shook her head, determined to wait for a better time, when they were alone and could be honest. But it felt as if they were alone now, even as they passed through a gauntlet of spectators. Everyone stared at the horses and riders, not their handlers. Julie sat high in the saddle, knotting her reins and smiling at her fans as they called out encouragement.

Eve realized she was clutching her stomach and dropped her hand. "Scott just told me you'd quit," she said.

"That's right," Rick said, totally unabashed. He alertly tightened Stinger's lead line, stopping the horse from nipping a foolhardy fan who'd reached out to touch Stinger's neck.

"Don't you like working as a PI?"

"He wanted me on another case," Rick said simply. "I didn't want to leave you."

"Oh, I see," she said. "Well, that's good," she added. And relief drained the pressure from her head, and her stomach stopped flipping. She even managed to smile at a little girl with braces and a pink horse tattoo on her cheek.

So Scott was mistaken. Rick wasn't running from anything, least of all Joey. But she didn't want Rick to give up his job. They could work something out, maybe meet in LA, or between racetracks, or she'd simply wait for him to finish his next case.

"Scott's agency is supposed to be the best," she said. "He has his pick of people. Don't you want that job?"

"I have a good horse in one hand," Rick said. "A good woman in the other. There's really nothing else I want."

She tripped. Would have fallen in the tunnel if he hadn't supported her, helping her keep pace with Stinger's prancing walk. He handed the lead line to Dana, mounted on her steady escort horse, and Stinger smoothly joined the post parade.

Then it was only her and Rick. But her legs felt too awkward to move. Because this was even better than she'd hoped. Rick was good with animals but she'd always suspected he preferred motorcycles over horses.

She must have spoken out loud because he winked. "You're right," he said. "I don't need any horse. Just you."

She noticed he didn't mention Joey, but he hadn't had a chance to meet her son yet. Once he did, he'd realize Joey was a great kid. And he'd see how happy they all could be.

"Let's find Joey and the others." She grabbed Rick's hand, excitedly tugging him behind her. She zigzagged through the crowd, her nausea replaced with anticipation. She'd never introduced a man as her boyfriend before. Joey would be ecstatic. Lately he'd looked wistful when he spotted other kids laughing with their fathers in the park.

She hurried toward the rail. Scott and Megan had staked out a good spot across from the finish line. Ashley and Miguel stood to Megan's right and Joey was bouncing on his toes, clearly thrilled at his proximity to so many horses.

He pulled away from Megan and charged toward Eve, flashing his gap-toothed grin. "Mommy, your horse is nice and shiny, but he looks mean. He tried to bite the other horse but Uncle Scott said the leather pad stopped his teeth."

Eve laughed, released Rick's hand and gave Joey an impulsive hug. "He's just eager to run," she said. "And he's not my horse. I'm only the trainer. Scott and Megan own Stinger."

She gestured behind her. "Joey, this is Rick. He's the one who made Stinger so shiny. He's a good friend, he—"

She turned but Rick was no longer beside her. He stood on the other side of Miguel, staring intently at the parade of horses. But naturally he wanted to see how Stinger behaved in the post parade.

She forced herself to remain patient. In a few minutes the horses would start their warm up. There'd be a better time for introductions.

"Is Stinger's jockey as good as you?" Joey asked.

"Even better," she said, pulling her gaze from Rick. Maybe he didn't want to talk right now. A lot of people were nervous before a race, including her.

"I hope she doesn't break her arm. Like you did." Joey wiggled in front of her, his feet moving as rapidly as his thoughts. "When will the race start?"

"Ten minutes," she said. "They're warming up now. The starting gate is right in front of us."

"I can't see." Joey hopped up and down, trying to peer over the rail.

She and Megan smiled, but Scott reached in, scooped Joey up and placed him on his shoulders.

"I can see everything now," Joey said, his eyes widening. He gripped Scott's hair. It must have hurt but Scott didn't say a word. In fact, both boy and man were grinning with delight.

Eve swallowed. She'd waited ten days to see Joey, to touch him, to hold his hand. It wouldn't hurt to wait a little longer. In a few hours, Megan and Scott would be gone. They were kind enough to kid-sit so she could concentrate on her job. She couldn't have it both ways.

And it was clear Joey loved Scott's company. Why wouldn't he? Joey needed a father figure. Someone kind and strong and smart. She peeked at Rick.

He was even taller than Scott, with shoulders every bit as broad. But he didn't look at all inclined to balance Joey on his shoulders. Instead, he remained ten feet away, just staring across the track.

"He's gorgeous," Megan whispered, following her gaze. "Not what I expected at all… Not based on what Scott said."

"He had a shave and hair cut," Eve said. She paused. Didn't want to pump for information. That wasn't fair, to Megan or Rick. Besides, Scott was tight lipped about company personnel. Megan probably didn't know much.

But the questions circled in Eve's head, clamoring to get out, and she couldn't keep her mouth shut. "What do you know about Rick?" she whispered. "What did Scott say?"

"Nothing." But Megan touched her earring, a sure sign she was flustered.

Eve's mouth tightened. "I think he's a really good guy."

"Of course he is. We just don't want you to get hurt."

She stared into Megan's familiar eyes, so like her brother's. There was no doubting her integrity. Megan had supported Eve from the day they met. True, her driving interest had been in little Joey, but she'd proven time and time again to be a rock solid friend.

Eve pulled in a resolute breath. "Then tell me what I need to know," she said, "so I don't get hurt."

"Isn't it obvious?" Megan's voice was gentle. "Look where he's standing. Has he even talked to Joey yet?"

"That's not fair. He was busy in the barn when you arrived. And then he had to take care of Stinger."

Megan just looked at her, her beautiful face full of sympathy. "Scott says Rick has an over-developed sense of responsibility. And there are things in his past he can't let go. No matter how hard he tries."

"The horses are approaching the gate," the announcer blared.

Eve pulled her head away and stared at the starting gate. Stinger looked blurry. She blinked several times, trying to rid her eyes of the annoying dust. The horse appeared on the muscle, yet composed. Rick had taught Stinger a little bit about respect, and he didn't even try to strike the assistant starter.

"You're wrong," she said, turning back to Megan. "Rick hung the swing, bought the soccer net. He's trying to make it nice for Joey. He wants this, just as much as I do."

"It's not that he doesn't want it," Megan said. "But he can't handle it. And you deserve more... Joey deserves more." And though her voice remained compassionate, there was a hint of steel in her voice. A warning.

"Hey." Ashley squeezed up beside them, waving her hand and brandishing two betting stubs. "Stinger has been behaving so well that I bet another twenty bucks. We can add any winnings to Camila's fund."

Eve made an agreeable noise in her throat. At twelve to one odds, Stinger was probably a decent bet. A longshot with a chance. Dana and Julie had warmed him up perfectly, keeping him composed and cooperative. Julie looked relaxed as the horse walked into the gate, and Stinger seemed to appreciate her nonchalance. He stood motionless, waiting for the doors to spring open.

This was an exciting time, the moment they'd all worked for—every one of her staff. But she felt empty.

She glanced once more at Rick, willing him to look at her. At Joey. But he just stared at the horses. Every time he acted weird it had been when there were children around. And she couldn't deny it any longer. Kids were his kryptonite.

"They're off!" the announcer called.

She swung her gaze back to the starting gate. Stinger burst from the four hole. But the number two horse was even quicker and shot to the front. For a moment it looked like Stinger would challenge for the lead. She could see Julie coaxing him, trying to persuade him to settle. But she didn't have a hammer hold on his face, wasn't turning it into a big battle. And by the time they entered the first turn, Stinger had relaxed and settled into fourth, running beside a white-faced bay on the rail. Running easy.

Eve blew out an admiring breath. The horse usually refused to conserve his speed. But today he was letting the jockey position him, seeming to understand that the rider knew best.

"I've never seen him rate like that," Megan said. "Thought he only knew one way to run."

Julie's reins were so loose they were almost flapping. Yet Stinger wasn't taking advantage and charging to the front. Instead, he galloped smoothly behind the front-runners, biding his time.

"She's an amazing rider," Eve said.

"Yes," Megan said. "But you taught Stinger patience."

"Rick helped," Eve said. "He showed Stinger he couldn't always be the boss."

She kept her gaze on the galloping horses. Julie was a better jockey than she'd ever been. But Eve's riding background certainly helped with training, and it left her with a sense of accomplishment. Maybe despite everything, she would make a good trainer.

"Run faster!" Joey called, wiggling from his perch on Scott's shoulders. "Pass those horses now, Stinger."

Stinger and Julie seemed to hear him. By the quarter pole, they'd moved up to the leader's flank, so effortlessly Eve's confidence swelled. If he could just keep running, he might hang on for second. Jackson would have to be happy, and so would Stinger's loyal owners.

She glanced sideways. Megan and Scott were both cheering but their incredulity was obvious. Clearly they hadn't expected their sprinter to handle the increased distance. But they hadn't once voiced any concern. They'd stood back and allowed her to train their horse. And even though they were interfering with Joey, she couldn't help but be grateful.

She could feel Ashley beside her, leaping up and down as Stinger thundered down the stretch. But Eve didn't look at her, or at Rick again. She was a trainer now and she needed to keep her eyes on the horse. Julie waved her whip once and it seemed Stinger had been waiting for her signal.

There was no question he had plenty in reserve. The two frontrunners were slowing and Stinger blew past them, widening the gap between him and the rest of the field. He crossed the wire a length in front, with Julie rising in the stirrups and patting his neck.

"I think he won!" Joey called, his voice gleeful.

And then Megan was hugging her, and Ashley too, and they were all jumping by the rail.

"Nice training job," Rick said into her ear. Then he looped the lead line over his shoulder and walked out to greet the horse.

"Do you win a trophy, Mommy?" Joey asked.

"Just money," she said. And even though most of it would go to the owners, she shared a relieved smile with Ashley and Miguel. Because the bonus Jackson had promised meant they'd just earned more from Tizzy and Stinger then they had after three weeks of work.

"Congratulations," Eve mouthed to them. And then she gestured for the Viper to join them in the winner's circle. Dana's steady gelding had been instrumental in teaching Stinger tolerance, and she wanted all his connections in the win picture.

Eve reached up for Joey, ignoring Scott's frown. Scott reluctantly lifted her son off his shoulders and set him on the ground by her feet.

"Let's meet Stinger in the winner's circle," she said to Joey. "Now I get to stand by you, instead of always being on the horse's back."

"I like this way better," Joey said, gripping her hand.

"Me too," she said.

CHAPTER FORTY-SEVEN

"Anyone still hungry?" Rick asked, expertly flipping a sizzling steak to the back of the barbecue.

"Are there any hotdogs left?" Joey scrambled off the swing and bolted to the grill. "I like those best."

"Don't run around the barbecue," Rick snapped. "It's not safe."

Eve stiffened. She felt Megan's accusing eyes, saw her son's hurt.

"Sorry." Joey kicked at the dirt with the toe of his cowboy boot. "I'm not hungry anyway." He scuffled back to the swing, his tiny shoulders slumped.

"Let me push you, buddy," Scott said, striding over to the swing. "Five more minutes, and then Aunt Megan and I have to go."

"Wish you could stay," Joey muttered. "And sleep in the RV with me and Mommy. Not *him*."

Eve couldn't hear Scott's low answer. Her face was too hot with anger, resentment and regret. It wasn't as if Rick was deliberately being mean. On the contrary, he seemed to obsess about Joey's safety. So much that Joey couldn't do anything right.

The meal was supposed to be a celebration. But it had been impossible for Rick to avoid Joey, and the results had been disastrous. If it hadn't been for Rick's pained expression and the wistful way he kept looking at Joey, she would have been even more furious.

She rose from the table and pried the barbecue tongs from Rick's tight hand. "Thanks for cooking. But it's probably time for you to check the horses."

He gave a lazy shrug of indifference but his eyes were so full of defeat, she felt like crying.

"Good idea," he said. He strode toward the barn, covering the ground with unusually jerky strides.

Eve turned and dropped the extra food onto a plate. Joey was laughing again, delighted with the tire swing and how Scott was spinning him in tight spirals. The tire was the perfect size, hung at exactly the right height. Rick clearly knew what a young boy liked.

He just couldn't be around them.

Megan rose from the table, her eyes grave. "What are you going to do?"

Eve swallowed, her throat too thick to talk. She pretended to be engrossed with rescuing a blackened hotdog from the side of the grill. Rick had burnt some food, probably so he had an excuse to feed the orange cat. The animal had long since wandered off, his belly rounded and content.

"What a waste," she muttered, studiously scraping burnt particles off the grill.

"Maybe he just needs more time," Megan said. "There's a Wounded Warrior program that uses retired racehorses. It's supposed to be effective for post traumatic stress."

Eve's hand was shaking, and she laid down the tongs. "Did someone die? Was it a child? Please tell me."

"It was one of his cases." Megan blew out a resigned sigh. "Scott won't say much. Just that it was the reason Rick quit the LAPD. And that he still feels responsible."

"He likes to look after everyone," Eve said. "People, horses, cats. He's just not so good with kids."

"He can't help it," Megan said. "What he's been through. He was sweating when Joey sat beside him. Even his hands were shaking."

"I know." A numbing despair spread through Eve's chest. "It's hard on everyone. Joey doesn't understand."

"At least you both tried," Megan said. "Scott said it was huge that Rick even cut his hair. He'd more or less retreated from polite society."

Eve's heart twisted. They both had tried. But maybe they could keep seeing each other, and she'd just keep him away from Joey. Give him time to heal. And that might work for her and Rick, but it certainly wouldn't help Joey.

She looked at her son, grinning up at Scott. Ketchup stained the side of his mouth, and his shirt was dirty and clearly he'd had a very fun day. He didn't ask for much, just a little attention. And a father figure.

"Scott would love to see more of Joey," Megan went on. "I know you don't have much interest in the jewelry business, but you could learn. And it would be a steady income. You'd be free of Victoria."

Eve closed the lid of the barbecue. She couldn't imagine life without horses. They'd always been her passion. She barely noticed jewelry, not even the shiny silver stuff around Megan's neck or the pretty green things swinging from her ears. She was more interested in types of race shoes and the size of the nails and the beautiful way a horse stepped out when his feet were feeling good.

But tonight everything seemed bleak. And a responsible mother needed a steady income. She glanced at Joey, and her heart gave that familiar kick of pure love. And she knew there wasn't anything she wouldn't do for him.

"Your jewelry is nice," she said slowly. "And I like the silver necklace you gave me. Do you still sell on the Internet? I wouldn't have to work in a store or anything?"

"No. Everything is online. But demand is growing. And I need to oversee the quality."

Eve stared dubiously at her fingers. She had good hands with a horse, a rider's hands. But she could barely thread a needle. And the idea of sitting inside a cramped room for hours at a time, doing some mumbo jumbo with silver and pointed tools almost made her stomach heave.

But she would have a steady income. And a boring but safe job. Besides, it was for a good cause since most profits from the Megan Spence Collection were donated to troubled teens. Megan had even set up a jockey fund in her brother's memory. That was certainly worth supporting.

"It would be good for everyone," Megan said. "Promise me you'll think about it."

Eve squeezed her eyes shut. Then she squared her shoulders and looked into Megan's hopeful face. "I will," she said.

CHAPTER FORTY-EIGHT

"Stinger has a cut on the inside of his left front ankle," Ashley said, stepping into the RV. "Rick doesn't think it's anything to worry about but he wanted you to know."

And he didn't want to come and tell me himself, Eve thought. She automatically poured Ashley a glass of water.

Ashley took the glass and plunked down at the kitchen table across from Joey. "Is that your bedtime snack?" she asked, eyeing Joey's carrot sticks.

"Yeah. And you can have some." He pushed the plate toward her. "Because I have lots."

"Thanks." Ashley snagged a piece of carrot. "I need to eat more of these. The guards don't have them around much. But I like them."

"Me too," Joey said happily. "And so does my pony. My real pony, not the one Mommy gave me."

"You have a real pony?"

He gave a crooked grin. "Yes, she's pretty and has white spots. But I can't keep her at my apartment. She has to live at the ranch where Aunt Megan lived when she was little."

"Wow, that's cool you have your own pony." Ashley crunched her carrot and glanced at Eve. "You're so lucky to have Scott and Megan. Wish I had godparents like that."

Eve gave a tight nod and continued rinsing the dishes. The toy pony she'd bought had been largely ignored. Joey had held it for a few seconds, pressed its belly once, then tossed it aside. But she understood his disinterest. A stuffed pony could never compete with the real thing.

"I need to give you the money we made betting." Ashley reached into her pocket and pulled out a crumpled wad of cash. "Eight-two dollars. Thank you, Stinger. Want me to stick it in the box Juanita left?"

"Better not," Eve said. "We're sending the fund through the bank. And Rick wants to check the contents again before the box is mailed."

"Looking for something, like a clue?"

"Camila had a diary. Kept daily notations of the horses she looked after. He wants to read through it in case there's something else."

"Well, you better take this money before I spend it." Ashley rose and pressed the bills into Eve's hand. "And tomorrow afternoon, I can stick around. Maybe take Joey over to barn nineteen and see the pot-bellied pig."

Joey's eyes widened. "I've never seen a real pig."

"Good. Then it's a date." Ashley reached out and gave him a high five. "We'll even take the pig something to eat. Something yucky that we don't mind sharing. Certainly not delicious carrots."

Eve gave a grateful smile. Everyone was being helpful, trying to make sure Joey enjoyed his stay. And Ashley was surprisingly good with kids.

"I can take him up to an hour," Ashley whispered, as she headed out the door. "After that, my patience disappears. That's why I don't know what to do. Liam says I have options. I only know that sometimes I want to keep this baby." She flattened her hand over her protruding belly. "Other times I'm thinking adoption is best."

You're going to have to decide soon, Eve thought, but refrained from voicing the words. She'd grown accustomed to Ashley's flip flopping. And pushing never helped. It was a monumental decision, made harder by financial constraints.

Luckily the horses had won this weekend. Not only would Ashley earn her eight hundred dollar salary but she'd also have a bonus this month.

"When will Jackson send our money?" Ashley paused in the doorway, as if reading Eve's mind. "He must be happy. Think he'll let us stay?"

"I left a bunch of messages," Eve said. "But I haven't talked to him yet."

He hadn't returned her calls, hadn't even commented on the win photo, but on the positive side Victoria hadn't picked up his phone.

"I'm sure he watched the replays," Eve added. "He must be proud of Tizzy and Stinger. And you and Miguel."

"Heard he lost a big owner yesterday," Ashley said. "Someone who had a public run-in with Victoria. Doesn't sound like she's helping his business much."

Eve gave a reluctant nod. According to her contacts, Victoria's unpleasantness hadn't been restricted to employees, and owners were definitely grumbling.

"After this meet is over," Eve said, "and we go back to Santa Anita, we might have to find other work. I figure we have a month or two. Maybe after the baby, you can ride for another stable."

"But what will you do?" Ashley's concerned gaze shot to Joey who was totally absorbed with dipping carrots in his glass of milk.

"Megan has a successful jewelry line. She said she needs help."

"That would totally suck." Ashley's eyes widened with horror. "I'd die away from the track."

Something in Eve's chest felt like it was dying too, but she forced a shrug. "At least Joey will be secure. And I'll have lots of nice jewelry."

"Except for a little silver necklace," Ashley said, "you don't even wear the stuff."

She yanked open the door, tramped down the three metal steps, then turned at the bottom. "Victoria really messed things up for everyone. How about I ask Liam about jobs for you and Miguel? He has lots of influence here."

"Ask about Miguel," Eve said. "He'd be a great pee catcher. He's good with horses. Loyal and steady."

Ashley smiled, but it was rather sad. "For once, you better worry about yourself. Because I can't see you happy sitting at a table stringing beads."

She shook her head and headed back toward the barn.

Eve closed the door, balled the dishrag in her hands, and tossed it into the sink. She didn't think she'd be stringing beads, more like jewels and feathers, although it probably didn't matter. And then she realized she hadn't even cared enough to ask.

"I can't wait to see the pig with the big belly," Joey said. A piece of orange carrot was stuck between his front teeth. "That lady's nice."

"Everyone here is nice." Eve picked up his empty plate.

"Not that big man. He's mean."

She yanked on the tap and rinsed the plate. There was no need to ask who Joey was talking about. "Rick's nice," she said. "He's just not used to children."

"Well, I don't like him. Can I sleep with the light on?" Joey asked, his mind already flipping to a different subject.

She wished it were that easy for her. "Of course," she said. "Rick left you a night light. It's in the shape of a soccer ball."

She reached for the bag on the counter, remembering his words earlier that day. 'There's no skylight in the spare bedroom,' he'd said. 'And it's really dark at night. Joey might not admit it, but he may want this.'

He'd placed the bag on the counter and then kissed her. And his concern was so genuine, and she thought everything would work out. But that was eight hours ago, before Joey arrived. Before it was apparent Rick didn't want anything to do with him. And that was his loss because Joey was the best kid in the world.

She stooped and gave Joey a heartfelt hug. He smelled of fresh air and soap and beloved boy, and it was impossible not to squeeze too tightly. "I'm glad you're here," she whispered.

"Me too, Mommy." He waited a polite moment before squirming away. "I better take my horse to bed with me." He grabbed the toy off the chair. "So he doesn't get scared being here alone."

Eve smiled.

Gravel crunched and she glanced out the window. A security vehicle pulled up in front of the barn, its engine running. She didn't like how the exhaust spewed so close to the barn door, but seconds later Ashley slipped into the passenger seat, and the Jeep rolled away. Liam might not be sensitive to air quality for the horses, but at least he was conscientious about keeping her staff safe.

She turned away. She didn't know where Rick planned to sleep tonight but it was obvious he was avoiding the RV.

Two hours later, long after she'd eased out of Joey's bed, a low rap sounded.

She rose from the kitchen table and pulled open the door. Rick stood on the steps. The light cast a shadow over his face and all she could see was his chiseled jaw. His mouth was hard and stern, and he looked more like a cop than any of the security guards.

"I need to pick up Camila's box," he said. "But not the money. You should send that to Guatemala. Quick as you can."

"Thanks." She gave a wobbly smile, but he didn't return it. In fact his mouth turned even more grim.

"Did you know it was me before you unlocked the door?" he asked.

"The door wasn't locked."

"It should be," he said. "Victoria may be neutralized but Camila's killer is still at large."

She swallowed back her hurt, not wanting to admit she'd left it unlocked in case he wanted to come and talk. Or even just to slip in later and have a more comfortable place to sleep. The two bedrooms were occupied but the kitchen bench folded into a bed. And it was his RV.

"Victims are often a product of their own negligence," he added, his voice clipped.

"There's no need to talk like a cop," she said, "just because you had a haircut."

She caught a glimmer of a smile before his face blanked. Clearly, he was shutting her out, along with Joey, but probably it was easier that way. After all, it wasn't a cop she'd fallen in love with.

"The box is still in the closet." She jabbed a thumb over her shoulder. "But I need to talk to you about this RV. It's not fair we're driving you out, but I was hoping you'd let us use it for the week. After Joey leaves, I'll move back in with Ashley. I'll pay you, of course, once Jackson sends our bonus money."

She tried to sound upbeat. But from what she'd heard, Jackson and Victoria were squabbling over every dollar. "I hope to pay you sometime soon," she added, squaring her shoulders. "You don't have a job either, and neither of us knew it would go like this—"

"Don't, Eve. I'm sorry. But I just can't do this. Not with him."

Something inside her withered, his bald statement killing any last kernel of hope. But she gave a nonchalant shrug, hiding that part of her had hoped they'd find a solution, some therapy that might help.

"It doesn't matter," she said. "Joey and I will be fine without you."

"Probably," he said. "But I won't."

She'd been trying hard to hold it together, but his bleak honesty made her crumble. And then she saw the spasms in his throat and realized he was feeling this every bit as much as her. Maybe more.

"I d-don't understand." Both her façade and voice broke at the same time. "Please, help me understand."

He'd been standing by the door, not leaving but not coming in either. But in seconds, he was up the steps and beside her. "I don't understand either." He buried his face in her hair. "I thought it would be all right. Thought I could do it. Want to do it. But my body shuts down. I can't breathe, can't think. When I get around children, around Joey, I just see them…" He stopped and shook his head.

"See them how?"

"I see them dead."

She recoiled. He immediately dropped his arms, his face turning to granite, and it was apparent her reaction had hurt him. But she didn't want him picturing Joey dead. She had a superstitious fear it might come true.

"That must be awful," she managed. And then the full import hit her. It must be utter agony. Especially for someone who cared about people as much as Rick.

Empathy swept away her aversion, and she reached out and hugged him. Could feel the pounding of his heart, his ragged breathing. He'd been living with this for two years. No wonder he preferred working the streets. But he shouldn't have been left alone to deal with it, and her anger swelled. "I can't believe the police department didn't provide support."

"They tried." He shook his head, his voice weary. "They have a list of approved therapists, specialists entrusted to hear details about their cases. Nothing helped."

"But maybe different doctors, different therapy—"

He placed a finger over her mouth, his eyes lifeless. "You deserve better. So does Joey."

They were almost the exact words Megan had spoken earlier. But coming from him they were even more heartbreaking. His finger traced her cheek, as if memorizing her face. "You ever need anything," he said gruffly, "anyone ever gives you trouble, you let Scott know. He'll be able to find me. And I'll come, fast as I can."

She didn't realize she was crying until she felt the wetness of his thumb. Didn't know how long they stood linked in the doorway before she could gather enough composure to speak.

"What will you do?" she asked.

"Probably head to Sacramento. A friend there needs some help with an Aryan gang."

The cynical part of her wondered if that had been the reason he cut his hair. Changed his look. Maybe he'd been preparing to run away, or at least been assembling a backup plan. He was a detail man. And his short hair and bike would make him a hit with the Aryans.

"So you're going to stay undercover?" she asked, desperation turning her words clipped. "Keep relationships short. Run from kids the rest of your life?"

The muscles in his arms tensed. "You don't understand."

"No," she said. "I don't."

"He…Ben, was only six."

"Ben was a relative?"

Rick shook his head. "Gang president's son. I was around a lot." He paused. She held her breath, not daring to move, her hands still splayed around his taut arms.

He took such a deep breath, his shirt molded around the ridges of his chest. "I'd been riding with that biker gang for almost nine months," he said. "My job was to find out who bought their stolen motorcycles. Gather enough evidence for convictions. I was handy with fixing things and after a while the gang trusted me. The president had a garage full of rebuilt bikes. I became their mechanic. Was there almost every day, stripping the Harleys, adding parts…babysitting." He paused, shaking his head, as if trying to wipe away the memories.

Then he started talking again, his voice detached, as if speaking about the weather. "Ben loved the bikes. Always wanted to help. His little hands would get so dirty. When we'd finish a job, he'd wipe them on Spike, the Rottie, but it never helped. Both the dog and kid would end up covered in grease, and his parents would get annoyed. Sometimes Ben and the dog were too dirty to be allowed inside so they'd curl up and sleep on the garage floor. I built a little bunkhouse in the yard so he'd always have a safe place." Rick swallowed, the only sign of emotion.

"By the ninth month, I'd gathered enough intel to put the gang away. They weren't heavy hitters, dabbling in theft, drugs, prostitution. But they were moving into tougher territory, from selling guns on the street to bigger players. They even worked a deal swapping three bikes with the Angels for some clean semis from Mexico. Brass was ecstatic, thinking they'd nail two gangs at the same time.

"They were nice bikes," Rick went on. "Two were custom built with Harley engines. Ben helped polish them up. I wanted to stay, but the police didn't want me around for the actual sale, afraid an unpatched mechanic might spook the Angels. So I told the president I had to meet with my parole officer.

"It was suppertime when I came back. The radio was on in the garage, the side door open. I thought Spike would smell the hamburgers I brought and come running. He and Ben always liked the same food.

"He didn't come out," Rick said. "I called the dog when I walked into the garage. But he never came."

Rick looked over Eve's head, staring at a spot on the wall, his voice turning even flatter. "At first it was hard to see. The three bikes had disappeared, but the president and another member were still there. Their eyes were open but the backs of their heads were gone. And the floor didn't look greasy anymore. It was just red.

"I ran into the house, calling Spike and Ben. But no one was there. His wife was in Vegas. I found the dog in a trail of blood by the bunkhouse. He did his best but—"

Rick's voice broke and he squeezed Eve so hard it hurt. "I'd hidden a camera in the garage. Caught it all. When they argued about the price, the deal went south. They didn't intend to kill Ben, but he and the dog had been in the bunkhouse. They wandered in at the wrong time. Turned out that bunkhouse wasn't safe at all.

"The Angels buried him back behind the trees. Thought no one would mourn two bikers but knew there'd be an uproar about a child."

Eve's nose was running along with her eyes. "You couldn't have stopped it."

"Maybe. Maybe not. But at least I could have tried."

"But you can't keep carrying the blame." She mopped at her eyes. "It's not your fault."

He just looked at her, his face so resigned it was clear he'd heard those words before. And they hadn't helped.

"I'll sleep in the barn." He dropped his arms and backed through the door and onto the top step. "I'm hoping to talk to Marcus tomorrow. Finish this up before I go."

She watched with blurry eyes as he turned away. "You won't leave though," she called, her voice breaking, "Not without saying good-bye?"

He didn't answer. In fact, he was in such a hurry to escape, he forgot to take Camila's box.

CHAPTER FORTY-NINE

Eve kept her reins loose and relaxed as she rode Bristol back toward the barn. The bossy bay mare was a bit lazy but she'd galloped strongly and appeared to be ready for her race on Wednesday.

Joey was playing with Juanita by the picnic table but he didn't look up, too engrossed with trying to balance a soccer ball on his knee. His teeth gleamed a brilliant white, and it seemed like the smile hadn't left his face. So far, his first morning here had been perfect.

Almost perfect.

She glanced sideways, checking for Rick's black and silver motorcycle. It wasn't in its usual spot, but his backpack and the extra helmet were still on the chair by the barn. Part of her was relieved. But another part wanted him gone so that the gaping hole in her chest would have a chance to heal.

At least the animals would keep her busy. She could almost pretend this was her barn, and she wasn't just an assistant on temporary assignment. If the horses kept running well, she wouldn't have to make jewelry. And she'd be able to pay Ashley and Miguel better wages. Having more stability might help Ashley reach a decision about her baby.

It was challenging raising a child alone, but Ashley didn't need a man. Neither did Eve. Maybe if a guy came along who was smart and fun and liked horses and made every part of her tingle, well, that might be a man worth keeping. She certainly didn't need someone like Rick who feared every child around him might die.

But just thinking of the love they'd found, then lost, made her tighten the reins in despair. And she couldn't bear to look at his pitifully small pile of belongings, packed and waiting on the chair.

Ashley rushed from the barn, as usual forgetting to call out, and the mare's head rose in alarm. Ashley gave an apologetic shrug and reached for the reins. "After I cool Bristol out," she said, "I'll take Joey over to see the pig."

Her eyes narrowed on Eve's face. "It must have been dusty out there. Your eyes are all red."

"Yes," Eve said. "Tomorrow I'll wear goggles." She dismounted and unsnapped her helmet.

The Viper had been even more blunt. 'Those better not be tears,' she'd said. 'Not after winning two races in one weekend.'

And of course Eve was happy about winning. It was especially gratifying that she'd done it without much help from Jackson. She still had three more horses scheduled to race, with high hopes for all of them.

Two wins wouldn't draw much recognition. But if the rest of the barn performed well, maybe Jackson would send her more horses. In fact, if he wanted time to fix his marital problems, he might let her stay here indefinitely and train.

That would be ideal. They wouldn't have to deal with Victoria's vindictiveness, Jackson could sort out his affairs and Eve would have more time to prove she was competent.

As a trainer, she didn't qualify to rent her own dorm room. They were assigned to grooms and hotwalkers. However, there must be affordable apartments close by. With Juanita's help, she could find a school and a good babysitter. She could be with Joey, make a little money…and not ache so much about Rick.

She unbuckled the girth then turned to Ashley. "Would you like to stay at this track?" she asked. "And ride here after your pregnancy?"

"Definitely." Ashley's head pumped with enthusiasm. "Then I wouldn't have to compete against big circuit riders, and I might become a top jock. At first, I didn't like it here. But this place has grown on me. The people are the best."

She had the grace to flush, and they both looked at Joey and Juanita playing beneath the protective shade of the oak tree. Juanita was tossing the soccer ball to Joey, who caught it on his knee, managing to bounce it twice before it rolled to the ground.

"I'm not sure if I want to join the parent club though," Ashley added. "Liam told me trainers don't like to ride jockeys who have babies. They worry about accidents. That's why male jockeys do a lot better."

Eve fought a flare of annoyance. "That's not true. I'd still use you."

"But most trainers aren't as supportive. And you're not a full trainer either. You work for Jackson."

"Yes." Eve pulled off her saddle. "And it takes time to build a clientele. But maybe Jackson will send me more horses. Rumor is that Victoria wants a divorce. There's a good chance he'll want to spread out his stable while he sorts things out."

"That would be awesome." Ashley reached up and scratched Bristol's damp neck. "Maybe Victoria was a blessing in disguise. She certainly can't cause any more problems now that everyone knows her game."

A white horse van rumbled down the road. It stopped in front of the barn close to where Miguel was emptying a wheelbarrow. Two men in blue coveralls stepped out, scaring the orange cat who arched his back in alarm, then scooted away.

"Looking for Eve Lewis," the driver called.

"You found her," Eve said. She stepped forward, shifting her saddle to the other arm, and met the man halfway across the grass.

He shoved a clipboard in her hand. She stared down at the typed sheet, scanning the Thoroughbred names, not their affectionate barn names, but their rarely-used race handles. Names like I'm Naturally Grey, Sugar Daddy, Oeste Wildfire and Bristol's Millie.

"What's this?" she asked, her mouth turning dry.

"We're picking up four horses." The man's voice roughened with impatience. "The animals are named below, along with all the required authorizations."

She pressed the clipboard to her chest, didn't want to look at the official papers stating the horses had been transferred to another trainer. "So everyone's going but Tizzy and Stinger," she managed.

Ashley groaned, but Eve didn't turn around. Couldn't. Her knees felt weak, as if in danger of buckling. Not only was Rick leaving but now their barn family was being ripped apart. The horses weren't going back to Jackson but to another trainer, where somebody else would oversee their feed, their exercise, their every mood. Someone else would help Banjo's sore back heal and clip Sugar Daddy's beautiful head and teach Bristol that she couldn't duck through the gap.

She'd given each horse her best, and they'd given her more, as horses do, and the pain of their loss was staggering.

"I just finished riding that mare," she said, her voice stronger than her legs. "She needs to be cooled out before she goes on any trailer."

"All right," the driver said. "But we'll load the other three now."

She squeezed her eyes shut. She should have anticipated that owners would move their horses. Nobody would put up with Victoria when there were so many other capable trainers around. And for a moment she felt sorry for Jackson. But only briefly.

Because when she opened her eyes she saw the shattered expressions of Ashley and Miguel. They were just as attached to these animals. Behind them her son was now burying the soccer ball in the sand, oblivious to the significance of the horse van.

And then the magnitude of the loss really hit, and her breath caught in a painful gasp. Because they weren't only losing four friends. Her business had just been destroyed. And the fact that others still depended on her for their livelihood left her feeling alone, helpless and totally terrified.

CHAPTER FIFTY

"Where are all the horses?" Joey asked, peering out from the feed room.

Eve bent over the grain bag, avoiding looking down the lonely aisle. Only two stalls were occupied. And Tizzy and Stinger kept poking anxious heads over their doors, clearly upset about the disappearance of their friends.

"Their owners sent them to a different track." She rationed out a second scoop of oats. "They're fine but they'll be trained by someone else."

"Good," Joey said. "Now you have more time to play. Can we go back and see the pig? Why did we have to leave the pig's barn so fast?"

"Ashley had to go with Miguel to the race office." Her voice was a little unsteady. "So we needed to feed the horses their lunch."

She made a fervent wish that someone there could help Ashley and Miguel find a job, along with a place to sleep. Maybe Rick would help. She didn't want to ask for anything else, but when he returned she was determined to swallow her pride. He knew almost every trainer on the grounds. Surely some other barn would have an opening. Track workers only qualified for dorm accommodation if they had a current job. Ashley and Miguel had literally been left in the cold.

She pulled in a pained breath, then blew it out, trying to hide her distress. When she spoke again, her voice sounded almost normal. "I just have to make one more call. Then we'll grab our lunch. After that, we can go back and see the pig. Maybe we'll take him an apple."

Joey gave a satisfied nod and wandered down the aisle.

She fed Tizzy and Stinger, then punched Jackson's number. As before, it went to voice mail. She left another message, her fifth today. But his silence spoke volumes. People spoke of trainers who abandoned their horses, their staff, their commitments, but she'd never imagined that of Jackson. Never thought it could happen. To her, or her friends.

Squaring her shoulders, she walked back into the feed room and took a last desperate inventory. Grain and supplements should last another week, and with only two horses to feed, there'd probably be enough hay. But since Tizzy and Stinger had just raced, they wouldn't be able to run for another month. Their food would be gone long before that.

And with no more horses to race, their chance of earning an income was dashed. Worse, since Jackson was the trainer on record, the purse money from the weekend would go to him. Victoria would never let him buy feed or make any more dispersals, even if Jackson intended to follow his agreement with Eve and pay out bonuses.

"When is Juanita coming back?" Joey asked, hopping on one foot in the doorway, and giggling when he lost his balance.

"Three o'clock." Eve gave her cheeks a quick swipe. "Then we'll drive to the bank and maybe stop for ice cream."

"Thought we were going to McDonalds?"

She jammed the scoop back into the grain bag. She had mentioned getting a hamburger. Thought it would be nice to buy Juanita supper and show appreciation for the excellent kid care today. But having the horses pulled changed everything.

Now she needed every cent to help her staff. For a few days, they could all sleep in the RV, but track management would soon insist that the trailer be moved. Soon they wouldn't have a horse left in the barn. They'd be squatters.

"Wouldn't it be more fun to eat here?" she asked, trying to inject the proper degree of enthusiasm. "With Juanita? We have leftover hotdogs and ice cream. And you can play outside. That way, we can invite Ashley and Miguel too."

Joey thought for a moment, then gave a swift nod. "Okay," he said. "But don't invite that mean man."

She winced. "Rick's not mean. But he won't be eating with us again." He'd have to come and collect Camila's box. However, it was clear he'd do that when Joey was either asleep or absent.

"That's good," Joey said. "And don't make peanut butter sandwiches for lunch. Juanita knows a boy who's allergic and he might get sick if it's on my mouth."

"Glad you're on the ball, buddy," she said, rumpling his hair. "Okay, we'll find something else for lunch. Race you home."

Joey turned and charged down the aisle, intent on winning. She followed, shooting an apologetic look at the two startled horses. It seemed another lifetime when running down the aisle was her biggest problem.

Joey sprinted toward the RV, his arms and legs pumping. She kept pace, careful to stay a few feet back, her steps muffled on the grass.

He reached the RV first. He whipped open the door, glanced over his shoulder and giggled with triumph.

"I won!" he said.

She followed him inside. "You did win. You're a fast runner."

She jerked to a stop, her smile fading. Liam sat in the middle of the kitchen floor, the contents of Camila's box dumped by his feet.

"What are you doing?" she asked.

Her gaze shot to the wad of bills stacked beside the cracker box. She doubted the security guard would be as compassionate as Rick. He'd probably insist she was withholding evidence and demand the money be turned over to the police. And Camila's sister needed every dollar.

"That's Camila's money," she said firmly. "We made it betting on the horses, along with the caps tournament." They'd made a couple hundred dollars betting, certainly not five thousand. But she didn't flinch at the lie.

"Where's your vehicle?" she added, glancing out the window at the empty road. Her voice sharpened. "What are you doing here? I don't recall inviting you in."

"Walked." He gave a dismissive shrug. "Sorry to barge in like this but I had an urgent request from the next of kin. Six calls in fact, all requesting we send Camila's diary."

"Everything she owns was in that box." Eve crossed her arms, still eyeing the money. It didn't sound as if he intended to confiscate it. But now her fear was replaced with annoyance. Even Rick never entered the RV without knocking. Not only had Liam walked in, he hadn't even removed his dirty boots. Now red clay littered the floor, marking his path like an arrow sign.

"Ashley told me you were going to see the pig," Liam said, his head still bent over the strewn contents. "And I know Rick is off trying to find Marcus."

He kept pawing through Camila's clothes, checking her jean pockets, even rifling through her undergarments. It looked all wrong. Rick had been far more orderly, more respectful. Liam seemed almost frantic.

"I'm not sure what you're looking for," she said. "There's no diary. Just that little notebook."

Liam picked up the notebook, skimmed through it, then tossed it aside. "That just has horse details. Ashley mentioned a diary. I thought… They thought it might have some personal entries, so they want me to find it."

"I'll help." Joey dropped to his knees and enthusiastically reached for the box.

Liam knocked his hand away. "Don't touch anything, kid. This is an official job."

Eve's jaw clenched. She dropped her arms and shot forward. "And I think it's time for you to leave. Now."

"Not yet," Liam said. He looked up at her, and something flickered in his eyes. Something ugly.

"Go to your room, Joey," she said, her voice clipped. "I'll see Liam out."

Joey rose, his face stricken. He shuffled down the hall and disappeared into the second bedroom.

She glowered at Liam. "Don't ever touch my son again."

"Sorry," he said, without sounding sorry at all. He picked up a tattered English-Spanish dictionary, flipped through the pages then tossed it aside. "But Camila's family is calling me all the time. Wanting some dumb diary. It's driving my security guards crazy."

He adjusted his gunbelt and emphasized the word 'security' as if reminding that he was the boss. As if that meant he was entitled to do whatever he wanted. She really didn't care how many phone calls the security office fielded. Camila had died in a tragic, unsolved murder. The family was bound to have questions, endless one. She remembered when Joey's father died, how many people it had affected… Yet Juanita said Camila only had one sister.

"Camila's mother?" she asked, keeping her voice casual. "Is that who's calling ?"

"Yeah," Liam said. "So that's why I had to hurry over."

"No problem." She turned toward the counter. "Take your time. I'll make us some coffee."

She reached for the coffee maker with her left hand. And with her right pulled out her phone. She kept it hidden in front of her, her fingers flying over the screen.

She smelled Liam's sour breath seconds before his hand squeezed her fingers, so forcefully she yelped. She wheeled. But he kept squeezing her hand, seeming to enjoy her pain.

For a moment, she was too shocked to move. Then she jerked her knee sharply toward his groin. But he was ready. He shoved her against the counter, until the edge bit into her back and she was pressed helplessly between his legs.

"Bitch," he growled, prying the phone from her fingers and slamming it against the counter. The case cracked. A colored circuit board and battery popped out like entrails. A vein throbbed in his neck, his face turned a mottled red and his explosive rage shocked her to silence.

"Bitch," he repeated. "Princess bitch. You ruined everything." Then he shook her, so hard it rattled her teeth.

"Liam," she managed, her breath ragged. "I was just texting Ashley. She's coming over…to babysit…to—"

"Shut up." He gave her another shake. "You screwed me over. Those were my babies. My money. You baby fuck-up bitch!"

Spittle formed around his mouth and something wet sprayed her cheek. He was incensed with rage, seemingly unable to speak except to call her a bitch. If she wasn't so terrified, she'd have poked fun at his limited vocabulary.

"Everything's okay, Liam," she said, desperate to keep her voice from squeaking. To act calm.

The drawer with the knives was only inches from her right hand. Once he loosened his grip, she'd grab a knife and chase this asshole from her RV. And then she'd make sure he lost his job and never was in a position of trust again and—

But his hand wrapped around her throat, and she couldn't think anymore about what she wanted to do. Could only gasp and twist and struggle to breathe.

"This is your fault." Tendons corded in his neck, and his lips pulled back, revealing bared teeth. "I didn't want it to come to this. I really didn't. I tried to make you leave."

She closed her eyes, didn't want to see his horrifying rage. His punishing grip relaxed slightly, and she grabbed a wheezy breath. And a few more. Enough that she could fight again.

She bent and sank her teeth into the fleshy part of his hand.

"Dammit," he roared. He released her neck but then grabbed her with his other hand and pounded her head against the counter. Once, twice, and then her eyes hurt and her head was spinning too much to keep count.

"Don't you hurt my mother!" Joey's voice sounded far, far away. But she could see him through a red haze. He was right there in the kitchen. His arms and legs were wrapped around Liam's leg, his face twisted with panic.

"No," she said. "Joey, run."

Liam tossed her to the floor, then pulled Joey off his ankle, holding him in the air with one arm. Joey's legs flailed helplessly.

"You want to tell the women how easy it is to have kids at the track," Liam said. "Well, go ahead. But be sure to tell them about this."

She saw his boot coming and curled into a ball seconds before his kick landed on her ribs. Pain knifed through her chest. Then he stomped on her left leg, and for a moment the agony was so intense she saw nothing but pinpoints of black.

"This is all your fault." His voice sounded above her. "Camila wouldn't have wanted her baby back if you hadn't filled her head with stupid ideas. And I had Ashley lined up. A blond woman!"

She lay unmoving, gasping, simply struggling to breathe. It felt like she'd fallen off a horse and then been trampled by the entire field. But she'd been hurt worse. And the knife drawer was close. She could get to it, with just a little recovery time.

Talking seemed to incense him, so she stayed silent, curled on the floor. She looked up at Joey's blurred face, trying to reassure him. And to warn him not to speak.

His little feet dangled in the air, his body pitifully small. And she couldn't not speak. Had to get him out of harm's way.

"Joey should go back to the pig's barn now," she managed. "Then I'll be able to tell the women they shouldn't keep their babies. And Ashley," she sucked in a breath that ripped the insides of her chest, "you can have her baby. That'll be a nice one. The father is blond too and blue-eyed."

She was lying like a lawyer. Had no idea who the father was, and she suspected Ashley didn't either. But when she was finally able to struggle to her feet, she was going for a knife. And she didn't want Joey anywhere in the vicinity.

Liam sneered. "Yeah, she listens to everything you say. All the women do. Making sandpits, spreading dumb ideas. Well, this is my track."

He prodded her ribs with his boot. "You're not so high and mighty now. Ashley thought five grand looked pretty good. I could have flipped her baby for thirty. Already have the deposit. Dammit. You should have left."

"It was you? Not Victoria?" She stared up, struggling to make her brain work.

"You women are all so stupid," he said, his face not quite so flushed.

"You stole my battery? The tack? Gave Miguel the liquor?"

He gave a superior smile, his arm relaxing. Now Joey's toes almost touched the floor. "Ashley made it easy. She babbled about everything. Even told me where the horse liked to roll. That stupid animal ripped open half his back. But you still wouldn't leave."

She stared in dawning horror. It was Liam? She gulped. "I'll leave now though," she squeaked.

"Too late."

"No, it's not," she said quickly. "No one can prove anything. You haven't hurt anyone."

He looked down at her, his eyes cold, the silence in the kitchen like a tomb. And she could see it in his expression even while the sound of her own heartbeat thrashed in her ears. "No," she whispered. "Not Camila."

"She wanted to buy back her baby. Too stupid to understand there's no going back. Even had the nerve to threaten me. Me!" His voice rose with scorn and Joey's feet lifted further from the floor.

Eve's cheek was flattened against a red footprint on the floor, the same color as the river bank. Yet Rick said they weren't allowed close to the crime scene. Her mind skittered away. She didn't want to accept that a killer was in her kitchen. With her son.

"You're right," she said, hating the quaver in her voice. "There is a real diary. But Rick already has it. So you should just run. He's coming back after he talks to Marcus. He knows it was you."

Liam snorted. "I knew Marcus would sing, that's why I needed him gone. Paid him a thousand bucks for each girl he lined up. But he didn't have the guts to see things through."

Eve tried to control her terror. She moved her legs a cautious inch. Her left leg didn't work, but her right leg twitched in response. That was the one she'd use to push for the drawer. Her head still reeled but Liam was a lightweight compared to a horse. And Rick would come once he saw her text. He'd promised he would if she ever needed help. He couldn't be too far away.

"Where's Marcus now?" she asked.

"Hiding somewhere in town. I can't find him."

"Oh." Her despair rose. "I thought he might be here at the track."

"No," Liam said. "So your hotshot investigator is far away. And you'll make sure he doesn't follow me."

"Yes." She nodded, so quickly pain shafted through the back of her head, and black spots dotted Liam's face. But her pain was tempered with relief.

"Because I'm taking your kid."

She stared up, frozen in horror. "No. Take me instead."

"The kid's easier. And you can't even walk. Besides, *he'd* come for you."

"He'll come for Joey too." But she shook her head, trying to clear her vision, as well as push back her doubt.

"Then you'll have to make sure he doesn't," Liam said. "I'll let your kid go in a couple days. Long as he's quiet and you don't go to the police. Or send that nosy prick after me."

"No, take me, please," she begged. "Joey can't walk far. He needs medication. He's only four—"

But Liam had already turned toward the door with Joey tucked under his arm like a sack of feed.

She pushed herself up, collapsed then grabbed the side of the sink. She hung on, frantically yanked open the drawer and pulled out a knife, the biggest one she saw.

"Wait!" She burst through the open door, the knife pressed against her leg. Tripped and bounced down the steps onto the grass. Didn't feel a bit of pain.

"Liam," she called brokenly. "Take me instead. Please."

She pushed herself up, hobbled a step then fell again. Liam and Joey were already beside the sand pit, close to the wooded path. Joey's beseeching eyes clung to hers. Despite his terror he didn't speak, was still trying to be quiet, as if confident she'd save him.

And then he was swallowed by the trees.

Moaning, she pushed herself up and stumbled forward. There was a rake by the barn door that could serve as a crutch. Liam must be taking the path up the hill, squeezing through the gap in the fence. She'd follow.

She turned toward the barn, crumpled, then pulled herself along the grass. Crawling was faster than her ineffective hobble, and fear galvanized her, so much that she didn't feel a shred of pain, other than the sheer terror that gripped her heart.

CHAPTER FIFTY-ONE

Rick parked his motorcycle by the guardhouse and cut the engine. The man inside smiled and slid open the window. "Coming in for a coffee?"

Rick shook his head. "Just looking for Liam."

He flattened his hands against his thighs, trying to keep them from fisting. He'd questioned Victoria's involvement, ever since the frustrated note on Eve's car. Victoria was cold and calculating, and that note had reeked of emotion.

But he'd completely overlooked Liam. Partly because of the guard's friendship with Ashley. But mainly because his brain always shut down whenever people spoke of kids and babies. If he weren't half a man, if he'd only stayed around the mothers and listened, he'd have figured this out much sooner.

As it was, Marcus's confession had barely surprised him. Liam and Marcus had a profitable gig, running a despicable baby market for almost three years. Marcus befriended pregnant immigrants, stoking their fear about losing their jobs in the States, while Liam fronted the sales.

If a woman hedged about turning over their baby, Liam ruthlessly severed all support. In Camila's case, he'd planted heroin in her boyfriend's dorm, forcing the man to flee to Mexico. Since many workers were illegals, Liam had wielded frightening power.

They'd paid five thousand to the girls, a huge sum for a track worker, and pocketed up to fifteen. When Ashley arrived, fair-haired and pregnant, Liam had hoped to clear twenty-five.

But Eve's support had united the women. Meeting friends at the sand pit, having a chance to talk and learn about support programs had boosted their confidence. They'd even started their own hair business. All had hoped to emulate Eve, a confident single mother who'd carved out a career in the competitive race industry and was all too happy to help other women do the same.

Liam had been infuriated and determined to run Eve off. It had been simple to cause problems. Especially since Ashley served as an information funnel. The self-absorbed girl had no idea Liam was using her information for sabotage. And ultimately murder.

Rick's fists tightened, his fingers pressing into his palms. He was determined to talk to Liam before the police were involved. Quite likely the man would turn belligerent and take a swing. Marcus said Liam was unraveling.

When Camila insisted on returning her money in exchange for getting her baby back, apparently Liam had exploded. Marcus hadn't remained by the river that night and claimed he never thought Liam would kill her. Marcus had sounded truly shaken. Kept insisting he shouldn't be blamed for her death. He'd known Liam was frustrated about the imploding baby business but hadn't dreamed he was capable of such brutality.

And Marcus could be telling the truth. He was too jumpy to meet Rick in person, opting to talk on the phone and claiming he wasn't safe from Liam. Rick hadn't been able to track down Marcus, not yet, so all he could do was listen.

But Liam was easy to find. And learning details about the backstretch babies only stoked Rick's anger. He despised anyone who exploited the weak, and Liam was a soulless predator. Little wonder people here thirsted for vengeance.

He'd listen to Liam's side of the story, but it was horrifying to imagine the families that had been ripped apart—the destruction, the despair, the heartache. And Camila.

"Coffee's fresh," the guard said, opening the door and gesturing. "Come on in and wait. We even have some of those maple doughnuts, the kind with apple—"

"Where's your boss?"

The guard's smile faded. "Don't know. But his Jeep's here. Guess he walked somewhere."

Rick scanned the parking lot. Eve and her son were visiting the fun-loving guys in barn nineteen where they kept a friendly pig named Benji as their mascot. She'd be safe there. But if Liam cut across the east end, he'd only be a five-minute walk from the barns. And Rick didn't want that man anywhere around women.

"Can you call him?" he asked.

The guard shook his head. "Tried. He's not answering the radio or his cell. But I can send car six out. They'll find him." He reached across the desk for his mouthpiece.

Rick dragged a hand over his jaw. He still wasn't used to the smooth skin and quickly dropped his hand. "Don't bother calling," he said. "I'll find him."

He didn't want to spook Liam. Neither did he want any other guards around. According to Marcus—and to Rick's instincts which he valued more—the rest of the guards were a decent bunch. But it would be safer, and infinitely more satisfying, to handle this alone.

"I'll come back later for that coffee," Rick added.

"Sure thing," the guard said, his amiable smile returning.

Rick's phone pinged, announcing an incoming text. He pulled it out and scanned the screen. And for a moment he quit breathing.

Help, was all Eve had written.

CHAPTER FIFTY-TWO

Rick cranked the throttle, roaring the motorcycle down a straight stretch. His heart pounded with terror, matching the pulsing throb of the bike. For Eve to ask for help, so succinctly, she had to be desperate. And his return call had gone straight to voice mail. She only turned her phone off when she was riding.

The paved drive split. He hesitated, not sure if she was still at the pig barn or walking back to the RV. He swerved left, deciding if she were close to the main barns she wouldn't be alone. Best to backtrack from the RV and check the walkway.

Probably there was no reason to panic. Maybe a horse was loose, or sick, or her car wouldn't start. Or maybe Joey had fallen off the swing—that tire should have been hung another inch lower—and knocked out a tooth.

But his sweating palms tightened around the rubber handles. Because Eve never asked for help. She squared her shoulders and fought her own battles. That gritty courage was one of the reasons he loved her.

And he'd left her alone with a killer on the grounds, a volatile sociopath who blamed her for rallying the women.

He blasted his bike around the last corner, craning to see the RV. The barn.

And then such a fierce pain rocked him, it felt like his gut had been lanced. His bike was making weird noises and it took several seconds to realize the moans were coming from him. He'd seen blood and carnage before, but when he spotted Eve's twisted form inching over the dirt, the sounds escaping his throat were inhuman.

He vaulted off, letting his cherished bike crash to the ground, the engine still running. Dropped in the dirt beside her, pressing 9-1-1 even as he called her name.

She barely looked at him. Kept crawling toward the barn.

"Don't move," he said, his voice rough with fear. He ached to touch her, wanted to stretch out on the ground and hold her and reassure himself that she was alive.

But he spoke crisply on the phone, detailing the situation, even as he assessed her injuries. Broken leg, bruised neck, shocked and traumatized. Blood on the mouth, possible broken ribs.

She needed to stay still so he could take her vitals. Luckily there was an ambulance on the grounds. First responders would be here in minutes.

But she wouldn't stop crawling. She kept shaking her head, even during his second call to the police. Tears stained her cheeks and the red welt on her forehead stood out in stark contrast to her bloodless face.

"No police," she repeated, her voice hoarse and whisper thin. "It's Liam."

"We know." Rick lowered the phone. "Police are blocking off the area now. They'll catch him. I'm going to get you a blanket."

"But he has Joey. And he said no police. They went through the path. I have to get him."

She dug her nails into the dirt and pulled herself another foot closer to the barn. And it was then he saw the serrated bread knife clutched in her hand.

"Don't move, Eve." He placed a knee on the ground in front of her, blocking her progress.

"But I need a crutch. I have to get Joey."

"Your leg is broken. And maybe your collarbone, some ribs—" His voice broke, overcome with guilt, fear and a white-hot rage.

"Then you get him," she said. "You go for me."

He shook his head, not wanting to leave her side. "You're hurt. I'll wait until the ambulance comes."

"No!" Her face twisted with anguish. "Liam killed Camila. He'll hurt Joey."

"Police will cordon off the area around the farmhouse. They'll bring in a negotiator. They're equipped for this."

She stared up at him, her eyes beseeching. "But Joey can't be with that man."

He shook his head, the movement in sync with the fresh helplessness worming through his gut. He wasn't the best choice for a hostage situation. And there was no way he'd risk going up that hill, and quite possibly losing Joey.

Liam was unhinged. If it went south, she'd hate him forever.

"You get him." Her voice firmed. "Scott says you're his best man. Go, bring him back."

But still Rick shook his head. "It's better if the police do it. Safer."

She reached out and gripped his hand. And even though the movement must have hurt, she gave him a nod full of nothing but confidence. "I know you can do this," she said, her voice fierce. "Get him for me. Please. I'll wait here until you come back."

A muscle spasmed in his jaw.

"Please, Rick," she whispered.

"All right," he said. "I'll get him."

He rose and yanked his Harley upright. Thrust his leg over the seat and gunned it toward the woods.

The path was narrow, barely wide enough for a single person but he bulled through, weaving in and out of trees and bouncing over exposed roots. He rode the bike like it was stolen, not caring about the polish or the shocks or the mirror that smashed the side of a gnarly tree and now hung uselessly.

He couldn't be more than ten minutes behind them, judging from the time of Eve's text. And he'd make up ground on the powerful bike.

He burst from the trees and throttled the bike even higher, heading for the hole beneath the chain link fence. The gap beneath the fence was surrounded by scuff marks. But the hill was bare, empty of everything except faded grass, their tips bleached to a familiar bone white.

He dropped his bike, barely slowing as he launched himself beneath the gap. A twisted link grabbed his back and he heard the rip of his shirt, felt the tear of skin. But it only spurred him. He could move a lot faster than most men, and Liam was carrying a forty-pound boy. Surely he could catch them.

He sprinted up the hill, fueled by adrenaline and a soul-sucking fear. A fear he hadn't faced since Ben. *Joey will be okay*, he told himself, desperate for reassurance. There was no reason for Liam to hurt the boy, to hide that little body beneath the dank earth.

Liam didn't even know anyone was coming.

He prayed the police would remain silent. Right now, Liam was probably confident of his escape. But if he heard wailing sirens, he'd realize the road below the farmhouse was blocked. He'd be cornered like a rat, with a rabid hatred for Eve and nothing to lose.

Rick's lungs were straining and his legs ached, but he didn't slow his ground-eating climb. Not until he reached the crest of the hill. He forced himself to stop and listen, taking precious seconds to picture the layout.

The farmhouse was approximately a hundred feet below, surrounded by a wide sweeping drive. Liam probably had his personal vehicle stashed there. No doubt, he'd been the one who dropped the beer cap. It was the perfect spot for a stalker. He'd known the best times to creep down to Eve's barn and wreak havoc.

Rick peered over the rim. The entire area was deathly still, and for a moment he feared he was too late. But possibly Liam had stashed Joey in a bedroom, or the cellar…or somewhere else.

He gave his head a shake. Couldn't let himself be weakened by thoughts of dirt and death and another innocent boy. Had to stay positive. Focused. Do his job.

I am going to find this kid in time.

But now his entire body was shaking, his muscles spasming with fear, and it had nothing to do with his frantic climb up the hill.

He took a deep breath, struggling to calm himself, then rose and eased toward the farmhouse.

A rusty lock hung on the front door, forlorn and caked with cobwebs. Brittle boards covered the windows. The porch was thick with undisturbed dust. He was too late. Obviously Joey wasn't stashed inside.

From the back of the house a car door clicked. Then a voice rumbled.

He edged around the side of the house, pressing against the weathered wood, not sure if he was using the house for cover or if it was holding him up. Sweat beaded on his forehead. Liam was a snake. If he spotted Rick, the first thing he'd do would be to point the revolver at Joey. And threaten to shoot the kid.

He swallowed, hating the trembling in his body that he was powerless to control. He shouldn't even be here. It would be impossible to free Joey safely. The boy could end up shot, merely because of Liam's volatility.

At this point, it was best to wait for the police. They had negotiators who were better able to extract hostages. He could call and coordinate a rescue from his vantage point.

They'd definitely order him to stand back. Which was what he wanted too.

He reached for the phone in his pocket then pressed back against the wall, struggling with his sense of worthlessness. And his indecision. But the last time he'd let orders overrule his instincts, Ben had been murdered.

Liam's curt voice sounded again, and Rick couldn't resist inching forward and peering around the corner.

A Nissan Maxima was parked behind the house, the nose of the sedan pointing toward the road. The trunk gaped open. Liam's hand was clamped around Joey's neck. The man was still in his khaki uniform, a gunbelt buckled around his hips.

Twenty-five feet away, Rick estimated. Much too far. He couldn't do this.

Joey looked up, his eyes widening. Rick forced a reassuring nod and raised a finger to his lips just as Liam scooped up the boy. Rick expected Joey to call out, anybody would, but the boy never said a word. He just stared with hopeful eyes. Eve's eyes.

"Stay quiet, kid," Liam said, stuffing Joey into the trunk. "Or you'll probably suffocate."

He slammed the trunk with a satisfied grunt.

Rick stiffened. The boy wouldn't last more than a few hours in the sweltering trunk. And Liam knew it. He probably intended to ditch the car and kid, steal a vehicle and flee to Mexico.

On the positive side, Joey was safe in the trunk, out of Liam's reach. Now it was just between the two men.

He steadied his breathing, drew his knife from his boot and stepped out.

Liam wheeled in alarm, nostrils flaring. His eyes shot to Rick, then beyond, scanning the sides of the house, the empty hilltop. The alarm on his face disappeared, replaced with smug satisfaction.

"Looks like you're alone," Liam said.

Rick stepped closer, gauging the distance. Twenty feet now. He needed fourteen.

Liam unsnapped his holster.

"Better not," Rick said, moving forward with slow but deceptively long strides.

Liam's lip curled over his teeth in a feral grin. "Ever heard the joke about the idiot who brought a knife to a gunfight? Well you're the fool—"

He was still sneering when Rick whipped his knife. The man's cocky smile changed to a yowl of pain. His gun barely cleared his holster before it thudded harmlessly to the gravel.

"Goddamn." Liam whimpered, clasping his shoulder and staring down in horror.

Rick glided forward. He wrapped one hand around Liam's throat, the other around his shoulder, holding the man still while he pulled out his knife. It was his favorite, good metal, well balanced, and it fit perfectly in his hand.

He wiped the blade on Liam's khaki uniform, ignoring the man's shriek. Then replaced it in his boot sheath.

"Sonofabitch." Liam groaned, clutching his bloodied shoulder. "Thought you were supposed to leave it in. Not pull them out."

"Then they just get in the way," Rick said. "I don't want to chip it. Break the tip."

Liam stared, uncomprehending, until Rick let loose with a flurry of fists. The guard was in bodybuilder shape, his stomach flat and knuckle hard. So Rick worked him over from the sides, thinking of Camila, the innocent babies, the countless families destroyed. But most of all, he thought of Eve.

Liam didn't have much bottom. He kept dropping, trying to curl like a whipped rat, and that only angered Rick more.

He yanked Liam up and propped him against the hood. The man begged and blubbered like a baby, even though Rick took considerable care to stay away from his reddening shoulder.

"Those were for Camila," Rick said, his mouth clenched. "Need a couple more, for what you did to Eve." He draped Liam's leg against the bumper then eased back to line it up.

"God, no." Liam whimpered, twisting away. "Don't break it."

He picked Liam up by the shoulders and repositioned him against the bumper. "If you're going to last in prison," he said, shaking his head, "you'll have to toughen up. Eve and her kid are braver—" He paused, his gaze shooting toward the trunk.

"Don't move," he said, cuffing Liam's head.

He hurried around to the back of the car.

"Joey," he said softly. "It's Rick, your mom's friend. Everything's okay out here. We're just talking. I'm going to open the trunk now."

He clicked it open. Joey blinked up, his face drenched with sweat. Tear tracks smudged his cheeks. But the boy didn't move. Didn't speak. Didn't move a muscle.

"It's okay," Rick said, reaching in and scooping him out of the stifling trunk. He knew he shouldn't touch him, should let the boy come to him. But he couldn't stand seeing Joey curled in that cramped space. It reminded him too much of being buried. Like the dead.

"You're okay," he said, his throat so tight the words hurt. "You're safe now."

Joey remained stiff and unspeaking.

"You're safe now," Rick repeated.

"I know." Joey's voice was a reed-thin whisper. "Because you saved me." He sniffled once, as if trying to be stoic. Then his little face crumbled. He reached up and wrapped his arms around Rick's neck, sobbing and wailing and burrowing his head into Rick's chest.

Rick's own face felt warped, his chest so twisted with relief he could scarcely breathe. But this was a different feeling from usual, when his lungs didn't work and it felt like he was suffocating. On the other side of the car, Liam was groaning but the sounds faded, the man no longer important.

It was just Rick and the boy now, both clutching each other so tightly it was hard to know who was doing the actual holding. The sun beat down from a brilliant blue canopy and an eagle floated overhead, far removed from their struggles. The place was actually quite serene, no sound of sirens.

Police would be here soon though. And the aftermath would be brutal, with statements and recordings and prolonged interviews. And he'd deal with that, along with his reasons for going in. But right now he didn't want to let Joey go. Even punishing Liam no longer mattered.

Joey's crying turned to sniffs. "That man hurt my mom. It's mean to h-hit."

"Yes, but she'll be okay." Rick squeezed his eyes shut, wishing now he hadn't given Liam such a thrashing. And his regrets had nothing to do with the police or possible liability, and everything to do with scaring Joey.

The boy had been in the trunk. He hadn't seen anything but unfortunately Liam had been rather vocal, running the gauntlet from moaning to cursing to crying. And the sound of smacking flesh was unmistakable. Joey already didn't like Rick. No doubt he'd be even more terrified. Any second now he'd shrink away.

The kid was quiet for a moment.

Then, "I don't think you're mean anymore," Joey whispered, his voice muffled against Rick's shirt.

Rick swallowed.

"I know grownups sometimes talk cross," Joey went on. "So it's okay if you come for supper. And talk mean."

"Sorry," Rick said, his voice thick. "I just worry about people…about children. I'll work on that, okay?"

"That's all right. Nanny talks cross sometimes too." Joey peered up, wiping at his wet cheeks with his knuckles. "You can put me down now. I want to go home."

"But we have to wait. The police will be here soon."

"No." Joey shook his head, every bit as stubborn and brave as his mother. "I don't need any more help. And I have to go. Mommy will be worried."

"But I need to wait for the police. And you can't walk back alone."

"The police will only want that man." Joey looked at Liam then turned his head away. "But you can walk back with me. Then I won't be alone."

Rick thought for a moment, then gave a solemn nod. "Okay," he said. "That's a good plan."

He set Joey on the ground and pointed him toward the hill. "I'll just say good-bye to Liam and be right behind you."

Joey nodded and started walking past the farmhouse. But his steps dragged and he kept checking over his shoulder, and it was clear he was a little spooked, despite his determination to find his mother.

Rick strode around the car, grabbed Liam's arm and tugged him toward the back of the car.

Liam looked up, his voice fearful. "What are you doing? Are you going to break my leg?"

"Shut up," Rick said, waving at Joey. "Don't speak. Don't scare the boy."

He bent down, picked up Liam's legs and jammed him into the trunk.

"Wait." Liam tried to sit up, his voice rising. "You can't do this. It's too hot. Where are the police? I want the real ones."

"Quit talking," Rick said, shoving the man's head back down. "Or you'll probably run out of air."

He clicked the trunk shut. Then he scooped Liam's gun off the ground, stuck it in the back of his waistband and hurried after Joey.

The boy was waiting by the side of the farmhouse. He glanced at the car with solemn eyes. Then he reached up and took Rick's hand.

"I can't wait to see my mom," he said.

Rick nodded, stunned by the gift of those tiny trusting fingers wrapped beneath his bruised knuckles. They walked several steps before he managed to speak.

"I can't wait to see her either," he said.

He shortened his steps to match Joey's smaller ones. And together they climbed over the hill, their hands linked.

EPILOGUE

Eve's cell phone rang just as the timer in the huge kitchen beeped. She grabbed the oven mitts, then tucked the phone between her shoulder and ear.

"Sorry to keep calling," Ashley said. "I just wondered if they arrived yet?"

"Not yet." Eve glanced out the window. The RV was parked a hundred feet from the farmhouse, but it was clearly empty.

"Megan said little Jessie's close to walking," Ashley said. "Do you think she'll start tonight? Because the cupboards in the RV aren't baby proof, and the floor might not be safe. Some of those cleaners have way too many chemicals."

"Don't worry," Eve said, pulling a hot pan from the oven and filling the air with the smell of homemade biscuits. "Scott already took care of that. He sent in an eco-friendly cleaning company. And some other agency that makes sure everything is toddler safe. They're the same people that put in the playground by the sandpit."

"Oh, good." Ashley blew out a relieved sigh.

Eve checked the biscuits with her left hand. Golden brown and flaky. Perfect. Juanita had been giving her cooking lessons, and the recipes were always delicious. It was a good thing they were quick and easy too, as Eve had never experienced such over-protective mothers. Ashley and Megan both needed oodles of reassurance, just like first-time horse owners.

But Ashley's baby was definitely well loved. And the open adoption they'd agreed upon left everyone ecstatic. Megan and Scott cared for Jessie five days a week, and the other two days—when there were no races and the track was dark—Ashley walked up from the dorms and stayed with Jessie in the RV.

Of course, for those two days Megan and Scott could be counted on to meekly ask if they could stay in the farmhouse. Just in case Ashley needed any help. Which she usually did since her jockey career was on the upswing and trainers were always calling offering mounts.

"You're still riding the filly for me Wednesday night?" Eve asked, grabbing a spatula and shifting the hot biscuits to a cooling rack. "Even though Jackson has been calling?"

"Definitely," Ashley said. "I'm glad he's single again and back in business but I told him to call my agent. You know I'll always ride first call for you. You've made my life awesome."

Eve just smiled, accustomed to Ashley's effusiveness. Amazingly though, Megan said the same thing, only in a more refined manner. Eve couldn't imagine sharing a baby, but it worked for them. Now Jessie had two doting mothers and a smitten dad. Ashley couldn't have chosen better people.

It meant that Eve had to watch her words around Scott and Megan, as they were simply unable to temper their gratitude. When she'd mentioned it would be nice to knock down the kitchen wall and add a sunroom that would open to the verandah, a ten-man construction crew had arrived the very next day. Rick was forever starting jobs that he didn't have the chance to finish, simply because Scott was falling over himself to help.

She noticed though, that Rick managed to protect the jobs he most enjoyed. He and Scott were always tinkering with the cars and bikes. No outside mechanics allowed. Rick called it male bonding time although she suspected their talks centered around Scott's firm and his ongoing cases.

Joey laughed, a delighted ringing sound that carried across the field and into the kitchen. She walked to the window, craning her head and scanning the field. Rick had built several turnouts with shaded run-ins so she could walk the horses up the hill and give them a mental break from the track. Joey's pony, Bubbles, certainly appreciated the company. But when Joey laughed, as he was doing now, it generally meant mischief.

She hurried into the sunroom, still carrying the phone and looking for a window with a better vantage point. "I have to go, Ashley. Joey's outside and it sounds like he's having too much fun."

She cut the connection, relieved it was Tizzy who was visiting Bubbles this week, and not Stinger. She believed Stinger was reformed and deserved a hill visit—he hadn't bitten anyone in over six months—but Rick remained cautious.

With Tizzy though, it was like Joey had a second babysitter. Joey could lead Bubbles beneath the horse's belly and Tizzy always stood rock still. Once Miguel had placed a ladder against Tizzy's back so Joey could climb on. The obliging horse hadn't even swished his tail. There was no doubt Tizzy had earned his pasture turnout, and Dex and Dani were delighted that the consistent racehorse now enjoyed the best of both worlds.

However, Joey's high-pitched laugh was a mother's alarm bell. And she still couldn't see him, even though the new sunroom gave a panoramic view of most of their property.

But then she caught sight of a man's broad shoulders, and her tension eased. Rick must have driven up the hill from the track. Now that the fence was gone, it was a scant two-minute drive.

And clearly Rick had been here for a while, long enough to rig up a cat-riding pad. He'd fastened it to Bubbles and Marmalade, the orange cat, perched on the pony's back. Joey was leading the two of them around the grass, still laughing uproariously. The cat and pony looked surprisingly content with the situation, although all the animals would jump through fire for Rick.

She gave a quick and fervent prayer, something she hadn't stopped doing since the day Rick led Joey to the back of the ambulance, proving that Joey was really free from Liam's clutches. Then she waved, knowing they weren't even looking, but it was just so nice to be able to see her son play. And in the middle of a training day.

The smell of biscuits wafted into the sunroom, and she hurried back into the kitchen, opened the oven and rescued the second pan. Soon it would be time to walk down the hill and check the eight horses in her race barn. But there was no hurry. She'd ridden five this morning—the ones that were racing next week—and Miguel could be relied on to supervise their staff and let her know how each horse was feeling. Besides, life was too busy with friends and family to waste energy fretting.

She didn't hear the click of the screen door or the sound of his steps, but her skin was tingling before Rick's hand even touched her waist. She'd grown accustomed to his silent way of moving, but she doubted she'd ever be unaffected by his touch.

"Why are you here?" she asked, placing the spatula on the counter and spinning around. "Aren't you working this afternoon?"

"Thought I better check the hill for intruders." He slid his palm over the small of her back then reached out with his other hand and snagged a warm biscuit. "Plus I could smell these way over by the track."

"I made extra," she said. "So you can take some back to the guardhouse."

"The boys will appreciate them. They've been burning a lot more calories lately." He took a big bite, grinning at her as he chewed.

There'd been several changes since Rick accepted the job as head of track security. He'd parked the Jeeps, encouraging the guards to conduct more foot patrols. A few of them even rode bicycles. As a result, relations between the workers and guards were at an all-time high. The ladies who operated Camila's Corner even cut their hair for free, and for the first time ever, the guards had been invited to enter a team in the caps tournament. Woody, of course, insisted that Rick remain with him.

"Don't tell Scott about fixing the guest room for your mom," Rick said. "He'll have a slew of carpenters in, and that's something I want to do myself."

She nodded. While it was great to have Megan and Scott as regular visitors, their generosity was often overwhelming. Since purchasing the farmhouse, Rick had made a lot of improvements, and there were some areas where he simply didn't want help.

"Joey and I plan to build a dog run tomorrow," he went on, reaching for the butter dish. "So Megan's dog has a safe place to hang out. Joey thought a puppy run would be good too…you know, if we have enough material."

She could tell he was being deliberately casual, and even caught him studying her reaction out of the corner of his eye.

"You two want a puppy?" She gave a mock frown. "So you can train Bubbles to carry a cat and a dog?"

"Saw us, did you?" He chuckled and slathered some butter on a biscuit. But then he sobered. "If Joey's having fun on the ground, he's less likely to climb on that pony and get hurt."

She gave an understanding nod. Bubbles was as bomb proof as any pony could be, but she doubted Rick would ever stop worrying. His therapist thought differently, but Rick was a man who needed to keep things safe. And she loved that about him. Loved everything about him.

"A good dog is important for a farm," he went on, buttering three biscuits, then wrapping them in a napkin and sticking them in his pocket. She suspected he intended to split the third biscuit between the horse, pony and cat. Joey had already reported, quite proudly, that Bubbles was not a fussy eater.

"A dog can look after you and Joey when I'm working," Rick added, his eyes on her face.

"I suppose one that barks when people come would be helpful." She gave an agreeable nod. "Like a poodle or something."

"A poodle?" His jaw tightened, but only for a second, and if she'd hadn't been alert, she wouldn't have caught it. "I was thinking something a bit bigger."

"But poodles can be big," she said. "And they're one of the smartest breeds. A white poodle will stay cool in the heat too, and the ladies could practice their clipping, and you could even take her on your rounds." She gave a more emphatic nod. "Okay, I'll tell Joey. A poodle will be great."

"Maybe we don't have time for a puppy right now," he said.

She hid her smile, figuring she'd wait until they were in bed tonight to let him know she'd be happy with any kind of dog, or a pig, or a goat, or maybe they could even adopt something.

But he tilted her head, his eyes twinkling. "I do believe you're messing with me again, sweetheart."

Then he smiled and kissed her, his mouth tasting of biscuit and butter, and he made her so deliciously happy, she guessed there'd be a puppy in the house by the end of the week.

He raised his head. "I came up because someone found me a saddle pad that the cat's claws wouldn't poke through. But mainly, I wanted a biscuit."

She sniffed and tried to inch away from the hardness of his gunbelt, but he held her still. "And," he sobered, "I wanted to tell you how happy you and Joey make me."

She reached up and touched his smooth jaw. She could hear his heart pounding beneath the crisp khaki, could feel his utter sincerity. And she was filled with such an overwhelming love, there was no way she could make him wait until tonight.

"We can get a puppy," she said. "I'll love anything. Even a Rottweiler would be great."

He stared for a moment, his eyes reflecting her emotion. "Admit it," he said, his voice gruff. "You just can't resist a man in uniform."

Then his head dipped again, and there was really no need to answer.

***

ABOUT THE AUTHOR

Bev Pettersen is a three-time nominee in the National Readers Choice Award as well as a two-time finalist in the Romance Writers of America's Golden Heart® Contest. She competed for five years on the Alberta Thoroughbred race circuit and is an Equine Canada certified coach. She lives in Nova Scotia with her family and when not writing novels, she's riding. Visit her at http://www.bevpettersen.com